Praise for MAL

'MALICIOUS INTENT will keep you gripped from start to finish. Author Fox displays the deft hand of a natural writer, whether she's weaving her break-neck plots, imparting fascinating medical and police procedural details or breathing life into her characters – both good and bad. What a compelling new talent!'

JEFFERY DEAVER, author of
The Bone Collector and *The Vanished Man*

'Kathryn Fox has created a forensic physician who readers of Patricia Cornwell will adore. MALICIOUS INTENT is chock full of interesting information and also has several nifty twists and turns.'

JAMES PATTERSON, author of *3rd Degree*

'Fox is clearly in her element on the scientific side of things . . . Her slow build-up of forensic evidence linking all these women is absolutely fascinating and, forensically speaking, MALICIOUS INTENT is top-notch in its genre.' *Sunday Telegraph (Sydney)*

'It is a wonderful moment when you track down something that's really worth reading. And Kathryn Fox's first novel, MALICIOUS INTENT, is just that. A forensic thriller, it has just the right balance of pathological detail and tight plotting. Think *ER* meets *CSI: Crime Scene Investigation* . . . a fine novel.

About the Author

Kathryn Fox is a general practitioner with a special interest in forensic medicine. She lives in Sydney where she also works as a freelance medical journalist, having written regularly for publications including *Australian Doctor*, *CLEO* magazine and the *Sun-Herald*. Kathryn is currently working on a TV project and her second novel in the Anya Crichton series.

KATHRYN FOX

Malicious Intent

HODDER

Copyright © 2004 by Kathryn Fox

First published in Great Britain in 2005 by Hodder and Stoughton
A division of Hodder Headline

The right of Kathryn Fox to be identified as the Author
of the Work has been asserted by her in accordance with the
Copyright, Designs and Patents Act 1988

5

A CIP catalogue record for this title is
available from the British Library

ISBN 0 340 89584 5

Typeset in Plantin Light by Palimpest Book Production Limited,
Polmont, Stirlingshire
Printed and bound by Clays Ltd, St Ives plc

Author photograph: Mark Strachan

Hodder Headline's policy is to use papers that are natural, renewable
and recyclable products and made from wood grown in sustainable
forests. The logging and manufacturing processes are expected to
conform to the environmental regulations of the country of origin.

Hodder and Stoughton Ltd
A division of Hodder Headline
338 Euston Road
London NW1 3BH

Acknowledgments

There are numerous people who have contributed in many ways to this book, and who deserve special mention.

For their generosity in research and technical advice I sincerely thank Detective Sergeant Mal Lanyon, Detective Chief Inspector Mark Sweeney, Dr Julienne Grace, Dr Jo Duflou, Dr Martin Pallus Dr Peter Ellis, Dr Dianne Little, Dr Jean Edwards, Dr Dominic Dwyer, Dr John Clarke, Mark Marion, Ken Marslew from Enough is Enough, and Siobhan Mullany for her invaluable legal and procedural input, but especially those mackerel skies! Thank you, too, to others who freely shared their opinions, experience and expertise along the way, begining with Ian Foster, Sandra Lambert, Frank McKone and Lance Chapman.

In addition, Sarana Behan, Colleen Daly, Michael Pribula, Dr Kathryn Fluker, Dianne Russell, Judy Benson, Graham Benson, Dr Anica Vasic, Katrina Newey, Janice Wykes, Lynne Ryan, Sarah Ryan, Howard Charles and Dr Bob Futcher have all contributed their time, energy and enthusiasm to assist during the long and challenging process, for which I am grateful.

To Tara Moss, Paula Timm, Michelle Page, Anne Rennie and the former Hornsby Shire Writers Group, thank you for firing the passion and providing such positive support. Special thanks go to Robyn Behan, Margaret Cronin and Carolyn Jensen for helping maintain sanity and being such wonderful role models. To Jeffery Deaver for his tremendous generosity and graciousness, thanks again for setting the bar so high.

An award for outstanding tolerance, encouragement and support goes to fellow writer Helen Mateer for the number of times she cheerfully read, re-read and critiqued drafts and plot points.

Special appreciation to Shauna Crowley for taking a chance, and Hal and Di McElroy, for believing, and the magnificent Marg McAlister at writing4 success – the best teacher and mentor any writer could hope for.

Finally, thanks to my agent, Fiona Inglis, and the wonderful staff at Pan Macmillan – Brianne Tunnicliffe, for her insightful editing, unbridled enthusiasm and humour, but mostly to Cate Paterson, for her faith, patience and friendship. The world definitely needs more people like Cate!

To Mum and Dad for giving me the
heart, soul and wings to fly.
With eternal thanks, respect and love.

Prologue

Clare Matthews was cold, wet and late for dinner – again. As the train pulled into Seven Hills station, she peered along the empty platform through teeming rain and braced herself to dash for cover. Two or three steps later, the full force of the storm unleashed itself, snapping her umbrella inside out. Dodging puddles, she sprinted up the stairs, along the overpass and down the ramp to the multi-level car park. Safely inside the entrance, she had a coughing spasm, and wiped her nose with a sodden cardigan sleeve. A group of teenage boys on the stairs above wolf whistled.

Clare's pulse pounded. She'd worked with girls who'd been raped in situations like this. Turning around brought the realisation: no-one else had left the train. The usual peak-hour crowds had long gone, escaping early for the weekend.

Just keep walking; don't bother them and they won't bother you.

'Look what we got here.' One slid down the metal railing and landed in her path. 'How about a gang-bang?' He leant forward and trailed a finger down her arm.

Repulsed, Clare turned and pulled away, but he grabbed her from behind, thrusting his pelvis into her back. The others laughed. She swung her bag at him and ran up the stairs. Halfway up, two more appeared and blocked the way while a pair of hands groped her breasts.

'Leave me alone!' she screamed, struggling to push them back.

The one in front pulled her skirt up to her waist and shoved a fist between her legs. With one hand fending off the fist, she used the other to ram the broken umbrella spoke into what she hoped was his groin. He instantly withdrew, clutching himself. She ran up the remaining flight of stairs as fast as her legs would allow. Swearing followed by loud laughter echoed through the concrete stairwell.

Clare pulled open the doorway to the car park's second level as pain stabbed at her ribcage. Suppressing another cough, she frantically tried to remember where she'd parked her car. Back on the stairwell, the laughter and noise stopped. The silence frightened her more.

Grabbing the house keys from her bag, she crouched behind a cement pillar, unable to see her car.

As soon as they come out that door and start looking, I'll get down the stairs and back to the platform. There's got to be someone there by now.

Raucous laughing started again, and grew louder. Then she saw the man. Thank God she wasn't alone. Holding her chest with one hand, she hurried to where he was standing.

He looked like a lawyer: long black coat, expensive shoes, impeccable hair.

'This is the third time I've called.' He spoke loudly into his mobile as she walked briskly towards her Volkswagen. 'It's a black BMW.'

The man managed a harrowed smile before moving away to continue his conversation. Clare turned around. No-one was following. Her body shuddered with relief. Her car was just down this aisle.

She took some slow, deep breaths and looked back at the man. A broken-down BMW. So God had a sense of humour, after all.

Hands trembling, she fumbled with the key and opened the door of her yellow VW. Leaning in, she quickly threw her bag onto the back seat. Shards of glass covered the seat and floor.

What?

'They've been at my car too.' The lawyer approached, briefcase in hand. 'Only they tried to steal mine and destroyed the ignition barrel in the process. It won't start.'

Clare's eyes flicked to the stairwell door. No-one else was on the level – yet. 'We should call the police,' she managed, feeling a pang of guilt about thinking he'd broken down.

'I've done all that. With the storm and the Friday night exodus, they're caught up with accidents, and the Motor Club will be at least two hours.

They said the best thing is to drive to the local police station.' He glanced around the near-empty car park.

Clare couldn't stop watching for signs of the gang.

'We can give a statement and at least get home tonight.' He paused as if waiting for an offer. 'Is there any chance you could drive us? Ordinarily I wouldn't impose, but I've already been here an hour and no-one else would help. With that pack of hoons on the loose, who knows what they'll do next?'

After the way they grabbed her in the stairwell, Clare didn't waste time. 'Okay,' she agreed, reaching in to pull a rug from the back seat. 'Quick. You can use this to wipe off the glass.'

'Thank you.'

With a grateful smile, the man brushed at the broken fragments and climbed into the passenger seat. An isolated car park was the last place either of them wanted to be.

Still shaking, Clare climbed in and started the ignition. The engine turned over and cut out. The man leant forward, almost willing the car to move.

'Don't worry, she almost never starts first time.'

Clare took a deep breath, reached down and pulled out the choke, continuing to pump the accelerator pedal.

'It's good of you to do this. After all, we're both victims of a sort . . .' the man said.

A screech of tyres startled them both. Someone

was racing around the car park above; the next screech was much closer.

'Come on!' Clare urged. This time the engine hummed and she released the handbrake. 'May not be a Beemer, but she's reliable.'

The man twisted around in his seat and stared out of the intact rear window as they headed for the exit.

'I don't think they're following us,' Clare said, unsure who needed more reassurance.

Out of the car park she waited at a stop sign for an opportunity to break into the dispersing traffic.

Eventually, the man spoke. 'Well, Clare. I was beginning to worry about you. You're not usually this late off the train.'

1

Dr Anya Crichton sat in the witness box and surveyed the room. Her gaze quickly found the teenager in the dock. Scott Barker sat, round-shouldered and eyes downcast. The university student was like any other, except for two things. His family was one of the most prominent in the state, but more importantly, Scott was on trial for murder.

Judge Little took command. 'Please proceed, Mr Brody.'

Anya concentrated on Dan Brody. The barrister seemed more impressive in court than he did on any of his television appearances.

'Thank you, Your Honour.' Smiling, Brody stood from behind the table, rising to his full six feet four inches. 'Could you please state your name and qualifications for the jury?'

'Anya Rose Crichton.' Her voice remained even. Controlled breathing always helped. 'I am a medical practitioner, with specialist qualifications in forensic pathology and forensic medicine.'

'For the benefit of the jury, doctor, could you explain what your job entails?'

'As a forensic pathologist, I have conducted thousands of post-mortems to establish cause of death. As a forensic physician, I assess wounds and injuries of people who have been assaulted or involved in an assault and survived.'

'Could you please tell the court where you gained your experience?'

'After completing my medical degree at the University of Newcastle –'

'Yes, yes, Your Honour,' interjected the prosecutor from his seat. 'There is no issue as to the expertise of this witness.' Alistair Fraser sat shrouded in black silks, hands on his paunch.

Anya's back straightened. Fraser was already on the back foot. He had no intention of letting the jury hear the breadth of her experience and qualifications, her work at the State Forensic Institute or two years in England specialising in wound analysis.

Brody placed both hands firmly on the lectern and addressed his witness. 'Doctor, could you please describe the circumstances under which you came to meet the defendant?'

'I was called by the family solicitor to examine Scott Barker on the twelfth of December. He was in hospital for injuries following an alleged assault. I documented Scott's wounds in case of permanent injury and/or further police investigation.'

'And what did you find?'

'Scott Barker was in the emergency department with a series of wounds to his arms, hands and fingers. The incisions were deep and extensive.

One particular injury severed the web between the base of his right thumb and index finger, as well as tendons in the right hand.'

Brody tendered photographs of Scott's injuries to be shown later to the jury.

'And, doctor, in your opinion, how were these wounds inflicted?'

'They are classic defence injuries.'

'Could you please explain what you mean?' Brody asked.

Looking to the jury, Anya carefully chose her words. 'These wounds result from attempts to ward off someone brandishing a sharp weapon. The victim instinctively raises his hands and forearms to protect his eyes, face and head.' Lifting her arms to demonstrate, she glanced at the twelve jurors. Three took notes, the others sat forward in their seats. 'In the process, the victim sustains the characteristic deep incisions to those areas.' She paused. 'Exactly like the ones Scott suffered on the twelfth of December.'

Seeing Scott triggered vivid memories of that night. The shy youth claimed to be the victim of an unprovoked attack by two drunks outside a pub in Glebe. The attack wasn't difficult to imagine; the forensic evidence supported Scott's version of events. As he walked home from Sydney University, two men stopped him, wanting to know what he had in his bag. In the confrontation, Scott's laptop computer was smashed. When he yelled for someone to call the police, one of the men pulled out a switchblade. In the scuffle, the knife pierced the chest and heart of the larger man, killing him. The dead man had a blood alcohol reading three times the legal limit. The police case rested on the testimony of the second man, who alleged Scott had gone berserk, broken his own computer and attacked the two men.

Brody continued, 'Could you please explain why Scott would have such a deep cut to one palm only?'

'When someone is under attack they'll do anything to defend themselves, even if it seems irrational. That includes grabbing the weapon by the blade. When the hand is closed around the blade, movement by the assailant results in cuts across the flexures of the phalanges, the palm side of the victim's fingers. The blade slices through the skin, tissues and even tendons. In the process of grabbing the knife, Scott suffered permanent damage to that hand.'

Fraser jumped to his feet. 'Objection, Your Honour,' he boomed. 'This is conjecture. The witness was not present and could not know who grabbed what, where or when.'

Judge Little curtly reminded Fraser he had accepted Dr Crichton as an expert in this field and overruled the objection. The prosecutor flopped into his chair. Anya breathed out, appreciating the minor victory.

'So, doctor.' Brody put a hand on one hip, just below his bar jacket. 'Scott Barker is accused of cold-blooded murder, but you are saying Scott's wounds suggest that he was, in fact, fighting for his own life.' He paused for maximum effect. 'How likely is it that someone claiming to defend himself against a knife attack could suffer no defence injuries?'

'It would be unlikely.' Anya clasped her hands as Brody prepared the final blow to Fraser's case.

'You reviewed the post-mortem report on the deceased?' Brody underlined something in his notes. 'Did the *alleged* victim, the deceased, sustain any injuries to his arms or hands to suggest he fought off a knife attack?'

'No.'

'That's all, doctor.'

A murmur rumbled through the courtroom and in their gallery the press scribbled notes.

Anya's adrenalin surged as she watched the prosecutor haul himself to his feet. She wondered if this was how gladiators felt during combat.

'You say that Scott was the *victim*, and yet another man died during this incident.' Fraser faced the jury. 'I would have thought the dead man is the only real victim in this case.' He slapped the desk and barked, '*And* we have an eyewitness account of Mr Barker initiating a vicious and premeditated attack on two friends, drinking after a hard day's work.' The seasoned barrister spat the words out as he leant over the desk, knuckles white with the weight of his bulk. 'Now, the deceased was two metres in height and the defendant is 1.6

metres tall. Let's talk about the fatal wound.' Pulling on half-glasses, he flicked through some papers and lowered his voice. 'The autopsy report states that the weapon pierced the fourth left intercostal space and penetrated the right ventricle of the heart, causing massive bleeding into the sac around the heart. This, of course, caused death.' Head down, Fraser stared over his spectacles. 'Do you agree with that, Ms Crichton?'

Brody rose to object but the judge was already berating Fraser for failing to address Anya by her professional title.

Pulling a handkerchief from beneath his robe, Fraser wiped his ruddy face.

'Now, do you agree that, taking into account the angle of the wound, it had to be inflicted from below, for example, by someone who reached up to stab the deceased?' His face glistened with perspiration.

'No, I do not agree.' Anya realised Fraser's strategy. 'Guessing trajectories of weapons is notoriously unreliable because people, hands, bodies and the weapon are all moving at the same time when the weapon makes contact with the body.' Staring directly at the prosecutor, she added, 'In other words, no competent expert could say the fatal wound was inflicted by a shorter person.'

Clearing his throat, Fraser responded. 'Now, as you were not actually present at the post-mortem, could you please explain how you are in any position to comment on the wounds described in the report?' He peeled off his glasses with a smug look of victory.

Fraser had gaffed again. He obviously hoped she would try to discredit the pathologists at the State Forensic Institute, giving the jury the impression that her opinions were based on bitchiness, not fact.

'As a forensic pathologist and physician, I am an expert in wounds, and the autopsy report is quite explicit in the wound descriptions. Having worked closely with the doctors at the State Forensic Institute, I believe their findings to be above reproach. The fact that I was not present at the post-mortem makes no difference to my ability to understand or interpret the wounds, which were clearly and expertly described by the pathologist.'

Fraser's tight-lipped expression confirmed his irritation. 'No further questions, Your Honour.' He collected up his papers as Judge Little excused Anya.

Stepping towards the door, she looked over to see Scott mouthing 'Thank you' as she passed the dock. It was the first time she had seen him smile. Outside the court, she walked quickly to the ladies' room, past the camera crews and reporters milling outside the gates. She turned on the cold tap and let the water flow over her wrists.

A familiar voice echoed through the bathroom. 'Still getting stagefright, I see.'

Anya grabbed a paper towel and turned to see

Detective Sergeant Kate Farrer sauntering towards the basins.

'You look like shit.' Kate dug her hands into the trouser pockets of her fawn suit and leant against the bathroom wall. 'But you still did well in there. God, it's amazing the way juries trust you.'

Too exhausted to argue, Anya wet the paper towel and dabbed it under her cream blouse, cooling her neck. Her temples pounded. This case had been more stressful than she'd realised. All she wanted was to go home and sleep.

'We still have to wait and see whether the jury acquits,' Anya replied, throwing the paper towel into the bin.

Kate raised one eyebrow. 'Anyone with an ounce of sense could see that kid is innocent. The only thing he's guilty of is being related to his old man's money. Next there'll be a wrongful death suit by the drunk's family.'

Anya watched Kate run a hand through her short black bob. The detective was smart and arrogant, with a reputation as a troubleshooter, among other things. The two had worked together on a number of homicides over the last few years and Anya had been impressed by the twenty-eight-year-old detective's straightforward approach. Gradually, they had become friends. Anya did wonder, however, why Kate went out of her way to intimidate everyone she met.

'When the kid gets off, you should make the most of the father's gratitude and double your fee.

13

That'd stick it up everyone who thought you couldn't make it on your own.'

Anya smiled. 'Good to see you've taken my advice and had those diplomacy lessons.'

Kate was one of the few who knew her reason for the job change. The marriage breakdown and losing custody of Ben, her three-year-old son, were still painful. Anya pulled a lipstick from her purse, reapplied the terracotta gloss and walked towards the door.

Kate followed. 'You look like you could use a coffee. My shout.'

Anya hesitated. Solo work was isolating and she hadn't seen Kate for weeks. 'Only if I can choose the place. Don't want to end up with salmonella or worse.'

The pair walked out the court gates, ran the gauntlet through the media pack and crossed Oxford Street. They stopped at the second café they came to. Inside, Kate glanced at the blackboard menu and grabbed a window table. The waitress pounced.

'We'll have a mineral water and . . .'

'A short black, thanks,' chimed Kate.

They sat and watched the activity on the street until their drinks arrived. Across the road, Alistair Fraser left the courthouse, a camera crew in his wake.

Anya sipped her water. 'You look exhausted.'

'No choice. Without enough staff, I've been involved with homicide jobs all over the bloody state. As far as the brass is concerned, I'm only "consulting". Problem is, the local detectives wouldn't know shit from clay half the time.'

'And you still have your own case load.' Typical police, Anya thought. The hierarchy cut staff, increased workloads and still expected more arrests and reduced crime stats. 'Something else is bothering you.'

'A coronial inquest.' Kate heaped two sugars in her coffee. 'The case was treated as an apparent suicide off the Gap. Right from the start, it didn't add up. This one was all dolled up in designer gear, Dinnigan kind of stuff, but lots of cheap, chunky jewellery – very cheap.' She paused to lick the spoon. 'Not something you'd put on to swan-dive off a cliff.'

'Maybe she bought an expensive outfit on a credit card to go out in style.' Anya had seen women do this many times. Sometimes they'd pay for an expensive hotel room on credit, rack up huge bills then kill themselves in the room. 'The jewellery could have had sentimental value.'

'It's possible. She must have been attached to the shoes, too. They went with her into the water.'

'Granted, that's unusual, but doesn't prove anything,' Anya said. 'What do you know about her social circumstances?'

'Well, that's the interesting bit.' Kate caught the eye of a passing waiter and ordered a hamburger with the lot. 'She went missing for a couple of months prior to her death.'

'Was it out of character?'

'Totally. She was about to take her final vows. The "I'm going to carry rosary beads and pray a lot" kind of vows.'

Anya had read about the case in the papers. 'The nun with the double life.'

'That's her. The stuff tabloid dreams are made of. She disappeared two months before her death. Went to work and never came home. Next thing she is found dead, all done up.' Kate looked around the busy café and lowered her voice. 'And that's not all; she was six weeks pregnant.'

'Priests don't have the monopoly on sex scandals,' Anya mockingly whispered. 'Nuns have been known to have sex!'

'Funny. But for added drama, this woman tried to claw her own ears off before taking the plunge.'

Anya had to admit the scenario was bizarre, but there may have been a logical explanation. 'What did the coroner say?'

'He returned an open finding. He says it is probable she threw herself off the cliff, but there isn't enough evidence to support the finding.'

'I'm tutoring at the institute tomorrow.' Anya smiled. 'I'll see what I can find out about the autopsy – unofficially, of course.' She lifted a notebook from her handbag. 'I'll ask Peter Latham to dig out the file. What's her name?'

Kate drained her coffee.

'Matthews with two T's. Clare Matthews.'

2

Anya entered the histology lab at the State Forensic Institute and placed her briefcase beside one of the benches. From a side room came the voice of the institute's director and the unmistakable sneezes of Derek, a technician who continued to work in the department despite an allergy to the preservative chemical.

Anya popped her head into their room. Derek sat encased in a white bodysuit, his face hidden beneath a mask with a personal ventilation system as he sliced pathology specimens. Beside him at a microscope was Peter Latham. Like so many pathologists, Peter had unique fashion sense. Today he'd chosen his favourite paisley tie, pale yellow shirt and dark green trousers – a stark contrast to the blue surgical scrubs he wore most days. For court appearances, he liked to formalise his outfit with a brown corduroy jacket.

'Need a second opinion?' Anya asked.

Peter looked up and grinned through a salt-and-pepper beard.

'Anya, come in. We'll be just a minute.'

Derek muffled 'Hello' and made his usual joke about being an alien under the mask.

The shelves around the room contained jars of specimens marked with Peter's name for reporting. There were more specimens than usual. He had either fallen behind or taken on the extra cases when Anya resigned. It wasn't in his nature to delegate to the already overworked staff.

After dictating into a hand-held tape recorder, Peter placed a slide back into its cardboard folder. 'How does it feel to be back?'

'I'm only here to tutor.' Anya thought she sounded defensive and forced a cheerful tone. 'Teaching pays better than legal aid.'

'You're just going through a lean time; a settling-in period,' he said softly.

'I only wish you were right.'

'Give it time. You've only been at it a few months.' Peter removed his glasses and began to clean the lenses with the end of his tie. 'Anyway, an acquittal in the Barker case would establish your reputation. You'll be turning down referrals before long.'

Dan Brody had been supportive, but more government forensic employees were using their rights to private practice, which meant stiff competition for the only freelance woman in the field.

Peter held his glasses up to the light. 'How's my favourite godson?'

Anya smiled. 'Ben's doing well. Thanks again for the train set. He absolutely loves it.'

Out of the corner of her eye, she noticed an Amazonian figure enter the lab with a couple of books clutched under one arm. Sneakers scuffing on the tiled floor announced her arrival as she flicked a long plait from her shoulder. Anya could easily imagine this woman dominating a sporting arena such as a hockey field.

Peter was quick with the introductions. 'Zara, I'd like you to meet Dr Crichton, well-respected forensic pathologist and now forensic physician.' Turning to Anya, he added, 'This is Zara Chambers, our medical student. She'll be with us for the rest of the year.'

There hadn't been a student willing to complete a Bachelor of Medical Science project in years and Anya knew how much Peter revelled in an opportunity to teach.

'Zara's comparing diatoms in various water locations to those found in victims of drowning.'

Anya shook the student's hand. 'You're brave to take this one on. It's not an easy thing to do.'

'So far, collecting water specimens with the Water Police hasn't been very challenging.' Zara's confidence belied her inexperience. 'But tomorrow I'll start the real pathology.'

Anya wondered how long the enthusiasm could last. The concept was simple but the project involved dissolving bone in nitric acid, a process Zara was bound to find both difficult and unpleasant.

'Dr Crichton, you're the first forensic physician I've ever met.'

'That's probably because the institute's Victorian counterpart led the way and has a staff of forensic medical officers, whereas New South Wales has been a bit slow to recognise us. I'm doing my best to change that.'

The medical student's watch alarm beeped. 'I'm sorry to cut this short, Dr Crichton, but I have a tutorial in fifteen minutes and Dr Latham's secretary said there are some slides he wanted me to see first.'

'Yes, yes, of course.' Peter scratched his beard and led the way down the corridor. 'Very interesting slides, from the case you called me about, Anya.'

'Anything I can help with?' Anya enquired with a wink at Peter and grabbed her case.

'I'd appreciate a second opinion.'

Peter walked through the lab and into the corridor, followed by the two women. As they passed the first block of stainless steel fridges and plastic double doors, the familiar smell of stale blood wafted from the morgue. The incongruous sound of rock music reminded Anya what she had left behind.

'Sounds busy,' Zara said.

'We've had a run of hospital PMs lately,' Peter commented, distracted from another thought.

In the director's office, papers were piled on every surface. Framed degrees hung on the wall, along with photos of Peter's work with the United Nations. His citizenship certificate, dated 1994, took pride of place. Beneath it stood a dual-headed microscope, used for teaching and demonstrating significant findings for police investigators.

Peter pulled a slide from a cardboard folder and held it up to the light. After ensuring he had the correct specimen, he lifted the microscope's plastic cover. 'This is from the lung of a thirty-five-year-old female found at the base of the Gap a while back. Macroscopically, both lungs had some unusual streaky patches that appeared pale compared with the rest of the lung tissue.' Peter slid his glasses above his forehead and focused the eyepieces. 'Anya, what do you make of this?'

Anya rolled a chair forward and peered into the lens. Stained with haematoxylin and eosin, multiple golden-brown, needle-shaped structures spread throughout the tissue.

'Did she have any relevant medical history?' Anya asked. Like a piece in a jigsaw, histology meant nothing without the full picture.

'Not to our knowledge.' Peter adjusted his chair. 'She lived in a convent, but it's anybody's guess what kind of insulation's been used in those old buildings.'

'I heard it was an open finding.'

'True. After you called, I went over the reports again. This woman died from multiple trauma. The injuries are consistent with falling from a height. Based on what we know, the coroner couldn't have come to any other conclusion.'

Zara interrupted. 'What does the slide prove?'

Anya moved away to let the student view the slide. 'What do you see?'

'There appears to be a group of small needles.'

'Any idea what sort of fibres are found in lungs?' Anya remembered one of her old tutors at university saying that seventy-five per cent of what a doctor learnt was through humiliation in front of colleagues. She had sworn never to humiliate a student, believing that problem-solving and understanding were the best ways to learn.

'Well, it's rather obvious. Asbestos!' Zara declared.

Anya considered making an exception to her rule. 'You're close. They resemble asbestos, but are a little unusual. Asbestos fibres are usually dumb-bell shaped, skinny with round bits on each end. These are more hourglass shaped.'

'But wouldn't you expect to see fibres in older people who've had a long history of dust exposure through their jobs, like brake mechanics and asbestos workers?'

Anya glanced at Peter and said, 'Normally, yes. It's extremely unusual to see them in such a young woman.'

'I agree,' Peter said, replacing the slide with another. 'Fibres are normally very difficult to see, even under a microscope. Luckily for us, the body coats the fibres with iron protein. What you are looking at is the haemosiderin deposit.' He propelled his chair back to a pile of books on a shelf.

'Is it like the body mounting an immune response to an infection?' Zara asked.

'Not really,' Anya responded. 'More like a primitive chemical reaction.'

'Does this mean the nun was dying of asbestosis?' Zara looked up, thirsty for a new diagnosis.

Peter handed her a textbook open at a page displaying a colour photograph of asbestos fibres. 'You see, these are a little different. The woman died of the injuries she sustained in the fall, and the fibres are merely an incidental finding to note.' He returned the slides to their folder. 'Besides, it could be any of a number of fibres used in buildings over the years.'

'Shouldn't we try to find out what it is?' Zara glanced at the two pathologists. 'I mean, won't the police want to know?'

Anya watched her old mentor rub his eyes.

'Our job is to identify the cause of death, which we have done in this woman's case. Chasing red herrings is not our role.' He scratched his collar-length grey hair. 'The coroner and the police wanted to know what killed this woman. The fall off the Gap did that.'

'Peter's right. The institute has to limit itself to investigating only what's necessary. There are one to two suicides from the Gap every week in addition to all the other coronial cases. Concurrent illness in a multi-trauma isn't really relevant and doesn't help the coroner.'

'Thanks anyway for showing me the slides.' Zara

stood, replaced the microscope cover and headed for the door. 'Nice to meet you, Dr Crichton.'

Anya closed the office door behind Zara. 'Peter, is the new coroner causing problems?'

'He wants to clear the backlog and doesn't want cases deferred unless absolutely necessary. Reports have to be in ASAP.'

'I heard there was something odd about this death.'

'Something about it doesn't sit right.' Peter clasped both hands behind his head. 'Did you know the woman was six weeks pregnant?'

Anya nodded. 'Any evidence of sexual assault?'

'No, but that doesn't tell us anything this far down the track. We can't even be sure she *knew* she was pregnant.' He wheeled across the carpet again and pulled a file from the top of a pile. 'It gets more interesting,' he said, opening the folder.

'I heard her ears had been clawed.' Anya sat on the table next to the microscope. 'Any signs of asphyxiation?'

'That was my first thought. We had the usual twenty cases that morning and I allocated it to a registrar, who panicked when he saw crescent-shaped scratch marks on her neck, involving her ears. Of course everything stopped. The crime scene guys turned up and immediately called Homicide. But when I had a close look, there was nothing to suggest strangulation – no congestion of the face, petechial haemorrhages, or bruising, and certainly no ligature mark.'

'Laryngeal trauma?'

'None.'

'That is odd. Any history of self-abuse or mental illness?'

'Suicide in the context of depression would be logical, but that doesn't explain the self-mutilation.'

'What about schizophrenia or depression with delusions?' Anya had always been shocked when historians suggested that Vincent Van Gogh had cut off his ear because of his love for a woman. She believed, most likely, that he suffered from schizophrenia and the self-mutilation was supposed to stop auditory hallucinations. 'Maybe she scratched her ears in an attempt to stop voices.' Anya had seen many odd deaths, but the image of a tormented religious woman still seemed particularly disturbing. 'Any evidence of antidepressants or antipsychotics on toxicology?'

'Nothing. For all we know, she knew about the pregnancy and couldn't cope with the guilt, or the baby's father simply left her. Even if she tried to damage her ears in a psychotic state, the result is still the same.' Peter glanced around the office before locating his glasses on his head. 'It makes no difference at this point. The circumstances surrounding the death may be suspicious, but the cause of death is straightforward. The coroner can instruct the police to take it further if more evidence comes to light.'

Anya thought aloud. 'To a Catholic, suicide is a mortal sin.'

'I'd forgotten you were a convent schoolgirl.'

'A mortal sin can't be forgiven by God without repentance. I was taught that suicide and murder are mortal sins, which means the sinner is condemned to hell, fire and brimstone, for eternity. A murderer can still get to heaven if he repents, but someone who kills himself goes straight to hell. If this woman knew she was pregnant and killed a foetus as well . . .'

'This doesn't mean much to me, I'm afraid.' Peter had always respected people with religious faith, despite being unable to understand it.

Anya continued. 'Surely it makes the probability of mental illness, or at least an irrational frame of mind, stronger.'

'Doesn't everyone who suicides have an irrational state of mind? I've reviewed the case, and the cause of death is clear. There's no physical evidence to suggest interference.'

Anya glanced at the wall clock. 'Tutorial time.'

'What's today's topic?'

'Autoerotic asphyxia.'

'Zara and her colleagues will love it,' Peter grinned, and walked Anya to the door.

3

Two days after her court appearance, Anya caught up with Kate by phone to tell her about the Clare Matthews' PM report. Kate didn't say much, which probably meant she was in the Homicide office. Or else she wasn't impressed that Anya had concurred with Peter Latham. After hanging up, Anya flopped on the waiting room lounge in her Annandale office and bit into an apple. Beside her lay the newspaper with the photograph of Scott Barker hugging her outside his father's office complex. She looked awkward, which was exactly how she felt at being invited to celebrate the acquittal. Publicly displaying a private moment with Scott made her uncomfortable.

She didn't hear her secretary tap on the open door.

'What's it like being famous? A front-page girl?' Elaine Morton walked in and sat on the padded arm, grinning at the photo of her boss.

'I look like an old schoolmarm.'

Elaine scoffed and picked up the paper. 'You look professional. Besides, the photo is quite touching; shows the public that the Barkers know how to say thank you.' She poked at the apple. 'Another health binge, or are you out of everything else?'

'I had a big meal last night.'

Elaine sniffed the air. 'Chinese takeaway, I'd say.'

Anya prepared for another lecture on looking after herself, and the perennial favourite, how much weight she had lost since the divorce.

Kicking off her shoes, Anya lay across the calico-covered lounge. Bought at a second-hand sale, it was a temporary fixture until the business could afford a leather Chesterfield. In the meantime it was serviceable, as were the ex-government computer desk and swivel chair in the corner. The high ceilings and ornate plaster cornices gave the room an elegant feel, unaffected by the cobbled collection of furniture. Monet prints on two walls disguised a fading lemon paint job.

Back at her desk, Elaine switched off the answering machine. She replaced new cross-trainers with blue courts and pulled a perfume from the drawer. The sickly fragrance was designed to obscure any smell of stale tobacco. Anya couldn't decide which odour was worse.

'Sperm Man paid another visit yesterday,' Elaine said as she rummaged through her handbag.

'The one with his wife's underwear?'

'That's our man. This time he brought the bed sheets – red flannel.'

Anya rolled her eyes and groaned. 'Is he still convinced his wife's having an affair?' She sat up and took the lid off a water bottle. 'Why can't he accept we don't do that sort of work?'

'I tell him every time he comes. He wants us to help catch his wife out. All we have to do is check the panties – and now the bed sheets – for sperm.' Elaine combed her neatly trimmed ash-blonde hair. 'I don't suppose we could do this one, and charge a consultant's fee for passing it on?'

Instinctively, Anya touched the necklace her son had chosen and felt a lump rise in her throat. Only weeks ago Benjamin had beamed back at his mother in the jewellery shop as he picked the cheap gold chain for her thirty-fourth birthday. He proudly handed over the two dollars she had given him and hadn't noticed when she paid the shop assistant the difference.

To afford another custody challenge, she needed more work, which meant improving her profile. Insurance cases paid well, but too many of them could ruin her reputation in legal circles. If things didn't improve in the next few weeks, she'd have to reconsider *all* options.

'We're not taking on Sperm Man.' Anya sipped the water. 'Just keep giving him the names of the private testing laboratories in North Sydney and Lidcombe.'

Elaine walked to the doorway. 'By the way, you have a nine o'clock appointment who should be here soon, a Mr Deab. He wouldn't tell me what it was about over the phone but kept saying how urgent it was that he see you.'

'Let's hope he doesn't bring underwear.'

Elaine chuckled. 'Coffee?' she asked, not waiting for an answer before wandering down the corridor to the kitchen. Unable to afford a separate office, Anya lived at the back of the terrace house. She slept in an attic bedroom and kept a smaller upstairs room for Ben's visits. A functional lounge room, bathroom and kitchen became common property during business hours.

At five past nine Elaine brought Anoub Deab from the waiting room into the main office. During a quick tidy up, Anya found under the lounge a Matchbox car, a Lego block and a plastic road worker left from Ben's last visit. She deposited the bounty on her desk just as the man entered the room.

Elaine offered freshly brewed coffee, which they both declined, before leaving to answer the phone.

Anya shook the young man's hand, which was bathed in perspiration. He must have been in his early twenties, with soot-black hair, olive skin and dark eyes. The neatly ironed jeans and an impeccably pressed white shirt meant he was either obsessively neat or still lived with his mother.

'What can I do for you, Mr Deab?' Anya offered the chair opposite her desk, sat and opened a notebook.

He cleared his throat a couple of times and lowered himself into the seat. 'I want to find out about my sister, Fatima. She disappeared seven weeks ago. No-one knows where she went. My father, he was angry – he thought she ran away with a boy. My mother . . .' Anoub lowered his head. 'Almost a month had passed since Fatima went missing. And then one night the police came and told my parents she was dead.'

Anya felt some of the young man's pain. She knew too well what it was like to lose a family member. She wrote 'missing 4/52, found dead 3/52 ago' and underlined them in her book.

Anoub stood and paced the small room. 'It was drugs, but I want you to find out what else happened.'

Anya spoke quietly. 'Do you think there's more to the story than you've been told?'

'That's what I want to know.' He sighed loudly. 'How can you understand what it is like, not knowing who to trust? You, with your pale skin and green eyes –' His voice was so bitter. 'Since September 11, we have been persecuted by police. Before then we were tolerated. Now people despise us. The papers say we go around in gangs causing violence. Just because we are Lebanese the police pull us over, search and threaten us. For no reason.' He ran a hand through his hair and stared at Anya. 'How can we believe anything they say?'

The man had a point. Talk-back radio had vilified Islamic immigrants since the devastation of New York's World Trade Center towers, and, closer to home, the suicide bombings in Bali.

'What do you think happened to your sister?'

'That's what I need to find out! This has brought

great shame to my father and our family. My father's business is suffering because our own community disowns us. Many say she died of AIDS. My mother does not speak about it but I hear her crying . . .' He stopped himself from saying anything more about his mother. 'Fatima was promised in marriage to a man from our home village. Now my father is disgraced there as well. You cannot understand what this means for us.'

Anya wasn't sure whether he was more aggrieved by his sister's death or the social implications of the way in which she died.

He reached into his back pocket and placed an envelope on the desk. 'I want you to take this and talk to the police. Find out the truth. Did Fatima have AIDS, like some people are saying? Was she with a man when she ran away? Who gave her the drugs and left her to die?'

Anya opened the envelope. Stuffed inside were ten- and twenty-dollar bills, amounting to thousands. Almost unrecognisable were wads of pound notes, which hadn't been in circulation for about forty years.

She replaced the contents. 'I am very sorry for your loss, but I think you're mistaken. I'm not a private investigator.'

'But Mr Brody said he would ask you to look into it.'

'Dan Brody, the lawyer?'

'Yes. He handles my father's affairs.'

Anya wondered what sort of 'affairs' needed a criminal defence barrister. 'As yet, he's not asked me to be involved,' she said.

The young man lifted his chin as though it gave him more authority.

'I want you involved. You'll work for me, not Brody.'

'I'm afraid I don't think I can help you.' Anya stood up and pushed the envelope away. With a reputation to build and the custody fight for Ben, now more than ever, she couldn't afford to be implicated in anything suspicious or illegal. And she didn't like Deab's attitude towards her.

Anoub refused to take back the money. 'I am prepared to pay to find out what the police know.'

'I choose whether or not to accept a client.' Her voice was firm.

'I didn't steal the money, if that is what you think. My mother has been putting aside a little each week, in case anything happened to my father. She has it hidden around the house and asked me to give some to you. There is more if you need it.' He sounded desperate, almost pleading. 'If I can prove that Fatima didn't have AIDS, it would help my family a great deal.'

Anya studied the grieving brother. He appeared so arrogant, but when he spoke of his mother he became surprisingly vulnerable. His defensiveness and paranoia didn't justify his arrogance, but could explain why he came across as so abrasive. She took a deep breath. 'Presumably, if the police were involved, the coroner requested a post-mortem, an autopsy, on your sister.'

'The pigs would not let us bury Fatima when we wanted. They defiled her body.'

Anya was aware of the Islamic tradition of burying the dead as quickly as possible. In a suspected overdose, screening for infections such as HIV prior to the autopsy further delayed proceedings, despite efforts by the coroner and pathologists to respect the family's wishes. For families, the wait could be devastating and poorly understood.

'If a doctor can't complete a death certificate,' she explained, 'or the cause of death is unknown, the coroner requests a post-mortem. Particularly if the circumstances surrounding the death are suspicious. It's the law.'

'Fatima,' Anoub faltered for a moment, 'died with a needle in her arm in a filthy toilet block.' He sat again and stared at a bookshelf of medical texts before speaking.

'My parents came here as teenagers. They wanted us to have a better and safer life but made sure we followed Islamic law. After Fatima left school, my father allowed her to work as a medical secretary in Merrylands. This made her see how much trouble Western immorality caused. She despised women who came to the practice with pregnancies and diseases caused by debauchery.'

Anoub took a deep breath, and tightly clasped his hands. 'She looked forward to marrying my father's cousin until that last night.' His facial muscles tightened. 'She said the train was late but my father did not believe her. He says she had a boyfriend and forbade her to return to that workplace.'

'How did Fatima respond?' Anya gently probed.

Anoub was matter-of-fact. 'She cried and went to her room. In the night, she left and no-one saw her again – alive.'

'I'm very sorry about your sister,' she repeated. The way her brother spoke, Fatima's life couldn't have been easy. It was not surprising she ran away if her father forbade her to have freedoms other people took for granted. 'But I don't know how I can help.'

'Did the person who left her give her an infection?'

Anya wondered why Brody hadn't discussed the case with her. Anoub Deab's motivation seemed odd. He seemed far more worried about infection than how or why his sister died. Reputation meant more to his family than she'd appreciated. It occurred to her that he might have wanted to pursue his own version of justice for the person who left Fatima in the toilet. She hoped she was wrong.

'Do *you* think she had a boyfriend?'

'That's part of what I want you to find out,' Anoub snapped.

'You must realise I can interpret the pathologist's report and find out what I can from the police, but that's about all I can do. Like I said before, I'm not a private investigator. I review medical evidence.'

Anoub straightened. 'Because of Fatima, people think we are drug dealers. My father is being followed and we have had threats on the phone.'

Anya suspected the man was paranoid, but then again, his father required the services of an expensive criminal barrister. 'I know some of the police investigators who cover western Sydney. If you're being threatened, you can tell them about the calls. They may be able to trace them.'

'We cannot do that. My father forbids it.'

Anoub's attitude made Anya uncomfortable, but his request was straightforward. She looked at the small car on her desk and thought of Ben and the lack of work offers. Anoub would obviously pay for her time, and she didn't *have* to like him or the way his family treated women. She felt sorry for the mother, wanting to know what had really happened to her daughter and the anguish of unanswered questions.

'Okay. I can talk to the police about the circumstances of Fatima's death and look through the post-mortem report. Then we can speak again.' Anya stood up and pushed her chair back. 'I may not find out anything you don't already know, but I'll keep your family informed.'

Anoub stood up. 'No! You will report to me and no-one else. Not even Brody.'

His authoritative outburst annoyed Anya. 'Does

36

your father know you're here?' she said, sounding like her own mother.

Anoub straightened and lifted his chin. 'No, he would not approve. My mother agreed, but my father is not to know.'

'Fine, I respect confidentiality. I'll see what I can do.' Anya moved from the desk. Handing back his mother's savings, she explained that Elaine would take his details and discuss a schedule of fees.

Dan Brody, she thought, had some explaining to do. Why had he mentioned her name, and what was really going on with this case?

For a moment she studied her volatile client, wondering whether he had disclosed everything he knew. Gut feeling told her he hadn't.

4

Senior Sergeant John Ziegler had been on call the night Fatima died. Anya's only chance to catch up with him was on a job. He'd postponed their meeting once already and she wanted to clear up the details of Fatima Deab's death quickly. With Dan Brody tied up in court for the rest of the week, she decided to find out what she could about the Deab girl's death.

Crossing the station footbridge, Anya was jostled by school-age voyeurs straining to get a view. Exhaust fumes and diesel from the adjacent main road clouded the air. She pushed to gain a position at the hand rail. Blue and white police tape cordoned off the far end of Platform 1. Parallel to the sleepers, a grey blanket covered the remains of a body. As a train pulled in to Westmead station, a lanky figure in dark blue police overalls and baseball cap moved away from the tracks and was immediately obscured by the carriage. A couple of minutes later the city-bound train continued and the head of the crime scene unit resumed his examination.

Anya pitied the lowly constable who had to notify

the family how their loved one had died. She descended the steps and walked along the platform towards the restricted area. As she surveyed the scene below, the senior sergeant waved a gloved hand and instructed the local police constable to let her enter.

John Ziegler was the senior scene of the crime officer, or SOCO. He photographed the position of the body parts, walked to a distant point, and squatted to zoom in on something on the ground. It was probably the site at which a wallet or some other personal possession was found. After taking photos from a number of perspectives, he began sketching the area. SOCOs were notorious for being methodical and pedantic. The process of examining a scene took time. Anything missed on the initial and most critical attendance could come back to haunt the officers later. It wasn't a spectator sport, Anya thought, wishing she'd worn more practical footwear.

'Sorry about making you come all this way,' the senior sergeant shouted as he approached the platform.

'No problem,' she called back, and shifted her weight between both feet. From her vantage point she could see what appeared to be a limb lying about twenty metres away from the bulk of the covered remains.

Ziegler walked over to the platform, camera hanging from his neck, and squinted up at Anya. 'Just finishing up. Be about five minutes. Hey, how are the drum lessons going?'

'Let's say I'm not ready to join the Police Band yet.' She glanced down at what looked like an arm on the gravel. 'Anything suspicious?'

'The driver is pretty shaken but saw the whole thing. The young bloke jumped from the far end of the platform just as the train was leaving the station and picking up speed.' He turned the page in his sketchbook. 'Lucky he didn't bounce off the platform and end up spread over a hundred metres or more.'

It occurred to Anya that someone dismembered and killed by a train wouldn't normally be considered lucky.

'Find any identification?'

'His bus pass, of all things, was thrown clear.' Ziegler smirked at the irony, and returned to his sketching. 'Grab a seat and I'll be with you in a minute.'

After instructing the government contractors to remove the remains of the body, Ziegler scaled the wall to the platform and planted himself on the bench alongside Anya.

'What's up?' he asked, peeling off his gloves.

'I need to ask you about a scene you attended.'

'Stabbing, shooting, sexual assault?' He leant back and wiped the sweat from his forehead.

'Drug overdose.'

'Dr C, I go to three or four each week I'm on call.' Looking at Anya with weary blue eyes, he softened. 'Can you narrow it down a bit?'

'It was a few weeks ago, a young woman in a toilet block.'

'The Deab case. Seems half the force is in a flap over that one.' Ziegler took off his cap and ruffled his wavy blond hair.

'What do you mean?'

'We treated it like any routine OD and then the shit hit the fan a week later when some anonymous caller claimed the girl had been murdered.' He shook his head slowly from side to side. 'Stuffs your day when that call comes through. We went back to the toilet block, which was a waste of bloody time, and collected up some cigarette butts and a couple of used condoms and that was about it.'

An express train rattled past without stopping and he raised his voice to be heard. 'What's it to you, anyway? I heard you defected to the dark side.'

Anya ignored the barb, pulled a notebook from her bag and waited for the final carriage to pass. 'Was the caller male or female?'

'A bloke, apparently, rang from a public phone box in the shopping centre.'

'Can you tell me anything about the girl's death, like where exactly she was found?'

'In a cubicle.' For a moment he stared into space as though visualising the details.

'Did anything seem suspicious at the time?'

'Nothing at all. Like I said, I do three or four of these a week.' He crossed his arms tightly and sat forward.

'Was the toilet door locked or open?'

'Wide open. The cleaner found the body but denied touching anything.'

'Did she look like a regular user?'

'I'm not sure.' He squinted as though staring at the dead girl. 'She had all the paraphernalia, but there was only one puncture mark obvious on her arm, below a shoelace tourniquet. Other than that she looked clean.'

'Anything unusual about the scene?'

'An OD in Merrylands is a bit of a novelty. We usually find them in Fairfield or Cabramatta,' he said. 'There is a bad batch of heroin going around. We've lost about forty junkies over the last few months. We put out an alert, but the pushers aren't exactly chatty about where the stuff came from.' Ziegler paused and watched a van drive onto the other side of the tracks.

Anya continued. 'What position was the body in?'

'Sitting on the toilet – slumped forward. Like I said, she had all the gear – syringe, water ampoule, spoon, lighter. She used a tampon as a filter.' He rubbed some dirt off his black lace-up boot. 'Never ceases to amaze me how junkies worry about filtering out the crap but don't give a shit about the poison they inject.'

Anya took brief notes. 'Was the syringe within reach?'

'Yeah, right next to her hand. One of those one-mil jobs, orange lid.'

She tried to picture the girl. Fatima could have

known users and learnt how to inject the heroin. The standard approach was to heat the back of a teaspoon filled with water from the ampoule and dissolve the powder. Cotton wool, cigarette filters and even tampons were used to filter out any lumps, and the drug was drawn into the syringe through the makeshift filter.

Anya was curious about the anonymous call. 'Could it have been anything other than an accidental drug death or suicide?'

He frowned and rubbed the cleft in his chin. 'She was clean, smelt like lavender. Oh yeah, she was wearing jeans with this see-through blouse. A hundred dollars was stuffed in a frilly red bra. When we found the money, we figured she was a working girl.'

Ziegler stood and took command of his scene. The government contractors opened the back door of the van and moved to collect the body. The SOCO's attention turned to the contractors. He walked forward and called out more instructions, reminding them to collect the severed limb. 'Someone treated her badly no matter what she was,' he said, turning back towards Anya.

'In what way?'

'She had bruises consistent with belt marks on her back.'

'From a beating?'

'Or beatings. They were old and discoloured. Didn't seem fresh. You know what scars and marks are like, they always look enhanced in the post-state.'

'Any evidence of head injury or restraint marks?'

'Looked for all that but didn't find anything. Lividity matched the position of the body and rigor mortis had started to set in.'

The evidence confirmed that Fatima had died where she was found. So far Ziegler had said nothing to arouse suspicion about the girl's death. She could have been assaulted by anyone if she'd been mixing with pushers and junkies, and an old beating was difficult to relate to the cause of death.

'Anything to suggest someone else was with her in the toilet?'

'Nothing. When we found the money, we figured robbery didn't have anything to do with the death. Any other user would have taken the lot so we treated it as a routine overdose.' He turned and looked down at Anya. 'Unlucky, if it was her first time.'

Anya wondered why a young woman would choose to experiment with drugs on her own, without peer pressure, or whether she intended to harm herself. The autopsy toxicology report might have some more answers.

'What sort of state were her jeans in? And how about her nails?'

Ziegler turned to face Anya. 'Why do you want to know that?'

'She ran away from home a month before she was found dead and no-one knows if she'd been on the street or living with a friend.'

'Didn't look like she'd been on the street. The

jeans were clean and ironed, come to think of it, and the face and nails were painted. What's this all about?' He sounded uncomfortable, as though he'd said too much. 'Why are you involved in the case, anyway?'

'A family member has asked me to look into the death, I think to help understand what happened.'

'Let me guess. They can't believe where they went wrong and why their little angel took drugs.' He sneered. Clearly, he was yet to discover the anguish synonymous with parenting.

'For some reason they're concerned they may have been misinformed,' Anya said, tentatively.

'Am I being investigated?' he demanded.

Following revelations of extensive police corruption, all officers, it seemed, were immediately on the defensive if any question of impropriety arose.

'Of course not! It's nothing like that. I'm trying to find out what I can, to help them deal with Fatima's death. I'm talking to you because you were there.' The pair watched silently as the bright blue body bag was placed into the government van before Anya spoke again. 'The signs of a beating are odd. The family didn't mention that or the money you found, so they probably don't even know. They also didn't mention homicide but seem to think something isn't right about the death. They want to know who took the girl into the toilet.'

'Sorry, can't help you out there. I don't even know what's happening in the investigation. I only find out if I have to appear in court. Anyway,' he said, tilting his head and raising both eyebrows, 'suppose now you're the enemy I shouldn't be talking to you.'

'You wouldn't be the first to think like that.' Anya knew the police resented anyone they believed worked for criminals. Too often, cases fell apart on technicalities, particularly if the crime scene was disturbed or protocol wasn't followed to the last letter. After the Barker trial, she expected the animosity towards her to increase.

'Come on, doc, only kidding. I'll walk you back to your car. Anyone who can play the drums is okay with me.' The SOCO placed a guiding hand on Anya's elbow. 'Why don't you talk to Alf Carney? He's filling in at Western Forensics for a few months. Odd bloke, but he may clue you in some more.'

'Thanks for your help. I appreciate it.'

'You'll just have to owe me a jam session. My sax and your drumming could sound pretty good together.'

Anya accepted that like so many policemen, Ziegler was a compulsive flirt.

Ziegler bowed his head. 'Seriously, I hope this all blows over and turns out to be a crank call. You know how it is; we go on automatic pilot when drugs are involved. It's only a matter of time before one comes back to bite us.'

At eight o'clock the following morning, Anya stood in Dan Brody's oak-lined chambers. Brody, ever stylish in a double-breasted suit, greeted her with a kiss on the cheek. The gesture took her by surprise.

'Thanks for coming this early, I've got to be in court this morning.' He offered Anya a seat facing his desk and unbuttoned his jacket. 'I'm sorry you were bailed up by Anoub Deab. I had no idea he'd go and see you himself.'

'I was surprised when he mentioned your name.'

Removing the suit-coat, he placed it on a hanger on a stand and smoothed the lapels. 'He's young, impulsive and angry. His sister's dead and he wants someone to blame. I told him I'd talk to you so he'd calm down. You are, after all, my star witness.'

'That's understandable,' Anya said, choosing not to contradict him right now. 'But your involvement has me stumped.'

'In what way?' he said, sitting in a high-backed leather seat.

'The family aren't high profile, don't live in the

eastern suburbs and haven't attracted much media attention so far.'

'That's a little harsh, even from you.' He grinned. 'Let's just say I've known the family for a long time and owe them a favour.'

Anya felt hot air from a floor vent. She took off her navy jacket and slung it over the arm of her chair. 'So why are you involved in an overdose?'

'It may not be that straightforward. Mohammed has been asked to give swabs for DNA.'

Anya sat back. If the police wanted DNA samples, there had to be evidence at the scene or on the body itself. 'I spoke to the SOCO. The death was treated like any other OD until an anonymous caller claimed Fatima was murdered. Crime scene went back a week later but didn't find much. Only what you'd expect in a toilet block.'

'I can see the panic on their faces now.' Brody seemed to take a childish delight in the possibility that the police messed up. 'Presuming this "evidence" is old and collected from a public place, they haven't got a chance in hell of implicating my clients.'

'You sound as though you think the Deabs could be involved.'

'You don't know these people.' Brody poured a glass of water from a pitcher on a glass tray to his right and placed it on a pewter coaster across the table. 'I'm merely considering all possibilities.'

'That's what I wanted to discuss with you. There's something odd about Anoub. He only seems interested in what happened to his sister before the death, and how much the police know. He's also convinced the family are being followed.'

'Yeah, well, he might have a point. A source in the department tells me they've been doing a lot of checking up on Mohammed. Even had him under surveillance.'

With the cost of surveillance, there had to be a damn good reason. Anoub may have been using her to find out whether the police had any evidence implicating his father. Obviously, Brody had the same thought. 'Was there something in the PM report?' she asked.

'That's what I'm asking you.' Brody shuffled through a file and handed her a pile of papers.

Sifting through, she identified a copy of the pathology report received by the coroner. The cause of death was listed as 'acute narcotism due to administration of opiate – morphine or heroin'. Turning the page, she quickly surveyed the external examination findings. The body was that of a female adult 160 centimetres in height and weighing forty-five kilograms, dressed in a white blouse, black high-heels, jeans, underpants and red bra.

She read aloud: 'There is a recent puncture mark in the right antecubital fossa, associated with an ill-defined area of reddish-blue bruising approximately three centimetres in diameter.' Looking across the table, she concluded, 'Pretty standard finding. The drug was injected into the front of her right arm.' Her eyes remained fixed to the page as she added what she thought was a rhetorical statement. 'Presumably Fatima was left-handed.'

'So I believe.'

Anya continued reading, her fingers trailing over the words. 'The pathologist mentions a number of yellowish bruises on the back of the body. The largest one measured five centimetres in diameter and was located over the lower part of the right scapula, or shoulder blade.' She glanced at Brody. 'The SOCO talked about them. It looks as though she'd been badly beaten. Yellowing confirms they weren't fresh, and a number of ill-defined scars were noted on the back. Looks like there'd been more than one beating.'

'That's a potential problem. Mohammed Deab was witnessed assaulting Fatima the night she disappeared. A neighbour rang the Department of Family and Community Services, but the girl was over eighteen and didn't fall under their jurisdiction. The community officer knew the family and recommended calling the police, but the neighbour wished to remain anonymous and didn't make any more calls.' Brody doodled on some blotting paper with a gold-plated fountain pen. 'A couple of weeks after the girl's death, the community worker phoned the local detectives but they'd already received the anonymous call you mentioned. By that stage the coroner had ruled that the death was due to a lethal injection of opiate and found no suspicious circumstances, didn't even hold an inquest. Seems the family were very quick to bury her.'

'Bear in mind that's normal practice for Muslims,' Anya said.

'I take your point, but that could be interpreted as a desire to cover something up.'

Anya returned to the report. 'The upper part of the body and the head are congested, consistent with dependent post-mortem lividity, and there is some frothy blood-stained fluid around the mouth and nose.' She watched Brody drawing a series of boxes. 'So far it's straightforward. She died slumped forward where she was found. In opiate-related deaths we often see pulmonary oedema, or fluid on the lungs, caused by heart failure. The fluid sometimes comes up into the mouth.'

'What causes it?' The pen stopped scribbling but his eyes stayed focused on the paper.

'No-one knows exactly how heroin kills, but it may damage the heart muscle, which leads to sudden cardiac failure.'

'Could that in any way be related to the beating?'

Anya scanned the paragraphs headed 'Cardiovascular and respiratory systems'. 'It's a normal-size heart, no sign of any trauma, and the lungs are heavy from the congestion. There isn't anything to suggest a chest injury – no puncture or bruising of the lung, no rib fracture. The assault appears incidental.'

Brody tapped his pen on the notepad. 'Is there anything else that could be incriminating?'

'There's no evidence of head trauma or restraint marks, so it would be difficult to prove whether

51

anybody hit her or held her down before she took the drugs.'

She moved to the toxicology report on the back page.

Screening tests for drugs and poisons show the presence of opiate in blood and urine. Alcohol nil, morphine 0.2 mg/L, codeine <0.5 mg/L, bile – morphine 2 mg/L.

'Looks like Fatima wasn't a regular drug user,' she added.

Brody looked up. 'How can you tell?'

'Heroin is broken down into morphine very quickly, usually too fast to detect. So we tend to measure the level of morphine in the blood, urine and bile.'

'Why bile?' He wrote the word in bold letters.

Anya sat forward. 'Not all labs do it, but Western Forensics routinely takes bile samples. They sometimes end up being useful. Narcotics are concentrated in the liver and secreted into bile, and can be stored there for days or even weeks. Regular users often have very high bile levels.' Anya double-checked the figures. 'The results suggest she wasn't a regular user – could even have been her first time, judging by the lack of obvious injection sites noted by the police and pathologist.'

'Sounds a bit suspicious.'

'Not necessarily. It's easy for a first-timer to overdose. They haven't developed any tolerance to the drug.'

Brody pointed at the document. 'What do you make of page two, last paragraph – "genital vesicles"?'

Anya flipped back to the second page and scanned the description of the external genitalia. Pubic hair was notably absent. Multiple vesicles containing clear fluid were noted on the vulva measuring between two and five millimetres in diameter. Other lesions had progressed to areas of superficial ulceration. 'They're like blisters,' she said.

'Which means?'

'I'd have to check the swabs but it looks like Fatima had herpes.' If Anoub Deab was paranoid about AIDS, he was unlikely to be happy about his sister having a sexually transmitted infection.

Dan Brody smirked. 'Debunks the virgin myth, don't you think?'

Anya ignored the comment. 'A first episode of herpes can be extremely painful. The toxicology report doesn't say anything about acyclovir.'

'"A" what?'

'It's an antiviral medication used to treat herpes. It helps reduce the severity of an episode.'

'Are you suggesting the girl used heroin as a *painkiller*?'

Anya shrugged. 'Unlikely, but anything's possible. Morphine's widely used to treat severe pain.'

53

Brody threw down his pen and ruffled his hair. 'It's pretty clear the police suspect foul play. Unfortunately, there's a well-documented history of domestic violence.'

'Lots of drug users come from families where sexual abuse and domestic violence are a part of life.' Anya straightened the papers on her lap. 'That isn't enough to make anyone suspicious. The police must have something else to go on.'

'I agree. That's where I'd like you to become more involved. I thought I'd talk to the neighbour who called Community Services the night the Deab girl was last seen. So far I haven't had any luck. Fatima's colleagues might know whether or not she had a male companion.'

'I told Anoub Deab that I'd find out what I could about the circumstances surrounding her death. That's all I've agreed to. Now I'm wondering if he told me everything.'

'They're a dysfunctional family, but whose isn't?' Brody shrugged. 'Anoub is probably just flexing his muscles behind his father's back. I don't see a conflict of interest at this stage and you can bill this office for the work you do for me. Mohammed Deab knows I've asked for some expert input and has agreed to pay the bills. As far as I can guess, they both want to know why the police are targeting them.'

'All right, although I'll have to work out whom I'm working for when I send out invoices.' Flipping to the end of the pathology summary, Anya added,

'The histology report isn't here so I'll check the slides and swabs and get back to you.'

Brody rose and handed over a card imprinted with the name Dr Jennifer Wallace. 'This is the GP Fatima worked for. She might be able to give you some information about the girl's habits.' His jaw twitched, and his tone became serious. 'I am sorry Anoub went to see you. The Deabs are in with some pretty unsavoury kinds of people. Just chase the pathology, speak to the GP and don't meet Anoub again without talking to me first.'

'You almost sound worried.'

'Believe me Anya, you don't want to be involved with these people for any longer than necessary.'

As Brody escorted her from his chambers, Anya began to regret her decision to assist Anoub. In the corridor stood a well-dressed man who smiled at them both and greeted Brody with a handshake. Although a few centimetres shorter than the barrister, Vaughan Hunter was a striking figure in many ways.

'Nice piece of work you did on sexual assault victims for the MJA,' Hunter said to Anya.

'I'd forgotten you two worked on a couple of cases with me,' Brody said, a little too loudly. He turned to Anya. 'Vaughan's going to the conference for expert witnesses in Canberra I told you about.'

'Glad someone read my paper.' Each time she had worked with the psychiatrist she had found his composure under cross-examination even more impressive than his breadth of knowledge. She wondered how anyone had that much time to read journals. 'I'd like to go,' Anya lied, 'but I'm committed that weekend.' Two days and nights with her son were better than anything Brody could recommend.

'Go straight in, Vaughan.' Brody turned back to Anya. 'Remember what I said about the Deabs. Be careful.'

6

Dr Jennifer Wallace's surgery was nestled between a chemist the size of a supermarket and an accountant's office on the most congested stretch of Merrylands Road. Anya pushed open the front door and found herself in the middle of an empty reception area. Toys were scattered across the floor and torn women's magazines lay along a row of white plastic chairs. The morning session must have been busy.

A short, portly woman stuck her head out from one of the rooms off a long narrow corridor. 'Dr Crichton?'

The woman approached carrying a full rubbish bin in one hand and a plastic shopping bag in the other. 'I assume you're Dr Crichton. I'm Maria, Dr Wallace's secretary. She's been called out to a minor emergency but shouldn't be long.'

'I'll wait, if you don't mind.'

Maria emptied the rubbish into the plastic bag and tied the handles into a knot. 'It isn't often other doctors come to discuss patients in person.'

'Actually, I've come to talk about Fatima.'

'Jenny said you wanted to know what happened

to her.' Her voice trailed off as she began to pick up toys and dump them in a yellow crate.

Anya bent down to help. 'Did you know Fatima well?'

'Yes, she worked here, you know, until . . .' She lowered her chin and turned away.

'Had you known each other long?' Anya located pieces of a puzzle.

'Since she was a small girl. We used to live across the road from them. They moved to a bigger house when the family bought a smash repair business on Parramatta Road.'

'How long had she been a secretary?'

'Since things got worse. About a year.'

Maria threw the last of the toys into the crate and stood up stiffly. Anya followed her into a consulting room.

'Her father wanted her to leave school, even though her grades were wonderful. She is – was – a bright girl.' The receptionist reached for a spray bottle under the sink and pulled the crumpled sheet from the examination couch. 'She talked her father into letting her earn some money. Jenny gave her the job to help her out and keep an eye on –' She stopped mid-sentence and busied herself cleaning the couch and covering it with a pressed white sheet.

'Keep an eye on her because of the violence at home?'

'You know then, and you do want to find out what happened.' Maria seemed relieved to talk. 'We could hear the screaming and fighting when we were neighbours. The father would rant and rave in English, then his own language. Discipline, he called it. I say it's criminal. I once found her hiding in the bushes and brought her to see Jenny. He'd beaten her black and blue. Big man with his belt.'

Anya stifled a sneeze at the lingering antiseptic and thought of the marks and pattern of bruising on Fatima's back. 'Did the violence lessen?'

'Got worse. The father was convinced she was seeing some boy and had the brother drop her off and pick her up. She even ate her lunch inside.'

Anoub had obviously lied about Fatima missing her train. Anya wondered why. 'So she didn't have a boyfriend that you knew of?'

Maria laughed sarcastically. 'Fatima wouldn't even eat without her father's permission. That girl was terrified of talking to boys.' She puffed the pillow and placed a paper sheet on top. 'Fatima knew if her father found out, he'd kill her and the boy. She was supposed to marry someone in Lebanon.'

'An arranged marriage.'

'Yes, only this man was in his late fifties and already had five children. Fatima was only nineteen, for heaven's sake.' Maria sprayed the sink in the corner.

'What did Fatima do?'

Maria stopped cleaning. 'As far as I know, she was going to go through with it. Her father wanted his cousin to migrate and that is how they do it.'

Anya had seen the fatal consequences of abused women who tried to escape. 'Do you think she may have panicked and run away?'

'Oh no, she would never do that. She had no money and nowhere to go . . .'

Presumably, the father took all the wages, ensuring his daughter's financial dependence.

'Was she an unhappy girl?'

'I don't think so. She didn't know any other kind of life.'

A piercing tone sounded from the room next door.

Maria flinched at the noise and wiped the basin. 'It's the autoclave. I need to release the valve before the door sticks shut.'

Anya sensed that Maria was keen for a temporary distraction and moved into the treatment room. Posters on the walls promoted immunisation, increasing iron intake for 'little Ironsteins' and, ironically, a crisis centre for victims of abuse. She silently watched Maria turn the wheel-shaped handle and release the door of the bench-top autoclave.

'Do you know if she had used drugs before?'

When Maria spoke, it was quietly, as though someone could have been listening. 'I don't believe it. That poor child couldn't even bear to look at needles.' She removed the sterilised instruments with artery forceps, placed them into sterile packs and sealed and dated each one. 'I can't believe she's gone.' Maria began to tremble and dropped the pair of forceps. 'She should have come to me – she promised.' The woman put her hands over her face and wept. 'She'd still be alive . . .'

Anya reached over and put a hand on the woman's shoulder. 'You're not responsible,' she said softly. 'It's not your fault.'

A woman's voice interrupted from the corridor. 'Maria? Are you all right?'

The receptionist grabbed a tissue from the box on the bench and wiped her eyes.

'Dr Crichton is here, I'm fine.'

Anya moved towards the door and greeted Jennifer Wallace.

The GP was a small yet imposing woman with long red hair and grey eyes. A bodysuit stretched to cover shoulders disproportionately large for her frame. She was businesslike in her apology for being detained but softened to address her secretary.

'Harry's in the waiting room. I can look after him, so why don't you have lunch and I'll see you back at three.'

Maria excused herself and left the room.

Dr Wallace spoke first. 'I hoped we could talk in private but one of my patients fell and lacerated his forehead. Harry's pretty deaf and there's no danger he'll have his hearing aid turned on.'

'Let me guess, he's saving the batteries?' Anya asked, familiar with the common elderly habit.

'Exactly.' The GP gave a relaxed smile. 'We can talk while I suture him. Unfortunately it's the best I can do today.'

61

Anya was unused to discussing cases in front of a patient. 'If Harry doesn't mind, of course.'

Dr Wallace returned to the waiting room and helped the elderly man onto the treatment room bed. A blood-soaked hand towel moved to reveal a deep gash above his left eyebrow. Touching his shoulder, she shouted into his right ear her intention to stitch the wound. He raised a hand in agreement.

On a silver trolley beside the bed, she unwrapped a plastic dressing pack, careful not to contaminate the contents. She scrubbed her hands and turned off the long-handled taps with her elbows.

Anya waited before breaking the silence. 'Obviously this is a difficult time for you all, but I'd like to ask you some questions about Fatima Deab.'

'I've already spoken to the police at length.' The GP dried her hands with a sterile paper towel from the open pack. 'So you agree the death warrants further investigation?'

'I am not actually working with the police. Fatima's family has asked me to clarify what happened.'

'In that case, I don't see how I can help you.' She snapped on surgical gloves.

'The family has asked me to find out more about the circumstances of her death and what condition she was in since she'd been missing. Both the crime scene officer and the post-mortem suggest the death appeared routine.'

'Are you sure that's what the family wants? I would have thought they'd want it all hushed up. This may look like a straightforward overdose, but not when you put it in context.'

'Are you talking about the history of abuse?'

'It's more than that. Perhaps there's something you don't understand. Fatima's family is fundamentalist. We're talking about a group within a culture that condoned the murder of a fourteen-year-old girl, whom they accused of sleeping with a local boy. The uncle chained her to a bed and beat her to death. Even when the autopsy found an imperforate hymen, men within the community proclaimed the death a moral victory. The family's honour was at stake and to them, honour is everything.'

Anya tried to hide her revulsion at the inhumanity. 'How severe was Fatima's abuse?'

'See for yourself. Her file and X-rays are on the shelf near the wall. Maria used to bring her here secretly when the father was at work. The mother doesn't drive or speak English.'

While Dr Wallace irrigated the man's wound and injected local anaesthetic, Anya opened the file. Notes dated back seven years. There were multiple entries for soft tissue injuries, bruising and suspected fractures. Anya held some X-rays up to the light. Fractured forearms, jaw, cheekbones and ribs were alarmingly evident on dates spanning the period of treatment. She felt pity for a girl who had known little tenderness in her short life. 'It seems as though the violence escalated the older Fatima became,' Anya said.

'That's right. She had another hairline fracture of the ulna not long before she disappeared.'

'There was no cast on her arm when she was found.'

'That's because I didn't plaster it. She let me treat her on the proviso that no-one else found out. The father believed that her bruises should remind her of the wrong she was supposed to have done. I'd bandage the wrist when she came to work, but she'd take it off before going home.'

'Didn't Community Services get involved?'

'With respect, Dr Crichton, you may not understand some of the complex issues we're dealing with. I'm obliged by law to notify Family and Community Services. I tried it once for Fatima and never again. The father was so enraged by the department's attempted interference, the beatings got worse and Fatima was kept under lock and key. It was two years before she was allowed out on her own. Every visit had to remain confidential. I made the decision to support her rather than provoke more violence. You have to remember that Fatima was a victim, sure, but she *wanted* to stay at home.'

Anya wondered how many more young women were like Fatima Deab.

Dr Wallace sutured the wound with a semicircular needle. 'This isn't an isolated case. Domestic violence is a way of life in many cultures. Look at African-American women, Aboriginal communities. We Anglo-Saxons can't be proud of our record either. Domestic violence rates are horrific but it's difficult to help when women don't want to isolate themselves from their communities and prefer to stay where there is financial and social support. As doctors, all we can do is be there to patch them up, wait for the next crisis and hope something like this doesn't happen.' She finished tying the stitch. 'Do you mind cutting?'

Anya picked up the pair of scissors and snipped the end of the stitch. 'Did you know if she experimented with drugs?'

'There was nothing to support that. She looked anaemic so I took a blood count and iron levels when she had the last fracture. I'd have noticed track marks if there were any. Besides, she was needle-phobic.'

Suicide remained a possibility, Anya thought. She thought about the nun suiciding off the Gap and wondered if Fatima had felt as desperate. 'Was she depressed?'

'Not clinically.' The doctor inserted another suture.

'To your knowledge was she sexually active?'

'I discussed contraception and pap smears but she denied any sexual activity. There was never a suggestion of sexual abuse.'

'Or herpes?'

'Definitely not.' The GP slowly tied off the last stitch and looked at Anya. 'Is that what they found at autopsy?'

'It looks like it.' Anya averted her eyes.

'Oh, God. Did the father know?'

'I'm not sure.' Suddenly Anya felt as though she'd breached a confidence.

Dr Wallace wiped the closed wound and applied a waterproof dressing.

'What that poor child must have gone through. Now, herpes is so common. There's not supposed to be a stigma attached to something that affects one in eight adults. But none of that applied to Fatima.' The doctor's eyes moistened as she spoke. 'For a girl like Fatima, herpes was akin to a death sentence.'

7

Debbie Finch watched the little boy's chest rise and fall with each artificial respiration. A cardiac monitor lauded one hundred beats per minute. He could have been any other sleeping five-year-old except for the ventilation tube in his neck. She reached down and tucked his tiny cold hand under the cotton blanket.

The night doctor approached. 'The CareFlight team will be another twenty minutes. You might as well hand over and go home,' he said before moving on to the next patient.

Debbie checked the fluid dripping into the boy's vein, unable to move her eyes from her little patient who, only a few hours ago, no-one thought would survive. He had choked on a cherry tomato and lay limp in his mother's arms.

When the doctor had tried to intubate, the fragile tomato broke into pieces and completely occluded the windpipe, rendering him without oxygen for three more agonising minutes. The doctor performed a tracheotomy and inserted a breathing tube into the child's motionless neck, bypassing the obstruction. Debbie had deftly handed him sterile equipment, connected up the ventilator and administered medications efficiently and accurately.

Her hands were still warm from the nervous excitement. She couldn't remember feeling this charged, not in all her nursing career at Gosford Regional Hospital. She didn't want to go home, not to her father, not tonight.

She glanced down at the watch pinned to her blue uniform. The carer had to leave at 11 pm, so she'd better make a move.

Debbie pushed through thick plastic doors to the corridor and turned into the staff room, where earlier that night the casualty team had celebrated her fortieth birthday. For once Debbie had been the centre of attention and people were waiting on her. It felt good.

Before leaving she indulged in one more piece of chocolate slice. It was funny, but even if she starved, her uniforms still needed letting out. The hospital laundry had a habit of shrinking them, or so she preferred to think. With a full mouth, she put the card in her bag, grabbed the bunch of flowers and headed out of the building.

Debbie glanced around for a security guard, but knew he'd be on rounds. She'd missed his 10.30 pm nurses' escort. At the bottom of the road she turned left and began the walk up the dimly lit street towards her car. Ahead of her she could make out the silhouette of a man.

He carried a baby capsule in one hand, two bags in the other and something else slung over his shoulder. Typical of a new father, he didn't look like he'd make it to wherever his car was parked.

He dropped one of the bags and arched his back.

'Excuse me,' Debbie called and caught up. A street lamp illuminated a nice-looking man dressed in a polo shirt and dark slacks. A baby teddy bear protruded from one of the bags.

'You look like you could do with a hand,' she offered.

'Thanks. I'm not used to this. Can't believe how much equipment you need to carry around.'

Debbie chuckled. 'From what they tell me, you're supposed to be an octopus to cope.' She picked up one of the bags, wondering why the father and child were leaving the hospital so late. 'Surely you haven't been discharged at this hour?' She leant over to peek at the baby, but the man was shielding the baby from the light with his side.

'My wife's been readmitted, some kind of infection, so I decided we would be better off at home.' He gestured with his free hand. 'The car is just around the corner.'

Debbie lifted the bag with the teddy bear and shuffled the flowers under her arm.

'They're beautiful. Are they from a grateful patient?'

Debbie felt her face flush. 'No, actually they're from workmates. A birthday present.'

'Happy birthday!' He began to walk and picked

up pace. As they turned into Faunce Street, Debbie started to puff, regretting the extra piece of cake.

'Not much further, it's the four-wheel drive up ahead.'

As they stopped at the vehicle, he unlocked both back doors. 'I haven't got used to the restraint yet, do you mind giving me a hand?' He lifted the capsule into the back seat on the driver's side.

Men were so useless, sometimes, she thought. Still slightly short of breath, she placed the bag behind the passenger seat and self-consciously hitched up her skirt just enough to climb onto the seat. The interior light didn't come on. She reached for the harness and tried to clip it in place. Curious to see the sleeping child, she leant across and gently peeled back the blanket. Inside the capsule her hand touched something cold and hard.

Heart hammering, panic filled her.

There was no baby.

8

The following evening, Anya finished some paperwork, edited two articles for a forensic journal and formalised the notes of her discussion with Dr Wallace. She had thought about Ben most of the day and wanted to hear his voice. Martin may have won custody but couldn't deny her that.

She finished her report, went straight to her room and phoned from the cordless handset. The call diverted to Martin's mobile.

'Martin, it's me. I'm calling to remind you about Friday. What time can I get Ben?'

Across the corridor, soft toys lay on a Harry Potter doona cover, ready for his fortnightly visit. A plastic tyrannosaurus sat propped on the red pillow, ready to attack a triceratops lying underneath. Only two days to go, or 'two big sleeps' as Ben would say. She walked in and straightened the doona. Being around his things helped sometimes, but it was nothing like being with him. If she closed her eyes she could almost smell his hair.

Martin's voice sounded strained. 'Something's come up. We won't be back for the weekend.'

'What do you mean you won't be back?' Anya's pulse quickened. 'Where are you?'

'Decided to have a bit of a break down the South Coast. We've been to Merimbula and thought we'd stop in Batemans Bay.'

It was just like Martin to disappear for days at a time, if he thought the surf was up. She'd heard it before, but this time he *knew* it was her turn to see Ben. 'You have no right . . .'

'Don't talk to me about rights. I look after the child. You come and go as you like, and it suits you to have him the occasional weekend. This time we wanted a bit of a holiday and Ben's having a ball. Do you want to ruin it because of your selfishness?'

'That's outrageous and you know it!' She struggled to regain composure. 'You should have told me, we could have organised another time. Maybe I could come to you.'

'That's *not* an option.'

Anya took a deep breath. Out of spite Martin once threatened to take Benjamin away – permanently – somewhere she'd never find him. It was what she feared most of all. She thought quickly. 'Who are you staying with?'

'A friend.'

Her clenched fist trembled. Martin would try to further manipulate the situation. He always did.

'Hey sport, come and say hi to your mum.'

Covering her face with her hand, Anya clutched the phone to her ear. She couldn't keep Martin offside for too long. While unemployed, he remained eligible for Legal Aid, whereas she wasn't because she earnt a living. Not only did she pay him maintenance but she supported a secretary's wages and paid off the Annandale house. She didn't have the extra money needed to legally fight Martin when he pulled stunts like this. Dan Brody had helped with some advice and recommended a lawyer friend – who charged more than he did! In some ways, being divorced was worse than being married. She still did all the work but Benjamin wasn't there when she came home.

'Hello, Mummy?'

Ben's voice almost made her cry.

'Hi there, sweetheart. Daddy said you're having a holiday?'

'We saw kangaroos that hop really fast! And there were lots of ducks going quack. One of the naughty ducks ate my lunch.'

'Did you like the kangaroos?' Suddenly the animals seemed more important than any feud with Martin.

'Uh-huh.' He paused, then added, 'I like kangaroos.' Benjamin panted with excitement. 'We are sleeping in a van with Nita. And I went into the water, all by myself. I went all by myself, Mummy. And Nita played golf with me and I hit the ball into the hole . . .'

Anya winced and held her breath. This woman even took her three-year-old to mini-golf. Her son loved the sea, being outside and playing ball sports.

She hoped that was all he had inherited from his father.

Benjamin chatted away, and then asked the painful question: 'Mummy, when are you coming to our van? I miss you.'

Trying to find the right words, she answered, 'I can't come to the van, darling. I have to talk to Daddy about seeing you as soon as you come back to Sydney.'

She could hear Martin in the background telling Ben to say goodbye and get ready for bed. Martin took back the receiver before Anya could say goodnight.

'There you go, you had a good chat. That should satisfy you.'

'You know damn well the court granted me access every second weekend.' She fought back tears.

'Go whinge to one of those fancy lawyers you hang around with.' His resentment was unmistakable. 'I'm not in the mood for an argument now. We can talk next week,' he said before hanging up.

'You bastard!' she screamed at the dead line. 'Everything's always on your terms.'

As she slammed down the phone, the framed photograph crashed off Ben's bedside table, shattering its glass cover. A piece sliced her finger as she brushed aside the shards. Ignoring the bleeding she picked up the photo of Benjamin squealing with delight as she lifted him into the air.

9

Early the next morning, Anya pulled into the car park outside the mortuary located at the Western Sydney Centre for Forensic Medicine. She entered the building through a glass door, buzzed the intercom and waited.

'Anya Crichton, here to see Jeff Sales.'

The door opened and Anya followed the sound of the Stryker saw, which echoed through the corridor to the post-mortem suite change rooms.

According to the clock on the wall, she was due to give an opinion in another coronial inquest in three hours. That left enough time to chase the Deab girl's histopathology, report back to Dan Brody and return to town. That was, if everything went to plan.

She exchanged her navy suit for blue surgical scrubs, pulled on a couple of shoe protectors and headed back along the corridor to the autopsy suite. She entered and cupped her hand over her nose. Only a decomposing body could smell that bad.

Holding the saw over the corpse was Gilbert Rowlands, the longest-serving pathology technician at the WSCFM. The Stryker had been superseded by gardening secateurs, which were effective, cheap and didn't cause bone dust. But Gilbert preferred to saw his way through a chest wall.

The room was brighter than normal, with spotlights glaring over each of the eight stainless steel tables.

Gilbert interrupted the ribcage separation to collect something from the body's hair with a pair of tweezers and held it up to his plastic goggles.

'Thought you'd got away, didn't you,' he said through a charcoal-filter face mask. The technician dissected each body and laid out the organs before the pathologist arrived. Collecting insect specimens on the job was a bonus.

'Hi Gilbert, is Jeff Sales around?' Anya almost shouted through her hand.

'No-one here but me and Ruby. They found her in a deck chair on her roof. And judging by these maggots, she's been working on her tan for quite a while.' Gilbert used the tweezers to transfer an insect from the woman's eye to a jar containing a small amount of organic material. A second, ethanol-filled jar sat sealed on the bench beside the table.

'Hey, did you hear about the intern who certified her?' Gilbert said, as though telling the first line in a joke. 'Threw up for half an hour outside Cas.'

According to hospital tradition, the most junior doctor was sent to certify bodies. She'd always remember climbing into the van and unzipping a body bag for the first time. A junior constable claimed the vagrant found floating in a local river had been there only a few hours, not two weeks as was later determined. One of the nurses offered a hospital stethoscope, but Anya had insisted on using her new Littmans Cardiology brand to listen for a heartbeat. When it sank through the chest wall, her initiation had begun.

'Any idea where Jeff might be? I am supposed to meet him here.'

'I don't need him until I'm done weighing the organs.'

Outside the autopsy suite, out of habit, Anya washed her hands in the corridor sink. Jeff Sales arrived wearing scrubs and white gumboots.

'What's with the spotlights? Looks like a solarium in there,' Anya said.

'Impressive, aren't they?' Jeff grinned. 'They've only been in a couple of weeks.' He rubbed his hands together. 'A real coup, considering we didn't pay for them.'

'Don't tell me there's a benefactor,' Anya said.

'No, the show put them in.' The interruption of a television crew filming a crime series based on a female pathologist was the talk of the hospital.

'Weren't the fluorescent lights bright enough?'

'On the contrary, they thought it was too light. Apparently, the viewing public expects morgues to be dark and gloomy.'

The reality was vastly different. Western Sydney

had windows just below the ceiling to let in as much natural light as possible without attracting voyeurs.

'They blackened the windows and only filmed once they'd installed the overhead spotlights. When they finished, they left the lights in place.'

'Just in case you ever want to grow hydroponics,' Anya joked.

'We all know the dead have never been a priority for hospital funding,' Jeff said, ushering Anya to the female change room. 'I'll get changed and meet you in the histology room. Sorry about the rush but I've got a plane to catch in a few hours. I'm presenting a paper at the Montreal conference, then the kids will join us for a holiday.'

Organising time off was difficult enough, Anya knew. With two pathologists from the same department in the household, joint holidays were almost impossible to arrange. No wonder Jeff seemed so excited.

'Fatima Deab, wasn't it?'

'Yes.'

In the histology lab, he bent over the computer terminal and typed in the name and identification number. 'Microbiology is back but there's no histology report in the file. Must be in the "to do" pile.' He walked over to the large sliding cabinet and removed the specimens mounted on slides. 'No rush once the coroner ruled the death routine on the basis of the initial PM report.' He took a slide out of its cardboard container. 'But since you're here, we might as well look at these and put them to bed.'

'Can we start with the vulva?' she asked, taking a notebook from her briefcase.

'I remember this one. On gross examination, the blisters were everywhere around the genitals. Given it was clearly an OD, we may not have noticed if she hadn't shaved the region.' He peered down the microscope. 'Okay, well, the features are typical of herpes simplex infection. There are your typical intranuclear inclusions, ballooning of cells and intra-epithelial vesicle formation.'

'Much inflammation?' Anya asked without looking up.

'Relatively sparse, as you'd expect. The swab came back positive for herpes simplex type two.'

'Do you remember if she had a cold sore at the time of her death?'

She had read of women with genital herpes who denied any sexual contacts. She could only surmise that they had accidentally infected themselves by touching both the cold sore and their own genitalia.

'Up to eighty per cent of genital infections are caused by type two. She didn't need to have a cold sore. And I don't recall seeing one on her face.'

'I know, but the question of sexual contact could be a problem for the family.'

Jeff was sympathetic but always pragmatic. 'Anya, in your experience, common things occur commonly, right? Herpes is common, adolescents commonly have sex. And if she was a drug user, her immune system was probably suppressed. You know the old adage, if it's yellow and it quacks . . .'

'Definitely no sign of sexual interference?' she said, hoping for Fatima's sake.

'None, but you wouldn't necessarily see any. As you know, it's pretty unusual to see signs of trauma even after a rape.' He looked across at Anya. 'Don't tell me the family want proof she was a virgin?'

'I'm sure they would if there was a way of proving it. What about Hep B and C, or HIV?'

'All negative. We ran them before the post-mortem.' Jeff removed the slide and replaced it in its protective case. 'What's next?'

'Well, the rest is likely to be normal, but –'

'I know, for thoroughness, let's go through them.' He sat reviewing the slides of blood, heart and brain. As he continued reporting, Alf Carney, the acting director, entered the room.

'What do you think you're doing?' he demanded.

Jeff stood up to introduce Anya, but was quickly interrupted.

'I know who she is. What does she think she's doing here, behind my back?'

'Excuse me? I'm not here behind anyone's back,' Anya said, stepping forward to meet his eye.

'I didn't see a written request for you to access any of our material.'

'I told her not to bother with formalities,' Jeff interjected.

'Well, you don't have the authority.' Carney

stabbed his index finger in Sales' direction. 'I am the one who grants or denies access to information protected by this office.'

Anya felt her face flush. 'The Royal College of Pathologists of Australasia has a policy relating to second opinions. A request to review material in a case by a bona fide expert in the area must not be refused.'

'I'm familiar with the policy. That access is only granted as long as it won't interfere with the functioning of the coroner in the case of a homicide, or confidential aspects of a police inquiry.'

'In practice, we've never refused a request,' Jeff offered. 'Besides, the coroner has already ruled this case a drug overdose.'

'This case is marked as a possible homicide,' Carney said before turning to Anya. 'I want you to leave now. You may send a written request and I'll review it as I see fit.'

Anya had heard that Alf Carney could be difficult. Rumour had it, he was even more so after a current affairs television program questioned his findings in relation to a number of cases. She decided that an argument right now would be futile. Carney was still acting head of Western Forensics for another six months, until the permanent director returned from a sabbatical working with the International War Crimes Tribunal. Besides, she had the information she needed. She did, though, wonder why he'd become so defensive about another pathologist looking at the case.

She picked up her briefcase, thanked Jeff for his courtesy and left.

Back in the car, along the M2 tollway, Anya's mobile rang. She slowed and pulled over.

'Anya, Jeff Sales. Sorry about the trouble earlier. Alf's under a bit of pressure with two of his cases being reopened. I tried to keep you away from him.' Anya heard crackling; the line was breaking up.

'I'm about to board the plane but I thought you should know. I finished going through those slides and it's probably nothing, but the lung tissue wasn't entirely normal.'

'In what way?'

'Fibres. Masses of fibres were embedded in the lung tissue.' The signal was interrupted. 'Don't know what the chances are, but –'

'Can you describe them?'

'They're unlike anything I've seen before. Looked like –' His voice dropped out. The phone crackled before it cut in again.

'. . . small hourglass shapes.'

The line went dead.

10

Anya studied the computer screen. On the desk lay the remainder of a half-eaten Lean Cuisine, forgotten when she downloaded the files. Jeff Sales had scanned the slides before he'd left for the airport and sent them attached to an e-mail. What a gem. She owed him one.

In the quiet of her office, she stared at the fibres. Why had there been two cases with similar findings in such a short space of time? The post-mortems on Clare Matthews and Fatima Deab had been conducted at different centres, so the specimens couldn't have been from the same person, and merely mislabelled. The odds of two young women inhaling the same fibres would have to be low, but how low? If it was a new fibre used in buildings, was this the start of an epidemic? She searched the web and failed to find a match for the hourglass fibres. Histopathology sites showed the usual asbestos, but no variants. A Medline search didn't help either. There were no journal articles of lung disease caused by anything resembling what Jeff had found.

The Central Sydney Public Health Unit and the Western Area branch websites didn't contain any warnings or press releases apart from the usual advice about Legionella infection.

She clicked on her discussion groups and sent a question to the forensic list group, along with the jpeg files of the slides. The list comprised crime scene police, forensic scientists, pathologists and criminal lawyers from all over the globe. The forum had proven useful over the last couple of years and meant invaluable access to some of the world's foremost forensic experts. Someone was bound to recognise the fibre, or give the name of someone who could.

Checking her inbox, she found a message from her father reminding her of the next Victims of Homicide meeting on Tuesday night. This time he hadn't phoned. She didn't know whether it was a relief, not having to give him a feeble excuse, or whether he'd given up asking. It was too late to ring – her stepmother loathed calls in the evening – and an e-mail seemed inadequate on what would have been her sister's thirty-second birthday.

She picked up the phone and dialled her mother in Launceston. The answering machine clicked in, saying that Dr Jocelyn Reynolds was on call for the practice. She was currently on a housecall and would be back as soon as possible. Anya decided not to leave a message and hung up. She couldn't think of anything that would make tomorrow more tolerable. There was only one day worse than Miriam's birthday – the anniversary of her disappearance.

Right now, the computer screen seemed strangely comforting. She had privacy and independence but could communicate with the world – on her terms.

The next fifty e-mails were spam. One click and they were banished to the black hole of cyberspace. If only dealing with family and the past was that simple.

Another e-mail appeared in the inbox, this one from Sabina Pryor, a lawyer with the indictable section of Legal Aid. Sabina congratulated Anya on the positive press for her testimony in the Barker case and wasted no time inviting her to provide opinions for a number of trial cases. At five hundred dollars per case involvement, the money wasn't worth it, but the work was interesting. She didn't have any pending court cases, so she typed a message agreeing to help where she could.

She glanced at her watch and realised it was 1 am. Time to clean up after dinner and throw the leftovers in the bin. After checking the locks on the doors and windows, she listened for any strange sounds. All she could hear was the silence of being alone.

The next morning, Anya found Peter Latham drinking coffee in the institute's tutorial room with

Zara. She loaded the floppy disk into one of the computers and showed them the e-mailed slides.

'Two sets of fibres is an unusual coincidence, particularly given the nature of the inflammation and the age of the women,' Peter said.

Zara interrupted. 'What are you saying? Do we have a serial killer?'

'No, that's not what we're suggesting at all!' Anya couldn't hide her irritation. 'These two young women have somehow been exposed to a fibre. If the fibre causes inflammation after a relatively short time, given these women's ages, who knows how much damage it could do over time? It's more likely to be a public health issue.'

'I agree,' said Peter. 'Whenever we see two similar cases in a short period, alarm bells ring.' He turned his attention to Zara. 'Two infants recently died from choking on the same brand of block. If we hadn't made the connection, the company wouldn't have recalled the blocks and more kids would have been at risk.'

'If the fibre is a hazard, shouldn't it be removed?' asked Zara.

'A large amount of asbestos in buildings has been, but in other cases it's safer to leave it in place,' Peter said. 'The danger lies in disrupting the dust in the process of removal, or in some cases, renovations.'

Zara fiddled with the elastic on her plait. 'But I thought this fibre wasn't asbestos.'

'We don't know what it is, exactly,' Anya said,

'but so far it appears to cause inflammation, like asbestos does.'

'What happens now you've got two similar lung cases?'

'A couple of problems,' Anya replied. For one, we don't know where the fibre came from, whether the women were exposed at work, home, or somewhere else.' She stood up, walked over to a portable whiteboard in the corner and pulled the lid off a marker.

'Firstly, we need to establish whether this is an artefact, or not.'

'Don't we want to know if anyone else has the same finding?' Zara asked.

'Yes. If the fibre appears in every lung slide, we can assume there's something wrong with the slide mounting process and take it from there. But if it isn't frequently occurring, it's important to determine whether there are any other cases.'

'How do we do that?'

'I'm glad you asked,' Anya said.

Peter gave her a familiar smile. 'I might leave you two to it, to see how you go. In the meantime I'll ask the other pathologists whether they remember seeing something like this.' He collected Zara's empty cup and left the room.

Anya continued. 'What we do know is that both women lived and worked in older buildings around Sydney. It's possible they were exposed in daily life, through either their jobs or home. Dilapidated buildings could be leaching something.'

'How are we going to prove that?'

'The first step is to establish whether the two women lived or spent time in the same places, and more importantly, if we've had anyone else through here with similar lung findings.' On the whiteboard she wrote a question mark, followed by 'number of cases', then turned to her student. 'We need to make some very subtle enquiries. This may be nothing at all, but it's a good opportunity to see how pathologists can make links and investigate unusual findings.'

'What can I do?' Zara asked.

'Let's start with a search of the departmental database. That way you can get some hands-on experience of the system.'

Zara sat at the computer, lowered the seat and logged on with Anya's instructions. She then typed the word 'fibre' with two fingers.

The computer took what Anya thought was far too long until she saw the search results. Thousands of entries contained the word 'fibre'. Hair fibres, muscle fibres and clothing fibres were mentioned in almost every post-mortem report, it seemed. This wasn't going to be easy. Zara typed in 'lung and fibre', locating all the references for lung as well.

'We have to think laterally,' Anya said.

'What about where the nun was found?'

Zara typed in 'the Gap'. Again, reams of references appeared on the screen. The word 'gap' appeared in thousands more references to teeth, distance between injuries, and lesions. It was impossible to manually search each entry.

Frustrated, Anya knew she'd have to wait until Jeff returned from overseas to access his department's records. Alf Carney was less than likely to be helpful, unless the approach came from Peter Latham. That was still one avenue that remained unchecked.

'What about the National Coroner's Information System?' Zara suggested. 'I don't know much about it, but we had a lecture saying it was set up.'

'That might be worth a try,' Anya agreed. 'It's based in Melbourne, at the Victorian Forensic Centre.' The NCIS was established in 1998 to collate post-mortem findings around Australia to identify clusters of similar cases and trends in order to reduce preventable death and injury. 'Ordinarily you need written permission to do a search, but this is in the interest of public health, after all.'

Anya located the website and typed in her password and access code. Zara read the entry screens and resumed the search. Again, the term 'fibre' yielded thousands of results. The full text of each PM report appeared with the relevant word highlighted on the screen. It made a visual scan easier, but the process remained time consuming, without any guarantee of a result.

Undeterred, Zara's determination seemed piqued by the challenge.

'How about "asbestosis"?'

89

The search yielded a couple of hundred cases. Zara would have to read the whole of each report to see if an hourglass-shaped fibre was mentioned.

'This is one of the problems with the database. Pathologists don't have a standardised way of reporting things. It's easy with something like toxicology, which has a protocol and terms with strict definitions, but our work is largely subjective, interpreting findings. What I describe as hourglass shaped might be called something else by a different pathologist.'

Zara baulked at the number of files on the screen.

Anya had a better idea. 'Let's take the slide and show the respiratory pathologist at Royal Prince Albert Hospital in town. She does most of our difficult lung cases. Maybe she can identify it for starters. Now, just to warn you, Dr Blenko is a stickler for detail and she is likely to ask questions we can't answer, and not too diplomatically.'

'Sounds like a scary woman.' Zara quickly logged off and grabbed her backpack from near the door.

'That's why I'm going with you.'

Professor Blenko sat at the microscope in her office with chained glasses hanging around a thick, wrinkled neck.

'Come,' the professor commanded without looking up.

Anya and Zara stopped inside the doorway, awaiting further instruction.

'What do you want?' demanded the gravelly voice.

Anya had always thought that manners and people skills were inversely proportional to levels of expertise. Judith Blenko's expertise remained unrivalled. 'Professor, thanks for making time to see us.'

'I don't have time to waste. Where is it?' She looked up and stuck out a hand.

Anya removed the Clare Matthews slide from her coat pocket and placed it in the professor's palm. Not invited to sit down, she and Zara remained standing.

The respiratory pathologist adjusted the slide and buried herself in the view. A few silent minutes passed.

'Clinical history?' she asked without disturbing her line of vision.

'This was an incidental finding on a young woman who committed suicide off the Gap. We've learnt of another case with a similar fibre and were wondering –'

'Did the patient have respiratory symptoms?'

'None recorded in the GP's notes,' Anya said, and thought she heard what sounded like a grunt.

'Where are the other specimens?'

Anya transferred weight from one foot to the other, anticipating a dressing down. She hated being made to feel like a naughty child, but being confrontational towards the Blenkos of the medical world was almost always counterproductive. 'There are no other specimens.'

Dr Blenko looked sideways with a scathing expression. 'When will you people understand the importance of obtaining quality slides?' She returned to the lens. 'What were the weights of the right and left ventricles?'

'They weren't recorded at PM,' Anya admitted.

This time the professor didn't bother to look up.

Recording the weight of the ventricles was helpful to a lung expert in establishing the significance of lung disease and pulmonary hypertension, but was unnecessary in a suicide. Anya had always wondered how to accurately record the weight of individual heart chambers when they shared a common wall.

'Can you identify the fibre?' she asked.

'I see very few post-mortem slides. Ninety-nine per cent of my work is from tissue biopsied during a diagnostic bronchoscopy, or taken during lung resection surgery. This fibre is probably an artefact. It doesn't look anything like asbestos. I suggest you review your slide preparation technique.'

'If it were an artefact, it should be appearing in other cases. At the moment it's the only one we have. The other suspected case was found at Western Forensics.'

Dr Blenko re-examined the slide before handing it back.

'This may be something that presents to occupational health and safety. I suggest you talk to someone at WorkCover or the Dust Diseases Board. If this is not, in fact, an artefact.'

With that, Anya and Zara were dismissed.

11

The man in the car watched Mohammed Deab park his vintage gold Mercedes. As usual, Deab lit a cigarette and looked up and down the street before entering the smash repair workshop. From what the man had seen, only two types of cars ever came in for repairs – the non-damaged, and others so smashed up, they would be a write-off in anyone else's book. Within minutes, a tow truck pulled in with a vehicle so mangled its make was unidentifiable. He relaxed and switched on the car radio. It could be a while before Deab showed his face again.

Outside the workshop, the daily parade of men smoking, loitering and arguing continued. Right on midday, a police car drove in and blocked the workshop entry. Before the two officers had closed their car doors, four men from outside had an urgent need to be somewhere else. No doubt about it, the boys in blue knew how to disperse a crowd. Half an hour passed before the constables came out, had a final look around and left.

Within minutes, Deab appeared again, talking into his mobile phone, waving his cigarette around as he spoke. Most of his conversations were animated, at least from a spectator's viewpoint, but this one was different. He almost looked excited, pacing around the driveway, with one hand on his hip. When the conversation finished, he shoved the phone into his shirt pocket and disappeared into his office. It wasn't long before he rushed out with a long, black sports bag and checked his watch.

A red Torana, its numberplate obscured, lurched into the driveway from the rear of the building with one of Deab's panel beaters behind the wheel. Mohammed looked up and down the road again, flicked his cigarette and got into the passenger seat. The Torana screeched back onto the main road, barely missing an oncoming bus.

Detective Constable Brian Hogan left his car and briskly headed over to where Mohammed Deab had last stood. The place was strangely quiet after the constables' visit. He bent and pretended to tie a shoelace. Scanning the ground, he pulled on a latex glove.

Bingo!

Hogan picked up the discarded cigarette butt and placed it inside a brown paper envelope.

This time, Deab, you're going down.

The white Ford Falcon slowed about fifty metres behind the parked red Torana, then drove past the grey brick house, turned right into the adjacent side street and parked in the shade of a tree two houses down. Constable Wheeler positioned his side mirror to get a good view of the front of the property. From his rear-view mirror, he could see Deab's car.

He wound down the driver's window and watched. He didn't recognise this street. Deab hadn't been here in the last two weeks, but that didn't mean much. Mohammed Deab was a busy boy with his extracurricular activities. This could have been business or pleasure; the object of surveillance overindulged in both. Either way, the plain-clothes constable didn't care.

After the driver walked around to the passenger side, Deab climbed out of the Torana and reached into the back seat. He pulled out an iron bar and the two men headed for the house.

'Shit!'

Constable Wheeler scrambled for the mobile phone by his side and dialled.

'Detective Farrer, we've got a problem. Deab and an accomplice just entered a house. 5120 Greystanes Road. He's carrying an iron bar of some kind and looks pissed off.'

He listened to the instructions.

'Don't get involved, Wheeler. I'll call the local police and arrange an ambulance. Do you understand me? Do *not* get involved.'

The young constable knew better than to argue with 'The Bitch' from Homicide. She may have been short in stature but she had bigger balls than most blokes he'd met. At least he always knew where he stood with her, and she'd already proven that she wasn't afraid of carrying the can. If things stuffed up now, she'd be carrying more than that.

'Okay.' He tried to sound comfortable about the situation.

'Don't compromise the surveillance. We've put a lot into this and I don't want you to blow it now.'

'Okay,' the young constable repeated, 'I understand.'

Waiting and staying out of sight were what Wheeler did best. As a child with a terrible stutter, he'd been too afraid to speak. At each new school, the other children had treated him as if he were invisible. Even though the stuttering had been controlled for years, Shaun Wheeler chose to make a career out of being 'the invisible kid'. But now the idea of sitting by while a crime took place unnerved him. It's where the ethics became blurry. He studied the side mirror, hoping to catch a glimpse of what was going on. His fingers tapped the dashboard.

Three minutes and forty seconds later Deab left the house, carrying his makeshift weapon. His mate was a couple of steps ahead and seemed in a big hurry to get away.

A woman ran out to the front yard, screaming for help, hitting Deab with her fists. The older man shoved her to the ground and got into the car. The driver must have kept the engine running, because he pulled out quickly, swiping a parked van in his path.

'Shit! Where are the uniforms?' Constable Wheeler

threw open the car door and sprinted towards the woman. As he hurdled the low fence, he saw that her hands were covered in blood. She kept screaming.

He grabbed her by the shoulders and asked her where she'd been hurt. It took until a police car screeched to a halt in the middle of the road for him to realise she wasn't injured.

'Inside!' Wheeler shouted above the woman's screams. 'Two suspects absconded in a red Torana.'

An officer wrote down the details. Wheeler's priority was to disappear but the woman wouldn't let him go. She dragged him to the open front door, clawing at his arms.

'Listen, lady,' he pleaded, 'the police are here now.' He tried to release her grip. 'I can't get involved.'

Inside the entrance lay a body in a pool of blood, the face unrecognisable. From somewhere came the hissing of air.

'Jesus! He's alive!' Wheeler shouted.

The woman wailed over the battered body, only to be drowned out by the ambulance siren outside.

The two ambulance officers rushed inside with tackle boxes and an oxygen cylinder. One gave orders and the other held a mask over the swollen and bleeding face. Wheeler staggered from the house.

He stared at the blood on his own hands and wanted to throw up.

12

Anya put the suitcase in the boot and slammed it shut. With Ben still down the South Coast with his father, she'd thought she might as well brave the expert-witness conference Brody had recommended. It was the only way she could think of to make the weekend pass more quickly. The morning was crisp, clear, and the sun hadn't yet risen to its full glory. At this time of year, 5 am was her favourite time of day, when the raucous calls of parrots beckoned young children (and by default, mothers) from their beds. She went back to the house to check the locked windows, and deadlock the front and back doors. She resisted the urge to check again. Martin complained that she was obsessive about safety. This came from a man who couldn't close a door, let alone lock one. The thought of him opening windows day and night was a constant worry. Fresh air could get you burgled, or worse.

She stopped herself from phoning Martin and leaving a message on his voicemail, to remind him to lock the caravan for Ben's sake. There was no point aggravating him right now.

The car was one of the few places she felt both safe and free. She locked the driver's door from the inside and cleared Liverpool within half an hour. Once out of the suburbs, Canberra was less than three hours away. On the freeway past Mittagong, the sign for the Sutton State Forest appeared. There she had examined the remains of a retired couple reported missing on a camping trip around Australia. The sight and smell of the decomposed bodies would always stay with her. For the first time in her career, she'd wanted to cover the bodies, to give them a modicum of dignity in death. From the severity and extent of their injuries, it was something they were deprived of in their last hours or days. The murderer had never been caught, and from the diffuse and extensive injuries, Anya remained convinced the injuries were caused by two different people.

Her thoughts turned to the family of the couple. The only comfort to the four grown children was that they had some closure and could bury what was left of their parents. The bodies, if not the family, could rest in peace.

Anya switched on the Radio National classical station and tried to enjoy the trip. The last half hour of the drive to the nation's capital, past Lake George, was the most relaxing. Planned roads made everything easy to find – Lake Burley Griffin and the Captain Cook memorial fountain, sights she always enjoyed. Once over the bridge, she saw the

Hyatt Hotel on the other side of Commonwealth Avenue. She turned right into a side street, drove back onto the main road, pulled in and parked her car outside the entrance.

At reception she entrusted her suitcase to a bellboy, then located the registration desk for the conference. Linda from the legal firm Mulholland and Chater introduced herself with a smile and polished white teeth. Linda had almost perfect dimensions and immaculate 'presentation', as she flashed her eyes around for the men and barely gave Anya the rundown. The conference would begin at 9 am sharp and had a full program, including a mock cross-examination of each dele-gate, which would be videotaped and assessed for feedback by the group.

'The weekend will be great,' Linda said, beaming through bright red lipstick.

Anya had a flashback to the days of Newcastle University and the torture of watching herself on videotape as a group of people she barely knew dissected her professional and personal skills. She felt her blood chill.

The process was non-threatening, or so the tutors said. The only thing remotely more threat-ening would be going through the whole thing naked.

She suddenly regretted coming. The object of the conference was to be less intimidated by lawyers, not humiliated by them in front of peers, and pay a fortune for the privilege. So far, the weekend was shaping up to be appalling, courtesy of her ex-husband and Dan Brody.

She thanked the human Barbie Doll from the firm and collected her information package. Turning, she noticed a familiar face standing beside her at the registration table. An older delegate sidled up and patted him on the shoulder. 'Good to see you back, Vaughan. You're looking well.'

'Thanks, Tom. It's good to be here, or anywhere, for that matter,' he said, as the man caught the eye of someone else and moved on. Vaughan's gaze fell on Anya.

'Excuse me, have we met?' he asked jokingly. He smiled warmly and extended his right hand.

'Hello Vaughan.' Anya shook his hand firmly.

'I thought you told Dan you weren't coming?'

'Plans change.' She quickly added, 'Couldn't beat a weekend of masochism. Embarrassing yourself in court doesn't endure. So I thought for posterity's sake, I'd record it on video.'

'Come on, it isn't that bad. This course is designed to help expert witnesses,' he said.

'Don't tell me you actually believe the propaganda in the brochure?'

'I'm one of the organisers, and a speaker.'

'Please don't say you testify for Mulholland and Chater, the greatest conjurers of class actions in the country?'

'No.'

'That's lucky, because I could have put my foot in it with a comment about the company's public persona,' she said, glancing at Barbie giggling with a man old enough to be her grandfather.

'Is there a problem with my wife?'

Anya felt her cheeks go a deeper shade of red. *Oh God, me and my mouth.*

'I'm sorry. I didn't know. I mean, I'm not sorry for you. I mean –'

Vaughan laughed and touched her arm. 'No need to apologise, I was kidding. I've never been married. I've always preferred what a woman has to offer from the neck up. Animated mannequins,' he said, glancing in Barbie's direction, 'don't hold interest for long.'

Anya was dumbstruck. She breathed a quiet sigh when one of the waiters asked delegates to make their way to the dining room for the introductory session.

Stopping at the first table, she filled a Styrofoam cup with black coffee and grabbed a chocolate-filled croissant from the pastry table. Vaughan watched her with a curious expression.

'What? Aren't the condemned allowed a last meal?' Anya said defensively.

Vaughan let her walk through the door first and whispered, 'The video session's not until tomorrow.'

The morning sessions included talks by crown prosecutors and defence lawyers. Anya had seen many of them in court, and had been on the receiving end of their semantic games and caustic tongues. She did have to admit, though, that compared to other witnesses, they treated her with respect on the stand. The police constables were routinely made to look like bumbling idiots for the jury.

Before lunch, the slowest session of any conference, Vaughan Hunter made a presentation entitled, 'Mind games – verbal and non-verbal communication in the courtroom'. His imitation of lawyers' and witnesses' body language had the audience laughing, although the underlying message was clear. Juries always sense when someone is uncomfortable, unsure or out of their depth. Arrogance, pretentiousness, over-confidence and under-confidence were fast ways to alienate jurors. Anya wrote the words 'Competent, sympathetic, authoritative, but be humble' and wondered if she would ever become confident in a courtroom.

She looked around the room at the people chuckling while they squirmed, a sure sign they recognised themselves in Dr Hunter's role plays. Among the thirty or so participants, she recognised a couple of forensic physicians from Melbourne, a professor of pharmacology, a cardiothoracic surgeon she'd seen testify on gunshot wounds, and a ballistics technician from the crime lab. Each was fixed on the speaker. No-one in the room dozed, testament to Vaughan Hunter's ability to hold an audience's attention after a morning tea of pastries and tepid tea.

'The final take-home message is never be coerced into giving an opinion out of your area of expertise. Don't guess. You'll only dig yourself into a hole and a lawyer with half a brain cell will bury you before you realise it's happening. Apart from that, have fun on the stand! And good luck tomorrow.'

The room applauded and everyone recessed for lunch.

Anya rose and headed for the door, keen to avoid polite conversation with people she barely knew. She took lunch to her room and decided to miss the last two sessions – one discussing the ethics of expert witnesses and the other covering legalities of subpoenas and medical records. Instead, she thought she'd look at the National Gallery's exhibition of John Glover's paintings of colonial Tasmania, and explore Questacon, the hands-on science centre by the lake.

She changed into a denim shirt, jeans and sandshoes and walked the few blocks, past the National Library. Canberra was often described as sterile, but Anya liked its clean, uncluttered feel. Unlike being in Sydney, she didn't feel grime under her fingernails or on her skin at the end of the day. The bike tracks around the lake and huge areas of grass and parkland within walking distance of the city centre meant that in the fine Saturday weather, families were out cycling, walking, scootering or picnicking as the bells of the Carillon rang across the water.

The gallery never failed to delight, and John Glover's depictions of Anya's home state were mesmerising. She made her way to the exit after staring at Jackson Pollock's 'Blue Poles' with even less appreciation than ever and walked over to Questacon. Inside, she strolled up a long ramp into a gallery of sideshow exhibits. Children squealed with delight as they took turns to slide down what, to the naked eye, appeared to be a six-metre vertical drop.

Anya watched two people sitting on either end of a turning boom arm, trying to throw a ball to each other. They laughed as they found the task impossible. From behind, it looked as though the ball was travelling in a curve, away from the catcher.

'Great optical illusion, don't you think?'

Anya looked up to see Vaughan Hunter at her side. She felt her cheeks redden.

'It's about relative motion. The ball looks like it's curving, but it actually moves in a straight line. If you watch carefully, the people are moving in a curve.

Eminent psychiatrist, part-time physicist and a know-it-all in your spare time. She resisted the impulse to speak aloud.

'You can see what I mean when you go upstairs and look down from above.' He wandered off and Anya wondered whether she should follow. Curiosity got the better of her.

'Have you been here before?' she asked.

'Once. This place is amazing. Look at the enthusiasm on all the faces. Even the parents are enjoying themselves.'

He was right. Children of all ages were involved in the displays. No-one stood idle.

They reached the upstairs level and looked down on the next pair throwing the ball from the boom arm. The ball did go straight every time. Anya made a mental note to bring Ben here one weekend. He'd love it.

'Did you know this place started off in a former public school to bring science out of the big white buildings and into the suburbs? It became a victim of its own success. Pretty soon the building couldn't cope with the number of visitors, so it –'

'Let me guess, moved to a big white building away from the suburbs.'

Vaughan smiled and nodded. 'Hope you don't think I'm following you, but I wanted to come back in my afternoon off.'

Anya felt like a schoolgirl playing hookey. 'I couldn't quite face the afternoon sessions. Thought a walk would do more good.'

'I thought the same thing.'

Anya studied the man, who she'd never before seen outside work. They'd both been involved in a case of child sexual abuse, during which she'd seen a video of him interviewing the child and been impressed by his kindness and gentleness towards the young girl. Later, he had asked her to discuss the girl's injuries as reported by the mother. He had asked highly intelligent questions, which showed his degree of concern for the impact his assessment had on this child and her family. From memory, he'd even done the report for no charge.

'Have you seen the sports section upstairs?' he

asked. 'You can challenge Cathy Freeman to a race.'

'Running against an Olympic gold medallist sprinter? No challenge for her at all, I'd say.'

'What about seeing how fast you can throw a tennis ball?'

'That, I could do.' Anya suddenly felt comfortable. This man had a relaxed manner and the ability to put people at ease. She envied him.

They moved up the spiral ramp past another gallery and heard loud cracking and buzzing.

'That's the Tesla coil. It's fantastic. Over three million volts to make lightning.'

Anya had seen what lightning could do to a human body and opted for sports instead. Inside Gallery 6, people rode stationary bicycles alongside a display of bone movement. The skeleton riding a bike resembled something from an old Don Knotts comedy.

A man with an over-developed upper body crouched down into starter position to race Cathy Freeman.

Vaughan shot Anya a look that said, *Don't say a word.*

'I've always wondered why they crouch like that. It looks incredibly uncomfortable,' she pondered.

'You accelerate faster than if you start standing upright. In the crouched position your body is so close to being off-balance, it's easier to move forward. Take someone out of their comfort zone and they can do things they never imagined.'

'Give me balance and comfort any day.'

Mr Muscles was barely in a standing position by the time Cathy Freeman's image had finished. As if disputing the result, he lined up to race again.

In a corner, a staff member in a blue coat introduced herself as an 'explainer' and asked if they'd like to learn about angular momentum. Anya reluctantly agreed and stood up to the platform. In the middle of a large turntable was a T-shaped bar to which she was strapped with a seatbelt around her hips. The Questacon employee turned the table and told Anya to stick out her arms. The turntable slowed. When she pulled them in close to her body, the platform spun faster. Vaughan laughed at the face she pulled as his face spun in and out of focus.

'Try the ice-skater spin,' he goaded.

She tentatively lifted her leg in an arabesque position and held her arms out wide. The assistant spun the platform hard. Anya waited before pulling her arms to her chest and her legs together. She spun faster than ever and didn't like the feeling.

'Can you stop it now?' she asked, her voice a pitch higher than she expected.

'Just hold your arms and leg out again and you'll slow down,' the explainer said as she answered a question from the milling group about why cats always fall on their feet.

Anya was dizzy from spinning. Vaughan applauded before helping her down.

'You were in control the whole time. You just didn't realise it.'

'Somehow that's no consolation. Now it's your turn.'

'No way, I get car sick at the movies. Let's try something else.'

The pair moved on to magnets, then a simulated earthquake, before exploring a cybercity. Two hours later, Anya couldn't remember how long it had been since she'd enjoyed herself this much. She'd forgotten how much fun science could be, having spent most of her life taking it so seriously.

'Coffee?' she suggested.

They collected their coffees from the downstairs café and sat at a table outside with a perfect view of the lake. Anya felt the sun warm her skin.

Vaughan sat initially with his eyes closed, as though thinking the same thing about the sun. She studied the laugh lines around his eyes and realised how unusual it was to be around someone who enjoyed such simple pleasures. The camel-coloured polo neck looked expensive, as did the long woollen coat he carried, but he didn't come across as vain or egotistical. Anya wondered why he'd never married.

Vaughan spoke first. 'Are you originally from Canberra?'

'No, why do you ask?'

'Profiling is part of what I do. I like to work out where people are from, where they came in the family order, what they do for a living.'

'All right, you tell me where I'm from.'

'That's difficult to say because your clothes this

110

morning screamed city, yet you have the air of someone from the country.'

'Air?' Did he mean like a country bumpkin? Suddenly, she felt defensive.

'It's naivety, or innocence, I assume. Don't tell me I've offended you.'

On second thought, he was probably right. 'I grew up in Launceston in Tasmania, trained in Newcastle and Sydney, had three years in London and moved back to Sydney at the beginning of the year. I'm not sure what you mean by naivety?'

'Perhaps "naivety" isn't the best word. Launceston and Newcastle are both big cities but still have that rural feel about them. People from larger cities usually have more confidence, self-assuredness to the point of arrogance.'

Anya felt her lip tighten. So far she'd made a great impression.

'When Dan first introduced us, I tried to work out what you did for a living. Medicine, without question. Too articulate for anaesthetics, too polite for a surgeon. Some kind of physician. Maybe haematology? That's what I guessed. Then, of course, Dan explained your role in that first case.'

'You're weren't too far off.' She took a sip of lukewarm coffee. 'I can just see you as a psychiatrist, lulling people into feeling secure then picking their brains.' She unconsciously crossed her arms.

'I'm not at work now, and I was intrigued, that's all. Sorry if that makes you defensive.'

Anya looked at her arms and uncrossed them.

111

Suddenly they felt stuck on, unnatural. She shoved her hands into her jeans pockets. 'It makes sense, what you say. I lived in a town where everyone knew each other. My mother was the only female GP for years and my dad was a well-known solicitor.'

'My guess is you're the eldest and have one, probably two siblings. High achievers often have competition in the family and something to prove. How am I doing?'

'Close. I have – or had – two siblings.'

Anya looked out across the lake and watched a cruising restaurant pass by. A wedding party sang and danced on the top deck. Vaughan remained silent. Most people felt uncomfortable when they heard someone had died and quickly changed the subject. He seemed to be waiting to let Anya say what she felt comfortable with. Words started pouring from her mouth.

'Dad has always been a crusader. He campaigns against violence. Spends half his time in prisons and schools trying to teach people to take responsibility for their actions.'

Vaughan nodded. 'He sounds like someone I met through grief counselling. This fellow is amazing and is doing some groundbreaking work coordinating visits between offenders and their victims. Bob, or is it Richard Reynolds, from Enough is Enough?'

Anya nodded. 'It's Bob Reynolds.'

'Oh, you know his work?'

'You could say that.' She quietly added, 'He's my father.'

Three cheers came from the cruise boat as it disappeared around the bend.

'He's an incredibly strong man, and you don't exactly come across as weak.' He drew an imaginary circle on the table. 'Why do you worry so much about court appearances?'

This guy didn't waste time getting to the point, thought Anya. 'I don't like being the centre of attention.'

'There's no-one with your experience doing the things you do, so Dan Brody says. He thinks you're quite a find.'

Anya felt self-conscious again, and Vaughan seemed to notice.

'What I meant was, he mentioned that that was why he wanted your advice on the Deab case. He asked me about perpetrators of domestic violence and it sounds as though you and I might end up working together again.'

She could think of worse things.

Just then a toddler ran past and fell heavily on the concrete.

Anya quickly reached down and helped him up. 'You're all right, darling, just got a bit of a shock.' Anya brushed down the toddler's clothes. 'Where's Mummy?'

He stopped crying as his mother ran up from inside the café, juggling a baby on one hip and an older child in the other hand. The woman

113

apologised for her child and scolded him for running off.

Anya checked her watch. She hoped to ring Ben before dinner. 'We'd better get back. I need an early night if I'm going to survive tomorrow.'

Vaughan touched her elbow. 'Every experience is meant to be helpful, not hurtful.'

For a moment she almost believed him.

13

Moot court began at eight-thirty the next morning. Each delegate received an envelope with a case scenario and information relevant to their field of expertise. Anya was second-last on the list. While the others devoured a buffet breakfast, she washed down a beta-blocker tablet with a glass of juice. Although she didn't have high blood pressure to control, the tablet stopped the racing heart, perspiration and uncontrollable nervous tremor; it gave her a chance to think clearly.

Dressed in a red shirt, black jacket and tailored trousers, Anya watched as the speakers grilled each expert witness. She almost felt reassured that many of them were intimidated by the video camera and performed worse than expected. The panel of three lawyers and a psychiatrist were highly critical of over- or under-confidence.

For the women delegates, the lawyers used sexist language, questioned their authority and attempted to extract opinions in subjects outside their areas of expertise. Having observed the mock witnesses, Anya felt better prepared, but still panic welled inside her. She sat in the makeshift witness box and took a deep breath, making sure her shoulders were level, not hunched.

Vaughan outlined the case scenario. The owner of a liquor shop called the police to tell them he had been robbed at knife point at 10.30 pm on Sunday night. He had just deposited the weekend takings in the safe situated beneath the floor of the back office when he heard a noise in the shop. When he went to investigate, a thickset man in a balaclava forced him back into the office to open the safe. In his statement to the police, the owner described being pushed to the ground with the knife in his face. When the owner failed to comply, the assailant pushed his captive's head forward and sliced his cheek with the knife. After that, the shop owner opened the safe and handed over $24,000 in cash. The thief had not been located.

The first lawyer rose. 'Dr Crichton has three photographs of the shop owner's injuries and the scene of the alleged crime. Could you please describe for us what you see in picture one?'

'This is a photo of a man's left cheek,' Anya replied, 'with three to four linear, parallel cuts of three to four centimetres extending from the midline to the base of the left earlobe. The cuts appear superficial.'

'Now, could you look at the photo of the open safe and tell us what you see?'

'An open safe with what looks like two large drops of blood in front of the safe about fifteen centimetres apart.'

'Could you describe the likely mechanism of injury?'

'These appear to be hesitation injuries, which occur when a knife is used for the sole purpose of breaking the skin and causing superficial, as opposed to serious, injury.'

'Are you suggesting that we have a thief who is sensitive and is afraid of hurting anyone?'

'No –'

'Let's move on to the crime scene photos.'

Less than two minutes and Anya was already being discredited. She had to focus and stay calm.

'The blood spots on the floor. If the victim had been kneeling down with his head forward, as described, how do you explain the distribution of the blood?'

'Providing there were no other injuries, it could be explained by movement of the victim's head as his cheek bled.'

'Is it customary for someone who is being held down at knife point to thrash his head around?'

'No –'

'Well, then, why was the safe free of blood if the cheek injury was bleeding?'

Anya wasn't being allowed to effectively answer a question. 'On the information available, it's not possible to say.'

Vaughan Hunter stepped forward and took over the examination.

'Well, doctor, what *can* you say?'

'I can say that the photos are inconsistent with

117

the history given by the shop owner. The wounds on his cheek are almost certainly hesitation injuries, which are characteristic of self-inflicted wounds. That would account for the lack of blood on and near the safe.'

'Thank you, doctor.'

The second lawyer stood. 'Dr Crichton. In your opinion, is this a fraudulent insurance claim?'

'Based on the information I have been given, I am unable to comment on that. I have been asked to give an opinion on the cause and extent of the injuries, and whether they correlate with the history given by the alleged victim.'

'Come on, you've seen cases like this before. Surely, it's a classic case of fraud. You and I both know it, even the jury knows it. So in your opinion, is this a classic case of a shop owner staging a robbery, cutting his own face, but not sufficiently to cause damage, for the purpose of rorting the insurance system?'

Anya refused to be baited. 'As I said before, I am unable to comment on fraudulent activity. Only on the information supplied to me for an opinion.'

'So with all your training and expertise, not to mention your exorbitant fees for an opinion, you can't tell us if it's likely that the owner staged the whole robbery or not?'

Anya calmly restated, 'The wounds in the picture are typical of self-inflicted injuries. That is all I can say.'

'Thank you. That is all.'

When it came to feedback, Vaughan praised Anya's performance, freezing the video on her posture, hands clasped on her lap, and the calm tone of her voice. He described her as a credible and sympathetic witness who had enough authority to convince a jury without seeming arrogant. The lawyers praised her for refusing to be drawn into an argument, or comment on points irrelevant to her task. Anya felt both relief and a sense of proud embarrassment.

At the end of the session, Vaughan left before she could thank him or say goodbye. She handed in her key at reception and received an envelope with her name handwritten on it.

Inside, the note read:

See how quickly you move forward when you're off balance? Who knows what you're capable of outside your comfort zone! Thanks for making the weekend a success. Vaughan.

Anya felt her face blush again.

14

At four o'clock the following morning, the high-pitched beep of a pager penetrated Anya's consciousness. Heart jolting, she rolled over and fumbled for the source of the noise on her bedside table. The prefix of blurry red numbers belonged to Northern Base Hospital's sexual assault unit. With a shortage of doctors qualified to examine a rape victim, Anya had agreed to be on call as often as possible at night. She understood why so few doctors volunteered for the training but, at this hour, she still cursed the abstainers for being so selfish.

She hit the touch lamp and dialled the unit, who confirmed they had a woman requiring examination ASAP. Anya climbed back into her jeans and the clean bra and cotton shirt laid out in case of a call out. With casual attire appropriate in the middle of the night, she combed her hair into a loose bun with her fingers and secured it with a large clip. She quickly glanced in the mirror and removed the black smears from yesterday's eye make-up.

Within twenty minutes she was at the hospital,

outside the unit located between occupational therapy and dietetics, away from the main hospital building. An eccentric-looking, middle-aged woman unlocked the entrance door.

'Good to meet you. I'm Mary Singer – the one you spoke to, in case you weren't totally awake.' She closed and locked the door behind Anya. 'We've got Gloria Havelock, a fifty-five-year-old who works as a night packer in a supermarket. She finished work at midnight and was attacked as she unlocked her car. Two men forced her to drive to Lane Cove park at knife point and assaulted her. She's in pretty bad shape. Took a hell of a beating,' the counsellor almost whispered. 'She's more worried about her teenage daughters than herself. The rapists stole her handbag with her licence, address, house keys and photos of the girls. They threatened to rape them if she told the police.'

'Is anyone with them?' Anya pulled some sleep from her lower eyelid.

'The police went round straightaway. The husband's overseas at a family funeral.'

Anya could already picture Gloria Havelock. A middle-aged mother who put her family first, even working nights to supplement the family income. 'Have the injuries been assessed?'

'The lacerations on her head and face have been sutured. Cerebral CT scan was clear. Put up a pretty good fight, by the looks of her.'

'Any analgesia on board?'

'Just the local anaesthetic.'

121

'What about orally?'

'Nothing by mouth, as per the protocol.'

'Thanks. We'd better start with the consent. By the way, who found her?'

'She crawled to Fullers Road and knocked on the door of the first house she came to. The old couple who live there were too scared to open the door and called the police. The patrol car brought her to emergency.'

Anya was relieved to be dealing with an experienced counsellor who understood the need to preserve evidence. Well-wishers making a cup of tea for a distraught victim could do more harm than good in the long term. If oral sex had taken place, a simple drink of water could destroy vital evidence that could mean the difference between conviction or acquittal. Anyone involved had to remember that Gloria's body was in fact part of a crime scene and had to be treated as exactly that in case she wanted further police involvement.

The two women entered the room, united in their difficult task. Mary locked the only other door to the outside world.

'Gloria, this is Dr Crichton, the one I told you about.'

'Please, it's Anya, if you'd prefer.'

The woman sat on a blue lounge chair, draped in a hospital gown and blanket. Stitches zigzagged across her nose, forehead and chin, which were only briefly visible when she looked at Anya. The rest of the time she was hunched with her face close to her lap. Blood matted the dark, wavy hair on her crown.

Gloria's demeanour was typical of the many sexual assault victims Anya had seen in England. Although she'd only been called in to this unit once before, she knew one thing: irrespective of religion or age, women responded in similar ways to the incredible violation of rape.

Anya moved slowly closer and touched the woman's forearm. 'You're shivering. Would you like another blanket?' Before waiting for an answer, Mary pulled a polar fleece blanket from the cupboard and placed it across Gloria's lap.

'Thank you,' she mouthed.

Anya sat in one of the two armchairs on the other side of a coffee table. Mary Singer occupied the other.

'I'm here for two main purposes,' Anya began. 'The first and most important reason is to look after you, to make sure you're okay and safe. The second is to do a forensic examination, but only if you want it. That means an examination to see if there has been any transfer of material onto your body from the men who did this to you. This is necessary if you are thinking that you might want the police involved. You don't have to make a decision about the police now, but the examination needs to be done as soon as possible to ensure that the material is collected. One thing we look for is traces of DNA, which is like a genetic fingerprint. DNA may be present if the attackers lick, bite, kiss, ejaculate or bleed, if you struggled with them. It can even be found in hair.'

Gloria looked up and Anya caught a glimpse of dark brown eyes, wounded and pleading for mercy.

'It may not seem like it, Gloria, but you have choices right now. We offer counselling, medical treatment with or without a physical examination, and a full medical and forensic examination. I won't do anything without your permission, so I'll explain what is involved every step of the way. If you agree, then we can go ahead, but you can also withdraw your consent at any time.'

Gloria looked across at Anya.

'What if I want you to stop?'

'I will. You're in control. It's important you know that agreeing to be examined in no way means that the information and samples I obtain go straight to the police. I can't do that without your express written permission, but before you make up your mind, you need to know and understand the implications of a decision either way.'

The woman shook her head. 'I don't want my daughters to hear what happened.'

'That's all right. There's no rush; you don't have to decide right now. I'd say about seventy per cent of women need time to think about it. So for now, why don't we talk about the examination, what it involves and what the samples mean.'

The woman nodded, suddenly subservient. She stared at the blanket again. 'Do what you have to do.'

Anya opened the Sexual Assault Investigation Kit at the second page. She moved next to Gloria with a pen and explained the booklet and first consent form.

'Remember, you can stop at any time, and this is only a consent to be examined, not a consent to release the information or samples to the police. The booklet is a record that can be produced in court, if you decide to go to the police. It is separate from your hospital records and stays here in the sexual assault unit. The only way anyone else will see it is if it's subpoenaed, and that only happens if you go to the police and make a statement.

'There's a separate consent form at the back if you decide you want the police involved. That one's a legal document and has to be witnessed, but can be signed later. Do you understand everything I've said?'

'Yes, you've explained it clearly,' Gloria said. She read and signed the first consent form.

Anya silently documented the apparent facial bruising and injuries in the medical records booklet. She glanced at the blood on a plastic-backed sheet placed on the bench above the cupboards to dry. Underwear should be collected but if the attackers took it, the next best thing was the sheet on which a woman bled after an attack.

'I'm going to have to ask you some things about your medical history, and what happened to you tonight. Some of the questions are about your gynaecological history. Do you still get periods?'

'I haven't had one for two years, until . . .' Gloria said in a quiet voice, and then stood quickly. 'I don't want to bleed on your lounge.'

'Don't worry,' Mary said. 'There's a blue-backed sheet underneath you that is waterproof. Not much longer now and we can get you showered and into some fresh clothes. We keep some here just for this purpose.'

Gloria sat down again and resumed her defensive posture. Anya followed the protocol, asking about gynaecological surgery and relevant medical problems before broaching the exact details of the assault, which she knew would be difficult.

After driving to the park with a knife at her throat, Gloria had been dragged into the park and assaulted by the men, whose faces she didn't recognise. One of the men held her down on the ground with her arms above her head, while the other used the knife to cut open her clothes, before he raped her vaginally with his fingers, followed by his penis. The other man took his turn. She had no idea how long she'd been with the men, but they raped her six times before beating her, holding up her keys and promising to rape her daughters. If she went to the police, they'd kill her. Like so many rapists, they threatened to hunt her down. Like so many victims, she believed them.

Anya paraphrased Gloria's words, careful not to quote her directly in the notes. She'd learnt from experience that defence lawyers could use her documentation to discredit the victim, if it didn't match exactly with the police statement.

Following such a brutal attack, the vaginal bleeding concerned Anya. She needed to identify the source and severity, for Gloria's sake.

'I'd like to know where the bleeding is coming from, and how bad it is. With assaults like this, sometimes women get bladder and bowel problems, which can become medical emergencies if not detected and picked up quickly.'

'I'll let you check me, but I don't want to answer any more of the police's questions.'

'That's fine. You don't have to decide right now. You've got a couple of days to make that decision.'

Mary helped Gloria to her feet and into the adjacent room. An examination bed, cupboard full of new clothes in various sizes, and a small ensuite with shower had more of a motel feel than that of a hospital. Mary and Anya did everything possible to make sure the examination did not feel like a continuation of the assault.

Anya put on gloves, opened the rest of the kit and lined up the sample tubes. She examined Gloria's head first, careful to keep her covered for as long as possible and only revealing what was necessary at the time. Each bruise, scratch and mark was thoroughly documented in words and on a body chart in the booklet. Grass seeds from her hair were collected to compare with those at the scene of the assault.

Gloria's fingernails held some blood and dirt beneath them. Red and black marks circled both wrists, consistent with her being held down and scratching at dirt and her attackers.

'It looks like you got some tissue from at least one of the men who did this to you,' Anya noted.

Mary sounded impressed. 'That's a very smart thing to do. It also means you put up a good fight.'

Gloria seemed unfazed by the compliment.

'May I swab your fingernails, and cut them too? That's the best way to obtain this evidence. While we're at it, I need to take some blood to distinguish between your DNA and your attackers'.'

Gloria Havelock nodded again and compliantly held out both hands.

After the venepuncture and nail collection, the examination was almost complete – except for the genital exam.

With rape victims often not having signs of genital trauma, and women involved in consensual intercourse likely to have abrasions, this part of the examination was of vital importance. At this point, Anya always thought back to a young mother raped and murdered on the outskirts of London. Two other rape victims in the same area lived to tell their story. At the trial of the man identified by both surviving women and charged with the murder, Anya had testified as a forensic pathologist. She'd been disturbed by the poor collection of evidence, particularly as the two other women had been examined by inexperienced practitioners. The man had subsequently been acquitted and, from that moment on, Anya had offered her services for clinical examinations of rape victims. As a member of what was now the Association of Forensic Physicians in the UK, examining surviving victims was how she had crossed over to forensic medicine. Her expertise in wounds meant she quickly became recognised as a leading authority on physical and sexual assault. A year later, her evidence helped convict the same man of another rape and murder.

Mary moved to the head of the bed to support Gloria. After gently positioning her patient, Anya swabbed the vulva for semen and smeared the swab onto a slide before placing it into the labelled container. She chose the smallest possible speculum to examine the vagina and explained each step in the process.

'It's easier if you remember to breathe,' Anya reminded Gloria. 'Most people hold their breath and all the muscles tense. If you breathe deeply, it helps a lot. Please tell me, too, if you're too uncomfortable. I'll stop whenever you want me to.'

Gloria took a deep breath. 'Do what you have to.'

Mary offered her hand and Gloria held it.

Inside the vagina, against the posterior wall, Anya saw a superficial tear about two centimetres long. 'I've found the reason you've been bleeding. It's a small tear, very shallow, and not likely to cause problems. They usually heal themselves in one or two days.'

Mary and Gloria sighed at the same time. Relieved by the findings, but more so, relieved that the examination was over.

Anya removed the speculum and pulled the blanket down to cover her patient's legs. 'You're going to be very sore tomorrow from your bruises and injuries. I can give you some pain relief and a certificate for work. I'd like you to come back tomorrow and have that tear checked, just in case.'

'I'd like to see how you're doing, anyway,' Mary said softly. 'Have you thought about what you'll tell your family?'

'I'll say I was mugged. That's all they need to know.' The battered woman sat up and, for the first time, her voice broke and her eyes filled with tears. 'Promise me you won't tell them anything about the . . . what really happened.'

'We respect your decisions, Gloria, and we're also bound by confidentiality,' Anya reassured. 'Now how about that shower?'

Gloria refused help with the shower and washed and scrubbed her hair and body in privacy. Within half an hour, she was clean and dressed in a new bra, underpants and a black tracksuit, the most popular choice for rape victims, who inevitably threw them away when they returned home. Most of her wounds were hidden, but there was little they could do about her face.

'You still have at least forty-eight hours to

decide whether or not you consent to the samples going to the police. Mary can go through the process again with you after you've had some rest. You'll also need to be checked again in a couple of weeks, to exclude infections. It's too early for anything to show up yet, which is why we don't test you for that today.' Anya thought again of Fatima Deab's herpes and hoped this poor woman wouldn't suffer the added horror of having to explain to her husband how she'd caught herpes or some other sexually transmitted infection.

Mary said, 'We can make a time. I'll call you later today, if that's okay.'

Gloria clutched Anya's hand tightly. 'Thank you for what you did. I'm sorry you had to see this.'

'Gloria, my job is to look after you.'

She withdrew her hand and took a step towards the door, before looking back.

Anya lowered her eyes and silently wished she could make every bit of this woman's pain disappear. The pain was one of loss. Great loss. It was like the look she'd seen on her own mother's face for the last thirty years.

Mary unlocked the door and led Gloria out to the waiting area. Anya continued writing up the last of her notes in the booklet, and placed it and the labelled specimens in the sealed SAI kit. Finally, she secured the evidence in the forensic fridge and entered the date, time and Gloria's name in the logbook.

Mary returned just as she finished. 'I think we're going to get on well, Anya. That was one of the gentlest and most thorough examinations I've seen. Whether or not she goes to the police, the respect you showed her will make a real difference to Gloria's recovery.'

Anya gave a feeble smile and stretched her back in the chair. 'Let's hope she does go the police. Those two aren't going to rape just once.' Anya rubbed her eyes. 'With that degree of violence, it's only a matter of time before they kill someone.'

'That may be so, but it isn't Gloria's responsibility. She has to do what is right for her.'

Anya found this part of the job the most frustrating. She believed that every man who committed this crime was a serial rapist. No-one raped just once. It was part of a pattern of behaviour, not an isolated incident, or 'aberration'. If more women agreed to make statements, the police would be better placed to make cases against the perpetrators. No longer would rapists serve sentences that lasted less time than the medical treatment and counselling of their victims. 'I know that Gloria isn't responsible for other victims, but what if she decides not to make a statement and more women suffer like she has, or worse?'

Mary scratched her thick head of wiry grey hair. 'As difficult as that is to accept, we have to look after Gloria, and what's in *her* best interest, not society's, or other women's. That's our job.'

132

Anya nodded silently.

Four hours soon became five due to the debriefing process. When they walked outside, the world had woken up. Hospital staff ambled from building to building, visitors sat on the grassy areas, students carried piles of textbooks in backpacks, oblivious to the horrors the darkness had brought.

'I wondered where you'd got to this morning, the phones haven't stopped since I opened up,' Elaine said as Anya threw her bag on the kitchen table. 'I assumed you'd been called out to something.'

'If it's Sperm Man, I don't want to know.'

'No! These were serious calls – work calls! The publicity you got over the Barker trial has been priceless.' She referred to the Post-it notes in her hand. 'Three lawyers want your opinion for their cases; one's an assault, the other is a question of child abuse and the other was about a wrongful death. And Sabina Pryor from Legal Aid has called. Some reporter's also been ringing about a rape case. And Anoub Deab has called twice. He seems very persistent.'

Anya sat at the table and rubbed her eyes.

'Actually, he's very rude over the phone,' the secretary continued. 'Treats me like some kind of servant. I told him we'd let him know when your report had been completed but he still called back. Anyway, if you need to catch up on some sleep, the rest can wait.' She handed her boss the final Post-it note. 'Except Dan Brody. He would like to

133

meet at five o'clock today in his chambers. It's amazing. Business is finally taking off.'

Anya didn't answer, distracted by thoughts of Gloria lying to her family to protect them.

Elaine sat on the other side of the table. 'Rough night?'

'You could say that. Call out to a sexual assault.'

'How about a pot of tea? It always tastes better when someone else makes it.'

Anya felt a strange comfort having someone in her home right now. She watched Elaine grab a tin of Earl Grey from the cupboard and fill the teapot with hot water from the tap to warm the pot before the kettle boiled.

'Would it help to talk about this one?'

Anya sighed. 'One minute this woman's life is fine. She's working, taking care of the kids, doing what she always does, the way she always does it, not hurting anyone. She's probably never hurt anyone in her life. Then out of the blue these two psychopaths pick *her* to rape, beat and leave for dead. They stole her purse, so they have her keys, bank account details, family snaps. They know where she lives, and their parting words were how they were off to rape her sleeping children, using her keys to enter the house. From now on, she'll go through emotional torture every day and night, wondering when they'll be back. They didn't just rape this woman, they raped her entire life.'

Elaine emptied the pot and dropped in three

teaspoons of tea. 'You can't stop evil people doing evil things.'

'Minimising the damage is like plugging a sieve with tissue paper.'

'What you do is so important. You're the one who says how empowering women immediately after an attack helps them recover.' Elaine filled the pot with boiling water and placed it on a trivet at the table.

'There is one victim but a lot more people suffer from the crime.' Anya turned the teapot three times, just like her grandmother always did. 'The family, friends, almost every relationship. No-one's going to slap you on the back and say, "Gee, that was a great exam of my private bits", but if it's done poorly, there's no end to the damage it could do. I can only speak for Pap smears, but a bad one can make you feel like the doctor drove a forklift truck up there.' Anya stared at the pattern on the china teapot. 'That poor woman could have been –' She stopped herself.

Elaine fiddled with the buttons on her shirt that pulled across her large bust. 'Any one of us. Will she be all right?'

'Physically, her wounds will heal.'

'You did everything you could. God knows I couldn't do what you do, but if anything positive can come of this, it's that someone as experienced as you did the examination.' Elaine sniffed and poured the tea. 'You need a rest and a long, hot shower. If the reporters ring back, I'll tell them you're in court all day. Maybe they can e-mail their questions, to save you time. The lawyers can send the info with a formal letter. That just leaves Dan Brody's meeting.'

'I'll be fine by this afternoon. Give me a couple of hours and I'll be back downstairs.' Anya carried her cup down the corridor. 'And I never do press interviews. Never.'

Elaine stopped her at the stairs. 'I'm sure what you did helped that poor woman.'

'How do you help someone whose soul was the scene of the crime?'

15

Dan Brody ushered Anya into his office. 'Sorry to call you here so late in the afternoon.'

Arriving at the same time was a solicitor she had previously met.

'Grant, good to see you. How's that little girl of yours?' Brody enquired, a master at feigning interest.

Every one of Grant Bourne's freckles glowed with pride. 'Five months yesterday and doing all the right things.'

'Excellent. Do you remember Dr Crichton?'

Anya remembered Grant Bourne, the melanoma waiting to happen. He'd be the pin-up boy for Skin Cancer Awareness with his red hair and almost alabaster skin. Out of habit, she looked at his hands and face for any malignant lesions. He noticed and cleared his throat.

'Certainly do, hello doctor.'

'Both of you, have a seat. On Friday afternoon, Mohammed Deab was arrested and charged with attempted murder, or more accurately, grievous bodily harm with intent to commit murder. That's where medical advice comes in.'

He handed Anya the police and emergency reports. 'This one's on Mohammed's bill.'

Grant proceeded, 'The victim of the alleged assault was a nineteen-year-old Maltese boy from Merrylands. George. Galea. He had often enquired about Fatima at her place of work.' He opened his brown leather satchel and pulled out a legal pad, along with a large chocolate-chip muffin.

Brody stared at the food. Grant didn't seem to notice and took a bite, dropping crumbs on his lap. Brody plucked a handful of tissues from the box on his desk and passed them across the table. The solicitor placed them next to his notes beneath the muffin and larger crumbs.

'If he pleads guilty, I plan to argue malicious wounding with intent to commit GBH,' Brody announced. 'It's more likely to attract a lesser sentence. And there are mitigating circumstances. Deab was pushed to the brink by Galea, who we're fairly sure had sex with his daughter. The adolescent had destroyed Fatima's life, the family's hopes and any dreams of grandchildren.'

'Problem is, this isn't his first offence.' Grant handed out a detailed list, outlining all the offences for which Deab had been charged, convicted and acquitted. 'Charges range from drink-driving, speeding, and rebirthing stolen cars, to assault and grievous bodily harm. Four charges of assault were dropped when witnesses either failed to appear or came down with a debilitating case of amnesia. He was up for losing his licence twice, but his wife signed statutory declarations saying she was the driver for each speeding offence.'

Anya shook her head. 'In other words, she had her licence cancelled instead of him.' She wondered what life lessons he'd passed to his children, in particular, to Anoub.

Grant added, 'The police chose Friday 4 pm for the arrest so he had to wait for weekend court. He was denied bail at the station and we didn't have any luck in court either.'

'Based on the severity of the assault?' Anya asked.

'And the chance he could intimidate Galea's mother,' Grant answered without emotion.

Brody began his familiar doodling. 'When is the committal hearing?'

'The brief is supposed to be finished in six weeks. We'll have to ride them or they'll drag it out again.' Grant licked a crumb from between his teeth. He and Brody couldn't have been more different, but they worked well together.

Brody drew rows of boxes. 'What about witnesses?'

'The fact sheet just says he was seen entering and leaving the premises, but doesn't say who saw him. He could have been under surveillance again.'

'You mean the police might have seen him do it?' Anya asked.

'Let's not jump to conclusions,' Grant continued. 'Someone saw him enter the house with a colleague and come out a few minutes later.'

'Did anyone hear him threaten to kill the boy?' Brody frowned.

'The mother is still under sedation. We're not sure what she said to the police, but the DPP could argue intent was implied from the injuries sustained.'

'If it comes to that, we respond that someone as experienced as Deab in assault knew when to stop before the boy died.'

'Does anything else place him at the scene?' Anya asked, suspecting the police had some physical evidence.

'There's the matter of the company car swiping the parked van. Our client says he heard sirens and thought there could have been an accident, so drove off quickly.' Grant explained this for Anya's benefit: 'Chasing sirens is how tow trucks get a lot of business.'

Brody stopped writing. 'What about a weapon?'

'The police couldn't find a crowbar when they searched the business or his home. Although that may look suspicious – a smash repairer without a crowbar on site.'

'He's not charged with workplace incompetence,' Brody declared.

Grant grinned and returned to his notes. 'He's also up for malicious damage and assault. The surgery on Merrylands Road, where his daughter worked.'

Anya interjected. 'Was anyone –'

'No-one was hurt,' Brody assured her. 'The

doctor and her secretary cowered under a desk while two men with balaclavas smashed up the place. The assault was an implied threat. Human faeces was deposited at the back door as a farewell gift.'

'Doctors are often targeted by angry patients or relatives, or anyone looking for drugs or cash,' Anya said. Her mother had been assaulted at least twice and the surgery vandalised three or four times to her knowledge. 'What evidence do the police have?'

Brody answered, 'Just the calling card faeces. Although our client denies involvement, we're assuming they won't bother extracting DNA from the afore-mentioned bodily excrement.'

Both men laughed. Anal humour – the one thing boys never outgrew.

Brody referred to the hospital notes. 'I'd like to talk about the injuries to the Galea boy. He's still unconscious, and in no position to provide a statement at this stage. How serious are the injuries, Anya? What are the chances he'll survive?'

Anya scanned the emergency doctors' and surgeons' summaries. Broken ribs, ruptured spleen, renal trauma, description of a bootmark on the front of his shirt when he arrived. The most significant injuries were to his head. A CT scan showed a subdural haematoma and a ruptured vessel at the base of his skull. The neurosurgeon drained the haematoma but nothing could treat the ruptured vessel.

'Slim. At this stage. He's critical.'

Brody drew heavy lines through his row of boxes.

'What happened to the shirt?' she asked, skimming the rest of the report.

Brody smirked. 'The guys in Casualty cut it open to treat the injuries. It got lost in all the excitement. No chance of a clear bootmark comparison now.'

Anya remembered what working in Casualty was like. The priority was to save a life. It was bad enough knowing these injuries were deliberately inflicted but finding out that the person who did it could get off because the patient, not the shirt, was the priority, beggared belief.

'Any chance some of the injuries were pre-existing or idiosyncratic?' Brody asked.

Defence lawyers automatically looked for a predisposing problem with the victim. Mohammed Deab regularly beat his own daughter, intimidated witnesses to his assaults, and had no qualms about bashing someone to death. She began to feel uncomfortable about where the conversation was going. 'What in particular are you thinking about?'

'Anything that could predispose him to more serious injury than anticipated?'

'Are you asking whether his skull is a millimetre thinner than the average so your client can say, "Oops, it's a mistake anyone could make. I only meant to kick his head around. How was I supposed to know the guy was thin-skulled and couldn't handle the usual amount of kicks?" Is that what you mean by "idiosyncratic"?'

Brody straightened. 'In a manner of speaking, but we can do without the editorialising.'

Bourne quietly finished his muffin.

'He didn't just happen to run into that boy.' Anya's temper flared. 'He found out where Galea lived, took a thug along and hunted him down. That's premeditation, not a spur-of-the-moment thing.'

The barrister asked Grant to organise some coffee. The solicitor quickly left and closed the door behind him.

Brody clasped his hands on the desk. 'This isn't helping.'

'How can you do this?' She dropped the notes on the desk. 'Defend bastards like Deab and sleep at night?'

'It's complicated.' He rose and walked to the bookshelf. 'The whole purpose of the defence is to give the accused – who is innocent until proven guilty, in case you'd forgotten – the chance for fair representation. That's what the law is for – to protect us all.'

'What about the victims? Who's protecting them?' She stood with her hands on the desk, trying to remain calm. 'Last night I examined a middle-aged woman who'd been raped by two men who promised to do the same to her daughters.' She felt a rage welling, one that hadn't surfaced for years. 'Who protects that woman and her family? Who gives her fair representation?'

143

Brody remained calm. 'In the eyes of the law, no-one. The prosecution represents the community, not individuals. Rightly or wrongly, that is how the law operates. Our job is to make sure we do the best job to defend our client within the letter of the law.'

'Your job, not mine. In case *you'd* forgotten, I don't work for the defence. I give expert opinion on what is presented to me. My role is tell the truth, not manufacture a version of events that makes someone seem innocent.'

'The truth? We each have our version of the truth, Anya. The only thing that matters is fact. And fact is whatever I can prove in a courtroom.'

'How's this for fact? The man you are defending has a long history of violence. It's not restricted to men who cross him. This man brutalised his own child every day of her life and got away with it. Now's he's caught for damn near killing someone and you're playing semantic games. Tell me, Dan. Are your clients above the law, or just beyond justice?'

Grant Bourne re-entered the room with a cardboard tray containing three plastic cups.

Brody stood. 'Philosophical debate isn't getting us anywhere.'

Anya collected her briefcase. 'Galea's condition is stable, but critical. There's a good chance he'll die from those injuries and you'll be defending a murder charge. Then how will you feel?'

'No different. My role remains the same. If Deab

is acquitted then I am happy because there's a chance he is innocent.'

'And if he's convicted?'

'I'll console myself with the fact that there's a fair chance he is guilty.'

Anya left an open door in her wake.

16

Peter Latham looked at the pile of work on his desk and reached for an antacid. He was beginning to feel every one of his fifty-five years and each joint begged for at least one early night. His wife had long ago given up on shared meals and usually ate before he'd finished for the day.

He found this time of the evening the most efficient. No phone calls, interruptions or meetings. The morgue technicians had gone home and the upstairs offices remained quiet. Nothing but paperwork to deal with.

He read and signed the reports his secretary had deciphered and typed. His duties also included reviewing post-mortem reports from other centres as a part of quality assurance. As tedious as it seemed, it kept everyone honest.

The Newcastle file contained autopsy findings on two road trauma deaths, a homeless man found in a bus shelter, a young mother strangled by her ex-husband, a two-year-old child drowning, and a murder–suicide from the Central Coast. Under greater scrutiny than ever, reports were becoming more detailed and Peter plodded through each one.

The murder–suicide immediately grabbed his attention. An elderly man had been shot in his wheelchair. The bullet had travelled down and backwards from his collarbone, through the lung, and lodged in the back of his chest wall. Judging by the amount of blood in his pleural cavity, death had been slow, maybe up to half an hour. Of note was a large amount of red viscous substance, identified later as jam, in his mouth, oesophagus and stomach. It also extended to his large airways. Jam was smeared down his shirt front, and on his semi-exposed penis. Toxicology failed to identify any toxins or poisons, so the daughter must have poured almost two kilograms of strawberry jam down his throat *after* shooting him. In all his years, Peter Latham had never seen anything like it.

The suicide appeared straightforward. The woman, identified as the man's daughter, had a single bullet to the temple. Her death would have been quick. She had a small quantity of jam in the back of her throat, but none in her stomach contents.

Peter had long ago accepted that some scenarios would never be explained, although he was intrigued as to what had happened in the room that night.

He skimmed the histology pages and noted the findings that most interested him. The old man had a squamous cell carcinoma of the lung. The daughter had a mild inflammatory respiratory

147

condition, attributed to a series of irregularly shaped fibres in her lungs.

Peter e-mailed Gosford Regional Hospital pathology department and hoped David Connelly hadn't left yet. Within minutes, his colleague had scanned and sent the images of two lung slides. Peter enlarged the images. Filling the screen were multiple fibres, exactly like the hourglass shapes he'd seen on the nun.

Peter Latham flicked through the notes and found the name of the detective in charge of the case.

17

Anya pounded the treadmill and raised the incline. Sweat leached through her T-shirt and leggings as a revamped, decades-old disco song pulsated through the speakers. Anya had disliked 'Staying Alive' back then and the second – or was it the third? – remake irritated her even more.

'What's up?' Kate Farrer threw her towel on the bar and started up the adjacent treadmill. 'Martin piss you off again?'

'Not for a couple of days. This time I pissed myself off! Don't think I'll be working any more paying cases with Dan Brody.'

'Turn down a ride in his Ferrari, did you?'

'Worse. Got on my soapbox instead. You'd think I'd be able to bite my tongue at least until I can choose jobs.'

Kate increased to jogging pace. 'Don't flatter yourself. He's a lawyer; probably didn't even notice.'

Anya's legs ached but she increased the incline again.

Kate studied her friend. 'You really are pissed off. I wouldn't worry. You've stuck to your principles. Ben would be proud of you.'

'Pride doesn't pay the bills, as Martin keeps reminding me.'

Anya watched the clock on the wall. Forty minutes of torture had taken its toll. She pressed the control panel and returned to the flat position. Another button slowed the pace. 'I'll find the money another way.'

'It's bloody unfair. The only reason you lost custody is because you were the one out working to support the family. If Martin hadn't been so stupid, you wouldn't be stuck paying the bills.'

The treadmill stopped and Anya stood down, wiping her face, neck and hands with a towel. 'The Family Court doesn't care about fair. The magistrate awarded custody because Martin was, at the time, a stay-at-home parent, the primary carer.'

'Instead of the lazy shit who wouldn't work if his arse was on fire.' Kate was now jogging fast, without even raising a bead of perspiration. 'If you applied that logic, every babysitter in the country should be awarded custody.'

'After what happened in England, you can't blame him for quitting nursing.'

'So he stuffed up. Grown-ups own up and deal with it. He never has. He just gave up and decided to live off you for the rest of his life. I'm buggered if I know what you ever saw in him.'

'No matter what you think, he still fathered Ben.'

'Okay, he made a great sperm donor.' Kate stared up at the ceiling. 'Sorry. I shouldn't have said that. Guess I haven't helped your mood.' She slowed her machine and finished with a cool-down walk. 'Fancy Italian for dinner?'

'Thanks, but there's something I've got to do. Raincheck?'

'Sure.' Kate's mobile phone shrilled the theme from *The Magnificent Seven*, her favourite movie.

'Dr Latham, hi.' Kate paused. 'Officially, I'm consulting on that investigation.'

Anya raised her hand in a wave and took a step towards the change rooms, but Kate signalled her to stay.

'Do you think these fibres are *exactly* the same? . . . Sure. I can go over the crime scene video in the morning.'

Mention of fibres caught Anya's attention.

'Thanks again.' Kate put her mobile back into a case attached to her wrist. 'Peter Latham says you've been following a couple of cases with similar findings to something he's just found. Interested in watching a video tomorrow morning to cheer yourself up?'

'If it's one of yours, something tells me it's not going to have a happy ending.'

18

Once showered and changed, Anya drove through Newtown, past the airport and headed towards Brighton-le-Sands. She parked in a side street off the Grand Parade and met her father outside his hotel. The pair hugged and Bob Reynolds didn't seem to want to let go.

'Thanks for coming, Anya. It means a lot.'

Anya never knew how to respond to her father's displays of affection. She'd seen him hug victims, well-wishers and serial killers. She felt more like a stranger than his eldest child. Tonight's menu should put them on common ground.

'Hope you're hungry, Dad. There are some great Greek cafés along the main strip.'

'To be honest, I had my eyes on the seafood platter from the fish-and-chip shop on the corner. Thought we could eat on the beach if you don't mind slumming it.'

Anya wondered why she'd bothered at the gym. 'If you throw in some potato cakes, I'm in.'

They crossed the side road and ordered a smorgasbord of fried food. The smell alone made Anya's mouth water. They walked over to the beach and sat on a cement wall, legs dangling over the sand as they unwrapped their bounty. Anya's first bite of chip burnt the roof of her mouth. Her eyes watered.

'Your food tastes haven't changed,' her father said fondly.

Anya smiled. The beach and cold weather always made her feel like salty, hot chips.

'Remember whenever Damien played goalie I'd feed him hot dogs and chips when the ball was up the other end, just to keep him warm?'

'I do, and all the times we sat on the beach outside the shack at Low Head with the fish we'd caught and the battered scallops and chips we cooked in the deep-fryer.'

The breeze picked up as a red-tailed 747 gained altitude, climbing above the water. Watching planes from Sydney's major airport take off from a runway over the ocean seemed odd, when people made a pilgrimage to the beach to escape things man-made – except for fish-and-chip shops, that is. Bob Reynolds finished a prawn and gazed into the distance.

'Speaking of your brother, how did you like the drum kit?'

Anya smiled. 'Trust him to give me a divorce present. Then again, if he'd given it as a wedding present, we would have separated a lot earlier.'

'He knew you always wanted one, the way you used to drive us mad with your tapping everything in sight. When I think how much your mother hoped one day you'd develop a love of the violin or cello . . .' He paused as another plane left the ground. 'Are you having lessons?'

'I have a teacher and practise when I get the chance, as quietly as I can in a terrace.' The breeze picked up and blew a strand of hair in her face. She anchored the hair behind her ear and felt the salty residue in her ponytail. She knew her father had something more on his mind than music. 'Is everything all right?'

'A detective from Melbourne rang me last week about Miriam's disappearance.'

Anya froze, dreading news about her sister.

'They haven't found her. A task force has been assigned to re-investigate cold cases.'

'But Billy Vidor's in prison.'

'He's still in Risdon for killing the Campbelltown boy. They've had him under surveillance but he's never admitted anything to do with Miriam. They're wondering if the Launceston police put all their energies into a false lead, and failed to follow up other potential suspects. They're re-interviewing all those who gave statements. That is, those who are still alive.'

Anya felt a chip stick in her gullet. 'I'll expect a call, then.' She swallowed hard. 'Does Mum know? God knows what this'll do to her.' Anya's sister was a topic rarely discussed by her mother, and never between her parents.

'I assume so. I've accepted Miriam's gone. I just want to bring her home and give her a proper burial. Your mother –'

'I know, Dad. She's still waiting for Missy to walk in the door.'

A seagull landed nearby, hoping for leftovers. Anya broke off a piece of fish, peeled away the batter and threw it into the waiting beak.

'I phoned Damien this morning, London time. He hopes that this time fresh eyes can turn up something new.' Bob Reynolds took a sip of ginger beer and turned to face Anya.

Anya couldn't meet her father's gaze. She was responsible for what happened to Miriam, and everyone in the family knew it.

19

The taxi driver honked as Anya grabbed her keys. She climbed into the back seat and was met by a surly stare from the middle-aged man behind the wheel.

'Where to, madam?' he said, touching an imaginary forelock.

'Strawberry Hills, thanks.'

Experience had taught Anya to use the back seat. Rape crisis centres had seen enough women who, assuming they were safe next to the driver, had been molested or raped on the journey home.

One case remained vivid in her memory, partly because of its humbling effect. She'd been called out to examine a woman who staggered into a late-night supermarket, waving a G-string in her hand. With the amount of alcohol involved and the woman's unusually disinhibited manner, Anya had reservations about her vague description of being raped in a taxi. It was obvious this woman had had sexual intercourse that evening, but there was no bruising or injury to support her version of events.

When questioned by the police, the taxi driver boasted that he'd spent at least an hour with the woman. After picking her up at a pub, he'd driven to a bottle shop, then a local lookout. After a few drinks, he said, they had sexual intercourse at the woman's insistence. A diligent detective discovered surveillance cameras outside the local pub, which showed the woman being helped into the taxi, only fifteen minutes before she told staff at the supermarket about being raped. The camera proved the taxi driver had been lying about how long he spent with the woman. The case went to trial and a jury found him guilty of sexual assault. Without the camera evidence, the man would have been free to rape again, and again. Anya had resolved never to judge a woman by her behaviour, no matter how inappropriate it seemed at the time.

The taxi turned into Lansdowne Street and Anya noticed two young schoolgirls waiting at the traffic lights, hands entwined. They couldn't have been more than five and seven years old. The taller girl kept a constant lookout for cars while the little one stood obediently, never breaking the touch they shared.

Anya felt a crushing weight on her chest. Why had she let Miriam's hand go that day? Why did she have to prove she could run faster? They would have walked to school together just like that if things had been different. She thought of the years of torment never knowing whether her sister was alive, and the fear of facing the worst.

The smell of stale smoke in the taxi scalded her eyes as she thought about the house full of light where she and Missy played. She loved their matching bedrooms with lolly-pink walls, antique doll's houses, and pictures of The Monkees on the wardrobes. They'd jump on each other's beds and pretend to be pop stars, belting out tunes into a skipping-rope handle. They always ended up lying on the floor, laughing so hard their bellies ached.

After that day at the football ground, the house changed. The light stayed away and the house always felt cold. Instead of something she and Missy played in, the rain became a jailer, something to fear and resent. Aunts, uncles and cousins stopped visiting, and neighbours stopped saying hello when the family went to town. It felt like they had all disappeared without a trace, just like Miriam.

In hindsight, her parents had functioned like sleepwalkers, as though they'd become two-dimensional figures. Her mother's once-straight back bowed with the weight of invisible lead, her shiny-eyed smile disappeared into a distant memory and she stopped playing her beloved piano. Anya missed her parents even more than she missed her only sister. At least Miriam's spirit was alive in the house. Her smiling face greeted them from photo frames in every room. Everywhere except the back shed – the only sanctuary Anya had from the loneliness.

Their mother would set a place at every meal. 'To remember our Miriam, who can't join us today,' she'd say.

The reality was that no-one could ever forget.

On the wall behind Miriam's chair hung a framed, embroidered Latin phrase, '*Cruci Dum Spiro Fido*', meaning while there was life, there was hope. Another Catholic mantra used to justify false hope and denial, irrespective of the consequences.

On Missy's fourth birthday, their mother placed a wrapped present at the table, like she did for each and every birthday and Christmas. The presents were piled on Miriam's chenille bedspread, then later moved to the study, awaiting her return. After a while, it looked like a magic cave of cards and gifts to show how much her mother loved Missy.

Anya knew she wasn't loved nearly as much.

Jocelyn Reynolds buried herself in medicine, as though that would bring her beloved child back. A clairvoyant wrote to say that Miriam was safe and wanted to come home. Anya's father said people peddled cruel lies to the most vulnerable. That was one of the first lessons she could remember.

For a while, her mother smiled again, with the birth of a baby boy, Damien Patrick, with enormous blue eyes full of mischief, and a giggle that infected everyone who heard it. Anya turned six the day her brother arrived by caesarian section. She knew she didn't deserve him after what she had let happen to Miriam, but in a secret way, she hoped God had given her a second chance to make good.

Damien spent the first few years of his life following Anya around, playing with her in every waking moment they were together. Sometimes her father would find her asleep on the floor beside Damien's cot and carry her back to bed. Damien quickly learnt to climb and would crawl into Anya's bed when a nightmare or storm frightened him. She often wondered which was worse – being blamed by her mother for losing Miriam, or hated by her for monopolising Damien.

Bob Reynolds didn't seem to notice his daughter's pain. If he had, he wouldn't have left home the day after Anya's seventh birthday. She could vividly recall the argument over the memorial service. It was time, he said, to accept that Miriam was never coming back and achieve some form of closure.

For the first time, Jocelyn screamed at someone other than Anya.

'While God gives breath, he gives hope,' she would say. 'If you give up on your child, you're not fit to be a parent.'

Bob stood up with tears in his eyes and smashed a plate against the wall, sending the embroidered motto to the floor. Jocelyn sat down, said grace and served the meal. Bob Reynolds retreated to the bedroom and packed his belongings. The next morning he moved into his office in town.

As he drove away, Anya noticed that the mantra was back on the wall. She hated it, as though it were evil. Whatever it really meant tore apart what was left of her home.

Every night after that, Anya begged God to bring back Missy and take her instead. Sometimes she secretly hated Miriam for wandering away that day and causing so much pain. Before long, she despised herself even more.

The taxi driver switched on his radio and listened to the traffic reports.

'Every road's chock-a-block,' he said.

Anya rubbed her temples. Her mind flooded with memories she had worked hard to block out.

A new investigation meant dredging up the past. Wounds protected by layers of scar tissue were about to be sliced open again.

If only she hadn't let Miriam's hand go that day.

She took a staccato breath as the taxi arrived at Cleveland Street's Homicide office.

20

After clearing security and being escorted upstairs, Anya sat down at the computer screen on Kate Farrer's desk. The detective sergeant chomped into a chocolate bar and a bag of chips. Anya shined an apple she'd pulled from her bag.

Kate explained the background while she fiddled with the computer to start the Interactive Crime Scene Recording System, or ICSRS, as it was known.

Debbie Finch had taken off from work one night, without a word. Eight days later she went home, shot her demented father while the carer was buying groceries, then poured jam down his throat as he sat dying. Meanwhile, she ate some jam and shot herself. Her death, although considered weird, appeared to be suicide, but she now had something odd in her lungs, which warranted investigation.

'The neighbours say the old man only ever left the house for doctors' appointments, and only ever with his daughter,' Kate said. 'A carer came each evening while she worked. She always left on time and was never late getting back. After that night, when Debbie didn't come home, the agency phoned the police and organised full-time carers. The local doctor had him on the waiting list for a nursing home bed.' Kate excused herself to answer her mobile. Without losing her train of thought after the call, she picked up the story. 'The father was a widower and Debbie never married. According to the neighbour who lived next door for thirty-odd years, no-one had even seen a boy call for her. Wasn't overly social by colleagues' accounts, either.'

She pressed the enter button and the first scene appeared in 3D. The computer software had converted photographs taken at the crime scene into interactive 360-degree digitised views that could be watched on a normal computer screen. It effectively placed the police at a crime scene and could navigate around rooms, allowing them to look at aspects of the location from any angle. The technology still impressed Anya.

Kate directed the program through the entry, turned right into the dining room and through to a small, laminated kitchen. The sort of china figurines that only grandmothers pass down filled a glass cabinet in the lounge room. An ugly cat, an eagle, a figure of a lady nurse, and a male doctor took pride of place.

Anya felt like a voyeur. 'What do you know about the woman's lifestyle, her hobbies?'

'No-one knows much about her. According to reports, Debbie Finch was quiet, private and efficient. Just did her job. Didn't have anyone over to her home. Always met people at the movies, wouldn't let anyone pick her up from her house. Maybe she was ashamed of her old man,' Kate suggested as an afterthought.

Anya had always wondered why Kate had said little of her family or life, apart from the fact that she was an only child. Like Anya, Kate seemed to concentrate on the present.

'Could someone else have been there? Any restraint marks to suggest she'd been coerced?'

'Nope.'

Anya perused the photos in the file. A demented father may have been aggressive and difficult to look after. Elder abuse was on the rise, given the pressures of home care on a relative who sacrificed a social life to care for someone who was incapable of loving in return. The man wore a urodome on his penis attached to a urine collection bag, and had no control of his bowels. Anya felt sympathetic towards someone who had to bathe, feed and toilet her own father. Maybe she just couldn't give anymore.

Kate licked her salty fingers. 'Neighbours say he couldn't even recognise her, let alone celebrate her birthday. Maybe it all got too much. She just disappeared after a party for her at work.'

The kitchen looked immaculate. No cups, glasses or dirty dishes. Each plate stood in a rack, every cup positioned on a stand. On the bench sat an almost empty two-kilogram plastic tub of strawberry jam with a large spoon in it.

'Doesn't look anything like my place,' the detective declared, tearing open another chocolate bar.

'For one thing, you can see the carpet. There aren't clothes, books or CDs lying on every possible surface.' Anya chomped into the apple.

Kate fiddled with the computer settings. 'Very amusing. What are we looking for, in particular?'

'Signs of renovations, any work or damage that could have disturbed old fibres in the building.'

In the large, open-plan office, detectives arrived for the day's work – men in suits, women in grey or black skirts or slacks. 'Plain clothes' meant uniform by another name. Four rows of five desks gave the room a classroom feel. Each workstation displayed a phone, a computer, and a distinct lack of paperwork. The 'clean desk' policy at the end of the day seemed to be enforced by everyone but Kate Farrer and her team.

Brian Hogan greeted Kate. 'Isn't this the one you're consulting on? Thought it was open-shut.'

'Just thought we'd check it over. See if anything got missed. And Dr Crichton is interested in the environment. Seems there have been other deaths that showed up something in the lungs and she wants to know where that stuff could have come from.'

Hogan responded with as much interest as a child made to watch a geography program, and found an excuse to get coffee.

The original linoleum and carpets were in place, and the bathroom still had brown mosaic tiles around the basin, bath and shower. The room had been modified with a hand rail and a white plastic chair sat in the shower. The shower head detached, just like a hospital one. There were no renovations or extensions in this house, nothing to explain the lung fibres.

The phone on Kate's desk rang. She grabbed it on the second ring.

'Homicide, Detective Sergeant Farrer . . . Right, thanks. I'll send someone down.'

She leant back in her chair and looked around. 'Anyone seen Hogan?'

An attractive woman answered without looking up from her desk. 'Um, I think he ducked out for a coffee.'

Anya saw him disappear towards the toilets with a newspaper.

'Shit. All right. I'll have to do it.' Kate stood, wiped the crumbs from her trousers and asked Anya if there was any food in her teeth.

'There's a woman downstairs who says she's a cousin of Debbie Finch. The Gosford boys couldn't find any relatives up there. She's the only one anyone's heard of.' She grabbed her jacket. 'Won't be long. Need to tell her about the deaths and ask if she knows what state of mind Debbie was in when she died.'

Typical Kate. Breaking bad news and interviewing a grieving relative only took a minute. Anyone else would put at least half an hour aside. As Kate headed for the stairs, Anya returned to the computer screen.

She navigated her way around the dishevelled bathroom. Towels lay crumpled on the floor, the toilet seat was up, a patterned shower curtain hung off its rail. She wondered how Debbie Finch, who shunned visitors but took pride in her house, would feel having strangers prying into her intimate world.

Anya turned into the first bedroom, with Joseph Finch sitting upright in his chair, bullet hole almost obscured by the position of his slumped head. She used the computer mouse to move around the old man's body. Jam stained his cheeks and mouth, and spread over his shirt and trousers. Beside the double bed sat a toilet chair, a commode. Apart from that, the room had little furniture.

Down the corridor in the adjacent bedroom, dressed in navy trousers, sheer black shirt and black heels, lay the body of Debbie Finch. She could have been sleeping peacefully on her side. The view from above showed a small entry wound to the right temple and a gun beside her hand on the turquoise chenille bedspread.

Leanne Finch stood on the steps outside the building, chewing her fingernails. A mop of dyed straw hair wafted from black roots. A baggy shirt and harem pants did little to disguise the emaciated body beneath. Pustular acne made Kate suspect heroin addiction. The woman looked to be in her forties. 'Leanne, thanks for coming.'

'What do you want? My flatmate said you had some news.'

'I'm afraid it's bad news. There's no easy way to say it. Debbie and Joseph Finch were found dead in their house a few nights ago.'

'Shit. Both of 'em?'

Kate nodded. 'Looks like Debbie shot her father and then turned the gun on herself.'

Leanne chewed the rest of her nails in silence.

'When was the last time you saw them?'

'Not for years. Not since Aunt Rita's funeral.' Leanne sat down on the cement steps. 'I don't believe it.'

'Why do you say that?'

Kate looked around and sat on the same step.

'I shot through when Rita died. I'd lived with them for ten years and had had enough.'

'What did your aunt die of?'

'Alcohol poisoning, although no-one in the family wanted to admit it. She bled to death from the stomach or something, they said. But we all knew she drank. No-one talked about it, that's all.'

'When did your uncle become ill?'

'Dunno. I lost touch with the family after that. I move around a fair bit.'

'When was the last time you had contact with Debbie?'

'About a year ago. The old man was in a wheelchair by then. Deb was relieved he'd stopped wandering all over the place. Lost his marbles with the Parkinson's, she reckoned. He had this disgusting thing happening where he couldn't control his tongue or head. Deb said it was because of a medicine he had to take for being out of control.'

'Did she ever get help from other people, apart from the carers? It must have been a huge job looking after someone that ill and working in a high-stress job at the same time.'

'Deb never wanted anyone in the house.' She studied what was left of her stumped fingers. 'Where'd she shoot him?'

Kate studied the woman's face. 'In his bedroom.'

'No, I meant where on *him*?'

'In the neck.'

Leanne Finch shook her head. 'Did she make him suffer?'

Kate was unsure how to answer.

'Come on, did she make the old bastard suffer?'

Kate stood. 'I think you'd better come inside and have a chat.'

Upstairs, Kate showed Debbie Finch's cousin into a conference room and sat opposite her at the table. 'Debbie shot her father and stuffed jam down his throat before she killed herself.'

'Oh, Jesus.' The woman's eyes filled with tears. She wiped her nose with her sleeve. 'I didn't think Debbie knew.'

'Knew what?'

'Every time Rita and Debbie left the house, the old prick would lock me in the bathroom with him.'

'Leanne,' Kate lowered her voice, 'did your uncle sexually abuse you?'

The woman almost whispered the words. 'Usually it happened in the bathroom. If anyone else was at home, he'd pick me up from school and take me to the park. He called it having afternoon tea.'

'Did he ever do this to Debbie?'

'Don't reckon. He said afternoon tea was "just for us".'

Kate shifted in her chair. 'What did afternoon tea mean?'

'He'd pull down his pants, and make me . . .' The woman looked away, unable to face the detective.

Kate offered, 'Leanne, this is really important. Did it have anything to do with jam?'

The woman nodded, wiping her nose with the back of her hand. 'He put jam all over his dick. He made me lick it off. And then he used it on me.'

The detective let out a sigh and the mysterious murder–suicide made sense. She would have shoved a lot more than jam down the old man's throat.

Leanne startled. 'But Debbie never knew about the jam.'

'Looks like she must have.'

'But I never told her about it. I couldn't. He was her father and I was about to shoot through. I just said he touched me up and she said she'd look after things.' Leanne began hitting her forehead with her fist. 'How could she know about the jam?'

Kate knew the answer. 'We found it in her mouth, too. Looks like you weren't the only one your uncle had afternoon tea with.'

Kate saw Leanne out and straddled a chair next to Anya. She quietly explained about the abuse. Anya felt a heavy ache in her chest. The thought of what her own sister had probably endured was almost too much to bear. She refocused on the murder.

Kate frowned. 'I don't get the jam in Debbie's mouth. Surely she didn't eat it for old times' sake. The old man didn't seem fit to force her to go down on him.' She closed her eyes tightly. 'They didn't check Debbie's mouth for semen, did they?'

'Not unless they had reason to suspect something. They swabbed the jam in her pharynx, but it would be easy to miss semen if you weren't specifically looking for it. There weren't any poisons or toxins in the jam.' Anya checked again. 'There's nothing mentioned about swabbing anything else.'

'Looks like these fibres don't mean much,' Kate announced. 'We've got a motive for killing her father.'

'Hang on,' Anya held up her index finger. 'The toxicology report says his blood contained thioridazine, but the family doctor says he should have been taking dopamine for his Parkinson's disease. None showed up on the screen.'

Kate wheeled her chair forward to check. 'Yeah,

that was on the fax when I got here, but looked like gobbledygook to me. What's the difference?'

'The daughter was an efficient nurse. I'd be surprised if she forgot to give him his medication, or didn't stand over him while he took it.'

'Maybe she withheld it, to keep him in the wheelchair. Sexual abuse would give her one hell of a reason for keeping him incapacitated before killing him.'

Anya had an unpleasant thought. 'Is it too late to do a sexual assault kit on Debbie's remains?'

'As far as I know, no-one's claimed the bodies. That's why the Gosford guys were tracking down Leanne.'

'In that case,' Anya said, 'you could ask them to do it.'

'You're not suggesting the old man rose from his wheelchair, made her give him oral sex one last time and she flipped out?' Kate knew better than to expect an answer. 'I'll check it out with Connelly right away.'

While Kate made the call, Anya flicked through the file photos. Debbie Finch lay on the stainless steel table, free from any kind of abuse. The gunshot wound to the temple was the only evidence of trauma. This white, hairless body would never know childbirth, menopause or ageing. It seemed slightly odd that someone so private shaved her pubic region. She remembered what Jeff Sales had said about the genital blisters only being obvious on Fatima Deab because she'd shaved. It was suppos-

172

edly a fad in younger, sexually active girls, not someone devoid of intimate contact. Anya wondered what other secrets Debbie Finch and Fatima took with them when their lives ended.

Anya spun back to the computer and once again navigated her way to the bathroom. And then it became obvious.

If the old man was wheelchair-bound and incontinent of urine, who'd left the toilet seat up?

21

Brian Hogan shook his head. 'Shit. There could have been someone else there. How did that get missed?'

Kate was behind him before he got the words out. 'How many blokes do you know who put the toilet seat down? Bet you wouldn't even notice if the bloody thing was missing.'

'Remember, hindsight is always twenty–twenty,' Hogan retorted.

Kate hung her hands on her hips. 'Bit embarrassing having a ring-in find a stuff-up like that.'

Anya wasn't quite sure how to interpret that comment. At this point, she didn't really care. 'Did they fingerprint the place?'

'The entry and exits but only four sets of prints turned up – the three carers' and the deceased woman's.'

Anya's first thought was the police. 'Could one of your lot have urinated at the scene?'

'It wouldn't have been the first time someone pissed on the evidence. But this time a female constable and her partner were first on the scene. They both swore blind they didn't touch a thing.

174

One look at the bodies and the young guy bolted outside. Stayed there 'til the detectives arrived. Don't reckon you could have paid him to go back inside for a leak.'

Kate had obviously done her homework late last night.

'Had the commode been emptied? That might explain it.'

'Full. Made the detectives gag.'

'Okay,' Anya tried, 'so someone else has been there. What about friends, relatives, community nurses?'

'No-one. Colleagues didn't even know where she lived. She'd meet them out.'

'What about the carer?' Brian asked.

'The agency told the local detectives the carers Debbie Finch picked were all middle-aged women. Wouldn't have anyone young or pretty, and never a man in the house,' Kate answered.

'You'd think if she hated him that much, the old man would have had to be loaded for her to stay,' Hogan mumbled.

A young tanned detective, dressed in a navy, fine pinstriped suit, joined the conversation. He looked like he should have been patrolling a beach.

'I just checked the bank accounts,' he said, addressing Kate. 'The old bloke had nothing when he died. The daughter was the one who squirrelled money away. She was worth a mint – $350,000 in shares. Not only that, but she rented out four properties at prime locations on the coast. A local real estate agent reckons they're worth over two million.'

Kate smiled approvingly. 'Mick, don't suppose you found out who she left it all to?'

'Some centre for abused women.'

Hogan shrugged. 'Guess we can rule money out as a motive.'

Anya wondered why a woman like that had a firearm. 'What about the gun? Was it registered?'

Brian Hogan pulled out a crumpled hankie and wiped it across his nose. 'Could have been bought on the black market anywhere. We're checking the Gosford pubs and dealers now, but don't expect to get an answer,' he said, shoving the handkerchief back into his trouser pocket.

'Do we know what she did in her time off? Where she went?'

'The carer said she'd go to Sydney sometimes. She'd say she was going shopping but didn't seem to buy much.'

'That could mean anything,' Kate said. 'Maybe she had a man, a hobby, bought handguns. Hell, she could have spent her time at the bloody art gallery for all we know.'

Anya looked more closely at the photos. Who could blame her for getting away?

A phone rang and as Hogan answered it, Kate leant over Anya's shoulder. 'Maybe it all means nothing. Maybe the carer cleaned the bowl and just left the lid up.'

'If she'd been cleaning you'd think she'd have

picked up the towels and tidied the rest of the bath-room up, too,' Anya deduced.

Kate agreed. 'If there was someone else in the room, we'd better find out.'

The lung slides bothered Anya. 'What did Peter Latham say about the fibres?'

'There weren't any in the old man's lungs. Only in the daughter's.'

'That suggests she wasn't exposed to them in the house. So the father's lungs were clear?'

'I didn't say that. He had a whopping great lung cancer.'

'Mesothelioma?'

Kate handed her a pathology report. 'You can interpret. Looks like hieroglyphics to me.'

Anya read the words 'squamous cell carcinoma'. 'No luck. It's not the sort of cancer men who've worked with fibres in the past get. We can't blame him for bringing home the fibres in his clothes, which could have explained how his daughter inhaled them.' Anya read on. 'The tragedy is that with a cancer the size of this, he was dying anyway.'

Brian Hogan finished his phone conversation and rejoined Anya near the computer. 'Is this some kind of death or euthanasia pact?'

'Pretty unlikely,' Kate replied. 'His own doctor didn't even know about the cancer.'

The sweet-faced surfer looked surprised. 'So what you're saying is, whoever pulled the trigger killed a dead man.'

Anya was still worried about the fibres. 'We

haven't explained where the fibres came from, or why they've turned up in three different women.'

'Is that so unusual?' Mick seemed interested.

'The chances of three young women having them at autopsy have got to be a million to one against,' Anya explained. 'Coincidences like this don't just happen. The fibres don't occur normally. They have to have been inhaled from somewhere. Is there any chance the women spent time at the same place, or knew the same people? Do they have anything in common? That's what we need to find out.'

Hogan wheeled his chair alongside Anya's. 'Is this like one of those infections people get from air-conditioning? Legionnella or whatever they call it?'

Anya smelt the combination of coffee and cigarettes on his breath. 'Not exactly. None of the victims died from it, but they may have spent time in the same place. All we know is that three young women apparently committed suicide, all three were missing before their deaths and all of them had the fibres. Fatima Deab died of an OD in Merrylands and Clare Matthews jumped off the Gap earlier this year.'

'If you think the deaths are linked, shouldn't there be a task force to investigate?' Mick asked.

Kate took command. 'A link hasn't been established or ruled out. Before we get carried away, we need to find out a bit more about this case. I want phone records cross-checked, friends and neighbours re-interviewed. Did Debbie have a boyfriend, did the family have any enemies? Where did she bugger off to?' Kate took her jacket off and slung it over the back of a chair. 'Was anything missing from the house? I also want to know if she had anything to do with Fatima Deab or Clare Matthews. Any connection at all.'

22

The following day, Anya returned to Cleveland Street and met Kate in the foyer. Together they rode the lift to the third floor. During that time, Kate checked her watch four times and cleared her throat at least twice. Either she couldn't wait for the meeting, or couldn't wait for it to be over.

'Is there something I should know before we go in?' Anya broached.

'Just don't get your hopes up. These guys will do anything to avoid a bigger workload. Filano fancies himself as inspector material and won't risk stuffing up. He didn't like it when I got called to the morgue when Clare Matthews died. Just wanted to close the book and make himself look good. You can decide about Faulkner for yourself.'

'Fair enough. All I can do is try.'

They settled into the second meeting room, with a rectangular table, six chairs and a whiteboard. Vertical blinds on the glass wall adjoining the main office remained open. Anya was introduced to Detective Sergeant Ernie Faulkner, a pot-bellied man with a few grey hairs combed over his head to give the illusion he wasn't balding. More like self-delusion, Anya thought. Detective Constable Ray Filano stood and almost bowed a greeting. Aged in his thirties, he wore a black shirt and matching tie. It wasn't difficult to work out that Ernie Faulkner came from western Sydney's Merrylands branch and the immaculately dressed Detective Filano fitted right into the eastern suburbs locale.

Kate took a seat at the table. 'Thanks for coming in. I appreciate your input.'

'Happy to help, if we can.' Ernie Faulkner's chair sat directly under the air-conditioning vent as evidenced by two of his comb-over hairs floating skyward.

'We're looking into possible links between three of our cases. An OD in your territory, name of Fatima Deab; Clare Matthews, a nun who died off the Gap; and an apparent murder–suicide up the coast, name of Debbie Finch.'

'What sort of link?' Ray Filano enquired.

'Well, Dr Crichton has been looking into some unusual findings post-mortem. I'll let her explain.'

Anya stood up and pulled the lid off a marker.

'Each woman had an unusual finding – a lung fibre – which was deemed incidental on post-mortem. It is extemely rare to get this sort of finding in older people who've had a lifetime of exposure, let alone young women.' She drew an hourglass fibre in black ink. 'We have no idea where it's come from, but it may mean the women have spent time in the same place.'

Filano appeared interested. 'The stuff that spreads through air-conditioning?'

'I think you mean Legionnella, which is an infection. That's quite different from this fibre, but they are both acquired by inhalation.'

'Then is it a new kind of drug they're snorting or smoking?'

'No, that's a good thought, but it's more likely to be in some kind of building material. Air-conditioning is still a possible means of spread.'

'I thought that was something the unions or workers' compensation usually investigate. Are we looking at some form of *criminal* negligence?' Filano said, in a tone usually reserved for children.

Anya disliked him already. 'No, it's likely the owner of the source of the fibre is unaware of its –'

'Excuse me,' Ernie Faulkner interrupted, 'didn't you just say this was incidental, which means it has nothing to do with the deaths?'

'Technically speaking, but it may be highly significant. The chances of a young person having this pathology are so rare, to my knowledge, it hasn't even been recorded.'

Kate spoke. 'We're talking about Fatima Deab, a nineteen-year-old who overdosed after going missing for a few weeks. Clare Matthews was about to take her final vows as a nun when she disappeared and turned up off the Gap. Debbie Finch, the third woman, also disappeared, for a week.'

The Merrylands detective rolled his eyes and closed his notebook. 'Regarding the Deab case, we looked at the possibility that someone else may have been there in the toilet block and got *nothing*. We're more interested in her old man bashing the shit out of some poor kid.'

Kate folded her arms. 'We had the father under surveillance following a phone call from someone claiming the girl was murdered. While we had him under our noses, he committed GBH. This guy is brazen, violent, and teaches people lessons.'

'Yeah, when he's got his mates and an iron bar. Not with needles.'

'Okay,' Anya said, 'but you think it's possible the Deab girl wasn't alone when she overdosed? We have no idea where any of these women went before being found dead.'

'Comb-over' grunted. 'Isn't it a bit of a stretch linking these women? Do you know how many people are reported missing every week? Most of them turn up sooner or later, these just turned up dead. As far as I know, they died from different causes. The Deab case enquiries were based on a history of domestic abuse and threats to the girl. I wouldn't be surprised if the prick was there when she died, but there's not a damn thing we can do to prove it.'

Anya now understood why her friend had seemed edgy. 'It is, however, important to identify the source of the fibres. There could be other cases with similar findings that are related.'

As she spoke the words, Anya realised how unin- terested the detectives were.

Faulkner wriggled in his seat and the floaters on his head swayed in the flow of cool air. 'Last I heard, we're not research assistants who run around so you can make some great scientific discovery.'

'Where are your manners, Ern?' Filano said. 'Let's hear the lady out.'

'All right,' Kate said, 'I know this may seem a long shot, but let's at least go through what we've got. In the Finch murder–suicide –'

Filano interjected. 'We've all heard about what happened and what *went down* with that one.'

Faulkner slowly licked his lips. *For God's sake*, Anya thought. It was worse than dealing with pre-pubescent children.

Kate ignored the bait. 'We know someone left the toilet seat up in the house and we've pretty much excluded household members, domestic help and the police. We can't discount a third person being present when this woman and her father died.'

DS Faulkner forcefully clicked the tip of his pen. The hairs seem to dance on his head, mocking his superior tone. 'Remember the case in Maroochydore where someone twigged that the toilet seat was left up, the one where two losers knocked off a woman and tried to make it look like an OD? Only problem was they cleaned up all the gear. How was the victim supposed to have injected herself with enough crap to kill a horse, tidy up and, oh yeah, put all the stuff in the neighbour's bin before going inside, getting into her pyjamas and dying quickly not on her own bed, but her flatmate's one? Didn't need to be Einstein to figure something was wrong with that little scenario. The toilet seat was just a bonus but it got a hell of a lotta press at the time.'

Ray Filano became serious. 'What about the gunshot residue?'

Kate answered, 'Consistent with the Finch woman pulling the trigger.'

'Signs of struggle or theft?'

Anya described what she'd seen on the 3D images. 'A couple of things were knocked off a table and broken, like a vase and old family photos. We know they were knocked over after the father's shooting because the blood spatter marks were on the photo sides of the glass. There were two bloodied handprints on the carpet, so we think the daughter touched the old bloke and maybe tried to help him, then wiped her hands on the floor.'

'So she shoots the old man in haste, has second thoughts about what she's done and panics. When she realises he's dead, bang. Her handprints are on the floor. She kills herself.' Detective Filano made it sound so simple.

Anya decided to re-enact the shooting to make her point. She pointed at Ernie Faulkner's shortened neck and collarbone.

'The bullet caused extensive haemorrhage as it passed to the left, downwards and backwards. It went through the insertion of the sternocleidomastoid muscles, then down to the left brachiocephalic vein, then to the origin of the carotid artery. Here's where it does the most damage. Through the aorta, before it tore through the upper and lower lobes of the left lung. It fractured a couple of ribs and the shoulder blade before embedding in the tissue under the skin at the back of the chest wall.' Anya laid one hand on Faulkner's back at the site of the bullet's final location. 'He took a while to die, long enough for her to shove jam down his throat. I think it's more likely that a shot in anger would have been straight through his chest. She was, after all, a casualty nurse and would have seen her share of gunshot traumas.'

Kate added, 'If she'd had regrets, there was plenty of time to call an ambulance.'

'It's not a lot to go on,' Filano said. 'As for Clare Matthews, she was on my patch. Pathologist ruled out a struggle, which meant it was a job for us local boys, not Homicide. So she got pregnant, screwed up her life and took the easy way out. The family had trouble accepting that, but nothing points to foul play. Ah, Kate, you know that already. Didn't you consult on that case, too?'

Faulkner cleared his throat. 'If Deab's been dogged, wouldn't your boys have noticed if he popped in to have a piss on the Central Coast or took a nun up for a midnight leap?'

Anya moved over to the whiteboard and circled her drawing.

'We still can't explain why these women were exposed to the same type of fibre.'

'Are you implying that they knew each other?'

186

Filano asked. 'Even if they did, it doesn't mean much.'

'If they knew each other, the significance of the findings is even more important. Whatever is in their lungs could be quite harmful.'

Faulkner clicked his pen again. 'Doctor, I understand you work freelance. You can pick and choose your workload. Well, we can't. We've got thirty other jobs at the moment. Break-and-enters, robberies, sexual assaults, indecent assaults, and a record number of shitty cheques being passed. Not enough money to have the Fraud Squad interested, so we're lumbered with them too.

'The coroner signed off on the Deab kid, the anonymous call caused us a headache chasing our tails, and right now we don't have squat except for a cigarette butt that the DPP thinks would be thrown out in court since it could have been dropped in the toilet anything up to a week later. As far as we're concerned, we want if off the books. And now you expect us to drop everything to chase up something that doesn't mean anything? And who's gonna pay for all this? Our overtime budget doesn't cover the jobs we've already got. Kate, tell us you're kidding?'

Kate Farrer looked at the frenzy of activity in the office outside. With the sound muted by the thick glass wall, the scene resembled a silent movie. Inside the room, no subtitles were necessary. She turned to Faulkner. 'Before you go, could we compare phone records and at least see if there's anyone in common they called?'

'I can tell you right now. The Deab girl didn't have a mobile, didn't go out and didn't have friends. So there you go. No contacts, no connections. Is that all? I'm due at the crime lab.'

'Hang on Ern, let's finish this,' Filano said. 'The Matthews woman lived in a communal house and didn't have a mobile either. Not a lot of point checking phone records when half-a-dozen people use the phone. I don't know about your Commands, but mine can't afford to waste funds on non-essential record searches.'

'What about bank accounts?' Anya directed her question at all three detectives.

Filano had the answers. 'That's the interesting thing. The Matthews woman's account stayed active the whole time she was reported missing.'

Kate found a stain on the floor, which she scuffed with one foot. 'How do you know it was her accessing the account?'

'Law of averages. Not many kidnappers take the trouble to log on to the net to pay their victim's bills.'

Comb-over stood first and recaptured his mutinous hairs, the set of four again together, traversing the bald head. Anya wouldn't hesitate to cut them off given half a chance.

'Anything else?' he smirked.

'As far as we know,' Anya said, 'at least two of the women, Debbie Finch and Fatima Deab, had completely shaved pubic regions.' She regretted the comment as soon as the words came out.

Ernie Faulkner tried to look shocked.

'That *is* suspicious! It's something my ex-wife did too.' He loosened his tie. 'In your experience, doctor, do you find pubic shaves suggestive of dangerous or even lewd behaviour? If that's the case, I strongly suggest you contact the God Squad or even the Morals Police. They have unlimited time and resources to address your concerns.'

Anya felt her face flush as she tried to explain. 'Less than five per cent of women at autopsy have shaved pubic regions. Lots have partial shaves, like bikini lines. But unless they're models, swimmers or prostitutes, it's uncommon.'

'I don't know if Clare Matthews was shaved or not,' Filano replied, 'but if that's all you have . . .'

Faulkner turned towards Kate. 'If you're looking for stuff to do, you could always check every beautician in the state and see whether they remember waxing these particular pubes. Might make some good contacts.' He leant over her and whispered loudly enough for the others to hear, 'Maybe you should try a Brazilian. Never know, it could do wonders for you. They tell me walking to the letterbox is a whole new thrill.'

Anya moved quickly to intervene in case a fight broke out. Instead, Kate stood, her jaw clenched. 'The point is, it's another coincidence. And I don't believe in coincidences.'

Faulkner moved his face closer. 'I find it co-incidental that out of everyone who's been involved in these cases, you two are the only ones who think

189

the deaths are sinister. You obviously spent a lot of time on this one *together*.'

Kate breathed through flared nostrils and Anya expected her to throw a punch this time. Thankfully, she reconsidered.

'I think you guys have had your say. We all know where we stand. Oh, and Faulkner, next time you go perving at the Pussy Club, try to make sure you're not caught in a drug raid. It's appalling public relations, and such a bad example to every officer in the service.' She waited for a reaction, then added, 'Television really does add ten pounds, even when you hide your face. On my screen it looked more like twenty.'

Anya's eyes widened. She'd heard about a detective being caught in a compromising position during a raid but had no idea who it was. This was justice, of a sort. Faulkner's speedy exit proved it.

Ray Filano uncrossed his legs, stood and bowed again to Anya. 'Sorry about Ernie, he's got a lot on his plate. Next time we should meet over lunch.' As he stood in the doorway, he added, 'I wouldn't lose heart. There's always the chance that all of us are wrong and you two are right. Who knows? You may have stumbled onto three perfect murders.'

'If they were perfect, I wouldn't be investigating them.'

Anya closed the door.

Kate walked to the glass window and slouched, hands on her hips. 'I know they're arseholes, but you've got to see it from their point of view. They're drowning in work. Unless we come up with something a lot better than incidental findings, these cases are closed.'

23

'Mummy!' Ben jumped out of the back seat and ran to Anya, leaping into her arms. Neither minded the spitting rain.

'I've missed you so much.' She held her son tightly and drank in the scent from his apple shampoo.

'I've missed you too. Mummy, I've got big again! See my muscles?'

Benjamin slid to his feet and flexed his biceps.

'They're huge! You must have been eating meat, fruit AND vegetables.'

'Uh-huh, except brussel sprouts. They're disgusting.'

'Fair enough,' she said, tickling his ribs. 'No brussel sprouts this weekend. If you go up to your room, there's a surprise waiting for you.'

'Wow. Let's go see,' he said, steering her arm towards the house. 'Dad, you come and see, too.'

Martin pulled a duffle bag from the front seat and placed it on the footpath. 'You go on in, matey,' he said. 'I'll be there in a minute.'

Anya waited until Ben was inside the house. Martin wore a grey suit and mauve tie she didn't recognise. 'You're late. Two hours late this time.'

Martin pulled a face and waved at the house next door. 'Mrs Bugalugs is at it again.'

Anya turned to see the upstairs curtain moving. The old woman was obviously nowhere near as deaf or blind as she constantly made out.

'I wish you wouldn't call her that. Ben thinks it's her real name.'

'Please don't start with me, Annie.' He tugged at his tie as though it were the enemy. 'I'm stressed enough after going through a long interview.'

Martin hadn't worn a tie in years, it seemed. Anya wanted to know what his work plans were and where they would take him and their son. If she asked, Martin would accuse her of prying. She decided to wait and see if he brought up the job himself.

'How's work?' He glanced up the street. 'We saw you on the news one night.'

'That case went well. The rest is slow but I knew it would be for a while.' Anya touched his arm and pulled back when he moved away. 'Before you go, we need to talk about Ben. Where he's going for pre-school and school?'

'We've been through this. He'll go wherever is close to our place.' Martin picked up the bag and swung it over his shoulder, just missing a cyclist riding on the path. 'Ride on the road, you idiot. And get a helmet!' he called after him.

'Forget the bike. Look, our son has special needs,' Anya pleaded. 'We have to make sure they're met. We owe that to him.'

'As far as I'm concerned, he's normal. I don't

want you using words like "gifted" around him. Life's got enough pressures without us labelling kids and expecting things from them.'

Ben tapped excitedly on the bedroom window and gestured for Martin to come. His father held up three fingers, so Ben would know he wouldn't be long. Anya suspected Ben wanted them to stop talking so they wouldn't fight.

'I know, but I didn't label him that. The teachers at his old day care wanted him assessed. You must know he's miles ahead of his age group. He needs to be stimulated, constantly challenged. There's a progressive school not far from here.'

'Sure, the kids learn the names of places and what flags look like. But how much running around do they do? Playing soccer, footie, climbing, learning how to be a boy. He's not a computer, he's a child who needs to play. I won't let anyone set that kid up for failure. Life's going to kick him in the guts soon enough.'

Anya had been through this with Martin before. She understood his point, but felt as though Ben should be given the best opportunities, or she would have failed as a parent. The difficulty was that Martin was exceptionally intelligent, but viewed himself as a failure. He compensated by lowering his expectations of others.

'Will you please consider talking to the school and see what they do?'

Martin looked at Anya. 'I'm not agreeing to anything, but I will think about it.'

Ben managed to push open the window. 'Dad, Dad, it's a castle with knights, a door that's a ramp and everything. And there's a new rug on the floor with a town on it.'

'Sounds great. I've got to meet Nita so I've got to go. You be good for your mum.'

'I will, Dad.' Ben ran downstairs and threw his arms around his father's leg. 'I love you.'

'Me too.' Martin looked over at Anya, who pretended not to notice. She still felt the pain of separation from her own father and couldn't believe her son went through the same thing.

She decided not to let him leave without asking, 'You mentioned an interview.'

Martin stroked his tie with one hand and picked up Ben with the other. 'It's with a pharmaceutical company at Ryde, as a drug rep.'

Anya tried to conceal her excitement. 'Does this mean you and Ben might be moving closer?'

'No promises, but they told me I was virtually guaranteed the job.' For the first time in two years, he seemed positive about his future. Arms around his son, he patted down a divot in the grass next to the path with his foot. 'Being a single parent isn't always easy. It's pretty hard on Ben, packing up his stuff all the time. I've been doing a lot of thinking lately about what he needs.'

Maybe Martin had decided to grow up and act responsibly, Anya thought. 'Good luck,' she said, and kissed his cheek, surprising them both.

'Annie, I am trying,' Martin said. 'Honestly.'

This time Anya believed it.

He waved again at the window next door and shouted, 'Mrs Bugalugs. Good to see your beak's still sticky.'

Anya pinched his bicep hard.

He smirked. 'Lighten up. Just checking how deaf the old busybody really is.'

Martin hadn't changed. He still enjoyed flouting convention and disturbing the status quo. Years ago, it had been incredibly exciting. Now, it seemed annoyingly childish. She had to live with the old woman as a neighbour whether she liked it or not.

'Thanks for the toys, Mum.' Ben wriggled to the ground. 'Can I play your drums now, PLEEAAAASE?'

As Ben waved to his father, Anya thought of 'Mrs Bugalugs' next door having a gripe at the noise and suppressed a grin. She carried Ben up the stairs and into a small annex off her bedroom. He gasped at the full set of drums, complete with newly purchased sound silencers on the skins, to dampen the sound.

'Hey, what are these?' he asked, tentatively touching one of the padded coverings.

'They're supposed to make the playing quiet. So the old lady next door doesn't get upset when we practise.'

The few occasions Anya had attempted to play had led to visits from the cranky woman next door, complaining about the noise. Anya found this ironic given that the same neighbour complained that she couldn't watch television because of terrible deafness, and couldn't read the teletext because of poor eyesight. She had a habit of whingeing about everything and everyone.

'Would you like to have a go?' Anya placed him on one of the two stools and pressed play on a CD player beside her bed. The Commitments belted out 'Mustang Sally'.

Ben picked up one pair of sticks and banged them together over his head. 'One, Two, Three, Four.'

Anya used her left foot for the high-hat, locked down to dampen the noise. That foot tapped the rhythm and her right-hand stick accentuated the downbeat. With her left hand, she controlled the snare drum and cymbal. Her right foot kept time with the kick drum base pedal.

Ben banged away furiously, oblivious to rhythm. He sang loudly, but, like his father, Ben sang flat, as though he were tone deaf. It didn't matter, though. When they played the drums together, Anya couldn't be happier. This was the sound of a child and parent uninhibitedly enjoying themselves, feeling secure – having fun – together. The sound of unconditional love and both of them knew it.

Ben's blond hair had grown and with each movement, his fringe flicked across sparkling blue eyes. Anya made a mental note not to say anything to Martin. Last time she did, he marched their son off for a crew cut. The soft, shiny hair that Anya loved to run her fingers through had been shaved and had only just grown back.

The song ended and Ben hit the crash cymbal. Mother and son sat clapping as the next song started.

'Mummy! I've missed you sooooooooooooo much.'

'I missed you, too. Hey, you must be starving, with all those muscles to feed.'

'Yeah. Let's eat.'

Anya lifted him off the seat and they held hands on the way to the kitchen. She plonked him on the bench-top and grilled fish fingers and steamed peas, carrots and cauliflower.

Ben talked about the beach, his swimming, and rattled off the names of countries he knew. Anya had to keep reminding herself that this chatterbox was only three years old.

To protests, she lifted him down to a chair at the dining table. She was forgiven when she poured tomato sauce on his plate, next to, not on, the fish.

As she filled her own plate with the leftovers, the phone in the lounge room rang.

'I won't be long, Speedie, you start without me.'

Ben didn't need to be told twice. Anya picked up the receiver and didn't recognise the male voice.

'Is that Dr Crichton, formerly Anya Reynolds, of Launceston, Tasmania?'

Only close friends and the Tasmanian police knew her family name. She held her breath.

'Who is this?'

'Trent Wilkinson, from the *Herald Tribune*.'

Bloody reporter.

Anya snapped, 'I don't give interviews, and don't appreciate being called after hours.'

'Please don't hang up. I just wanted to ask you some questions about the investigation into your sister's disappearance. I have spoken to former neighbours who believe you were involved. Do you have any comment?'

Anya felt light-headed as her pulse galloped.

The voice continued, 'I understand you lost custody of your own child, too. Do you ever worry about having unsupervised access to him?'

Anya dropped the phone and watched her hands tremble. The voice kept talking until she kicked the handset and the sound stopped.

She took a few deep breaths, disconnected the phone and returned to Ben, who was counting peas on his plate.

'Who was it, Mum?'

She tried to sound calm. 'No-one we know, darling.'

Anya sat and watched her son play with his food. With a new investigation, the media were bound to become interested again, just as they had at the time. Half of Launceston knew who she was and could have told the reporter. What was his name? He was probably young and looking for a new angle to make a name for himself. Even so, the call rattled her. She wasn't ready for all the attention again, not after working so hard to distance herself from the past.

She told Ben to finish up.

'It's time for bath, pyjamas, clean teeth and if you're lucky, one story.'

'Oh, Mum . . .'

'Just for that, Speedie, you're going to get cuddled to bits!' She grabbed him tightly and carried him upstairs as he laughed and squealed.

Within forty-five minutes he was safely tucked into his bed. After a story, two songs, three books and a game of shadow puppets, Ben threw his arms around her.

'I don't want to let you go, Mummy.'

'Neither do I. But you have to get some sleep sometime.' She cradled him and stroked his down-like hair.

'I want to stay with you tonight.'

'I thought you'd want to sleep in your room with your new rug and toys.'

'I do. Will you sleep here with me? PLEEEAAASE?'

Despite protesting, Anya adored these moments. Ben was *the* love of her life, and the most accepting person she'd ever known.

'How about I sing you one more song? I'll even rub your back if you'd like.'

'Okay, but I still want you to stay.' Ben's eyelids were already starting to droop. She lay beside him under the covers. By the time she'd finished 'Rock-a-bye Your Bear', he had drifted into a peaceful sleep. She lay holding him until the sleep deepened, and each breath lengthened.

Leaving the room, Anya tried to avoid the creakiest floorboards, and went downstairs to clean the kitchen and check her e-mail. Channel-surfing didn't yield any interesting TV shows, so she made sure the doors and windows were locked.

Stopping in the study, she turned on the light and took some notes about the three women with the fibres. In separate columns, she wrote 'pubic hair', 'fibres', 'missing' and 'no social life'. Beside Debbie Finch's name, she ticked all four and added 'long-term sexual abuse'. Fatima Deab scored four ticks and 'physical abuse'. Clare Matthews was the only one who didn't fit. No-one had talked about her upbringing and whether or not she'd been abused. Maybe she did have something else in common with the others. There was nothing mentioned about pubic hair in her PM report. Shaved genitals weren't unusual markings like tattoos, not something you'd record in a passport as an identifying feature. Maybe it was a coincidence and she was making something out of nothing. Detectives Faulkner and Filano might have had a point, even though they'd been so offensive about the whole thing. She'd have to ask Peter Latham and hope he remembered about the Matthews woman. The conservative Fatima that the GP receptionist described wouldn't have worn see-through clothes and gaudy underwear. She had learnt that you can't ever predict how people will behave. Anya hadn't believed Martin would ever change his attitude or that Miriam's disappearance would be re-investigated.

Thoughts of tonight's call filled her mind. She could phone the paper tomorrow and complain about the intrusion. Then again, that would just inflame the reporter. Profiting from people's misery should be a crime. Private suffering was bad enough. Doing it in the public domain was even more devastating. With a throbbing headache, she headed upstairs.

Looking in on Ben, she found his bed empty. As her eyes flicked towards the bathroom, she caught a glimpse of him lying sideways in her double bed. The urge to reprimand him was quickly replaced with an overwhelming desire to hold him. She intended to lift him back into his room, but paused to watch her son, so peaceful. He'd grown in the three weeks since she'd seen him. Apart from the physical changes, she'd also missed a litany of thoughts, feelings and discoveries. Irreplaceable moments.

She undressed, pulled on a T-shirt and climbed into bed. After turning him so his head rested on the pillow, Anya held her little man and fell asleep.

Without letting go.

24

On Monday morning, Elaine arrived during the second bowl of cereal. 'Let me see. It's Monday. Coco Pops. Ah, you finally got to spend the weekend with Ben.'

Anya crunched a mouthful and smiled.

'I'm really glad Martin didn't let you down again. Did you have a good time?'

'It was great. We went to the craft markets, played charades, ate lots of junk, and spent hours talking about countries on his blow-up globe. He's growing up so quickly . . .'

Anya couldn't hide her sadness from Elaine, who mirrored it with a look generally reserved for someone who had suffered great loss.

A loud rap on the front door saved Anya from sympathy that would only have upset her more. Elaine excused herself and went to investigate.

Anya heard Dan Brody's booming laugh and wiped the milk from her chin just as he entered the kitchen waving a white hankie.

Elaine stepped forward and commandeered the bowl. 'I was helping myself to some cereal and Anya was about to cook something more substantial.' Elaine came from the 1950s era of housewives who believed that men's stomach's stimulated their hearts.

Anya shot her a steely stare. Brody didn't seem to notice.

'Good, I'm famished. But if you'll permit me, I'd like to save you the trouble and buy you breakfast.'

Anya hesitated. 'I'm surprised you're even speaking to me after the other day.'

'We both became a little heated and I can, I'm told, on rare occasions, be a little bombastic.'

'A little?!'

Elaine interjected. 'Well, it sounds like you've got work to discuss. Anya would be delighted to go with you. That'll give me a chance to catch up on paperwork while you're gone.'

'But I've got to lecture the med students at ten o'clock.'

'That's nearly two hours from now,' Brody told her. 'I'll have you back in plenty of time.'

Feeling like a schoolgirl being herded out on her first date, Anya grabbed her shoes from inside the door. As they walked down the street, she could hear the swish of his faded Levis as he took one stride for every two of hers. Even without the dramatic effect of an Italian suit, she could see why gossip columnists loved him.

'Do you ever hear from Brenda?' she asked.

'Not since I asked for my ski boots to be returned and one came back full of cement. Not in both, mind you, just one of them. I wouldn't have cared but they were custom-made for my paddle-sized feet.'

'I gather she's still angry about the divorce.'

'I wasn't the one who strayed.'

'This time.' Anya cringed at her spitfire tongue.

'Point taken,' he said, not seeming to mind.

Anya had last spoken to Brenda before the separation. They had been friends at university, both living in Edwards Hall, the student quarters. Brenda studied economics and law, which is how she'd met the young, idealistic solicitor she would marry within months. Anya wasn't surprised when the union soured.

'I think I went too far the other day, accusing you of being some kind of devil incarnate for doing your job.'

Brody laughed. 'I took it as a compliment. One day you just may find yourself sleeping with the enemy.'

Anya opened her mouth but couldn't think of anything witty to say. Her silence only made her feel more inept.

They crossed the road and stopped at a café. A blackboard menu boasted smoked salmon, scrambled eggs, bacon, grilled tomato and sausages. Brody patted his stomach.

'Looks good to me,' he said, pulling a chair out for Anya.

A waitress arrived at the table.

'I'll have one of your full breakfasts from the blackboard, with a macchiato and . . .'

Anya surveyed a laminated menu on the table. 'Wholemeal toast and a poached egg for me, with a soft yolk. And could you put it beside the toast, please, not on it. And a pot of tea as well, thanks.'

The waitress wrote down the order, wiped the table with a wet cloth, collected the menu and wandered back inside without saying a word.

Brody swept up some left-over crumbs from the table with his hand. 'We were all a bit tense the other day, and for good reason.'

Tense was an understatement. She was keen to make peace.

'How's the Galea boy?'

'Alive and out of critical condition, they tell me.'

She thought of the boy as someone's son. 'Suppose that's good news for your client.'

'Better than looking at a murder charge. Which is one of the reasons I came to see you. I'm going to the prison to see Mohammed this afternoon and wondered whether you'd come with me.'

'In what capacity?' Anya assumed Brody had a strategy in place.

'Mohammed's been assaulted. The prison doctor claims the injuries are superficial, but I'd like you to take a look and give me your opinion. He may be in serious risk if he stays put.'

'You want me to find his injuries more serious than the prison doctor?'

'No, I want an honest opinion.'

'Fair enough. Has Mohammed consented to my examination?'

206

'Not exactly.' Brody looked more interested in someone else's breakfast. 'I haven't told him you're coming yet.'

The coffee and pot of tea arrived.

Anya poured, and tea dribbled down the spout into the saucer. She was yet to meet a spill-proof stainless steel teapot. Brody handed her a couple of serviettes from a dispenser on the next table.

'Thanks. While we're discussing Deab, I've been looking into the fibres that Fatima had in her lungs. They've turned up in at least two other women who died in what at first glance looked like suicide.'

Brody slurped his coffee. 'Go on.'

'The odds are miniscule that young women have these findings. I met with Homicide detectives, who didn't want to know about it. All they want to do is close the cases and move on.'

'Ah, our diligent constabulary. At least they make my job easier.' Brody winked at the waitress as she delivered his plate of cholesterol.

The still mute woman placed the egg and toast in front of Anya.

'I'm concerned that these women might have spent time at the same place, or somewhere similar, where they were exposed to some sort of environmental hazard.'

'If there's anything relating these women, it won't affect our case. Our defence is going to have to focus on Mohammed's state of mind following the death of his daughter, whether we can argue aggravation by the Galea boy's actions, or even an automated response by Deab, where he didn't fully understand the results of his actions due to his overwhelming distress.' He shoved a forkful of bacon and eggs into his mouth.

Anya had always been amazed at the detachment defence lawyers had from the crimes their clients were charged with committing.

'Why do you think these fibres are relevant?' Brody asked, finishing off the grilled tomato.

'They may be a clue as to where Fatima stayed in the period between going missing and over-dosing. If Mohammed is angry enough to almost kill someone he thinks touched her, he may want to know what really happened to his daughter. Anoub certainly does. He's been calling non-stop to see if I've found anything out.'

Brody raised one eyebrow. 'Okay, do what you have to do to find out about these fibres. Don't worry about the cost, the Deabs will pay for it.'

Anya left the toast on her plate and finished the lukewarm tea. She wondered whether Mohammed Deab had agreed to psychiatric evaluation. If he pleaded not guilty, he may never be assessed. In the unlikely event of him claiming diminished responsibility, the prosecution was compelled to have him examined by a psychiatrist. Once on the record, Brody would know what sort of psychopathology he was dealing with. 'I know it's out of my area, but have you thought about getting Vaughan Hunter to review Deab? The man sounds as though he's got some kind of personality disorder and Vaughan does seem to know a lot about domestic violence situations.'

'Hadn't decided that yet, but you're right. I'll see if I can get Mohammed to agree to an assessment.'

'Thanks for breakfast.' Anya wiped her mouth with the serviette and stood. 'What time will I meet you at Long Bay?'

'I'll save you the drive and pick you up around two.'

25

Anya plugged in her PowerPoint presentation and glanced around the lecture theatre as stragglers filled the remaining empty seats. More faces appeared each week. Put the word 'forensic' in a lecture's title and it pretty much guaranteed a full house. Anya introduced the day's topic and a croaky voice from the back row interrupted.

'Excuse me, but will this be in the exams?'

The most predictable question had taken all but thirty seconds to be asked. All these students cared about was passing exams, jumping through the right coloured hoops in the right order. If something wasn't open to examination, they didn't want to know about it. It often frustrated Anya that the medical system perpetuated exam-obsessed students who lost sight of the real reason for learning.

Anya addressed the man with uncombed shoulder-length hair and a five o'clock shadow despite the early hour. 'If you graduate, what area do you hope to specialise in?'

'Emergency medicine,' he answered.

A couple of people in his vicinity snickered.

'You don't believe that forensic pathology is worth investing effort in?'

'I didn't mean that. It's just, unless you want to deal with dead, not live people, it doesn't seem all that big a priority.'

Anya felt a surge of annoyance, but kept her tone reasonable.

'Learning about death, procedures families go through when their loved one has to have a post-mortem, decisions crime scene police and medical examiners make is highly relevant and should be a priority for you. What happens when you have to inform the relatives of the young motorcyclist killed by a car, that the death is now before the coroner? How do you prepare them for what lies ahead? Your emergency medicine couldn't save him, but knowledge about what happens next might prevent his family suffering unnecessarily.' She let her gaze scan the room. 'How many of you hope to enter general practice?'

Half-a-dozen hands shot up.

'There's an area that doesn't have much to do with forensic pathology, or does it? What if you arrive for a routine house call and find your elderly diabetic patient dead on the floor? The surgery's full, you're running late. He was a bit doddery and often confused his doses. You conclude he died of an accidental insulin overdose and write out a death certificate, thereby saving the grieving wife the trauma of a post-mortem. All in all, you've done a good job. No pathology involved.

'Within days of the cremation, you notice the house up for sale and his wife flaunting a much younger man. You begin to wonder about the death and call the pathologist. Thinking back, there were two vials next to the bed, one half full, the other almost empty. You check the scripts with the chemist. He'd only filled the vial the day before because the wife had said she'd broken one.' The room had fallen silent, and she knew they were all listening. 'Congratulations. You just helped someone get away with murder.

'What I have to teach you is highly relevant to your future practice of medicine, even though it's not in the exams.'

A chorus of pens clicked into the off position and three people, excluding the scruffy one, elected to leave by the back door. Anya couldn't blame them. With first-term exams only weeks away, each student faced days and nights of study to survive the course. Right now practising seemed lifetimes away.

For the next forty-five minutes, Anya showed slides from a multitude of perplexing homicide cases and fielded questions about rape, murder and the process families endured to bury homicide victims. She always tried to humanise the victims to help students appreciate loss of life but stressed that there was a fine line between sympathy and empathy that should never be crossed. Sympathy was appropriate. Feeling pain *for* someone else was human and revealed compassion. But if doctors put themselves emotionally in the families' position, and felt the *same* pain, they lost all objectivity. And that spelt disaster for an investigation.

She concluded with a quiz accompanying the photo of a deceased elderly male lying on his back in a room. The body appeared intact, but the muscles and some of the bones in the face and neck were exposed, the skin notably absent. One student quoted the case of a psychopath with a fetish for removing faces. Another thought the attack had to be personal, given the degree of facial disfigurement. They argued amongst themselves about whether or not the culprit had prior surgical knowledge.

Anya enjoyed the power that came with knowledge as she showed the next slide – two cats sat next to the body. No-one offered any further explanation for the mutilation.

Finally, Anya admitted that the man had died of natural causes. A female voice loudly proclaimed, 'It's obvious. The cats ate their owner.'

A collective gasp filled the room.

'Zara is correct. That's exactly what happened. When the owner died, the cats, locked inside, had to fend for themselves. That meant feeding on the only meat available. As the slide shows, they went for accessible areas like the face and neck.'

Anya couldn't tell whether the distasteful expressions in the front row were in response to the gory details, or to the fact that a beloved 'Fluffy' wouldn't think twice about eating the hand, or face, that had fed him.

'That's it for today, and before you discount pathology as a career option, just remember, we're the ones called when even the best doctors have failed.'

The group applauded loudly. Two fresh-faced women asked about postgraduate employment opportunities. Anya explained the training requisites and the relatively new field of forensic medicine.

As she unplugged her laptop and gave the two women the website addresses for the local forensic societies, she noticed Zara Chambers waiting with a piece of paper folded in her hand.

'What's new in the world of diatoms?' Anya asked.

'Not much. I've actually been going through some old slides and I think I've found another case involving those fibres we looked at.'

Anya abandoned her computer. 'Exactly the same?'

'I thought they looked identical and Dr Latham agreed.'

'Do you know the age, history, condition of the person?'

Zara propped herself against the lecture table, backpack between her legs.

'Name was Alison Blakehurst, a doctor who died in a hotel room about six months ago. Toxicology showed a combination of alcohol, benzodiazepines and codeine.'

Another suicide. Another woman, this one by different means. Anya sat on an adjacent stool and tried to approach the case logically. 'Did she have any history of mental health problems?'

'Not that I know of. She was being sued by the family of a teenager who bled to death after a pregnancy termination.'

That was enough to drive even the most rational person to despair, as she knew from living with Martin in England during the investigation of a death in intensive care. Along with the victim's loved ones, the toll on the staff involved and their families was enormous.

Zara dug around in her backpack and retrieved the crumpled articles and some handwritten notes.

'I did a search on some of the newspaper websites and found a couple of stories on her. One is about when she was found, and the other is a feature from the *Australian*. They interviewed her parents and husband. Her dad just happened to be a professor of paediatrics and an active member of the Right to Life association.'

Anya had to admit to being impressed by Zara's diligence and resourcefulness.

'I didn't know you could print off old stories. I've always used microfiche at the library.'

Zara smiled to reveal slightly crooked top teeth. 'No-one's used microfiche since the Dark Ages. They're fossils compared to the net. You can print just about anything – law reports, transcripts from TV and radio, lectures from other unis. I would have thought you'd use it all the time in your job.'

The student's lack of tact didn't surprise Anya. 'Any more on Dr Blakehurst?'

'Oh, yeah.' She recited from her own notes. 'Apparently Alison had a drug addiction as an intern and was put on restrictions by the medical board. She married a gastroenterologist and, throughout the marriage, agreed to regular drug screens. She worked at a women's health centre and was allowed to prescribe anything but Schedule 8 drugs, which I guess are narcotics. That's where she referred the patient to an abortion clinic. I don't think she was there during the procedure and the paper doesn't say why she got sued instead of the surgeon.'

'It's usual for the lawyers to name every doctor in the suit, including the referring GP.'

Zara appeared taken aback, then returned to her story.

'The article goes on to quote someone from a consumers' group demanding mandatory drug testing for doctors.' She rolled her eyes as if bored. 'And the Doctors' Benevolent Society says how much stress doctors are under, and how they have such high addiction rates to drugs and alcohol, and how they have a high suicide rate, blahdy, blahdy.'

Zara had a lot to learn. She was just the type of self-driven over-achiever who could run into problems herself, and not through too much empathy.

'How did the case finish up?'

'A week after the suicide, the coroner exonerated the doctors. Apparently the teenage girl had a bleeding disorder that hadn't been diagnosed. She'd never had surgery before and rarely got periods so there wasn't any way of knowing she'd be a bleeder. Turns out her mother had Von Willebrand's disease too, and the daughter didn't know. If she'd told her mother about the abortion, it could have saved a lot of hassle.'

Anya wondered if Zara had somehow missed adolescence. Surely, she could at least sympathise with a teenager's decision to keep a pregnancy secret. The girl may have wanted to protect her family, or even have been scared of their reaction. Anya tried to imagine Zara's family and could only picture a field full of hockey players elbowing each other out of the way. Because winning was all that counted.

Zara picked up her bag and swung it over one shoulder, flicking her plait out of the way. 'One of the articles mentions that the husband thought she'd gone off with some sort of cult or commune, judging by the way she was dressed in a cheesecloth outfit the night she died.'

'Gone off, as in gone missing?'

'Yeah, by the sounds of it. I've got to go to a class, but if there's anything else I can do –'

'Yes, there is. You might be on to something important.'

Four relatively young women, four sets of

unusual fibres. Each disappeared for a time before coming back to commit suicide. Anya felt the hairs on her arms and neck stand on end.

'I'm going to need you to search the system and database for any other cases.'

'The computer system doesn't help. We tried that already. Things aren't labelled consistently. The word "fibre" appears in almost everything.'

Anya didn't envy the task but it had to be done. These women weren't dying of natural causes. The fibres said something about where the women had been – and they might have inhaled them from the same place.

'It'll have to be done manually, or you'll have to read each computerised PM report and decide whether the fibres mentioned are the ones we're after.'

'That's thousands of reports!' Zara sighed. 'It'll take months, and I've still got my nitric acid project to do.'

'Maybe Peter can give you some time off. I'll see if we can get electron microscopy on the sample we took to Professor Blenko. If we can get a breakdown of the constituents, we can compare it to charts and hopefully find out where it comes from. With this many cases, the cost is justifiable. Besides, if we find out what it is, you might want to write it up for one of the medical journals.'

Zara's back straightened. The ultimate carrot – a published paper – was enough to entice any ambitious medical student; she'd be scoring a match-winning goal.

'I'll get onto it first thing in the morning,' she said, and scuffed off.

On her way back to Annandale, Anya thought about the four women. What did they have in common? They came from vastly different religious, cultural and social backgrounds. Even so, each had a lot to lose, in terms of face, family and community life. Zara had mentioned a cult. That could explain their disappearances and failure to contact families, and even their odd behaviour and clothes. Clare Matthews and Fatima Deab had strict, non-forgiving families. The doctor had a lot to live up to morally and medically. Debbie Finch had a sexual predator for a father. In that context, a commune made a lot of sense. The women were just the type to escape their lives and join a welcoming, touchy-feely group. They were all vulnerable.

But what sort of commune trained its members to kill themselves?

26

Searing pain shot through the woman's chest and left shoulder. Any movement made the pain almost unbearable. Despite desperately trying to keep still, her body rocked up and down. In her line of sight, branches above thrashed in the wind and speckles of sunlight shot through tiny holes they left in their wake. She could hear someone breathing quickly, panting, and realised it was her own body fighting for breath. Suddenly, a crack sounded and the ground dropped a few centimetres, her contorted body lurching with the movement. She tried to move her legs but nothing happened. There was no feeling in them. Were they broken? She had no idea where they even were relative to the rest of her body. Trying to scream seemed futile. All that came out was a whimper. She licked her dry lips and tasted something metallic. Blood. Before she could wonder where the blood came from, her body jerked with what had to be the branch threatening to snap under her weight. With her right hand, she clawed at a branch up higher. Pain shot through her again, and the sunlight faded to black.

*

'Can you hear me?!'

The woman imagined floating in a dinghy, with a rescuer rowing up close.

'Can you hear me?'

Opening her eyes snapped her back to reality. The voice was real! She tried to roll her head to see.

'No! Don't move! Stay still.'

Whoever he was, she dared not disobey him.

'You've had a bad fall and we're going to fly you to hospital. The updraft's too dangerous to get you out by chopper from here. Instead we're going to winch you up to the top. But first I'm going to get you stable. You've lost a lot of blood.'

The wind buffeted her more and the man shouted above the noise.

'Could be a broken pelvis and your thigh is in pretty bad shape. I'm going to get some fluids into you and put you into an extractor device. We call it a RED. It's like a whole-body splint to protect you. Got to make sure you're okay for the ride up to the top. And hey, my name's Ryan. I'm a para-medic.'

'The tree won't hold us both.' Her mouth was so dry her tongue couldn't make the words clear.

'It's okay. I'm on a winch. Don't worry about a thing. Everything's going to be all right.'

By now she knew it wouldn't.

27

As a passenger in Dan Brody's Ferrari, Anya noticed things she missed when driving. She closed her eyes and felt the warm leather seat contour to the shape of her back. The interior still had that new-car smell, a combination of leather and Armorall spray, the one teenage males spend hours using to polish the dashboards and blacken the tyres. She wondered why women spent half their lives cleaning, making things 'whiter than white', whereas the only cleaning job men took obsessive care with made something black look even darker.

Brody hummed to 'Scotland the Brave' from his CD of the Royal Military Tattoo. Anya unconsciously drummed her fingers on her lap. Brody was a bit of an enigma: fast cars, stunning women and an ardent appreciation of the bagpipes. She would have picked him more as a Led Zeppelin fan.

'We're almost there,' Brody said, turning off the music.

Anya opened her eyes and blinked a couple of times in the bright sunlight. They approached the perimeter fence on Anzac Parade. Adjacent to the complex was a childcare centre. Years ago it would have been unheard of to have a prison on the community's doorstep, but urban sprawl and increasing numbers of prisoners meant the two worlds were no longer separate – something locals had to come to terms with.

Long Bay ensured that sex offenders, super-grasses, as informants were known, people on remand and violent offenders in rehab programs were kept in separate blocks.

Brody turned left onto the road to the main entrance and announced himself to the guard at the boom gate, who curtly reminded him that mobile phones must be left in cars.

'New rules, I'm afraid,' Brody said as the boom gate lifted, 'thanks to a prisoner who robbed the prison credit union and phoned his mate on a mobile to pick up the proceeds.'

'One of yours?' Anya asked.

'The phone wasn't mine, but I'm afraid the defendant is. Court case comes up soon.'

He turned right, then left into a car park outside the regional office where he parked his Ferrari, straddling two spaces, making it more conspicuous than usual.

Funny, it wouldn't occur to Anya to bring a flash car to a jail in case it was stolen. Maybe this was actually a safe place to leave valuables, although the credit union members had probably thought the same thing.

As they stepped out of the car, the gusty wind

flicked and whipped Anya's hair about her face. She buttoned her jacket to lock out the cold but still felt the chill in her muscles. It seemed almost farcical to build a prison on such a scenic part of the coast, when the height of walls obliterated any view, where the weather could be so inhospitable, it made people *want* to be inside.

At the remand centre, they walked to a door beside the visitors' entrance and pressed the button.

The door opened automatically to a short corridor with a gate inside the doorway. A prison officer arrived and unlocked the gate, admitting visitors and their children. Anya noticed a girl of about ten wearing shoes that swam on her feet. The boy with her had on a floral shirt about two sizes too large for him. She assumed they had borrowed clothes to dress up for their father. The woman accompanying them wore a cotton shift dress and more make-up than necessary.

'Sorry,' Brody said quietly. 'It's a mistake to come on family visit days. Slows everything down.'

They signed forms stating their names, the prisoner they intended to visit, reason for the visit and who they worked for. Brody wrote his car rego alongside the time – LAW4L.

The forms were inserted into plastic covers and pinned to their jackets. Anya pulled out her driver's licence with a photo that made her appear so bloated that the officer looked twice to confirm she was in fact the same person.

Brody flashed a Bar Association ID with what

must have been a ten-year-old photograph. Vanity wasn't the sole domain of women.

They handed more forms to an officer inside a glass cage who entered the information into a computer database, which recorded details of every visit.

Finally, the guard started looking Deab up on the computer. Brody folded his arms and waited, watching him. The frown on his face deepened as the minutes ticked by.

'Not here, mate. You must have the wrong section,' the guard finally announced.

Brody's mouth tightened. 'I assure you he *is* here. He was assaulted yesterday, Officer –' He stared down the other man. 'May I document your name for future reference, particularly as I'll be seeing the Minister at lunch tomorrow?'

The guard looked back to the computer screen. Within a short time, he'd miraculously discovered Deab in the section after all.

'Go through the metal detector then out that door over there,' he instructed, not making eye contact. 'You'll have to cloak everything but paper and pens.'

Beyond the door, they headed in silence along a narrow walkway between a two-storey window-less building and a wall covered with razor wire. Judging by the mould on the path, even sunlight had an aversion to the place.

Visiting prisons always made Anya feel claustrophobic, despite knowing she could leave at any time. Brody didn't seem bothered by the process, or didn't let on if he was.

They passed through a gate to the outside visiting area. Anya eyed the drab furniture and umbrellas fixed in concrete. To think this was the highlight of an inmate's week.

Prisoners dressed in white overalls that zipped up the back sat and walked with their partners and children. No chance of hiding contraband, so the authorities assumed. The little boy with the floral shirt shook hands with a stocky man, tattooed on the side of his neck. A father and son with so little physical and emotional contact was painful to witness.

Brody walked towards a set of caged stairs that led to a basement.

'It's the dungeon for us, today,' he quipped.

They walked down and along a corridor that smelt like stagnant water. Peeling paint showed it hadn't been tended to in years. On one side stood a stained toilet bowl, not connected to anything. The place felt like a mausoleum.

'God knows what went on down here in the past,' Brody said. 'It's where I usually interview protected prisoners.'

They entered a concrete room containing a mirror. Brody waved to the officers on the other side. At one of the tables, a man and wife seemed oblivious to them, making the most of the opportunity for physical contact.

'Don't worry. These aren't conjugal visits, but

the guards have a good look before they break it up.'

Mohammed Deab entered the room accompanied by a guard who didn't look more than about twenty. Anya expected to see a large man, huge in stature. Instead she stood to face a shorter, plumper version of his son. Mohammed's features were coarser than Anoub's but the resemblance was striking. In his younger days he might have been considered good looking, but time and, judging by the nicotine-stained fingers on his right hand, tobacco, hadn't been kind.

He nodded at Brody but didn't acknowledge Anya as he sat at the plastic table.

Brody introduced his colleague and explained the rationale for a medical examination, but Deab merely stared at the table.

'She can examine only what she can see,' he said without looking up. 'I will not undress in front of her.'

'Fine, that is your prerogative,' Anya agreed. 'I can't do anything without your permission.'

Anya took notes of the facial bruising and asked him to extend his hands. She drew the blackish-brown bruises over both sets of knuckles, which were understandably more prominent on the right side, his smoking and dominant hand.

'Can you make a fist with each hand, please?'

Deab complied.

'Good. That suggests your metacarpals, the long bones in your hand, are okay.'

'Would you mind standing up for a moment? I'd like to check your face.'

Deab shot Brody a cold stare, reminding him of the conditions.

In heels, Anya stood slightly taller than Deab and bent down to get a better look at his face. His breath reeked of sickly sweet tobacco, which he made no attempt to hide.

'You have extensive bruising of this cheek and eye area. I'd like to feel the bone if that's all right.'

Deab grunted, which she took as tacit approval. She palpated the bony prominences on his face, looking for boggy swelling, an indication of a fracture. Conjunctival haemorrhage covered most of the white part of one eye but didn't extend to the sclera's outermost part. She felt the skull and located a firm swelling on the back of his head on the left. Probably from where he hit the ground after being punched.

'It's unlikely you have a fractured cheek, although the bruising is quite impressive. Both pupils are equal in constriction and reaction to light. Mr Brody said you didn't lose consciousness. If that's the case, even with the lump on your head, a significant head injury this long after the assault is unlikely. How's your neck?'

Deab copied Anya's lead and moved his neck from side to side, up and down so that his chin came close to his chest.

'Good. Were you hurt anywhere else?'

'I have a sore back, that is all,' he said, touching his left lower ribs at the back. 'And a bruise.'

'Any shortness of breath or pain when you breathe?'

'A little pain.'

Anya placed her hands on either side of his chest. 'I'm going to spring your ribs. If you have a broken rib this could hurt.' She gave two short sharp pushes inwards and Deab failed to react.

'Can you take some deep breaths?'

Deab exhaled in her face. 'No more.'

Dan Brody shifted in his seat, as if bored. Anya returned to the table to document her findings on a body chart diagram in her notepad.

'My guess is, the bruise on his back was caused by a boot after he hit the ground. Do you know if the medical officer tested your urine for blood?'

Deab addressed Brody. 'He said test was good.'

'You are either very lucky or whoever did this didn't intend to kill you. You have soft tissue injuries, which will heal in a few weeks.'

Dan Brody asked, 'Why would anyone assault you?'

'Someone knew the Galea family. I tell him that boy deserves to die for the dishonour he has brought my family. I tell him I will spit on his grave.'

Brody sighed. 'That might explain the assault. You can't go around making verbal threats against the person you've been accused of putting in intensive care.'

Deab stared at the table again. Anya suspected he wasn't used to being reprimanded.

'We can talk about your plea in a minute, but first Dr Crichton has some questions to ask you about your daughter.'

'I have no daughter,' he said calmly.

'We need to know about Fatima, Mr Deab,' Anya urged. 'It may explain what happened to her.'

'I once had a daughter who shamed me. She is dead. That's how it should be.'

Brody flicked Anya a concerned look but she ignored it.

'Your daughter died alone in an awful place. Don't you want to know why?'

'You sit there thinking you are better.' He clenched his fists. 'You with your loose morals. I didn't go to university but I know things you don't.'

She spoke quietly. 'I am not passing judgment. I am trying to find out how Fatima breathed in something that could be quite dangerous. Your workshop, for example. Did she spend much time there?'

'I look after my workers, just like I look after my family,' he said through closed teeth.

'Like you looked after Fatima?' she said, a little too aggressively. Anya couldn't help feeling he knew more than he was letting on, the same way she felt Anoub had been hiding something the day he came to her office. She watched the dark parts of his eyes fill with a blackness she would have feared if they were alone.

'No-one is accusing you of anything,' Brody said. 'The doctor is asking some questions that may or may not turn out to be important later on.'

'Fatima dishonoured me. You look at me like I am some kind of animal but I am not ashamed of anything I have done. I will tell you and anyone else. Just like with Galea, I took care of my family. No-one will shame me again.'

Anya spoke on reflex. 'How did you take care of the family, of Fatima?'

Deab looked up from the table at her.

'I make sure she can no longer bring shame upon my family.'

Brody interjected. 'Mohammed, we don't need to know about this. Don't say another thing. Anya, I'm terminating this interview.'

She wasn't about to protect this man from himself. 'What did you do that you hadn't done to her before? You'd already beaten her, broken her bones, locked her up and thrown her out on the street.'

Dan Brody called the guard but Deab stood up and spat on the ground, barely missing Anya's legs.

Deab was a bully. He'd used force to control everyone around him. And it had to stop. She remained sitting to defy his attempts to frighten her.

'I'm advising you not to say another thing, Mohammed.' Brody stood and pushed back his chair.

'You made sure she didn't have a life from the day she was born. What more could you have done to her when she had nothing to live for?'

Deab raised a hand to strike Anya as Brody

231

yanked her from the chair and moved to block his client. Two guards burst into the room and Deab raised both arms in the air.

'You think you are so smart, lady? I tell you. I kill her. I did what I had to. I kill my slut daughter and make sure she never shames me again.'

Brody stood holding Anya's arm in silence as the guards led him out of the room. Anya shivered. Being physically threatened didn't frighten her nearly as much as seeing Mohammed Deab proudly confess; a father who had murdered his child to save his reputation.

28

She saw another white light, this one bright and warm as moist air brushed her face. Something pierced her shoulder as the light swung to her other eye and back. More pain.

Now she could only make out white spots when she closed her eyelids. And the sounds of chaos all around. Beeping noises, squeaking shoes, voices in the background, plastic crinkling. This place smelt like sickly disinfectant, the same nauseating smell she endured at Nanna's nursing home. She tried to roll over but couldn't move her head.

'She's rousing!' a male voice declared, and someone else shone lights in her eyes.

'More O Negative. Blood pressure's dropping. Get the surgical resident down here NOW!'

'I'll get the blood cross-matched right away. The wardsmen is already waiting. Blood bank knows it's urgent.'

'Where the hell is X-ray?'

'Right behind you. You're not the only ones having a bad day, you know.' The whirring of a machine stopped and a clunk sounded on her left.

'We'll need a cervical spine, chest and pelvis for starters. And make sure no-one else goes into CT. This girl's going as soon as she's stable.'

'No breath sounds on the right,' someone else said. 'We're going to have to put in a chest tube.'

'What about the chest X-ray?'

'No time. Can we have a chest drain set pronto?'

'Right here, Phil.'

She tried to focus but struggled to make sense of anything.

'BP is eighty over fifty. Oxygen saturation's ninety-three per cent.'

A woman with moist breath put her face about thirty centimetres from hers and spoke gently.

'You're in Casualty. You've got a lot of injuries from the fall. Don't try to move, we need you to keep still for now. We've got a collar on your neck until we've had the X-rays done. Dr Tan is going to put a special drain in your chest to help your breathing. One of your lungs has collapsed and isn't working properly.'

The smell of antiseptic filled her nostrils as someone said, 'This might hurt a bit and you'll feel some pressure.'

She felt a stab beneath her armpit and held her breath. It hurt like hell, then he pushed hard where it hurt. She thought he was trying to pop the other lung with whatever he was ramming in.

'Nearly there. Nearly . . . Good. Drain's in.'

A loud splash sounded and then she realised it came from her side.

234

'Let's connect your end to the water seal before I get any more blood on my shoes.'

The female voice said, 'This looks bad. I'll get thoracics.'

'Thanks. Tell them large haemopneumothorax. We're okay for X-ray. Can we get some more neuro obs, please?'

The woman's face appeared again and so did the light in her eyes. Were they trying to blind her or keep her confused?

'Can you squeeze my hand?' the face said through minted breath.

'I can't feel my legs, where are my legs?' she said, looking up from the bed.

'That's okay, darl. What's your name?'

Her mouth was too dry to form words. What did it matter? She wanted to die. Why wouldn't they leave her alone?

'Just try to squeeze my hand.'

She made what she thought was a fist and pain shot through her shoulder again.

'Did that hurt, darl?' the woman asked, as she felt a cool rush beneath her collarbone.

'We're giving you some blood through a tube into your vein. Your breathing looks easier already. Now, we're going to have to roll you for an X-ray. Everyone, on the count of three. One, two, three.'

She felt herself tip over, like a log rolling, and something cold and hard slipped behind her back. All she could see were the chests of the people moving her, and a silver curtain rail over the bed. They rolled her back. Pain ripped through the top half of her body.

'Jill, can we put in a catheter? I want to know if there's any blood in the urine,' a man said.

There must have been six people rushing around her, shoving tubes and needles anywhere they could find.

Everything went quiet for a moment. She was alone, which frightened her more. Then they came back.

'We've got to move you again, darl. Get the X-ray plate out.'

They rolled her again.

'Okay, darl. I'm going to put a thin plastic tube into your bladder so I need to cut off your knickers and sterilise the skin between your legs. This will feel cold.'

Cold? She couldn't feel anything from the waist down, especially not her legs. The voices kept talking, as though she wasn't there.

'Oh my God.' Then there was a silence as the nurse called, 'Philip, you'd better look at this. I can't put a catheter in, not with this.'

'What is it? Blood?'

'No, it's – you'd better look at the whole area.'

'Shit. Blisters everywhere,' said the man who gave all the orders. 'All right, there's only a small chance of spreading the infection if we catheterise, but at the moment she's going to die if we don't get her more stable. BP's still only seventy-eight.

The reasons for catheterising far outweigh the risks at this stage. Let's do it.'

'They must be agony,' she heard the nurse say. 'How on earth did she shave there?'

'I don't think they're causing pain now. She can't feel anything below her ribs, and there's no movement. My bet is it's a complete spinal cord injury. With the hypothermia she suffered, blood loss, and multiple fractures . . . Find out if the police have contacted her family. They need to get here fast.'

They talked about her as though she couldn't hear. 'No, no,' she muttered. 'No family.'

Someone bent over her. 'What are you trying to say?'

'No family. There's no-one.'

They ignored her.

'Better get some fluid from those vesicles,' the man said, 'and send it to micro just in case. And get orthopaedics down here. Where the hell are thoracics?'

29

The following week, Dan Brody thanked Grant
Bourne, Vaughan Hunter and Anya for agreeing to
meet over the Deab case.

'Vaughan, Anya suggested that you become
involved at this stage and I think it's a good idea.
As you all know, Deab confessed to killing his
daughter in the toilet block. So far he refuses to
disclose any details, such as how he acquired the
drugs or how he injected them. I have to say the
confession was unexpected, but I suspect he has
said something to his fellow inmates. If he did it
for honour, he has to let people know, to keep face.'

Grant curled his lip. 'In all the years I've been
working for him, he's claimed innocence, even after
he ran into that police car with a blood alcohol
level double the limit.'

'Something bothers me about this,' Brody said.
'It just doesn't seem like his style.'

'It isn't violent enough?' asked Anya as a quiet
knock on the door interrupted them.

'That'll be our cultural expert. Maybe she can
answer that.'

Brody stood as an attractive, middle-aged woman

dressed in a turquoise sari tentatively entered. She looked as though she had been born into the highest possible caste.

'Dr Gupta, please come in. You've met Mr Bourne. This is Dr Vaughan Hunter, psychiatrist and profiler, and Dr Anya Crichton, pathologist and thumb screw expert. She's the one who elicited the confession from my client.'

Dr Gupta shook hands with the group and stopped at Anya, lifting half-glasses from a chain around her neck onto the bridge of her nose for a better look.

'I believe you encouraged Mr Brody's client to discuss his feelings and he admitted to killing his daughter. That does not surprise me. You represent everything he wanted to protect his daughter from.'

Hardly a compliment, thought Anya.

'No, no, please do not misunderstand me,' Dr Gupta added, obviously reading Anya's face. 'I'm afraid I chose my words poorly. What I meant to explain was that men like Mr Deab feel they are morally superior to those they deem unworthy, which is how he appears to view Western women.'

Brody found her an extra chair.

'Dr Gupta is an associate professor in social studies from Sydney University and specialises in cultural differences. She knows a lot about honour killings, which is what I've asked her to discuss in relation to this case. She thought, and I agree, that it would be more efficient to meet together.'

The Indian expert removed her glasses and sat down. 'To give you some background, honour killings are recognised in many cultures, not just those of Islamic faith. It is estimated that 5000 women are killed by family members each year because of rumour or innuendo. Most commonly these killings occur in rural areas where the literacy level is low and fundamentalism has its strongest numbers. Many of the Islamic perpetrators kill having never read the Koran and hence are unable to understand the difference between indoctrination and the Prophet Mohammed's teachings. That makes the women in these communities extremely vulnerable.'

Deab's coldness had shocked Anya. He might as well have been slaughtering a lamb for dinner, the way he spoke. 'Are these men torn at all, having to decide what to do, or is it like a reflex action?'

Dr Gupta wound the chain from her glasses around her finger. 'If they are torn, they don't seem to show it. Most deny remorse and boast about their preservation of honour. In this country, we do not understand that to these men, honour is everything. In places like Pakistan, more often than not the men who kill family members get away with it, and suffer no punishment. The threat of jail doesn't deter them either. If they are imprisoned, they become heroes in their own communities.'

Brody doodled on his pad again. 'What exactly constitutes dishonouring a family?'

'Well, it may involve a woman being seen in the company of a man other than a family member, or even rumoured to have been seen. It doesn't matter if the woman is in a public place when she commits the alleged indiscretion, this still could affect a man's perception of honour. Of course, having a relationship with a man outside marriage or prior to marriage is deemed unacceptable, and in some areas, punishable by death. There have been instances in which women are accused of sexual relations when autopsy shows an intact hymen.'

The concept of an intact hymen confirming virginity was misleading, but Anya didn't wish to argue the point. She'd heard about honour killings but didn't believe they happened in a country where women supposedly had equal rights. 'Do other relatives, like the mother, have any say in the killings?' Anya couldn't believe they kept quiet about it.

The three men in the room listened intently as Dr Gupta explained.

'None at all. They may not even know until it is too late. They cannot report their husbands to authorities. They fear for their own lives if they do. In some instances, mothers agree with the killings, just as they do with female circumcision.'

Vaughan Hunter leant forward. 'I understand that these killings are usually by means such as stabbing, strangulation, or gunshot. Is that correct?'

'Yes, the deaths are particularly brutal and the woman endures suffering as well as seeing the face of her father, husband or brother when he kills her.'

'Well, I have an uncomfortable feeling about the confession,' Brody said. 'Deab is a hot-head. Killing Fatima with drugs would have taken time, planning, and then he had to make sure everyone knew what he'd done, anyway.'

'Maybe he wanted to avoid police involvement at the start,' Grant considered, 'which is why he made it look like a suicide for the coroner while he bragged about it to his Lebanese mates. I heard that a lot of people think she died of AIDS because of the toilet block, assuming promiscuity and drug use. If he killed her for honour, the message didn't filter through. Maybe he needed to let the world know by confessing.'

'Under the alleged circumstances,' Dr Gupta said, 'the mode of death is most unusual.'

Brody gripped the arms of his chair. 'Exactly my point. He bashed Galea after his daughter died a relatively peaceful death by injection. Wouldn't he have made it more obvious that he'd killed her if it was to show his community he valued honour? Why go to the trouble and suffer the indignity of having people think she died of a stigmatised sexually transmitted disease?'

'Criminals don't always think things through, as you know,' Anya said. 'Could Mohammed have said he killed his daughter to remove some of that stigma? I know it sounds crazy and illogical to us, but maybe it doesn't to him.'

242

Dr Gupta nodded. 'We are not dealing with what we consider logic in these matters.'

Brody turned in his chair to Vaughan. 'The question is whether or not we can argue provocation and mitigating circumstances in the Galea assault and the daughter's death. Is he capable of telling right from wrong?'

'From a psych viewpoint, he knows what is legal and not, but that doesn't correlate with his sense of right and wrong. He doesn't care what our law says. He lives by family law, the only way he knows.'

'You've interviewed Mohammed. What would you say about his state of mind?' Brody asked.

Vaughan seemed to relax as he spoke. 'I've no reason to think he is delusional. He avoided questions about his business dealings but made it clear he feels that he is in the right in the way he deals with business and family. This is where conclusions become interesting. He is, to my mind, a sociopath, but it could equally be argued that he is a fundamentalist Muslim who believes he is morally right. The Old Testament supports an eye for an eye, which is what he believes he's doing.'

'Surely a court isn't going to buy that?' Grant asked.

Dr Gupta polished her glasses with the end of her sari. 'This is not a phenomenon restricted to Islamic people. Fundamentalists and extremists exist in many religions – Judaism, Hinduism, Christianity. In general, the more extreme the beliefs, the more brutal the abuse of perceived transgressors.' Her left eye twitched as she spoke. 'There have been cases in which Aboriginal tribes have administered their own justice and the police have accepted that, in addition to our legal punishment. A youth accused of murder had both legs speared after killing another tribe member. Then our courts dealt with him, so he served double penalties, if you like.'

Grant shook his head. 'There's a big stretch from letting the tribe go around committing payback killings and GBH.'

'Or is it?' Brody said. As usual, his mind seemed to work quickly. 'Vaughan, how did you find Deab during the interview?'

'He's aggressive, intimidating, has poor impulse control and is difficult to predict. In addition to that, he doesn't exactly respect women, although any mention of his own mother makes him teary. That was the only hint of vulnerability he displayed. All in all, he's a pretty unsympathetic character.'

Brody poured himself a glass of water. 'He'll alienate a jury, or at least any women on it, without even trying.' He waved the jug at the others. 'Anyone?'

'Thank you.' Dr Gupta accepted a glass.

'What about Fatima's state of mind,' Brody asked, 'as a female in this environment? What do we know about her? If she had a boyfriend, why didn't she just take off with him?'

Dr Gupta took what barely constituted a sip. 'That's the difficult thing. To an abused person, an open door isn't necessarily seen as open. Women in these circumstances can be frightened of the violence escalating if they are caught leaving. In this case, it looks as though Fatima had good reason to be terrified. I have read the domestic violence history, which is not surprising, either.'

Grant interrupted. 'I don't get it. The girl had a GP boss prepared to protect her; there are plenty of social supports for women who live with violence. Why didn't she just go to a shelter so he couldn't find her, if the bashings were that bad?'

'With respect, Fatima belonged to a small, closed community. She hadn't been permitted to mix with anyone else, so she knew of no other options. Would you want to leave all your friends, family and possessions if you had no skills, no means of support? These women are often suffering from poor self-esteem, and leaving doesn't appear to be an option.'

'We're forgetting that Fatima disappeared for a few weeks prior to her death,' Anya said. 'No-one admits to seeing her in that time.'

Vaughan reached for the water jug. 'During our interview, Deab expressed disgust at how his daughter was dressed when she died. It didn't sound like the police had told him, so how else would he know unless he saw her that night?'

Anya said, 'Belongings and clothes are returned to the families.'

Vaughan filled a glass. 'I should have realised. Do the police have anything to tie him to the scene?'

'A cigarette butt found in the toilet block, which we all know is a very public place,' Brody said. 'It was collected a week after the death and was initially identified as an imported brand that Deab smokes.'

Anya had heard about the 'butt bible', an encyclopaedia of cigarette butts compiled by an officer in his spare time. It included details as well as photos of all the cigarettes available in Australia – and many from around the world. The officer had become the pin-up boy of obsessive compulsives in the police service, and a positive example of thorough, if tedious, investigation.

'Our Mohammed was then seen discarding a butt, which was collected, and the DNA found compared with that from the toilet block. It's a pretty good match, apparently. How reliable is that?' Brody asked Anya. 'I've had cases where no DNA was found on the butt.'

'Pretty accurate. As little as 0.6 millilitres of saliva could contain enough cells for a DNA comparison.'

Grant seemed sceptical. 'Under privacy laws, can we challenge the admissability of the sample the police found?'

'No, once he threw it away, it was deemed discarded and fair game for the police to collect.'

Something else bothered Anya about Fatima's death. 'A tampon was used as a filter. Why would Deab use that when he smoked and cigarette butts were equally good? If he knew enough about it to filter the stuff, why choose a tampon?'

'To make it look like suicide?' Grant offered.

'Which is what we don't understand if he wants the world to know what he did. Isn't using a tampon going too far?'

Brody rocked in his chair. 'I have doubts about the veracity of his confession.'

As much as Anya wanted men like Deab to spend their lives in prison, she had to agree. He could have been provoked into a confession, to an extent by her.

'Why would he confess to a crime that he didn't commit? We don't even know whether a crime took place, apart from illicit drug use, that is.'

'Anything's possible,' Brody said. 'We've got a few weeks before the brief goes to the DPP. I'll talk to him some more and get the son in too. Anya, I want you to focus on the fibres we discussed in case they're helpful. Vaughan, I'd like you to write a report on the personalities of victims of domestic violence. Incidence of anti-social behaviour, suicide, substance abuse. That sort of thing.

'Now, for the charges of GBH. We know Mohammed suspected the Galea boy of having a sexual relationship with his daughter. Grant, I'd like you to interview the girl's friends. See if you can get a statement substantiating his claim.'

Anya had a thought. 'You'll need to subpoena Galea's medical records, too.'

Brody looked perplexed. 'I've gone through them already and he doesn't have any previous head injuries or anatomical variants.'

'What about herpes?'

'Isn't syphilis the one that causes brain damage?' Grant Bourne smirked.

'If there's no mention of it in the local doctor's records,' Anya advised, 'I'd check the sexual health clinics. If he doesn't have it and was sexually involved with Fatima, the prosecution is bound to ask the question: who managed to give her genital herpes before she died? It's not going to look good for your client if he bashed the wrong man.'

Outside the chambers, Vaughan positioned himself next to Anya as the others walked ahead. She took the opportunity to ask if he knew anything about cults.

He leant closer and whispered, 'Thinking of joining one?'

Anya felt her face redden again. 'I'm looking into a series of deaths that may involve a cult of some kind and wondered if you know any good references or people to speak to.'

'Interestingly enough, I have some articles in my office. The behaviour techniques the leaders implement are not dissimilar to those used by perpetrators of domestic violence and sexual abuse. What specifically do you need to know?'

'Whether any cults encourage members to kill themselves outside the cult's premises, and whether any operate in Sydney or up the coast.'

'Sounds intriguing. I'll see what I can find for

248

you and let you know. How soon do you need the information?'

'Whenever you can manage would be great.'

Anya pulled a card from her jacket pocket and handed it to him.

Awkward silence took over. She felt like talking longer but had nothing to say. He seemed to be waiting for her to speak, which made it worse.

'I'll be in touch,' he said, saving her any more embarrassment, and left the building.

30

Anya answered the door, dressed in a striped T-shirt and capri pants.

'Bit formal for an agricultural show, don't you think?' she said, assessing Kate Farrer's caramel suit.

'Change of plan, sorry. Gotta work.'

'Ben'll be disappointed. You can be the bad guy and break the news. He's up tidying his room.'

'Fair enough. That gives us a minute.' She stepped back into the front yard, ensuring privacy from little ears. 'You were right about the Finch case. As if the case wasn't sick enough already with the old man's jam fetish, Polilight exam showed semen right up the back of Debbie's throat that wasn't picked up at the initial exam.'

'Semen in the throat isn't the first thing you look for in a shooting victim. If jam was in other parts of the mouth, it's understandable how it was missed.'

Kate put both hands on her hips. 'I know the old man had a history, but I got thinking about his state of mind, or lack of it. I asked for DNA. It confirmed the semen wasn't his.'

Anya's skin prickled. 'Someone else *was* there.'

'Yep, your gut feeling about the toilet seat was right.'

That raised more questions than it answered, Anya thought. 'Why would someone go to the trouble of making sure he didn't leave fingermarks on the doors, but not worry about having oral sex or urinating in the house?'

'That's what gets me. He must have cleaned himself up in there. You think if he'd worried about leaving evidence, he would have gone outside for a leak. Especially since the backyard is fairly private.'

Anya agreed. 'Did the neighbours hear anything?'

'The old lady a couple of doors down heard two loud bangs but had no idea when. She thought it was kids with firecrackers. So we don't know how far apart the shots were. Times of death can't be pinned down that closely to help.'

'Maybe this guy's pretty confident. If he's brazen enough to put jam on himself and make Debbie lick it off, he probably cleaned himself up, assuming no-one would check the toilet.'

'Obviously he knew about Daddy's little secret,' Kate said, glancing up at the stairs behind her, to check Ben wasn't within earshot. 'So the next question is, whether this guy killed them both. Or did he come along to help Debbie? Maybe he went along having no idea about the gun or her plans. Either way, I want to find this guy. I'll start with the DNA bank and see if he's got priors.'

Initially, Anya had concerns about privacy issues with the New South Wales DNA bank. In a flurry of publicity, police and victims of crime groups hailed it as a godsend. Her father had even campaigned for it. In the first year, over sixty cold cases were solved with DNA matches. It soon became clear to her that having that facility meant more victims could attain closure, which had to be a good thing. And Kate was right. This mystery man could be the key to finding the source of the lung fibres. And he could still be at risk from them if he wasn't found.

'By the way. You're the toast of the station,' Kate gloated, 'for getting Deab's confession. Bet Brody gave you a gold star for that little effort.' She laughed a deep, throaty chuckle.

Anya's cheeks burnt. 'Dan figured it was better to know now instead of Deab blurting it out mid-trial. For your information, as soon as he heard it, he went into ethical mode. There's no way he could plead not guilty for Deab once he'd heard him admit to killing Fatima.'

'Lawyer, ethical? You sound like you're going soft. He hasn't got to you, has he?' Kate teased. 'Buggers me what women see in him.'

'God, no.' Anya hadn't been interested in anyone since Martin. Seeing her ex-husband in a suit reminded her of how attractive he'd once seemed. She lowered her voice to share the news. 'Martin's had a second interview at Ryde for a pharmaceutical company. He's waiting for the official nod, but it sounds promising.'

'So you might see more of Ben? That really is great.'

'Aunty Kate!' Ben took two stairs at a time, galloped to the open door and leapt into Kate's outstretched arms.

'Hey buddy, how's it going? You are growing so quickly.'

Ben let go and fidgeted on the spot. 'Are you coming with us to the Easter Show?'

'Sorry, champ, I've got to work.'

Ben's face couldn't hide his disappointment.

'But tell you what. Next time you visit, we can kick a football around and even fly that kite in the park. Promise. What do you say?'

'O-KAY!' Ben threw his arms around the best footie player he knew and landed a big kiss on her mouth.

Kate returned the affection by hanging him upside down by the legs and tickling his exposed belly.

Anya put a change of clothes for Ben, jackets and snacks in the car and heard him scream, 'Stop!' then, 'Again, again!' from the doorstep.

'Are you catching baddies today and throwing them in jail?' he asked Kate from a semi-upright position.

'Sure hope so. You have fun and be good for your mum, okay?'

'I'm always good!'

Anya closed the car door and noticed Vaughan Hunter crossing the road towards her. Dressed in a pale blue shirt and khaki chinos, with a jumper draped across his shoulders, he carried a large yellow envelope. She quickly checked for stains on her capri pants that could have been put there by peanut butter fingers.

'Good morning,' he said cheerfully. 'Didn't expect you'd be at your office on a weekend, and I'm afraid I missed the post.'

'I live here. Makes commuting easy.' Anya wiped her palms on her pants.

'I was going to leave this at the door, but since you're here . . .' He handed over the envelope. 'It's the info you asked about.'

Kate stood with her arm firmly around Ben's shoulders.

'Thanks. Vaughan, this is a friend of mine, Kate Farrer. And my son, Benjamin.'

Kate didn't offer to shake hands. 'We've already met. Hunter, here, testified that a stalker wasn't fit to stand trial. The guy spent a few months in a cushy mental hospital. The day he was released, he walked up to the woman he'd stalked and . . .' she looked down at Ben. 'Let's just say they're still trying to rebuild her face. Pity the same can't be said for her brother. Yeah, we've met.'

'I felt horrifed about what happened, but I still stand by the original diagnosis,' he said with a hint of sadness. 'Unfortunately, the system isn't perfect.'

'That'll be a big comfort to the victim's family. I'll let them know when I see them next month.'

'I understand you're angry about what happened. I'm still happy to talk to the family if they'd like.' Vaughan knelt down, turning his attention to the young boy. 'Wow. Nice to meet you, Benjamin. You are so tall. What are you, four years old?'

The pair shook hands.

'I'm free.' Ben proclaimed, holding up three fingers.

'I'm off.' Kate remained unimpressed. 'Have fun, see you next time, Benny boy.'

She nodded at Anya and stepped towards her car. 'I'll let you know what we come up with.'

Vaughan stood again. 'I apologise if I upset your friend. She seems to have left in a hurry.'

Anya believed that in Kate's world, everything felt personal. She obviously blamed him for something he couldn't have predicted or prevented. Apart from work, Kate's world was becoming increasingly small, and Anya couldn't allow hers to do the same. 'She just isn't one for drawn-out goodbyes.'

Ben tugged at his mother's shirt-sleeve. 'Excuse me, Mummy, is this man coming with us?'

'Somehow, I don't think Vaughan would want to come to the Easter Show.'

'Hey, that is such a fun place.' He knelt down again. 'Did you know there are rides and lots of fun games to play? They even have a petting zoo and cows, sheep, horses, and my favourite, alpacas.'

'I love alpacas. They have nice eyes. I like them and giraffes.'

'They do have great eyes. A patient of mine has a cattle farm and has his prize-winning bulls at the Show.'

Ben grinned. 'Wow! They're huge, but not as high as the biggest slide in the whole world. Mummy doesn't like that, so I can't go on it.' He whispered, presumably so as not to embarrass his mother, 'She's scared, but I'm not.'

Ben had forgotten his usual shyness with strangers. Like mother, like son with this man.

'I love slides. They're my favourite ride.'

'Mine too!'

Even for a psychiatrist, Vaughan adapted well to his audience. If Anya closed her eyes, she would swear the two were the same age.

'Mum, please can this nice man come with us? He could show us the special bulls.'

Anya felt her ears heat up.

'Plleeaase, Mummy?'

'I'd love to come if your mum will have me.'

'This was going to be our day together, Ben,' she stammered.

'I know, but we're going to the museum to see the dinosaurs tomorrow. Pleaaaasse?'

Anya felt outnumbered by a small boy. Scientists denied the possibility, but every parent knew the reality. She wondered how anyone with more than one child coped. 'Okay. We'll need to go in our car. It's got the booster seat.'

'Just let me lock mine and we'll be off,' Vaughan said.

Anya grabbed a pack containing snacks, change of clothes and a camera.

Ben couldn't contain his excitement at having two people to play with, and Anya knew he'd beg Vaughan to go on the giant slide. Every child came out of the womb with skills of manipulation. Ben seemed to have a Masters degree in the field.

When they arrived at Homebush, Anya insisted that Ben sit in the stroller until they were inside the grounds, despite her son's protests.

'He's a really good kid,' Vaughan said. 'Incredibly bright and obviously very attached to you.'

Anya didn't know what to say so said nothing. She felt uncomfortable talking about how much Ben loved her, as though talking about it may dilute or devalue it in some way.

Inside the gates, they strolled around the showground, heading first for the showbag pavilion.

Anya had looked up the bags' prices and contents on the Internet and planned to buy a library book bag stuffed with kids' books. Instead, Ben begged for a Superheroes bag, which was double the amount she had intended to spend. A little boy suddenly forgot his passion to read and became just another boy wanting to be Batman. How could she refuse him that?

He saw a cowboy-themed bag with a gun and begged for that too.

'What are my rules about guns?'

'We're not allowed to have them in your house. But I can take it to Daddy's place.'

'No, Ben. I will never get you a gun and I don't want your father getting you one either. You know how I feel about them.'

'But Mum . . .'

'It's the Superheroes one or nothing.'

'Okay.'

Why was it that children made you feel mean when you were doing something nice in the first place? Another mother repeated the conversation with a boy dressed like Spiderman.

'Thanks, Mum!' Ben said, clutching his new prize in his stroller.

Vaughan disappeared and reappeared with a showbag.

'My treat. Something educational and fun.'

It was a bag full of *Star Wars* books, stickers and pull-out face masks.

'Wow, thanks Mr Hunter.'

Anya tried to protest but had to let it go. She'd make sure she paid Vaughan back later.

They moved on to the animal enclosures. Vaughan kindly took some photos of mother and son next to large bulls with blue ribbons worn proudly around their necks. Anya and Ben rode the merry-go-round three times to old Abba hits. After that, he refused to return to the stroller. Three-year-olds liked to walk – everywhere.

As they passed one ride, Ben stopped and almost

dislocated Anya's shoulder in his excitement. They looked up at a two-storey slippery-dip. Anya held her breath.

'Mummy, look, you slide down on those magic carpets.'

Vaughan didn't help. 'That is the best fun. How about I take you and we give your mum a break?'

'Yipppeeeeee!'

The look on her son's face made it impossible to refuse.

Anya stood where she could see the slide and promised to get an action photo for the scrapbook. She tried to stay calm and relaxed as Vaughan took her child's hand. For a moment the pair disappeared into the queue until she caught sight of them again, climbing the stairs.

Having a child was like having your heart outside your chest, permanently. She now understood some of what her own parents had gone through. Sometimes, though, she had to learn to let Ben be and not smother him. That was the most difficult part.

After a few minutes, the two went behind the slide, presumably where the carpet pieces lay. The queue climbing the stairs slowed. She took the lens cap off the camera and waited for the pair to reappear.

Spruikers selling 'genuine quality jewellery' for twenty dollars and vegetable peelers spoke through headset microphones, competing with balloon sellers and clowns hawking necklaces that glowed in the dark. All that was missing was the kewpie doll on a cane she'd always wanted from the Launceston Show.

The sun appeared from behind a cloud and she peeled off her jacket, stepping in chewing gum in the process.

'Shit,' she said, holding the camera up as she heard Ben's voice.

'Mummy!'

She looked up and snapped two photos of him speeding down the slide, Vaughan sitting behind, legs apart to accommodate his co-slider. They looked like a blur in real life, so she didn't hold out much hope for the shots.

Ben came running out of the side exit with red cheeks and 'windtunnel' hair. He took off his polar fleece jacket, put it in the stroller and took Anya's hand.

'This is so much fun, Mum. I was really brave.'

'You didn't look scared at all.' She squeezed his hand. 'You did really well.' Vaughan stopped on Ben's other side, short of breath and wheezy.

'Are you all right?' Anya asked, concerned. 'You look hypoxic.'

'Just a bit of asthma.' Vaughan pulled a ventolin puffer from his hip pocket, shook it and inhaled two doses. 'I'll be right in a moment. Must be the animal hair all around.'

His colour improved.

'We could sit, if you like, and have some lunch,' Anya suggested.

They joined a queue for hot food and Vaughan's breathing quickly returned to normal.

'He's a real talker, your son. Even asked me if I knew what a parasaurolophus eats.'

Anya laughed. She'd been quizzed on just about every topic. After ordering a kebab, hot chips, chicken nuggets and Vaughan's battered hot dog, they sat and ate at a picnic table in front of the cold drinks stand.

Fried food could be marketed as a sedative, Anya believed. Ben gorged himself and climbed back into the stroller, too tired to walk anymore and dodge the hordes of legs roaming around.

Putting the rubbish in the bin, a handbag bumped Anya's back. She turned to see a woman with fine red hair, white skin and freckles, wrestling with rubbish on a tray. The woman, who would have been about Miriam's age now, had similar features, minus the chubby face lost to maturity.

'Sorry,' the woman said.

Anya couldn't help staring and was about to speak when another woman, with curly red hair, appeared. Their body language intimated a closeness that came with living together, the kind shared by siblings.

It wasn't Miriam.

Back at the table, Vaughan rose. 'You look like you've seen a ghost.'

'For a moment I thought . . .' Anya pushed the stroller and they walked towards the agricultural displays.

261

'When you said Bob Reynolds was your father,' Vaughan said, 'I remembered going to a meeting where he spoke about psychological issues for parents of murder victims. He talked about having had two daughters, one of whom was abducted as a toddler. It must have been difficult growing up with that.'

'I'm told what I go through is "normal", whatever that means, but even though my brain says she's gone forever, sometimes I look into a crowd and . . . well, emotion takes over.'

'How did your family cope?'

Normally guarded, Anya didn't feel the question an intrusion.

'Mum struggled. She wouldn't let my brother or me go anywhere without her or Dad.' Anya found herself talking freely about her family, something she hadn't done since Damien moved to England.

'She even changed her surgery hours so she could drop us off and pick us up from school. Every patient knew that if they needed to be seen they had to wait for school hours. That wasn't too restrictive, but it got embarrassing as a teenager going on house calls with Mum. We could choose to have her come to parties and sit outside all night, or stay home. More often than not, it was easier not to go.'

'What happened when you left school?'

'I got as far away as possible. I applied for medicine at Newcastle University and got in. Within weeks I'd met Marty. He dropped out of medi-

cine at the end of first year, flirted with engineering and then did nursing. He should have
finished medicine because he was always trying to
prove himself. Anyway, we got married at the end
of second year.'

Entering the pavilion, they joined the crowds
meandering among stalls selling fresh produce,
pumpkins, honeys, macadamia nuts, juices, aloe
vera products and home-made jam. Anya's
thoughts flashed to poor Debbie Finch.

'You married your first boyfriend?'

'I think in many ways he provided an escape.
No-one in Newcastle knew me. By then I'd changed
my name to Crichton, my grandmother's maiden
name, and started with a clean slate. You probably
can't imagine what small-town gossip is like if you
haven't lived there. Everyone had a theory about
what happened to Miriam and who took her.'

'Where did you work after Newcastle?'

'I trained in pathology here in Sydney. After
that, we moved to England. Marty was working as
a nurse in intensive care for a while but ran into
problems. It's complicated, but by the time we came
back to Australia, we'd been living apart for months
and the marriage was over.'

'How did your parents take it?'

'Not well, the marriage or the divorce, but my
father understands now, I think.'

Ben roused and closed his eyes again.

'Sorry, here I am babbling on. Guess you're
good at your job, being so easy to talk to.'

'You're easy to listen to. Hey, let's have some grown-up fun while Ben snoozes. You up for sideshow alley?'

'You're kidding? What do you want to play?'

'Let's start with some video games and work our way up.'

They jostled their way to the area filled with teenagers trying to impress one another, and losing a fair bit of money in the process. Vaughan bowled over the skittles but didn't fare well at the ping-pong ball in the laughing clown's mouth. He challenged Anya to a game of target shooting.

'No thanks, I'll pass.'

'Why?'

'I don't like guns.'

'Come on, it's just a game,' he goaded, pushing her arm with his elbow. 'They're not real.'

'It doesn't matter. I don't like guns.' She stood, force of habit, with a leg touching the stroller. She'd automatically know if it moved.

'Guns don't have emotion. They only do what they're positioned to. People are the problem.'

'Encouraging, coming from a psychiatrist,' she said, smelling popcorn as a couple walked by with a large tub. 'How gullible do you think I am? Aren't the sights on these things rigged anyway?'

'You just have to get your eye in. That's half the challenge.'

He paid the large Tongan man working the stand enough for two players and handed Anya a rifle tied to the bench. 'You just aim and squeeze the

264

trigger. Besides, we're all capable of the same things. It doesn't mean we have to demonstrate those capabilities.'

Anya concentrated and missed the target by about a metre to her right. A couple of passers-by laughed.

'You're doing well. Try again,' Vaughan encouraged.

'What do you mean, "We're all capable"?'

'We're all capable of killing under the right circumstances. Surely you've experienced that in your line of work.'

Anya lined up and completely missed the target again.

'Not everyone murders their former abuser, or the pedophile priest who molested them as a child.'

Vaughan took aim and hit the target three times in the middle. 'Bullseye. Misspent childhood,' he said. 'Don't you think that under certain circumstances even the most convicted pacifist could kill? Mothers have been known to protect their children if it means killing to do so. Isn't there anything that would drive you to go against your value system, under the right circumstances?'

'Killing doesn't solve anything. And it hurts a lot more people than just the victim.'

'Impressive. You are opposed to the death penalty, even for the person who took your sister?'

'Capital punishment doesn't make sense. Aren't we better making these people's lives hell on earth in prison, rather than martyring them? Look at terrorists. If they're prepared to die in a suicide bombing, the death penalty is hardly a disincentive.'

Vaughan handed over more coins and reloaded. 'Is that why you chose a profession in which it is impossible to kill anyone?' he asked wryly. 'They're already dead, so even if you make a mistake, there's no harm done.'

Anya picked up her rifle again. She didn't manage to hit any of the targets with her next three shots.

'Why do psychiatrists have to pigeonhole people based on some archaic theories about id, ego and superego? I chose this career path because of the fascinating subject matter, and the fact that I can maybe help people to get closure in their lives. Help them find out what happened to their loved one, how they died. I also see rape and assault victims, so your theory about only looking after the dead doesn't hold. It's not the fear of incompetence or failure that drove me, as you imply.'

She fired one last time and missed again. 'And I believe guns do kill. Whether it's accidental or deliberate, the result is equally devastating. Can't recall a mass murderer killing thirty-five people with a shoelace and shoe, or even a machete, for that matter. The only way to kill on that sort of scale is with guns.'

Vaughan smiled broadly, with no hint of sarcasm. 'I stand corrected. Perhaps you have more faith in human nature than I do.'

'Maybe I have less.'

The Tongan man retrieved his rifle. 'Bad luck, lady. Mister, do you want a prize?'

'I'll take the large blue dinosaur for my little friend, thanks.'

Anya said, 'Only if you promise not to tell Ben I had a gun in my hands.'

'Agreed. We'd better get our stories straight about what kind of dinosaur this is and what it ate, who it mated with, who its friends were and what its favourite colour was, or you'll be in trouble tomorrow.'

Anya had already forgotten their discussion. Vaughan made her laugh and she enjoyed hearing herself sound and feel happy. They headed for the exit, with Ben stirring only as they arrived back in Annandale.

She carried her son inside, sat him on the lounge half asleep and returned to Vaughan, who waited at the door.

'Would you like to come in for a coffee? I'd offer dinner but I'm a terrible cook.'

'Thanks, but I might pass this time. I really should be going.'

'Of course.' Anya tried to hide her disappointment.

She wanted to make amends if she'd offended him. 'I sort of overreact sometimes and assault people with my opinions, especially about the gun issue. I get all worked up and just babble on –'

He took a step closer and she noticed his subtle aftershave. She stopped talking and inhaled slowly.

Vaughan leant down and her skin tingled as his face moved closer. Like a schoolgirl, she closed her eyes as he gently brushed the hair from her face and touched his lips to her cheek.

'It has nothing to do with that, believe me. There is nothing more attractive than an intelligent woman with strong opinions.' He took both of her hands. 'I'd love to come in, but this isn't the right time – for you.'

Anya stood there, like Oliver Twist, wanting more.

He stepped back down the path. 'Tell Ben I'd like to see him again sometime.'

She started to close the door and paused.

'Hey, it eats plants.'

'What does?'

'A parasaurolophus.'

He laughed, and was gone.

31

Anya couldn't get comfortable in bed. Neither hot nor cold, she tossed and turned with a feverishness that left the sheet strangling one leg.

Eventually, she decided to have a glass of water and check on Ben. After covering him with a light blanket, she padded downstairs. On the hallway table sat the thick yellow envelope Vaughan had left. She held the package for a few minutes before opening it.

Inside she found a wad of papers on cults and the psychology of recruitment. To Anya, cults had always conjured up images of disillusioned adolescents escaping society's ills by setting up their own communities. Eventually they grew up and moved back into mainstream life, which explained why no-one ever saw geriatric Hare Krishnas or wizened Orange People.

Although she hoped for a list of known cults in the area, the papers contained extracts from medical literature. *The Annals of Psychiatry*, *The Journal of Cultic Studies*, *Abnormal Psychology* were all represented, along with a series of titles unfamiliar to her.

The package also contained abstracts of over forty articles on related topics. Vaughan either had an extensive, well-organised library, or had gone to the trouble of doing a literature search and locating relevant articles. The least she could do was read some of them in case he asked what she thought. Psychiatric mumbo jumbo didn't hold much interest, but like anything, if it were applied, it became more interesting.

She took the stack to the living room, dimmed the light, turned on the muted television for company and curled up on the lounge.

Within a few pages, her assumptions about cults were proven false. Rather than outlining a series of benign and 'whacky' fads, the papers described a litany of cults dominated by psychopaths intent on violence to protect their concept of order. People like Charles Manson and David Koresh came to mind. She remembered seeing the siege at Waco on television, and the controversy surrounding the US government's management of the situation. Like so many other horrors, the memory had been filed somewhere in the section of the brain that dealt with tragedies that only affected other people.

She read on. Case studies compared cult members' behaviour to that of prisoners of war under the Koreans, Nazis and Japanese. Some of these prisoners, who had documented their incarceration and become aligned with their captors, described stages of behaviour that were often called 'brainwashing'.

The case of Patty Hearst, the American heiress who joined her kidnappers in committing an armed robbery, was compelling. Back then the jury had failed to accept that her behaviour could have been modified by torture and isolation, but the psychological changes she underwent made sense under the circumstances.

Anya couldn't think of any cults run by females, yet women were among the most committed followers. Were women less educated and psychologically weaker than men, and therefore incapable of analysing and rejecting the cult's beliefs? Judging by the next study in the pile, that couldn't be further from the truth.

The television flickered. On screen two trim bodies promoted the latest exercise machine. Without sound, they seemed more like satires of themselves.

Cults targeted better-educated, wealthier members. University campuses, religious colleges and many professional organisations were infiltrated to identify potential recruits. Anya wanted to understand why cults attracted strong, ambitious, intelligent women. It didn't make sense, but neither did so much of what she saw in life. A gadget to make perfect curls of zucchini skins flashed on the screen. Life was way too short to curl bloody zucchinis! She stretched her legs, wandered into the kitchen and boiled water for a hot chocolate.

Ben would be awake in six hours. Somehow

sleeping while he was in the house felt like a waste. It was silly, but she enjoyed being awake just knowing he was comfortable and safe. With an over-sized cup warming her hands, she returned to the lounge room and the articles.

One author hypothesised that people wanted acceptance, to belong to a group, especially if they had poor social skills. That fitted with the demands and wants of many of today's women, she thought. Cults tended to deceive members, just as people often did early in relationships. The similarities were remarkable. Being intelligent certainly didn't protect you from a destructive relationship. In the beginning they both offered satisfaction, affection and a wonderful life together. What woman didn't want to be seduced by love? The clincher seemed to be the cult leader convincing recruits that he had the answers to life's most difficult questions. If an intelligent person's questions were answered, they were likely to join and remain committed to the cause.

The next paper looked at behaviours in cults. Manipulative and deceitful actions were often implemented to recruit members who would 'volunteer' to join the group. That's when the isola-tion began. A typical pattern seemed to be to indoc-trinate, punish lack of commitment or wrong-doing, and make the member completely dependent on the cult.

Sounded just like army training, she thought, and took a sip. The liquid scalded her tongue.

'Shit!' She put down the cup and continued.

In each case, the individual's character was systematically destroyed by 'techniques' including deprivation of basic needs like sleep, food and cleanliness. Some groups locked people in rooms to watch the same video over and over again. Anya almost couldn't believe what she read. It seemed more like Orwellian fiction than something that happened in the twenty-first century.

The next step in the process was the most difficult to comprehend: why people stayed when the abuse of members that almost all the papers described was horrific. Women were often physically and sexually abused by the leaders and other members. In many cases, children born into the cult underwent similar abuse.

Anya couldn't understand how an intelligent mother could let that happen and not stop it. Surely her instinct was to protect her children above all else?

While a woman smiled and contorted herself into a yoga position from the screen, Anya read multiple descriptions of cults and mass killings. In 1978, over nine hundred people died when the Reverend Jim Jones ordered them to kill themselves. Children died first, babies fed the poison via syringes. In 1993 more than eighty followers died with David Koresh. The Order of the Solar Temple managed to murder child members before mass suicides. Suicide by cult members was the shocking, recurring theme.

Anya stretched her stiff back and felt the crack of a vertebra. She blew on, then sipped the chocolate and thought of the four dead women with lung fibres. The cases bothered her more than ever. Fibres, shaved pubic regions in at least two cases, a period of disappearance and probable suicide. Not much to go on, but they had to have something else in common. She scribbled a note to remind herself to ask Peter if Clare Matthews had been shaved. Moving into her office, she found the newspaper stories Zara had photocopied, about the woman doctor who overdosed.

A photo of a pretty, smiling brunette cuddling two children stared back at her. At least the children were alive. If all of these women joined the same cult they'd have lived in the same place, which is probably where they inhaled the fibres. It also meant that Fatima's death may have had nothing to do with Mohammed Deab at all.

Zara had attached a handwritten note about Alf Carney doing the autopsy. Great. She knew that Jeff Sales was in Montreal and wouldn't be back for another two weeks. Realistically that meant she had little chance of getting information until then. After Alf's performance about refusing her information, she decided to contact the doctor's husband on Tuesday morning and see if he would agree to a meeting. No-one else needed to know what she was exploring.

Anya finished her drink and decided to head back to bed. With Ben in the house, though, she couldn't leave papers strewn across the floor. While collecting them into a pile, she found one she'd missed – a study of domestic violence, which described thirteen behaviours used by perpetrators of domestic violence to manipulate their victims.

Many of the behaviours were identical to those used by cult leaders to control members. They isolated victims from friends and family, used economic abuse to deprive them of money to escape or go out. They coerced and threatened their victims and used their male position as 'king of the castle' to dominate the household. The list went on: sleep deprivation, unpredictability, and violent actions followed by displays of love and affection.

One paragraph in particular stunned her. Battered women might be forced to commit acts that went against their beliefs and values. They could be made to steal, sell drugs or prostitute themselves for the abuser.

She immediately thought of Fatima Deab. Crime scene assumed she was on the game when they found the money in her bra. She'd been cut off from social contact, had her salary confiscated, so her father knew exactly how much money she had. How could she have afforded to leave?

Mohammed had threatened her life and the

Galea boy. He'd been unpredictable in his violence, hitting Fatima when she hadn't done anything wrong. How did Fatima cope not knowing what would set her father off, knowing that following the rules didn't save her from being beaten?

Abusers denied fault and blamed their victims as well. Deab had accused his daughter of being a slut, and thought Fatima deserved to die.

Jesus! Deab could have written the textbook on battered woman syndrome. For someone who lacked formal education, he had a hell of an instinct for manipulation. He could have run his own cult. In a way, he did, from the comfort of his own home.

A cult was beginning to make more sense as a plausible link between the women with the lung fibres. Each was intelligent, vulnerable and at least three of them – Fatima, Debbie and Clare – were deprived of affection. Joining a cult could explain their sudden disappearances and the fact that no-one heard from them when they were missing.

Anya realised how ridiculous her theory would sound to the police. Deab's confession made the link more tenuous. Unless he was involved with more than one of the women, no-one would investigate another lead.

She went to bed wondering if Deab was capable of murdering anyone he deemed immoral and making it appear like suicide. If he'd done it once, was it possible he'd done it before? She hoped they hadn't seriously underestimated Mohammed Deab.

32

Anya drove along Old Northern Road, past a weatherboard school on the left with horses and bulls feeding in green fields opposite. The scene seemed anachronistic. She pulled over to the side and stopped outside a gated house, about where Glenhaven became Dural. After checking the address, she left her car on the side of the road and walked down a long, gravelled path that crunched beneath her shoes.

An overwhelming scent of manure filled the air, which she found oddly refreshing. It reminded her of Evandale markets in Tasmania, where she would go with Damien and her mother on weekends. Local farmers brought their trash, treasure, crafts and produce to sell on land surrounded by farms. In many ways, these parts of the Hills District were similar to Tasmania, where rural life was possible, close to city comforts. In this case, people could live on a couple of acres and be minutes from one of the largest shopping centres in the southern hemisphere. Unfortunately for Anya and Ben, real estate prices in this part of Sydney were prohibitive, for now.

She rang the doorbell of the sandstone brick

cottage, her arrival already announced by a dog barking loudly inside the house. A man in his early forties opened the door, restraining an excited Irish setter with both hands.

'He hasn't gone for his W-A-L-K yet and gets a bit impatient.'

The attempt at secrecy was redundant. The dog knew what a walk was, no matter how it was spelt.

'Come in. I'm Paul Blakehurst.'

'Thanks for seeing me.' Anya wiped her feet and entered. 'I appreciate it.'

The man steered the setter through a door that opened into the garage. 'He can get to the backyard from here so he won't bother us.'

On the hallway table stood a black and white photo of a striking Alison Blakehurst graduating from medicine. Beside it was a professional family portrait.

'We can talk in the kitchen. I'm just organising dinner.'

He led the way into an open-plan living room and timber kitchen. Two teenagers, older than their newspaper and portrait shots, sat at a dining table doing homework, still in school uniforms. They barely noticed the visitor.

'Could you two please clean off the table and get changed? I'll set the table tonight.'

'Great,' said the boy.

'I'll be on the phone,' said the girl.

In a blur, the books, laptops and owners were gone. No interest in introductions.

'Dinner will be in an hour,' their father called to an empty corridor.

He picked up a knife and continued chopping carrots as Anya took a seat at the kitchen bench.

'We eat together every evening. I don't want them getting into –' he took a deep breath, 'trouble of any sort. This is family time.'

'I understand. I know how special that is.'

He slid a bowl of peas across the bench for shelling. 'Would you mind? I'm curious as to why you've come now, when Alison died almost six months ago.'

Anya could see how painful each of those months has been. He probably knew how many days and hours had passed, too.

'I apologise for the timing, but I'm looking into some specific findings that occurred in your wife's case. They're not isolated and may tell more of a story about what happened to her.'

He slid the carrots from the board into a saucepan, filled it with water and placed it on a ceramic cooktop.

'Isn't it clear what happened? Once an addict, always an addict. I was too stupid to believe it. Everyone told me how addicts manipulate everyone to get what they want. God knows, I've seen it enough at work.'

'How long had she been abusing drugs?'

He pulled some potatoes out of the pantry and a peeler from the top drawer.

'Who knows? We met at uni. We both did medicine as mature-age students. I'd done science and she'd done economics. I knew she'd used heroin in her teens and her boyfriend died of kidney failure thanks to strychnine mixed in a batch. After that she swore off the stuff and never looked back. Or so we all thought. She even got honours.' He kept peeling. 'That's something I didn't manage.'

Anya felt he needed the distraction of doing something with his hands. She appreciated having a task herself.

'As an anaesthetic registrar,' he said, 'she ran the pain clinic at Southern General.'

'Do you think she was using drugs then?'

'Someone reported her to the medical board and she had conditional registration imposed. That's when she admitted to being dependent on codeine.'

Anya shelled another pea. 'How did she react?'

'Career-wise, well. She studied hard for her fellowship and enjoyed general practice. She said it was a wake-up call and, to save our marriage, agreed to regular urine tests. Do you know that when she got pregnant, she wouldn't even take a headache tablet? Said she wouldn't do anything to endanger her child. And I believed her. Again.' He chopped the potatoes into wedges and laid them in a baking dish.

'When your wife died, the PM found evidence of a fibre deposited in her lungs. Any idea if she had exposure to anything like asbestos?'

'Not to my knowledge, but then I didn't know everything.'

'What about a history of respiratory illness?'

'Mild asthma. She self-medicated and didn't seem to need much treatment, except when she caught the kids' colds.'

'What about where she grew up?'

'She lived at home until we got married. Her parents still own the home in Pennant Hills. A lovely old federation place on half an acre.'

'Did they renovate?'

'It still has a 1950s kitchen, if that's what you mean.' He wiped the scraps into a small container on the bench.

Anya shelled another pea. 'Somehow she inhaled an unusual fibre. Could her father have brought it home?'

'How do you mean?'

'We're finding a new generation of asbestosis sufferers. The kids who cuddled their fathers when they came home from work with fibres all over their clothes.'

'Look, where is all this going? Al's father owned a menswear store and made his money franchising.'

'I'm trying to source the fibres.' Anya continued shelling.

'While you're at it, how about you find out who she was sleeping with?' The knife slipped and the end of his finger oozed blood. 'Damn!' He sucked it and ran it under the tap.

Anya walked around the kitchen bench, looking for something to apply pressure with.

Paul Blakehurst stared at the water and blood

running down the sink. 'I always thought I'd know if my wife was involved with someone else. You hear about partners having late meetings, change of habits. Alison wasn't any good at lying. Her voice would go up an octave even if she lied about a surprise birthday party. Can't believe I had no idea. Nothing seemed different with me or the kids.'

Anya found a box of tissues on top of the fridge and pulled a handful out to press on the cut. Paul took the tissues and turned off the tap.

'One day I came home from work and she was gone. Can you believe she didn't even take her favourite photo of the kids?'

'What makes you so sure she chose to leave?'

'It's pretty obvious. The affair, running away. Initially I thought she'd joined some sort of cult but there were rumours around the clinic she was seeing an obstetrician.'

This man had lost his wife twice. Once to an unknown man, and then to drugs. Anya remembered being too busy working to notice Martin's early behaviour changes. Looking back, signs were there. Moodiness, starting fights as an excuse to walk out. The marriage counsellor called it transference, or projection, or some other clinical name. Anya just recognised it as guilty behaviour hiding infidelity.

'What makes you so sure she was having an affair and wasn't part of a cult?'

'A drug habit wasn't the only thing she picked

up. The children know their mother was found lying in vomit, dressed in a see-through cheesecloth dress and G-string in a hotel room.'

'That doesn't necessarily mean –'

'She *had* an affair. How do I know? I know because she had herpes and that's one thing I couldn't give her.'

33

Elaine opened the mail and presented Anya with a series of bills and a request from Sabina Pryor at Legal Aid. Attached was a photograph of the back of a ten-year-old girl. The child was covered in linear bruises down her spine, fanning out from the vertebrae.

'That poor child!' Elaine said, covering her mouth.

'Let's not jump to conclusions,' Anya said, reserving judgment.

She read the letter from Sabina, which explained that the parents of this girl moved from Vietnam two years ago. They were being investigated for child abuse and had little understanding of Australian law. Through an interpreter, they denied harming the child.

They came to the notice of Family Services when the child complained of pain in her ribs at school. The school teacher noted a fever, and saw the bruises on the girl's back. Mandatory notification laws meant she immediately contacted the department, which promptly intervened. The child was admitted to hospital with a right-sided pneumonia and was currently in foster care.

Sabina wanted a second opinion regarding the injuries to the girl's back – what most likely caused them and were they consistent with an Asian healing therapy, as the parents claimed.

'I've seen this before,' Anya said. 'The bruises are symmetrical and outline the ribs. It looks like someone has drawn on top of the backbone and ribs with a red marker.'

Elaine peered at the photos.

'These injuries weren't caused by hitting or striking. See, the skin isn't broken. They've been caused by a blunt injury, in this case, something rubbing against the skin. It's a common practice in Asia, especially Vietnam, to rub coins along the ribs to relieve pain. Pneumonia can cause inflammation of the pleura, which feels like pain in the ribs. The teacher automatically assumed the marks on the skin were the problem.'

'I'll be damned. The family thought they were doing the right thing, treating the pain. I'd have thought the same thing as the teacher.'

'So do many doctors in Casualty. Intravenous antibiotics and physiotherapy are obviously more effective and don't involve Family Services. It's a good, straightforward case. I'll dictate a letter this afternoon. So, what else have you got?'

'I'll type it but invoice Legal Aid before it's sent. That way you'll be paid for your effort, rather than donating your time again.' She referred to a list on her notepad. 'Dr Latham called while you were on the other line. He's on his way over with some files for you to look at. I'll go and put the kettle on. Lucky we've got some biscuits in the tin.'

Elaine seemed to be fussing more than usual.

'Has Anoub Deab been bothering you?' Anya asked.

'He turned up with a girlfriend draped all over him to find out if there was anything new, but didn't "bother" me. I just wish he wasn't so rude.'

On time, Peter arrived, and Elaine presented him with tea.

'Ah, perfect brew, just the way I like it. Thank you. And coffee creams, my favourite.'

Anya noticed that his normally woolly hair had been combed down.

For a moment, Elaine seemed coy. Anya wondered if the pair were flirting.

Peter quickly suggested it might be a good idea for Elaine to document the meeting. She flicked over a page on her pad and sat on the spare chair, beside Peter.

'I brought Alison Blakehurst's PM.' He seemed pleased with himself. 'Carney wasn't keen to let it go, but he could hardly refuse to send it when I mentioned a possible connection with other cases. He even included the tissue samples.'

'It's what we needed.' Anya sat, elbows resting on the arms of her chair. 'I suggested we meet here because I didn't want to talk in front of Zara or anyone else. Having an occupational health issue is one thing, but dealing with a possible serial offender is something I'd like to keep quiet until

287

we know more. Besides, I'd prefer that everyone at the State Forensic Institute didn't think I was out to show them up, looking for mistakes, to make a name for myself.'

'If we've missed something, we need to know so it doesn't happen again.' Peter frowned. 'They know I believe in quality assurance. But I agree. Meeting here is wise. After all the media attention on retention of body parts, everyone's more than a little paranoid right now. I looked at the fibres again and sent the slides along with tissue samples from both the Matthews girl and Alison Blakehurst. Electron microscopy confirmed the presence of pseudo-asbestos bodies.'

'Sorry, what sort of asbestos bodies?' Elaine asked without looking up.

Peter explained, '"Pseudo-asbestos", meaning they mimic the appearance but are chemically different in make-up from asbestos. I can give you a copy of the printouts.'

'Organic or man-made?' Anya asked.

'Man-made, it seems. Whatever the fibre, it is the same in both cases.'

Anya sat back. 'So, they *are* identical. Whatever we saw on Clare Matthews' slide was the same as Alison Blakehurst's.'

'Your judgment was sound. Nice bit of pathology work.'

'She's been trained by the best,' Elaine added.

Peter stuttered for a moment, something Anya had never before witnessed. Seeing her mentor vulnerable in the presence of her secretary didn't feel right.

'We have the chemical composition,' Peter added, 'but it doesn't match any of the controls. I checked with the Dust Diseases Board but they don't have records prior to 1967. It must be something that was in use before that.'

Elaine listened, then said, 'What about building suppliers? If you know what it's made of, can you find out where it was made?'

'Unfortunately, it isn't that simple,' Peter said. 'Asbestos and similar materials are found in a plethora of products. For example, asbestos can be found in roofing, sheeting for sheds, linoleum, brake linings. The list is almost endless.'

'What I don't understand,' Anya said, 'is if this fibre is old, why it is turning up now in young women?'

'That bothers me, too. The time lag for developing disease from these things is twenty to forty years and, of course, cigarettes exacerbate the condition. As far as I can tell, neither of these women smoked or had obvious exposure.'

'Clare Matthews was orphaned and grew up in foster homes, and Alison Blakehurst grew up around a clothes shop business.'

'We don't know if the fibre itself causes disease, but if the body coats it in protein, it has already induced an inflammatory response, even in young people. That is a genuine concern.'

'Maybe someone is recycling the material

without knowing what it contains,' Elaine suggested.

'We still need to identify the fibre to find out where the women came into contact with it. Did they do X-ray diffraction?'

Peter nodded. 'In addition to electron microscopy.' He pulled a page from the file. It included a graph of a continuous black line with a series of vertical peaks and troughs. 'There are several prominent peaks that correlate with those found in amosite asbestos, but the central ones,' he pointed with his pen, 'don't match any of the controls on record. We know the substance has a chrysotile core made of hydrated magnesium silicate, but the percentage of elements is unique.'

Elaine stopped writing. 'There must be other ways of finding out what it is.'

Anya tapped her desk. 'For that, you have to send it to Western Australia.'

The area of analysis had become so subspecialised, only one lab, located in Perth, was capable of performing the detailed molecular analysis.

'It's the only lab with the facilities to test it further.' Peter again turned to Elaine. 'They determine the molecular structure of the substance. That's the equivalent of a fingerprint, if you like, which can be matched to a larger database. It is, unfortunately, very expensive to do.'

'Why don't you pass it on to the public health unit? Surely they'll want to know about this fibre so they can warn people about it.'

'It's not that straightforward, Elaine. We're in a bit of a catch-22. The public health unit doesn't want to know about it unless it's a notifiable disease. And until we can confirm what it is and that is causes disease, they're not interested.'

'So by the time you find out what it is, it's already a public health problem. What is wrong with these bureaucrats?'

Anya pulled out some notes she'd taken. 'Could we talk about what we know about the dead women who inhaled the fibres? In terms of backgrounds, the women, including the overdose in Merrylands and the murder–suicide from the coast, have absolutely nothing in common. They didn't even grow up in the same place. What we do know is that they are all recorded as deaths by suicide, or in Fatima Deab's case, accidental overdose. All have the fibres and all went missing. And two of them had shaved pubic regions, that we know of.'

'Make that four,' Peter said. 'I checked. Neither Clare Matthews nor Alison Blakehurst had any pubic hair.'

Anya leant forward. 'Are you sure?'

'Alf Carney's registrar started the PM and he was keen to do all the right things, exactly by the book. He documented a complete absence of body hair. Seems he'd never seen completely hairless genitalia before. And sorry it took so long, but I had to track down the junior registrar who did Clare Matthews' PM. He's on holidays in Queensland, but remembered the case. He sounded pretty sure she had no pubic hair, even though that wasn't documented at the time. Unfortunately, I only examined the neck wounds on the body.'

Anya wondered if the police would still dismiss information that could prove so important. Identical fibres, shaved pubic regions, disappearances and suicides. She remembered Detectives Filano and Faulkner arguing about the coroner's rulings of suicide. They'd still consider the fibres and shavings as coincidence, and they believed the women left of their own choice. No mystery disappearace, apart from Clare Matthews. Her pregnancy and suicide could easily be explained by believing she screwed up her life and couldn't cope, as Filano put it. So far nothing connected Mohammed Deab to the other women. Anya needed more.

Peter continued. 'You mentioned herpes over the phone. As you know, we don't ordinarily do swabs, but the registrar for Alison Blakehurst was initially concerned about a streptococcal infection and questioned rare diagnoses such as pemphigus and pemphigoid as causes of sepsis.'

He addressed Elaine. 'Don't worry about writing down any of this. The woman was found in a hotel room. She'd swallowed a cocktail of pills and died after choking on her vomit. My senior registrar couldn't exclude overwhelming infection as a precipitant for the vomiting and aspiration, which caused death. Of course, he didn't have the benefit of a toxicology report at that stage. He diligently conducted the PM as he should have. Mind you,'

Peter added, glancing at Elaine, 'he once wrote that a deceased gentleman looked like Yoda from *Star Wars*. Turns out the poor chap had a rare syndrome that makes people look exactly like Yoda. Of course, we couldn't put that on the formal report, but we all had a clear image of exactly what he had seen.'

Elaine giggled.

Peter became serious again. 'The herpes culture came back drug-resistant. So now you have two of the four with drug-resistance and no obvious immune system suppression.'

Anya shook her head. 'It's like playing that game where A and B are the same, and A and C are the same, therefore B equals C.'

'Syllogistic logic, I believe it's called,' Peter said, stroking his beard.

Elaine drew three circles surrounded by a rectangle. 'Sounds more like those circles and sets we used to draw with subsets at school.'

Anya drew three large intersecting circles on her notes. In one she wrote 'lung fibres', 'herpes' in the second, and 'pubic hair' in the third. 'All four women had fibres and shaved pubic hair, but Fatima and Alison were the only ones known to have herpes.'

Elaine offered, 'Is it too late to check whether the other two had the virus?'

'Good thought, but unfortunately, the virus would have only survived in any blood samples for a few days, and if there weren't any obvious blistery lesions, the chances of culturing it at the time were pretty much zero, anyway. Debbie Finch's report didn't mention blisters.'

Peter Latham appeared to be deep in thought. 'Out of context, none of the findings means much. But when you look at the ages of the women, their disappearances and deaths, you can't help but suspect that they are very closely linked. I have had an uncomfortable feeling about the Matthews case from the start.'

'I know this is going to sound far-fetched,' Anya ventured, 'but I can't help thinking these women might have joined the same cult, religion, or whatever you choose to call it.'

Elaine looked shocked. 'A cult here in Sydney?'

Peter scratched his beard again. 'It's not implausible. Suicide seemed to go against Clare Matthews' beliefs, for one. Something or someone had a big influence on her.'

Anya began the instructions. 'Elaine, could you do some chasing up for me? I want to know if there are any cults in this part of the state. You could try searching the Internet, newspaper articles, maybe even consumer complaints, and checking with the police. Peter, could you arrange to have the fibres from the Finch woman and Fatima Deab tested, too? We don't have much unless we can confirm the fibres from the others are identical to these.'

'Of course.'

'Can I ask you both to keep this quiet until we know if there are any more cases? In the meantime, I'll have a chat to the microbiologist and see if there's a link between the two herpes infections. I'll also put another message on the histology forum and see if anyone recognises the fibre. The sooner we find out what we're dealing with, the better.'

After Peter had left, Anya wanted to discuss the new information with Kate and dialled her mobile. The call diverted to voicemail.

'Hi Kate, Anya. I know the other day at the station didn't go well, but I've some more info about those cases. It's important. Please call me back.'

34

At 1 pm Anya arrived at the desk in the outpatients department at Western District Hospital. Toddlers ran around and between rows of plastic chairs occupied by women at various stages of pregnancy and, judging by the trail of crushed crisps and biscuits on the carpet, the mothers-to-be had been waiting a while. Across the aisle, men and women with casts, crutches and slings filled the seats. Pretty much like the clinics Anya remembered from her resident years – too many patients and too few medical staff.

'Dr Crichton.' Professor Hammond came out of a side room and placed a file in a basket attached to the outside of the door. 'Don't tell me. Um, got it! You were a path registrar when we dealt with that outbreak of meningococcus in the pre-school down the road.'

He shoved both hands into the pockets of his knee-length white coat and rocked on his heels.

'That's right.' Anya clearly remembered. 'Ten or more children were admitted here and we had to examine and interview two hundred contacts in twelve hours. One of our more stressful days.'

'Even though we warned them about the side effects of the prophylactic antibiotics, the sight of all those toddlers crying orange tears panicked the staff. They closed it down for weeks, despite our reassurances.' He rocked one more time, as though remembering the episode with fondness.

'I'm sure you've come to discuss something other than old times, and I'm about to start an STD clinic.' He shrugged his shoulders. 'Or I should say "sexual health clinic", to be PC.'

Jules Hammond ran the microbiology department at one of the state's biggest pathology centres. He came from another time – when nurses trained in hospitals, not universities, his patients suffered from 'venereal disease' and doctors all wore white coats. Although he had accommodated most of the changes, the white coat, which he usually buttoned right up, had become the enduring image of a bygone era.

'I know you don't have much time so I'll be brief.' Anya stepped away from the desk and out of the nurses' hearing range. 'A couple of months ago your lab did some sensitivities on a herpes simplex virus detected on the genitals of a young woman who died of a drug overdose. The virus was multi-drug-resistant.'

'We do tend to see it in people who are immuno-compromised. Drug addicts' immune systems are exposed to an awful lot of abuse, not to mention innumerable infectious agents. Look at the high incidence of bacterial endocarditis and staphylococcal sepsis they get. Of course, nutrition is vital to maintaining the immune system so, if an addict is malnourished, immunocompromise is more likely.'

One thing about experts in fields of medicine, they never gave succinct answers. Anya listened patiently, careful not to offend him by interrupting a point. She spoke when he allowed.

'This girl wasn't an addict. Blood levels and absence of injection sites suggested it was her first time. She could have been undernourished with a body weight of forty-five kilograms, but was otherwise well.'

'Drug-resistant herpes is moderately rare in healthy people.' He rocked on his heels again.

'We've identified a second case of drug-resistance in another healthy woman.'

The pager in Hammond's top left pocket bleeped and he checked the number.

'Clinic's beginning around the other side. Do you mind walking with me?'

'No problem.'

They hurried along a badly worn blue carpet. Every section in the hospital was colour-coded so people could find their way. Anya felt like Dorothy following a 'blue brick road'.

'Now where were we?' Professor Hammond asked, overtaking a young woman in a wheelchair. 'We have seen that a bit around here, but you're more likely to see resistant strains in the inner city, where they treat greater numbers of end-stage HIV cases. Of course malignancy, and chemotherapy, can cause immunosuppression. You're sure the women weren't on treatments for auto-immune diseases? Arthritis, for example?'

'Nothing. What I'm trying to find out is whether both women had relations with the same contact.'

'We would use the swabs taken and do a plaque reduction assay. That way you take the virus and grow it up in the cells with differing concentrations of the antiviral drugs, and if the herpes is resistant, it continues to grow. If you isolate the same drug-resistant virus from other contacts, that would be unusual. If you have a cluster of people with acyclovir-resistant virus who have had some kind of contact with each other, then that would be pretty good circumstantial evidence that they've all got the same virus.'

'Actually, I am trying to establish whether these people shared a contact. They are both dead, so they can't answer that question. Is there any way you can work backwards, and confirm the viruses are the same strain?'

They turned into an uncarpeted corridor, Anya's heels clomped conspicuously on the hard floor.

Jules Hammond slowed his pace. 'Logically, you'd have to go to the molecular level to prove the viruses are related.'

'Is that possible?'

'Theoretically speaking, you could do a phylogenetic analysis.'

Anya stopped short of a yellow 'wet floor' sign

as a cleaner mopped the floor up ahead. 'What does that involve?'

'Three steps. First, you map out the genetic make-up of the herpes virus and that of your other suspected contact, which in this case is the two women you described. Then you compare it to a run-of-the-mill herpes virus found in other people in the community, presumably who had no contact with your two women.

'You look to see whether those viruses resemble each other at a molecular level. In other words, are they related strains? That process is called phylogenetic analysis. In fact, phylogenetic analysis is the only way you can really see whether the viruses are likely to have come from the same source.'

'Is it difficult to do?'

'Not really, it's usually done for HIV, to identify new and unusual strains. We don't ordinarily do it for herpes viruses, but there's no reason why we couldn't.' He paused and rubbed his chin. 'It's an expensive process. I'd need good reason to justify it.'

'I'm trying to determine whether these women contracted the infection from the same man, which would mean that their deaths, which were both initially ruled as suicides, may need re-investigation. Apart from that, if we're sourcing contacts as we are supposed to do, we should know if someone is practising unsafe sex and infecting partners with a drug-resistant strain of herpes. If he has a number of sexual contacts, we could see an outbreak of a pretty much untreatable condition.'

'You certainly do present a compelling case.' He smiled approvingly. 'Write down the names of the patients and give them to my secretary. I'll see what we can do.'

His pager beeped again.

'And please include your contact details so I can let you know the outcome. Might take a couple of weeks. Now, where was I? Oh yes. The clinic.'

Professor Hammond hurried off down the corridor, barely avoiding the cleaner. Only an infectious diseases specialist would scurry like that towards a sexual health clinic.

35

'While you were out, a medical student popped in.' Elaine blew her nose.

'Something about another case she'd found from four years ago. She was in a hurry to get to a lecture.'

'Did she say where she's going to be this afternoon?'

'Only that she had exams coming up and would be studying. She stayed long enough to write you this note.'

Anya put her bag down, kicked off her shoes and sat down to read Zara's message.

The woman had died aged forty-five years. The autopsy, performed on Lucinda Tait at Western Forensics' morgue, cited cause of death as pneumonia secondary to chronic airflow limitation. It noted large numbers of fibres in the lung peripheries. An addendum to the histology report said that the fibres remained unidentified. No records of such a fibre at the Dust Diseases Board or through the public health unit. The coroner deemed death by natural causes and released the body for cremation.

The place of death took Anya by surprise. Lucinda Tait had died at the Meadowbank Nursing Home in Pennant Hills.

Zara had phoned the nursing home for the name of any relatives but was told they would not release information unless requests went through the appropriate processes. Predictably, the staff couldn't tell Zara what that actually meant.

'She's a funny girl.' Elaine wiped her nose and replaced the tissue inside her cardigan sleeve. 'Can't imagine her as a doctor. A dentist, perhaps.'

'Zara's got a lot to learn, but she's determined. The intern year will make or break her. Non-stop patient contact is the best test of all.'

'The counsellor from the sexual assault unit phoned, Mary Singer. The woman you examined the other night has refused to make a police statement. She thought you should know.'

Anya quietly sighed. She had learnt to accept a victim's decision regarding police involvement but was always concerned when the evidence taken was disposed of. It could be useful for future or past cases, to compare with specimens taken from other women, or even used to compare with DNA from the state data bank. Mary had been right. Victims weren't responsible for their assault, or anyone else's, and had to do what they felt necessary to get on with their lives.

Still, Anya believed that two men who brutally raped a middle-aged woman in a park were bound to attack again.

She turned her thoughts to the nursing home where Lucinda Tait had died. Elaine handed her a note with the address and phone number of Meadowbank, and a print-out of the map showing the location, courtesy of the Internet.

'You're clear until four-thirty, and you have an appointment out there at two o'clock with the director of nursing. If you need more time, let me know and I'll reschedule your meeting at Legal Aid.'

People had always told Anya that she needed someone to organise her life. Elaine Morton was like a wife, personal trainer and coach all in one.

'Thanks. What would I do without you?'

'Let's hope you get enough work so you don't have to find out.'

The Meadowbank Nursing Home sat nestled behind a large ivy-covered wall on Pennant Hills Road, one of the city's busiest thoroughfares. Carefully manicured gardens gave the place a sense of grandeur that belied the state of the residents. The director of nursing, or DON as she liked to be known, greeted Anya with a forced smile and escorted her to a family room.

'It's the cosiest room in the place,' she boasted as they entered an open room with glass panels and single vinyl chairs lining three walls.

An elderly lady rocked a plastic baby doll in one of the chairs and sang an unintelligible lullaby.

'Now Maisie, isn't it time for activities? Off you go.'

Maisie kept singing, rose, clutched the baby more tightly and shuffled out down the corridor.

'Diversional therapy does wonders for the residents.'

If Maisie was a testament to therapy, Anya wondered how bad she had been before.

'I'm looking into a lung disease that afflicted one of your former residents, Lucinda Tait.'

'Ah, poor Lucy. We all have vivid memories of that woman. She didn't really accept living here, I'm afraid. The fact that she was so much younger than most of our residents didn't help.'

A woman in her mid forties surrounded by Maisies couldn't have been easy under any circumstances, Anya thought.

'Did she have family or friends who visited?'

'No. Working with the elderly has taught me one thing. The kind ones always seem to have someone visiting, whereas the others sit alone day after day.'

Anya didn't hide her surprise. 'No-one ever came?'

'Not that you could blame them. Lucy was, should I say, somewhat difficult to manage.'

'In what way?'

'Her lung disease was very aggressive and her smoking didn't help. When she came to us, Lucy was unable to walk more than a few steps because of her shortness of breath. She had twenty-four-hour oxygen via a mask and second-hourly nebulisers. Not the easiest woman to nurse, either. Lucy constantly argued with the staff about the smoking.

305

Once she set off the emergency exit alarm sneaking out for a cigarette. The staff caught her dragging the oxygen trolley with her. She needed the oxygen more than ever when she smoked, she said.'

The DON clasped both hands on her lap. 'We were concerned she'd blow herself up and us with her. Towards the end, we discussed transfer with her, due to the risk to other residents. Then she succumbed to pneumonia.'

Anya had seen a number of cases in which chronic smokers were unable or unwilling to break the habit, despite respiratory distress. Many had a terminal illness and, she suspected, wanted to accelerate the process.

'Was she widowed?'

'Never married, as far as I know, and no children. She lived at home until her mother died, which is how she came here. She was no longer independent with her ADLs.'

Anya remembered her mother talking about 'activities of daily living' when she assessed her elderly patients to establish whether they could shower, use the toilet, cook, and function independently. For someone so young, being completely dependent on carers must have been difficult. She may have had good reason to be resentful.

'Do you know if the disease was thought to be occupational?'

'No. She was just another smoking statistic. I recall the GP wanted her to have a bronchoscopy, but Lucy refused outright to have anyone probe her lungs from the inside. The local doctor suggested it may be due to some toxin and she may be entitled to compensation, but money meant nothing to Lucy, and she had no-one to leave anything to.'

The sounds of a piano playing 'Pack Up Your Troubles in Your Old Kit Bag' filtered from somewhere down the corridor. Male and female voices became louder as the song progressed.

The DON forced another smile. 'Some of our residents don't remember their names, but they can all remember the words to songs from the war.'

'Could you tell me the name of her treating doctor?'

'Wilfred Campbell, one of our best GPs. He had a time of it, with Lucy refusing investigation and most of his treatment suggestions. Still, he was with her at the end, when she needed it most.'

The thought of someone with an illness that might have been diagnosed earlier with appropriate investigation must have been frustrating for the doctors and staff. One of the basic tenets of medicine was, at times, the most difficult. You are there to treat patients, not yourself. All you can do is advise them of their options. The rest is up to them. The post-mortem was the only alternative to secure a diagnosis.

'Is it possible to have her former address?'

'The house was sold to pay for her place here. I don't see how that can help you now.'

Anya stood. 'It's actually vital to an ongoing

investigation into a potential public health problem.' She smiled wider than normal. 'I can always arrange a subpoena for the information. Besides, the information is in the public domain. All I'd have to do is search for title deeds but that would be a huge waste of my time.'

The older woman straightened the scarf accessorising her navy-blue blazer. 'Well, I suppose it wouldn't hurt to help if we can. I'll get the address for you if you don't mind waiting.'

Anya waited outside the office area. Further along, an elderly gentleman in striped pyjamas relieved himself in the middle of the corridor.

'Arthur, the toilet is in the bathroom, not out here,' groaned one of the nursing staff as she steered the resident back inside a room.

Anya averted her eyes out of respect for the man, who appeared embarrassed, just like a child who has an accident during toilet training.

The DON reappeared with an address. 'Lennox Crescent is off the main road. Turn left at the next set of lights and you'll find it. I'm not sure how far down number seventy-two is.' She noticed the puddle on the floor nearby. 'If you'll excuse me, I need to make sure no-one slips on that.'

Anya followed the directions to Lennox Crescent, aware there was no mystery disappearance for Lucy Tait and no suicide. She didn't fit the pattern of the others. This could have been a red herring, but still needed following up. A number of blond and brown brick homes sat back from the street on large blocks. Further along, developers had knocked down the original houses and replaced them with rows of medium-density, two-storey units. It was difficult to believe that councils approved the destruction of suburbs' characters to line the pockets of developers.

Halfway down the hill on the left, she saw numbers seventy to seventy-six, a series of town-houses, extending down each block. She stopped the car by the curb. Number seventy-two no longer existed. With it went the best clue to finding the source of the fibres.

36

Anya stepped out from the lift and saw Professor Jules Hammond sitting at the nurses' station, absorbed in a patient's notes. He startled when she spoke his name.

'Thought I'd be finished my rounds by the time you got here.' He closed the file. 'The clinic's about to start, but I wanted to discuss this in person, given the sensitive nature of the circumstances.'

'I appreciate it.'

Anya had hoped to talk somewhere private, but hospitals weren't designed for that. Most clinical exchanges took place at or around the nurses' station, the medical version of a central command post.

'The results of the phylogenetic analysis aren't yet back, but I have identified a drug-resistant viral infection, in a young woman, again with no obvious reason to develop resistance. I remembered what you said about the women committing suicide. In the context, I felt you should be aware. This one fell from a cliff somewhere up the mountains.'

Anya felt her chest tighten. Another suicide. The police would have to take this seriously. 'How long ago did this happen?'

'A couple of weeks. As yet, the woman is unidentified.'

'So we have no way of knowing who she was with or how she acquired the infection.'

A young female doctor extracted a number of files from the metal trolley behind the desk, while two older males checked a list. A ward round, with consultant, registrar and resident was about to begin.

Jules Hammond lowered his voice. 'As yet, she refuses to speak to anyone.'

Anya walked around the desk and knelt beside the professor's chair.

'She's alive? But you said she fell from a cliff.'

'Seems the trees caused deceleration injuries that she somehow managed to survive.'

'Where is she now?'

'I am not at liberty to say.' He pinched the bridge of his nose. 'Darned hay fever.' He sniffed. 'I can tell you she is safe and undergoing treatment.'

The young doctor nearby dropped some of her files and opted to take the whole trolley around. The senior pair didn't acknowledge her, or offer to help.

'Why the secrecy?' Anya asked. 'If it's possible, I'd really like to interview her.'

'I understand your desire to have her answer some questions but my duty of care is to my patient. If I disclose her whereabouts, I have breached confidentiality. Consider my position. Where would we be if people with sexually acquired infections could not be guaranteed anonymity? No-one would seek treatment and the effects on the community, not to mention the individuals, would be disastrous. No, I'm afraid I must respect her privacy.'

'I agree, but we are not talking about an isolated case here. If she were pushed from the cliff, would that make a difference?' A phone rang on the desk but Anya ignored it. 'It's too coincidental that four intelligent women, all with shaved pubic hair, abandon their loved ones and kill, or almost kill, themselves. And on PM, each had an identified fibre in their lungs.'

He sat back, seeming to digest the information. 'Did they *all* have the herpetic infection?'

'No, but we knew of two, now three. The others could have had latent infections that weren't obvious at the time of death.'

A uniformed nurse leant over the desk and muttered something rude about the ward clerk as she answered the phone.

'Unfortunately, that's conjecture. No matter how noble your cause, I cannot breach confidentiality.'

The nurse put down the handset and began calling along the corridor, 'Who's looking after bed eleven? There's a relative on the phone.'

Anya tried another approach. 'Irrespective of the cause of death, shouldn't the contacts be traced? I am, after all, a physician, and I often deal with sexually acquired infections in assault victims. Is it possible for me to at least talk to your patient, with you present if you prefer, to discuss sexual contacts so we can trace possible sources of the infection? I can offer another clinical viewpoint and go through the problems with drug-resistance. That isn't a breach of trust. It's clinically appropriate.'

A young woman placed a box of cornflowers and cream roses on the counter. 'Flowers for bed twenty-three.' She disappeared as the food trolley stopped at the station.

Hammond explained, 'She's refusing to give her name to anyone. The police have been informed but are so far unable to identify her. She has suffered horrific injuries from the fall, push, or whatever you call it. At the moment she's deemed fragile from a psychiatric viewpoint.'

'I'm used to dealing with sexual assault victims,' Anya persisted. 'If she's traumatised, there's a chance she's suffered some kind of abuse. Don't we owe it to her to give her the best treatment for her physical and emotional pain?'

Professor Hammond waited until the meals trolley moved on. Buzzers on the backboard were lighting up. Patients wanted nurses but no nurses were in sight. Lucky it wasn't visiting hours as well, Anya thought, trying to block out the distractions.

'I think the ethics are tenuous but you make a valid point. And, on examination, she, too, has no pubic hair. Under the circumstances, I've decided to test this herpetic infection against the others you mentioned.' He seemed to be struggling with his decision. 'But this poor woman is obviously terribly

313

private and I have to ask you to respect that in any dealings.'

'Of course.' Anya could have hugged him. She could finally meet this woman. 'Do you know anything about her background?'

'She has certainly had at least one pregnancy. The surgical team noticed a Caesarian scar. The only other marking is a tattoo with the initials J.E. So far the police haven't turned up anything on her ID. They've just put an article in the newspapers to see if anyone is missing her.'

Another nurse returned to the desk to answer the phone query, and seemed nonplussed that the caller had hung up.

Anya waited until they were alone again. 'May I see her now?'

Hammond thought about it, clicking one of the pens in his white coat pocket.

'She's in the single room down the hall. Bed twenty-three.'

37

Anya knocked and pushed open a large wooden door. Lying face upwards was a large-framed woman with a crown of mousey brown hair.

'Hello, my name is Dr Anya Crichton. Professor Hammond has asked if I could have a talk to you.'

The woman stared at the ceiling.

'Don't worry, I'm not a psychiatrist. I actually wanted to talk about your physical condition.'

Clear liquid dripped from a burette to a cannula in the woman's right arm. She remained silent, an occasional blink confirming she was conscious.

'It's all right. You're safe here. No-one's going to hurt you.'

Anya thought she saw the woman's face muscles tighten.

A young nurse with a bouncy ponytail wafted in, carrying a box of flowers and a kidney dish containing a syringe and glass vial. 'Looks like someone cares for you,' she said. 'These are absolutely gorgeous.' She placed the box on the windowsill then filled the burette with the syringe's contents.

'Antibiotic time. May sting a little in your arm, but it won't last long,' she added, without looking directly at her patient.

She attached a bright orange sticker to the plastic tubing and glanced at the food tray on a table beside the bed.

'You haven't touched your food,' she said. 'Do you need some help?'

The woman didn't answer. She kept staring at something on the white speckled ceiling.

'Come on now, your body has a lot of healing to do. If you don't start eating soon, we're going to have to tube feed you. Is that what you want?'

No response.

Anya watched the sorry scene. The mystery patient was helpless in the situation. Eating soggy fish and unrecognisable vegetables wouldn't have been a priority for her either. She waited until the nurse hurumphed and took the tray away.

'I don't blame you for turning that lunch down. If you like, I can organise a toasted sandwich for you from the café downstairs.'

The woman flicked her eyes in Anya's direction and frowned.

'I remember when I was in hospital with my son,' she went on, 'I came out lighter than my pre-pregnancy weight. I'm sure the food is meant to scare people into thinning down.'

The woman closed her eyes for a few seconds. Anya didn't know whether she'd struck a chord

316

about being in hospital with a child, or bored the woman more than the nurse had.

Four bouquets lined the shelf on one side of the room, two more sat on the windowsill. Anya walked around admiring them and noticing the card. No message, just the hospital florist's card on each arrangement. She wondered how anyone knew to send flowers when the woman hadn't disclosed her identity.

Anya moved a chair to the side of the bed and sat down.

'When you came into hospital, you had a blistering rash which the staff noticed when they put the catheter into your bladder. Those rashes are usually very painful. Even passing urine must have been agony.'

The woman closed her eyes again and held her breath.

'The lab found that this infection is very unusual. Part of my job is to work out how you acquired it. I can also help identify the person, or people spreading the infection, so they can be treated appropriately. It might help others from suffering the way you have.

'Usually,' Anya straightened the creases from the bed blanket with one hand, 'we try to locate sexual partners you have had in the last six months.'

Moments later, a sole tear slid from the woman's right eye onto the pillow.

Anya couldn't begin to wonder what pain this

woman had experienced, emotionally, physically and maybe even spiritually. She reached over and gently brushed her shoulder.

'I'm worried that someone tried to hurt you. And you're not the only one. There have been others.'

The woman's eyes became glassy and her breathing slowed.

'I hurt myself,' she whispered.

'You must have been suffering a lot at the time. Something drove you to it.' Anya wanted to find out more and tried to gain her confidence. 'Someone, or maybe even a group of people you trusted did this to you.'

'You don't understand,' the woman said softly. 'I did it to myself. No-one else is to blame.'

Anya wasn't accustomed to dealing with suicidal people. Someone who'd just been raped needed medical attention. The counsellors dealt with the long-term psychological problems. She wanted information, not to upset the woman, who was clearly emotionally fragile. She turned her attention to the flowers. 'These are all beautiful. Do you know who sent them?'

'You're wasting your time. I want you to leave.'

'All right. The least I can do is get you a sandwich from the café.' Anya placed a straw in a glass of water on the bedside table and offered it.

'I'd like to come back tomorrow and sit with you, if you don't mind.'

The woman took a sip and licked her cracked lips.

'You're wasting your time,' she said. 'He didn't want me to die. He tried to save me.'

38

'Who is he?' Anya pressed. 'Is he alone, or does he work in a group?'

The woman reached down to her side and and pressed the call button twice. The ponytailed nurse quickly arrived with some tablets.

'Still got pain? No wonder. It's well over four hours since the last dose.' The uniformed sister seemed to sense tension as she scrawled on the bedchart. 'Is everything all right?'

'I need to ask your patient some more questions.' Anya had to find out where she'd been and who the man was. The police could take it from there.

'I don't have anything to say. Make her go,' the woman begged.

'I'm sorry, but you'll have to come back another time.' The nurse put the tablets in a small paper vial on the bedside table. 'As soon as these are on board, it's time for a sponge bath.'

Anya didn't want to leave. This was the only woman so far who'd survived, and she'd only lived by sheer fluke. Once she'd had pain relief, she would probably become drowsy and less lucid. 'Could I please just have one more minute before you give the tablets?'

The ponytail swished. 'I think our patient has made it very clear she wants you to leave.'

Now wasn't the time to make a scene. Anya decided to come back when a different shift of nurses was on duty, and not at bathing time. Frustrated she left the room. Who the hell was *he*? She'd come so close to finding out. And why did he want to save this woman? Nothing made sense. If he'd pushed her from the cliff, why would she say he'd tried to rescue her? Had he done the same to the other women? Or was she talking about her soul being saved?

Outside the room, Anya brushed past a woman dressed in a burgundy suit, holding a young child on one hip. The woman didn't seem to notice Anya turn and watch as she peered in through the door of room twenty-three. The visitor pressed her forehead against the door but didn't go in.

Anya approached. 'Can I help you?'

'It's her. It's definitely her.' The woman said without looking up. 'It's Briony.'

The toddler buried her face in the suit.

'Do you know this patient?' Anya couldn't believe the lucky timing.

'Mummy? Where's Mummy?' the little girl called as her carer turned and hurried towards the lifts.

'Wait.' Anya followed. 'Please wait a moment.'

The woman stopped by the nurses' station and stared at the floor. 'I saw the picture in the paper and came to identify her. Briony Lovitt. There. It's done. Now, Georgia, we have to go.'

'Georgia's a pretty name,' Anya said, stepping fowards. 'And you are absolutely beautiful. Who have you got here?'

Georgia hid her face, sneaking a peek at her inquisitor as she held up a soft green dinosaur with bright yellow spots, white gloves and hat.

'I know who that is. It's Dorothy, from the Wiggles, isn't it?' Anya beamed. 'She's one of my favourites.'

The little girl turned her face and revealed two soulful blue eyes. 'Do you know my other mummy?'

'I'm not sure. Is your mother's name Briony?'

'It used to be, now it's just Julie,' the little girl stroked her carer's hair. Buzzers lit the backboard as nurses hurried past with bedpans and wet towels.

Patient names written on the whiteboard blurred in contrast with the block letters next to number twenty-three, which read, 'UNIDENTIFIED FEMALE'.

'I'm Julie Everingham,' the woman explained. 'Do I need to sign anything before we leave to say I've identified Briony?' Her eyes referred to the whiteboard. 'You can change that now.'

Her tone was defensive, but businesslike. This was a professional woman, judging by the Bally shoes and expensive suit, probably a Carla Zampatti design. Her fingernails were neat but unpainted, and her make-up and hair, low maintenance.

The nursing unit manager, whose uniform and

hair remained pristine each shift due to a lack of patient contact, appeared. 'Excuse me, but did you call from downstairs about our mystery patient?'

'Yes, but if you don't mind, I need a few minutes.'

The NUM seemed taken aback but had no choice.

'This must be very difficult for you,' Anya ventured. 'I think it's been difficult for Briony, too.'

'She has no-one to blame but herself,' Julie said, fighting back tears. She placed Georgia on the counter and pulled an embroidered handkerchief from her black leather tote bag. Georgia swung her legs and smiled.

Anya instinctively moved closer to protect the child from falling. 'What's your favourite song? I like "Do the Monkey".'

'Oo oo aa aa,' Georgia began singing softly, slapping her floral pinafore to the beat.

Since becoming a mother, Anya had learnt all the popular children's songs, games and television shows. It made the bond with her son even stronger, and gave her an instant advantage connecting to other children. The singing and dancing Wiggles quartet had become a universal hit. Anya believed they had done for kids' appreciation of music what J.K. Rowling had achieved for children's literacy.

With Georgia happy, she turned again to the woman. 'It's very important that I speak with you, if you have the time.'

Julie agreed and lifted her daughter from the counter. Anya informed the NUM they'd be back shortly and escorted them to a relatives' room on the same level. Once inside, Julie gave Georgia a small box of sultanas and a book from her bag. The trio found a lounge chair and sat.

'May I ask why Georgia said Briony used to be her mother?'

Julie's face couldn't disguise the hurt. 'She was, until she walked out on us. Georgia called us both Mum.'

Anya realised they were a single-sex couple. The 'J.E.' tattooed on Briony was for her lover. 'How long ago did she leave?'

'A few weeks ago. We were at a play gym in the local shopping centre. Briony said she wanted something from the car. After about half an hour, she sent me an SMS saying she had some thinking to do and would be gone for a few days. I suppose we should be grateful she left us the car.'

'You didn't have any warning that she wanted to leave?'

'None.' She combed Georgia's hair with her fingers. 'You think you know someone.'

Anya had experienced the same sense of desertion. 'May I ask about the biological father? Was he involved?'

'No. A male friend donated his sperm but didn't want to have anything to do with parenting. He moved to Singapore a year ago.'

Anya wanted to know more, without giving anything away about the other cases. 'The situation in which Briony was found isn't unique. I'm concerned she may not have left of her own free will.'

'Well, the letter she sent said it all. She'd found herself and realised she'd sinned by being with another woman. She wanted to redeem herself and purge all evil from her life. That meant leaving Georgia and me.' She twisted the toddler's hair into a plait as Georgia entertained herself with the book. 'How can this child be the work of the devil? It was Briony's idea to have a commitment ceremony and conceive. We shared the parenting and I thought things were great between us.'

'What if she didn't leave you voluntarily? What if she were abducted?'

'Is that what she claims?' Julie shook her head. 'Always could embellish a story, the original drama queen. Look. The letter was in her handwriting. In the end, it's all the same. What am I supposed to say to our daughter when she asks? I didn't plan on being a single parent, and financially everything's a mess. I just wish she'd thought of someone else other than herself when she left.'

Anya sympathised with the woman, so hurt at being abandoned by the person she thought was her life partner.

'Would you like to speak to her, for Georgia's sake?' Anya added, 'She's very ill. It might help you to get some answers.'

'No. I don't want anything to do with her. Briony's made her choice. My lawyer will take it from here.'

Julie Everingham was back in control, her strength and pride admirable. She collected some loose sultanas from the floor and wiped Georgia's hands and mouth with a wet towel from her bag.

'We'd better see that nurse and fill in the paperwork. Then we can get you home for a bath,' she said, and grabbing the book, toy and Georgia's hand she left the room.

The little girl turned and blew Anya a kiss. The tiny child would one day need to know why a parent had rejected her. For Georgia's sake, Anya hoped she could find the answers.

39

Returning to her office, Anya couldn't help
wondering why a woman would leave her child and
partner after finding religion. Briony obviously
thought of 'him' as some kind of saviour. How
could anyone reject little Georgia, such an innocent and loving child, and accuse her of being the
devil's work? It went against the most basic maternal
instinct. She wondered who the leader was, and
how he converted the women, encouraging them
to leave behind everyone they loved. Whoever he
was, he must have incredible charisma. He
commanded loyalty, even though Briony had almost
died in his care.

What was Briony doing in the mountains? Is
that where the group lived, the place it took new
recruits? There wasn't a cult mentioned out west
of Sydney, although the Blue Mountains had its
share of alternative lifestylers. If she tried to escape,
she might have fallen accidentally. So why was she
saying he saved her life?

Nothing about Briony Lovitt made sense. The
message and letter she had sent let Julie know she
had chosen to leave. But if she'd been taken,

anyone could have sent the message using her mobile phone. Kate Farrer might agree to find out where the letter was sent from, which may give a clue as to where Briony stayed after she'd disappeared.

Someone or a group was out there collecting women and managing to get them killed. If Debbie Finch had been abducted, maybe she hadn't shot her father by choice, and was forced to have oral sex with the man in the house. Anya thought of the women she'd examined who'd been subject to the same act during a sexual assault.

By the time Anya had put her bag down in her office, Elaine had printed out information on two local cults, along with a note about having to leave early. No messages from Kate yet.

Disappointed, Anya sat down to read. One group on the Central Coast had recently been raided for sexually abusing young girls in its compound. A self-proclaimed Messiah led the other cult and wanted to ascend to heaven with his followers when the Apocalypse came.

The computer on the desk made a ringing sound, indicating new e-mail. Vaughan's message, thanking her for a wonderful day at the Show, took her by surprise. He seemed more effusive than in person. She hit the reply button and typed a response, concentrating on the articles he had given her. She finished with a question.

'Are you aware of a phenomenon in which a

woman has been abducted by a cult and then adopted the cult's teachings, even refusing to contact her family, given the opportunity? I'm particularly interested in instances in which cult members had initially been abducted.' She hit the send button.

Immediately, an e-mail appeared in her inbox. Vaughan couldn't have answered that quickly. She clicked on the message, which was titled 'lung fibres', the subject header she'd used when posting questions about the fibres on the forensic list groups. Someone must have recognised the fibre!

The author introduced himself as Dr Felix Rosenbaum, a retired respiratory physician living in Bowral, two hours from Sydney. He explained that he had been in China for the last month and had only just checked his mail.

Anya could hardly believe what she read. The physician recalled a fibre similar to the one she scanned, in a case he had treated over forty years ago. It involved a sound engineer with lung cancer, if his memory served him correctly.

Clearly, Felix Rosenbaum was mentally and physically active if he travelled around China. He had the files from the case at his property. If she wanted to see them, they could arrange a meeting. He would prefer to meet in person if possible, because poor hearing made phone conversations difficult for him.

Anya checked her diary and sent a reply

suggesting they meet the day after tomorrow in Bowral. The sooner, the better, she thought.

Her inbox beeped again and she realised Vaughan Hunter had been online. His message had her baffled. All it said was 'Stockholm syndrome'. She vaguely remembered the name from a psychology lecture from years ago, which described people falling in love with their captors during sieges. Apart from that, her mind was blank on the topic. Typing the name of the syndrome into the search engine produced a list of hundreds of sites.

Damn! Anya tapped her fingers on the desk in frustration. She was no longer in the mood to sit and digest psychobabble. She needed to clear her mind and vent some frustration. Upstairs at the drums, she readjusted the stool and counted in time. Within minutes she felt her shoulders relax and her legs and arms work in rhythm as she played along to 'Unchain My Heart'. For once, she didn't worry about getting the song perfect. No stopping and starting again because of mistakes. Improvising, she played louder and longer than usual. Bugger Mrs Bugalugs next door. She smiled at the thought.

Half an hour and ten songs later, perspiration covered her forehead and chest. This was so much more relaxing than the gym. Putting down the sticks, she resolved to face the Internet again. With a sloppy joe covering the damp T-shirt, she headed downstairs to the office computer. This time she typed the term 'brainwashing with Stockholm syndrome'.

She clicked on an article about brainwashing victims into submission. It talked about prisoners of war, and referred to a young British woman who had been kidnapped for a ransom and was found out to have joined the terrorist group that held her hostage. The young woman had been imprisoned for bombing a police car in Northern Ireland, but her lawyer argued she'd been brainwashed during her time in captivity. While in prison, she had tried to smuggle love letters to the man who orchestrated her kidnapping.

Anya immediately focused on the woman's story. She searched for information on 'Wendy Privet' and found a number of articles in psychiatric journals dedicated to the case.

One described a syndrome in which abducted people were grateful to their kidnappers for not killing them. Through isolation, victims became dependent on their captors, and some developed an affinity for them, to the point of wanting to testify or raise money to defend their captors after being released.

The syndrome was named after a 1973 siege in a bank in Stockholm, Sweden. Four bank staff held captive in a bank vault for six days developed empathy with their machine-gun toting captor. They actually feared the police, who they saw as dangerous. Without intervention they could survive, but if the police provoked their captor, violence was the only likely outcome. It was assumed that they sided with the person holding them hostage out of fear and, in part, denial. Anya printed out the information and decided to show Kate Farrer in person.

40

Inside Kate's flat the following evening, Anya tried not to step on papers and CD cases littering the floor. Kate lifted a plate with a half-eaten taco on it and cleared a space for her friend on the couch.

'Aren't Virgos supposed to be obsessively tidy?' Anya asked.

'Do you believe in the tooth fairy, too? I haven't spent much time here lately,' Kate said, wandering into the kitchenette. 'Can I get you a drink? Light beer?'

'Great, thanks.'

Kate returned with two small bottles and unscrewed the lids, tossing them into the bin across the room.

'How was the Show last weekend?' she asked, handing one over and sitting cross-legged on the floor.

'We had fun. Vaughan Hunter's good company and was great with Ben.'

'Never trust anyone with a slimy handshake. If you ask me, he's a bit too smooth.'

Anya took a sip and used the bottle to catch a

dribble from her chin. 'Is there anyone you do trust?'

Kate changed the subject. 'Sorry I didn't get back to you. The boss was bawling me out about wasting time on closed cases. I don't think I can do much more about the Matthews or Deab cases.'

'We've located another woman who died with the same type of lung fibres. A doctor who simply disappeared and was found a while later overdosed in a hotel room. Not only did she have the identical lung fibres, and shaved pubic hair, but turns out she had genital herpes, drug-resistant, just like Fatima Deab's.'

Kate took a drink and raised her eyebrows. 'I'm listening.'

'There's more. A woman survived a fall from up near Govetts Leap. Number three case of drug-resistant herpes, which is, again, pretty uncommon. Turns out she left her child and female partner. Just disappeared one day, but sent a text message followed by a letter saying she'd started a new life. A few weeks later she is found, body shattered from a fall she shouldn't have survived.'

'I agree there are definite similarities.' Kate thought for a moment. 'I need more. Can the one who survived be interviewed?'

Anya knew this would cause a problem. 'She refused to speak up until today. Wouldn't even give her name in hospital. All she said to me was that he, whoever "he" is, tried to save her.'

'Did he try to catch her when she fell?'

'I don't think so. She didn't have any scratches or bruises on her hands that looked like someone had grabbed her.'

'What was she doing on the cliff in the first place?'

'I don't know.' Anya took a large sip and wiped her mouth. 'But the lab is testing the herpes virus she had which should determine if it's the exact same strain as Fatima's and the doctor's infections.'

'Hang on. Are you saying two other women had sexual contact with the Deab girl? This is getting sicker.'

'No. They might have had sex with the same man as one, or all of the others. It's possible the virus strain is being passed around a group of people.'

'That would ring some alarm bells. Same guy, two dead, the other nearly dead. If you can tie her to Clare Matthews, or Debbie Finch, we'd have more to go on to reopen the investigations into the deaths.'

Anya ran her finger over the condensation on the bottle. 'I've been reading about cults.'

Kate rolled her eyes. 'Now you're sounding crazy.'

'Hear me out. If the women joined a cult, by their own volition or by force, that could explain at least why the surviving woman seems to idolise some bloke she thinks wanted to save her. Often cult leaders sleep with the women followers, hoping to inseminate them with their genes, and as a way

335

of confirming the disciples' place in the group. It's also somewhere the women could live for weeks at a time, and may be the place they all inhaled the fibres. A cult is a definite possibility.'

'I can't take a bloody theory about cults to my commanding officer. We've got to have something more tangible. Some kind of physical evidence to link her to the other women. How about I start with the one who came off the cliff?' Kate reached across and grabbed a notebook and pen from beside the phone. 'What's her name and where is she?'

Anya hesitated. 'I can't tell you that.'

'Don't shit me. What's her name?'

'I'm serious, Kate. I can't breach confidentiality. She has to be guaranteed anonymity.'

The detective stood up. 'You doctors are full of bloody principles when it suits you. You have no problems naming a child abuser, or telling the Roads and Traffic Authority someone isn't fit to drive. So why the crap about confidentiality now?'

'It's different, and you know that.' Anya didn't find the decision as simple as her friend made it sound. 'We're legally bound to notify child abuse, and people who are potentially a danger to themselves or others.'

'What do you call someone who falls off a bloody cliff? Why don't you let her out and see if she'll do it again? See how safe she is to herself?'

Anya put down her bottle on an old *Police Journal*. She couldn't win an argument with Kate right now with emotion, so she tried logic. 'Maybe

336

there is a way to establish whether Clare and Debbie had contact with the same man.'

Kate stood sceptically, hands on her hips.

'Hear me out. Clare Matthews was initially ruled a suspicious death, because of scratch marks on her ears.'

'Yeah, I was called but it ended up a false alarm.'

'Once a death is deemed suspicious, all the specimens are labelled with a fluorescent orange sticker and the specimens kept. They're not discarded, like in routine cases.'

Kate crossed her arms, 'So . . . ?'

'She was pregnant and if I know Peter Latham, he would have wanted a sample taken of the foetus. The specimen would have been tagged with orange stickers and no-one would dare throw one of those out. That means we could compare the DNA from the foetus to the DNA in the semen from Debbie Finch's throat. If the two match, you've got some interesting physical evidence.'

'All right, I'll arrange it. We can get to the witness later. If Debbie and Clare both had sex with the same man and we can prove it, forget the cult stuff. We could be looking at a serial killer. One who finally made a mistake.'

41

The next morning, Anya arrived at the home of Dr Rosenbaum, five kilometres from the Bowral turnoff on the Hume Highway. Recent rains following one of the longest droughts on record meant much of the grassland had turned green, giving the place a warm, welcoming feel. She had stopped at a shop in town and bought some marmalade, plum jam and sourdough, as a token for morning tea.

A balding, slightly stooped gentleman opened an oak front door, flanked on both sides by green and red stained-glass panels. The glass probably originated in the late nineteenth century, as did the house. Felix Rosenbaum dug one hand into a grey cardigan pocket and with the other hand, ushered Anya into an elaborate foyer with black and white marble tiles laid in a chess-board pattern. Light shone through a skylight, one of the few modern accessories.

'You have a beautiful home,' she said, handing him the parcel of bread and condiments.

He seemed genuinely overwhelmed by the gesture. 'Your coming was enough, really.'

Anya took off her long jacket and placed it over

a chaise longue. 'With such high ceilings, how do you manage to keep the place warm in winter?' she asked.

'Since my wife died, I tend to stay pretty much in the kitchen, which gets the afternoon sun. The wood stove in there does the job.'

Mention of his wife seemed to make his shoulders droop a little.

Anya felt the temperature fall about ten degrees when he opened the glass sliding doors to a lounge room that boasted a bay window, in front of which stood a full-sized concert harp.

She stood in awe at the magnificence of the instrument. As for so many people, harps held an almost mythical quality for her. She put her hands behind her back to resist the temptation to touch it.

'Do you play?' Felix enquired.

'No,' she lamented, 'just an admirer. The gold decoration on the column is stunning.'

'My wife thought so, too. She used to play, you know. I could have sat here for hours as she practised. Mind you, I was prone to falling asleep on the odd occasion, if on call had been particularly busy. She was always insulted, of course, but I assured her that her music was so relaxing, falling asleep was indeed a compliment.'

Anya smiled. This man reminded her of many of the senior doctors she had learnt from. Always good for an anecdote, and devoted to the wives they 'widowed' until retirement.

He stood touching the instrument with tenderness, as though it were his wife, herself.

'This harp was used in a tour with Dame Joan Sutherland. Picked it up through the Harp Society over twenty years ago. Had it restored, naturally, but I'm afraid the changes in temperature play havoc with the strings. My Eva used to say that a harp had to be played, or both its soul and sound would rot.' He let go of the wood and wiped some dust off the soundboard with his cardigan sleeve. 'Maybe I'm a sentimental fool, but I can't bear to get rid of it. Now,' he said, straightening a fraction, 'about this case that has your interest.'

Dr Rosenbaum opened another set of sliding glass doors, these ones leading into an antique dining room. He pulled out a chair for her at one end of the cedar table buried beneath a stack of books and papers. He sat beside her and opened a faded envelope. It contained a pile of cards covered in obsessively neat handwriting, and carbon copies of typed correspondence.

'This fellow came to me with weight loss and shortness of breath in 1957. Phil Abbott. A nice fellow, I remember because he had a true passion for music. Chest X-ray showed calcification and pleural thickening. I trust you saw the slide images I e-mailed.'

'Yes. They were very clear.'

He carefully removed an X-ray from a package mended with yellowing sticky tape, handed it to his guest and walked to the doorway to switch on the chandelier. Anya held the X-ray towards the light source. White spots on the lung periphery looked exactly like calcium deposits seen in cancer. She noticed the patient had large lungs, and flat diaphragm markings, suggesting hyperinflation. He had signs of airflow obstruction such as emphysema as well. In cases like these, asbestos disease in smokers was far more dangerous than in non-smokers. 'Did he smoke?'

'Never. None of his family did, either, which was unusual back then. That's why his case played on my mind for so long.'

Dr Rosenbaum switched off the chandelier.

'Of course, we didn't have CT scans back then. There wasn't much we could do to detect soft tissue tumours, except in the brain. And we only diagnosed them by injecting air during a lumbar puncture and taking X-rays of the brain to show up any compression or obstruction to the air.' He sat back at the table and opened a textbook of radiographic procedures over the last century. He located an image of the procedure and slid the book to Anya. 'That's how George Gershwin, the greatest composer of our time, went. Did you know that he had headaches and used to smell burning rubber when he played piano? People thought him depressed or crazy back in '37. Today we recognise the symptoms as classic for temporal lobe pathology, but of course, that's with CAT scans and MRI. Back then they did the LP and made the poor fellow's headache worse in the process.'

Anya enjoyed the anecdotes, but knew it would take a while to answer all her questions. The doctor had the unenviable combination of knowledge and a gift of storytelling in a world where almost no-one remained to listen.

'Can you tell me what you remember about your patient's work?'

'Ah, he and his cousin were sound engineers with the ABC, back when that stood for Australian Broadcasting Commission. Of course, it's now a corporation. Phil did balance tests for the Sydney Symphony Orchestra. I remember, you see, because my brother was the ABC concert manager and used to get us tickets.'

'What was a balance test?'

'The sound engineer's job was to balance the sound so that one instrument didn't dominate the orchestra. That entailed using a VU meter, a small box, something with a needle on it – it looked a little like a battery tester, you could say, except it measured sound intensity. That way he could perfectly position the various microphones relative to the orchestra players. They use room-sized electronic mixers today, and I don't believe the sound is much better than we had.'

A grandfather clock chimed ten times. Felix pulled a small pillbox from his trouser pocket and swallowed a tablet dry.

'Did you have any idea where the fibre he inhaled could have come from?'

'For a while I wondered whether it was in the

speakers he worked on. You see, he was obsessed with perfecting an amplifier for the electric guitar. Cost him his marriage, and, who knows, possibly even his life.'

'Did you investigate the amplifiers as a potential source of the fibre?'

'No, his wife burnt everything after the funeral. I think they had a small daughter, from memory, he called her Meggie. I kept the lung slides and you may borrow them, if you wish, provided you return them.'

'I'd appreciate that. We've seen the fibres turn up in a number of women post-mortem and are trying to identify the source.'

'I hope you can. He suffered the horrid end we, as physicians, try desperately to prevent.'

Anya copied some of the details from Dr Rosenbaum's notes. Felix stood and rubbed his hands together.

'Now, for morning tea, if you'll do me the pleasure of joining me.'

'Just one cup, and then I have to go.' She smiled, knowing she'd be lucky to get away before lunch, and not until he'd regaled her with more stories from times and people long gone, people who may hold the key to mysteries of the present.

'Before you put the kettle on, do you recall the daughter's full name by any chance?'

'I used to always document family members, so I could ask about them by name. Always seemed more personal when we met.' He shuffled his file cards and deciphered a scribble in one corner, which he'd circled. 'That's it. He called her Meggie, but that's right, her name was Lucinda Margaret.'

'And the address?'

'Seventy-two Lennox Crescent, Pennant Hills.'

42

Anya stopped outside the hospital florist. A row of white buckets contained mixed bunches of gerberas, baby's breath, roses, and her favourite, deep purple irises. On a stand stood boxes of arrangements for all occasions, with red and yellow the dominant themes. Inside the small shop, a young woman put a lavender ribbon around an enormous white bouquet.

'Hi, I was wondering if you could help me with a couple of things. I'm Dr Crichton, and I noticed some gorgeous flowers of yours up in room twenty-three, third floor. Is that your design, or did the person who ordered them specify what they wanted?'

The young woman took a minute. 'Room twenty-three. We've done a new bunch every day for that patient. Someone is pretty keen to impress her. He leaves it up to me, but asks for something extra special.'

'He must be a nice guy.'

'I just talk to him on the phone. But he sounds so romantic, and pretty cute.' She stifled a giggle.

Kidnapping, brainwashing and killing weren't

Anya's ideas of romance. 'You mean he doesn't even see what he's ordered?'

'No, he says he's seen our work and loved it. What's the other thing I can do for you?' she asked, placing the bouquet to the side of the counter top.

'I'm trying to locate the person sending the flowers.' Anya knew she wasn't a good liar, but tried anyway. 'You see, I'm concerned he may be walking around totally unaware he has a serious medical condition.'

'Oh, my God! That's terrible.'

Anya felt guilty playing on the girl's emotions, but she needed more information. 'You may be his best chance of getting help.'

The girl plucked at her floral apron, to which the name badge 'Taylah' was pinned. 'We're not supposed to give out information about our clients.'

'I understand that, and respect that you have a strong code of confidentiality. Imagine the mess if people found out who sent them Valentine's roses?'

'That's right.' Taylah smiled. 'You do understand.'

'But in this case, it's very important that I find this person. He may be ill right now.'

'Gosh, I wish I could help,' she whispered, as a man browsed outside the shop window. 'But he does it all by phone and all I know is, an envelope with cash in it comes through internal mail. Last lot was enough to pay for two weeks' worth of flowers.'

'Do you have the envelope, by any chance?' Anya realised that the chances were minimal.

Taylah shook her head.

'Does he call you from inside the hospital?'

'I dunno.'

Anya pushed for any morsel. 'Sometimes phones have a double ring when it's an outside call. It only does it once if the call originates in the hospital.'

She tilted her head, as though listening. 'Come to think of it, you're right. It does have different rings. When my mum rings from her work, it always rings twice. He's definitely not in the hospital.'

Whoever 'he' is, this man phoned from outside, but paid via the internal mail system. So far, that could mean an employee, possibly a shift worker, who called during shop hours from outside. Then again, he might not even work at the hospital.

'Do you have any idea where the internal mail comes from?'

Taylah kept an eye on the fellow outside the shop. 'Could be anywhere. There's a big letterbox in the foyer and other places all over the departments. It's collected, sorted and delivered. Tons of it every day.'

Great, Anya thought. Try again.

'Do calls come directly to you, or do they come through the switch?'

'We've had problems with our line, so switch puts them through.'

Anya knew there was no chance of checking phone records. Switchboards at hospitals the size of Western District handled thousands of calls per day.

'Did he give a name?'

'No, but he calls me by my name, probably 'cause I say it when I answer.'

The man entered the shop carrying a box of red carnations.

'Excuse me, can I help you sir? Beautiful, aren't they?'

As he opened his wallet and exchanged pleasantries, Anya excused herself, left her card on the counter and asked if Taylah could let her know when he called again.

'I hope he'll be okay,' the florist said as she put the card in her apron pocket.

For whatever reason, it seemed pretty obvious. The mystery man didn't want to be found, and knew exactly how to stay anonymous. That made him even more disturbing.

Stopping at the cafeteria, Anya bought a vegetarian Turkish bread and took the lift to the third floor. With the door of room twenty-three ajar, she entered.

Briony Lovitt lay staring at the ceiling.

'May we talk for a few minutes? It's Dr Crichton.'

No response.

'I brought real food again, in case you're hungry.'

Briony glanced in the direction of the food and looked away again.

'I'll put it beside you, if you like,' Anya offered.

'What do you *want* from me?'

Anya moved a little closer. 'You've had a terrible time and I want to help.'

'I don't need your help.'

'At least, eat something. Some suffering can't be avoided. But if someone throws you relief from another hospital meal,' she bent forwards, 'for God's sake, don't pass it up.'

Slowly, Briony turned her eyes towards the peace offering. With one hand she took a half and tore off a small piece with her other hand. She seemed to be savouring the sight and smell of it.

'How are you feeling?' Anya asked.

'How am I supposed to feel? Stuck flat on my back, crippled, having to answer stupid, banal questions. How would you feel if every second person gave you perky platitudes? The regular nurses are full of them, telling me to be cheerful, no matter what's happened. Just like Polly-fucking-anna. Except in Disneyland, she walked again.' The woman rolled her eyes. 'Then there are the relief nurses. They look at me with pity. "Poor cripple, let's whisper around her in case she gets upset." I don't know which is worse. They all go home on both legs, while I'm stuck here.'

Anya pulled the curtain around the bed and forced Briony to make eye contact. She'd never been good at counselling and usually either resorted to giving medical information or sat silently. She couldn't even begin to imagine what this woman had gone through, or what she felt, and didn't pretend to.

'The emergency doctor might have thought you wouldn't walk again, but I've read your notes. Tests show there's a ninety per cent chance your spinal cord will recover and you'll regain use and feeling in your legs. You've suffered a type of spinal shock from the fall and the swelling needs to go down before anyone knows for sure what the prognosis is.'

'The bits I can feel are painful, but I don't care about that.' Briony chewed a bite of the bread.

'I met Georgia the other day.'

Briony froze and seemed to hold a swallow.

'She's the most beautiful child.' Anya studied the woman for a reaction – anything.

'She's better off without me.' The mother turned her face away.

'You can't really believe that?'

The door opened and the humming of a floor polisher became louder. The cleaner pushed the machine under the curtain, defeating the point of privacy. During her resident years, Anya had argued many times that if the curtains were closed, cleaners should come back later. She was usually met with comments like, 'We've all got our jobs to do. Yours isn't any more important than anybody else's.' Staff too frequently lost sight of the fact that hospitals were there to care for patients.

'You don't know anything about me.'

Anya pulled a chair closer to the bed and sat. 'You're right. You are a stranger, but I know what a mother feels. I have a son the same age and it aches to be away from your children. You'd die for them.'

'That's why she's better off the way things are.'

Anya poured water from a jug into a plastic cup and offered it, not wanting to cause any more distress. It would take time to gain Briony's trust. She hadn't said much, but at least she had spoken. The art of medicine came in listening to what people *didn't* say.

'Where do you think you'll go when you're discharged?'

Briony took a sip and ignored her interviewer.

'The herpes infection you had when you were admitted was pretty severe. Is there any chance you'd had episodes before?'

'Is that what this is about?' Briony almost spilt the drink. 'Julie doesn't have to worry. It's got nothing to do with her.'

'It's my job to notify anyone who has come in sexual contact with the virus. I realise this is very personal, but it's standard practice to try to curtail the spread. The type of herpes you have is resistant to drugs and quite difficult to treat.'

Briony didn't comment.

Anya decided to take a risk. 'Other women, in similar circumstances to you, had the same type of infection, only they were all found dead. I have to ask you this: were you sexually assaulted?'

Briony closed her eyes. 'No. I didn't refuse, if that's what you mean. Happy now?'

'I'm not judging you. Please understand that.'

A cheery woman with a clipboard knocked on the door and poked her head around the curtain.

351

'TV rental, would you like your set connected?'

Briony shot her an icy look. 'Leave me alone!'

'Okay, I'll be back tomorrow if you change your mind.' The woman rolled her eyes and left.

So much for privacy.

'I don't think your fall was an accident,' Anya said.

Briony clenched the bedclothes. 'You still don't get it, do you?'

'Then tell me,' Anya pleaded. 'Help me to understand.'

After a long silence, Briony began to speak. 'He took me up to the mountains, for a trip out, he said, somewhere private where no-one would see us. Suddenly, he changed, like he did in the beginning. I don't know what I did to make him so mad. It was like his whole face was different. His eyes turned black and so full of hate. I didn't know what to do. I tried making things okay again but he just got madder. I panicked and tried to run away, something I promised him I would never do.'

'What happened then?' Anya almost whispered.

'I slipped on a rock and fell onto a small ledge. All I could do was cling to a branch above my head. I begged him to help me but he just stared, like I was some dumb animal. I could feel my hand slipping. It was freezing. I kept begging him but he just stood there, staring.

'Then he said the time had come to make the choice. I'd done this to myself, betrayed my lover, child, everything I was supposed to believe in. I

352

didn't deserve to have a child. She didn't deserve someone pathetic and weak like me in her life.'

Briony sounded detached. She could have been discussing a grocery list.

'He was right. Everything he said was true. He told me my daughter would be better off with me dead. Never having to face a mother who had abandoned her, or deal with the grief of rejection. If I didn't go with him, it would have been someone else. If I died now, Georgia wouldn't remember. That way, she'd suffer less.'

She twisted the sheet tightly around her finger. The tip turned a dark red, then blue. 'Then he put his hands out to help me up. After saying all that.'

'None of what he said was true,' Anya stressed. 'He was lying. Some cruel, sick game.'

Briony took a breath and winced. 'He was right. Georgia is better off never knowing me. I failed her. And what about Julie? I heard her voice outside when she came. Julie doesn't forgive, ever. So what do I have left? My business can't have survived. Health, I don't have that. I have nothing.'

She began to cry. Tears turned to sobs and Anya, tempted to call a nurse, hesitated and put her hand on Briony's forehead. She sat silently, stroking the poor woman's forehead. She'd endured a hell of a trauma, but implied she was a willing participant, in sex, at least. A while later, the sobs subsided.

'I have to ask. Who is he?'

'I don't know. I don't even know his name.'

Anya held her hand, too. 'What about where he lives?'

'I don't know. He said it was a surprise and put a blindfold on my eyes.'

Anya wiped Briony's face with a hand towel from beside the bed. 'He played mind games with you. You're not the first one this has happened to.' She realised how callous this might have sounded but kept on. 'Did you meet any other people when you were with him?'

'No, he said I'd meet the others one day.'

Others? Anya wondered, was he part of a group, or was that another lie to manipulate women?

Briony closed her eyes. 'I don't want to talk anymore. Could you please ask the nurse if I can have some pain tablets?'

'Sure. Do you mind if I ask two more things? What made you go with him?'

Briony turned her head away. 'He said his baby was inside, and he'd accidentally locked the keys in the car. I went to help. There wasn't really a baby.'

So that's how he got women into his car. From there he could restrain, drug, or do anything to them, without anyone else knowing or seeing, even in a shopping-centre car park. 'How did you finally get away?'

Briony swallowed hard. 'I didn't get away. I let go.'

43

After leaving the hospital, Anya called the nursing home to ask about Lucy Tait's birth certificate. The director confirmed that Lucinda Abbott's mother had remarried after Phil's death from lung disease. Kel Tait adopted his stepdaughter, which was how she became known as Lucy Tait.

Anya felt drained from the visit with Briony. Driving back to Annandale gave her time to think and unwind without interruption. Lucy's mother's post-mortem showed death from a massive stroke, and no sign of lung disease or infiltration with fibrous material. Either she had been extremely lucky, or had never been exposed to the fibres, which meant they could have been inhaled some-where other than the family house.

Phil Abbott could have brought them home on his work clothes and transferred them to his young child through cuddling. Anya doubted that, as the mother would have been exposed when doing the washing, and she died with clear lungs, according to the records. Alternatively, Lucy could have spent time with her father while he was exposed. Maybe he had a workshop somewhere. She made a mental note to e-mail Dr Rosenbaum again, in case he recalled any more details.

Near the intersection with Old Windsor Road, her mobile phone rang. She pulled into a side street to answer, cursing herself for not bringing the hands-free set. Northern Base Hospital had a woman in Casualty, claiming to have been raped by a group of men. Ordinarily, Dr Beattie would handle this in office hours, but she'd been called to a family emergency and requested that Anya Crichton cover for her.

Anya checked her watch. With heavy traffic, it would take her over an hour to get there, even with the M2 tollway. She agreed and explained she'd be there as soon as possible.

Next, she dialled Elaine, who gave her a series of messages. Dan Brody wanted to talk to her but was in court all day. He asked that she keep trying him.

Sabina Prior from Legal Aid called to say thanks for the report about the alleged child abuse case, and Mick Hayes was available for a drum lesson this afternoon. He'd be teaching in the area and could manage a home lesson at 4 pm today, or on Monday.

As usual, she hadn't practised or done her theory homework. Every lesson, her teacher would politely say that at least she did him the courtesy of making different mistakes each time. She asked Elaine to call and rebook for Monday afternoon. That would give her time to practise, knowing that with Ben around over the weekend, the chances of playing music seriously were zero.

Finally, Martin wanted to know if he could bring Ben early on Friday. He was going away with Nita. Anya dialled his mobile and left a voicemail message. She planned to spend all day working in the office and would be happy to see Ben any time.

Her phone rang again. Elaine had forgotten to mention a fax from Professor Hammond. It said the results Anya had requested were back. He was ninety-nine per cent certain the viruses from the deceased patients and the in-patient came from the same source. Elaine complained that he hadn't mentioned names and hoped Anya understood what the message meant.

Hammond had wisely omitted the names of the women, in case the fax mistakenly went to another number. His commitment to confidentiality impressed her, and she wanted to respect that.

'I know exactly what he's talking about. Thanks Elaine.'

The herpes cultured from Fatima Deab, Alison Blakehurst and Briony Lovitt had the same molecular structure. It confirmed that the women had had sexual contact with the same source. She still needed more for a police investigation, especially since Briony refused to speak about what had happened to her while she was missing. Otherwise there'd be no chance of reinvestigating each woman's death.

Little doubt remained that Briony had had intercourse with the same man. If only she'd open up and talk about what had happened.

Anya turned the car around and headed for Northern Base Hospital. She'd let Kate know the herpes results tonight. In the morning she'd go back and find out whatever else Briony knew.

44

Anya arrived at Western District Hospital at 8.30 am. With nursing handover finished, most of the showers and baths were out of the way. On surgical wards, the doctors did the rounds before or after theatre lists, which meant she had the best chance of talking to Briony without interruption. At the desk, the nurse from the other day stood labelling blood vials.

'Good morning, doctor. Briony Lovitt's just had some blood taken. Took two goes because of the mood she's in this morning.'

'Is everything okay medically?' Anya tried to read the pathology request.

'She refused breakfast, which isn't unusual, but I thought she looked a bit yellow. I paged the resident and he wanted her liver function checked. He's in theatre all day and said he'd duck out to see her in between cases. Otherwise, Briony's her normal rude self. You'd think she was the Queen the way she dismissed me just then.' Looking up at a whiteboard that allowed the nursing staff to communicate non-urgent reminders to doctors without constantly paging them, she added, 'I'll write it there as well, so the resident doesn't forget.'

'What are her obs like?' Anya asked.

The nurse checked the bed chart on the desk. 'Temp is fine, pulse normal. BP 110 over 70. No more shortness of breath than yesterday. The resident thought it could be the antibiotics affecting her liver,' she said, placing the specimens in a plastic bag with the request form and sealing it. 'He's more worried about pulmonary emboli. Her lung function is poor enough as it is. Imagine surviving all those injuries and dying from a blood clot.' She deposited the plastic bag into a blue box and returned the bed chart. 'You'd have to be jinxed or something.'

Within a minute, she had returned. 'You can go in now, but she's in a foul mood. Lady Muck doesn't want to see anyone.'

'Thanks.' Anya would discuss the fibres later with the registrar. Briony may need a bronchoscopy if clots and infection were excluded. She also wondered whether this woman, now facing the reality of losing her business, partner and access to her child, could be experiencing depression.

She tapped on the door and entered. Predictably, Briony didn't acknowledge her presence.

'Good morning.' Anya pulled a small cardboard box from a carry bag. 'Thought you might like a bagel. There's a cheese and bacon roll, too.'

Briony continued to stare at the television attached to an overhead stand. In the light she did appear a little sallow.

'How are you feeling?'

Briony clicked off the remote. 'You've got a hide coming here. I could sue your arse off.'

Anya was taken aback. 'I don't understand. We talked the other day –'

'And you couldn't help yourself. Had to go and tell your friend all about me. You're a lying bitch. Get out!'

'What are you talking about? I kept your confidence.'

'You're using me to solve your precious case and get brownie points with your mates.'

Anya had no idea what had upset her so much. 'I don't understand what happened. Did someone come to see you?'

'As if you didn't know. Two homicide detectives forced their way in and threatened me if I didn't cooperate. They said they could charge me with obstructing a police investigation if I didn't tell them how to find him. They knew I'd already spoken to you.'

Anya felt her heart speed up. 'Was one of the detectives a woman? With short, dark hair?'

Briony bit her bottom lip.

'The thing that really pisses me off isn't your cop friend. You knew what I'd been through and pretended to care.' She held her side with one hand. 'I believed you.'

Anya had no idea how Kate had found Briony, but felt responsible.

'I'm sorry. The police asked for your name but I wouldn't give it to them.'

'How did they know you'd been here?'

Anya knew nothing she could say would help Briony now. 'I'm sorry. This wasn't supposed to happen.'

Briony became louder, sounding hysterical. 'Sorry doesn't fix anything. Get out now or I'll call for security. Get out!'

Anya opened the door to leave as the nurse from the desk rushed in.

'What's going on?'

'I was just leaving.'

Briony lowered her voice. 'You're no different from *him*, using people to get what you want. You'd make a great pair.'

Anya pulled up outside Homicide and phoned Kate. Within minutes, the detective appeared on the front steps and Anya headed her way.

'What the hell do you think you're doing, going to see her in hospital?'

'Hang on, I know you're pissed off.' Kate held her arms up in a pseudo surrender.

'Damn right I'm pissed off. Briony Lovitt just threatened me with legal action for betraying her confidence. And what about the emotional damage you've caused that woman?'

'Can we cut the melodramatics? She is pivotal to a possible homicide investigation. All I did was my job. If you weren't going to tell me, I had to do something. That way you weren't directly involved and you still have your precious ethics

362

intact. No penance or Hail Marys, or whatever it is Catholics do.'

'You deliberately used me to get to a patient. So how did you do it?' Anya paced along one step. 'Did you have me followed?'

Kate looked around. Uniformed officers and detectives on their way in and out of the building began to notice the pair. 'Can we talk about this somewhere more private?'

'Jesus. You *did*. You dogged me.' Anya knew exactly how betrayal felt. 'You compromised me. This could cost me my registration, my practice.'

Kate looked up at the sky. 'Don't be ridiculous. I'll say how I located the witness. No-one's going to hold you responsible.'

She couldn't believe that her friend had been so deceitful. Now the odds of getting anything from Briony were impossible. She'd be unlikely to open up to anyone again.

'I hope it was worth it.' Anya turned around and headed for her car.

Kate followed. 'Could you just stop and think for a minute? We know something is happening to these women. The DNA from the foetus came back. The kid was fathered by the same guy who sprogged into Debbie Finch's throat. It can't have been Mohammed Deab. You said the viruses were from the same source. I can connect two women to each other with herpes, and the other two to each other with DNA. What else was I supposed to do?'

Anya stopped at her car and swung around. 'That isn't the point. Any chance we had of finding out who Briony was with is gone. She's withdrawn and refuses to talk to anyone. We're back to square one. Some man slept with these women before they died. Suspicious, sure, but without a record, there's no chance of finding this guy, let alone charging him with a crime. He's smart. No-one sees him take the women, or they go voluntarily. We've got nothing. Briony was the key. She won't talk again.'

'This wasn't personal,' Kate said, throwing her hands up in the air. 'I made a decision under the circumstances. I did my job.'

'Like hell it wasn't personal.'

The detective's mobile rang and she walked over and grabbed Anya's arm as she answered the call. Anya pulled away and fumbled for her keys.

'Shit. Thanks, I'll be right there.' Kate hung up. 'You might want to come to the hospital. Briony Lovitt's been taken to intensive care. She's in some kind of coma.'

45

The director of intensive care came out of the unit and asked to speak to Detective Sergeant Farrer. Dr Jim Ho recognised Anya from medical school and was happy to include her in the conversation, turning more of his attention to his colleague than the policewoman.

'The patient's in a critical condition. It looks like paracetamol poisoning –'

Kate interrupted. 'Hang on, are you saying she has overdosed on *painkillers* in here?'

'I'm afraid that's what the blood tests show.'

Kate rubbed her chin. 'How does someone with a spinal cord injury, flat on her back, manage to get hold of enough tablets to kill herself? Did someone else poison her?'

Jim Ho spoke calmly and without sounding patronising. 'I suppose it's possible but, I suspect, unlikely. The psychiatrist believed she was depressed but didn't think she was a suicide risk. We can only assume that instead of taking her analgesia, she saved her tablets and took them all at once. Judging by the levels in her system and the degree of organ failure, I'm guessing the lethal dose was taken over the last couple of days.'

Kate paced, hands on hips again. 'How can you kill yourself in hospital? Aren't you people supposed to notice something?' Her voice was half an octave higher than normal. Anya recognised the anxiety signs, and so, it appeared, did the intensive care specialist.

'With paracetamol poisoning there may not be any symptoms until very late, and it can be done with as little as a dozen tablets,' he said, without sounding defensive. 'The notes suggest that Briony seemed all right this morning apart from mild jaundice.'

'I spoke to her and she was lucid. The jaundice was barely noticeable,' Anya confirmed.

'The blood tests showed she already had early renal failure, liver failure and her PT was over 180.' Again, Dr Ho addressed his former classmate.

'Excuse me?' Kate asked.

'PT's a test for bleeding time,' he said. 'The liver is responsible for clotting factors and if it fails, bleeding time increases. That means a risk of haemorrhages.'

'Is she conscious right now? I need to interview her.'

'I'm afraid not. She's developed encephalopathy, which is the effect the damage has on her brain, and is in a coma. We're trying haemodialysis, but we'll find out tonight if we're winning or not.'

Anya thought of Julie and little Georgia. 'Has the family been notified?'

'Yes, but no-one's come yet.'

A nurse hurried out of the unit and called for Dr Ho, just as his beeper went off and a loud-speaker announced a code one in the ICU. 'Excuse me, I have to go,' he said with urgency.

Within minutes, four doctors came sprinting along the corridor and ran into the unit.

'What's going on?' Kate waited for an answer from Anya.

The doctors must have been on the arrest team and answered the emergency page. Anya said a silent prayer for Briony. Minutes passed. No-one reappeared.

'Why the frig don't the nurses watch you take the stuff if it's so bloody dangerous?' Kate muttered.

Nurses habitually left tablets in a small paper cup by the bedside. For safety and legal reasons, two nurses checked the medication when dispensed, but they were too busy to stand there and ensure the pills were swallowed. Patients could have been in the bathroom, with a doctor, or may have had to take the pills with food and wait for the meal tray.

As they sat on a lounge outside the unit, Kate phoned the office. Anya knew Briony had faced death rather than return to the man. The poor woman had lost her child, partner, home, business, and the use of her legs. Of course she was a suicide risk. It just hadn't occurred to Anya that Briony had the means to commit suicide. It should have.

A couple of middle-aged men in dark suits

walked up to the intercom at the door and buzzed. One of them complained loudly how damaging a wrongful death lawsuit would be for the hospital. The other agreed that the cost would run into tens of millions. Classic administrators. Full of compassion and tenderness, Anya thought. What if we were the relatives hearing that?

They buzzed again and walked in. A few more minutes passed before Dr Ho came out. Judging by the lack of eye contact as he approached, the news wasn't good.

'I'm sorry to tell you this,' he said to Anya and Kate. 'Due to metabolic failure, Briony Lovitt suffered a series of cardiac arrests. Despite all our efforts to resuscitate her, I'm afraid she passed away a few moments ago.'

46

At seven o'clock on Saturday morning, Ben sat down to crunchy cornflakes, scrambled eggs – Anya's only specialty, done in the microwave – and thick crusty toast. He even had room for a chocolate-chip muffin intended for morning tea. Thankfully, he didn't seem to notice how little his mother ate.

She thought about Briony Lovitt and wished she could have done something different. No matter how she replayed the events of the last week, Anya felt responsible, in part, for Briony's death.

Sitting next to his latest prized possession – the blue dinosaur – Ben asked a barrage of questions about the world.

'If bodies are buried and people go to heaven, what's a ghost made of?' 'Why doesn't Superman stop wars?' 'Why is it called a swimsuit when I swim and it gets wet?' and 'Why do some words start with PH instead of F, when they make the F sound?'

No matter how much she prepared, Ben's questions left Anya stumped most of the time. Martin must have known how bright their son was, continually asking things that were impossible to explain.

Ben played with his dinosaur as another thought came to mind. He gulped the last of his milk.

'Mum, is Vaughan your boyfriend?'

Luckily, the phone interrupted.

'Hi Elaine,' Anya said into the receiver. 'No, not yet.'

Ben watched his mother. Unlike most children his age, he usually knew the instant that things weren't right.

'Thanks for the warning. I'll speak to you later.'

Hanging up, Anya tried to reassure Ben, who now had a furrowed brow.

'Elaine just wanted me to know about a story in the newspaper in case I forgot to read it, with you and me being so busy.'

Ben climbed off his chair, placed his plate and cup next to the sink and picked up his toy.

'Why don't you go upstairs and choose something to wear today, Speedie. We've got a big day planned.'

He was out of the room, clomping up the stairs before Anya had opened the front door to collect the Saturday newspaper. She unwrapped the plastic, flattened it and turned to the News Review section. Elaine couldn't have prepared her for the shock of the double-page spread.

'MURDER MOST FOUL, EXPERT IN PRIVATE AND IN PRACTICE', the headline screamed.

Dr Anya Crichton, prominent forensic pathologist and physician, can't seem to avoid murder in her private and working lives. Perhaps it's become second nature. Her life has been embroiled in controversy from the age of five, as Trent Wilkinson discovers . . .

In the middle of the page, in a box, was an old photo of Miriam, taken on her third birthday. It was the one used by the police all those years ago. 'Miriam Reynolds disappeared, presumed murdered. Family members were implicated but no charges were ever laid', the caption read.

There was no mention of Billy Vidor in Risdon jail. This was a hatchet piece designed to discredit her. Why?

Her eyes were drawn to a photo that stunned her.

Crichton's husband, Martin Hegarty, was dismissed from London's Royal Huntley Hospital for injecting a patient with a lethal dose of the narcotic, morphine. He resigned from the hospital only after a public campaign for justice by the dead woman's family. Hegarty failed to maintain nursing registration in Australia. The victim's family remain convinced there was a cover-up by the hospital and maintain that manslaughter charges should have been laid. They deny that the woman requested euthanasia. A close colleague of

Crichton's performed the autopsy on the victim, a fact condemned by lawyers acting for the family.

A few paragraphs down was the photo taken with Scott Barker.

Her testimony in the recent trial of Scott Barker was instrumental in getting the heir to the magnate's empire acquitted of murder. Crichton, it seems, has friends in high places.

Anya couldn't believe what she was seeing. The vilification went on.

Crichton's father is Bob Reynolds, who has recently lobbied the State Government for more rehabilitation, at taxpayers' expense, for prisoners convicted of violent crimes. Neighbours of her mother, Dr Jocelyn Reynolds, believe Crichton is estranged from her Tasmanian family, and hasn't been seen in Launceston since returning from England with her shamed husband. They say that depriving her mother of access to the only grandchild is one of the cruellest things Crichton could ever do.

Anya dropped the paper and sat on the chair. Her chest ached as she struggled to catch her breath. The public obsession with her life had started all over again. No matter how far she ran, it haunted her. And now it haunted Ben.

She called his name but he didn't answer.

Panicking, she started up the stairs as someone pounded on the door. She could hear raised voices outside.

Peering through the glass, she saw her ex-husband yelling at a photographer by the road. As soon as the door opened, Martin barged into the kitchen and threw his paper on the table.

'That job interview I told you about? Last night I was told, unofficially, that I got the job. Then I get a call this morning – on a Saturday – saying the position's already been filled and not to bother reapplying. Of course, I'm thinking this doesn't add up until I see the front page of today's paper advertising a feature on my ex-wife, which happens to describe me as a murderer. Not just any paper, mind you. The biggest-selling one in the country.' He sat down with both hands pulling his hair. He looked as though he'd been crying. 'You know she was ninety-six years old and in terrible pain – she didn't want the bowel operation and couldn't wait any longer for pain relief.' He looked up. 'For fuck's sake. Are you going after custody of Ben? Is that why you told them about me?'

'Martin, I had nothing to do with it.' Anya was shocked that he thought she could be so calculating. 'You know I would never talk to the press. A reporter rang here a couple of weeks ago, on a Friday night, and asked if I was Anya Reynolds from Tasmania. I refused to answer and he started asking me whether I killed my sister.'

'Your fucking work has caused this. It's always been the problem.'

Ben bounced down the stairs proudly sporting a *Star Wars* T-shirt and shorts.

'Dad! Hi! Are you coming with us?'

'No, Ben. Get your bag. We're leaving.'

Anya couldn't believe what he was saying. 'You can't take him. I have legal right to access.'

'I'm taking him to the coast, where nobody knows his name.'

'But Daddy, I want to stay. Mummy and I are going to the Powerhouse Museum.'

Martin took off up the stairs, two at a time, and Anya chased him.

He shoved Ben's pyjamas, toothbrush and spare clothes in the duffle bag and headed downstairs. Anya had never seen her ex-husband so angry.

She grabbed his arm to stop him and he pulled away, picking Ben up at the bottom of the stairs.

'We have to talk about this,' Anya pleaded, but Martin pushed past her.

Ben began to cry and squirmed in his father's arms. 'Put me down, Daddy. I want to be with Mummy! MUMMY!' he shrieked as Martin carried him away from the house and into the car. 'I want Mummy!'

Anya's eyes filled with tears. She felt pain tearing through her with every one of her son's sobs. She ran to comfort him.

'It's all right, Speedie, I love you. Daddy's just very upset right now.' She held his hand as Martin strapped him into the car seat before slamming the door.

He pressed his hands against the window. 'Mummy. I don't want to go.'

'I know you're angry, Martin,' she pleaded, 'but don't punish Ben. He's got nothing to do with this. Listen to him. This is really hurting him.'

Martin leant on the car and buried his face in his forearm.

'This isn't about us. It's about our child!' she said.

'Things were starting to fall into place. My job interview, the school you talked about. I really wanted to try to give Ben two parents, even if we didn't live together.'

A camera flashed in Anya's peripheral vision and she turned to see a camera crew heading her way. Martin saw them too.

'Look what you've done to us.'

He got in the car, closed the door and drove off before she could stop him. Ben's screams resonated through her as they rounded the corner.

47

Anya went back inside and locked the door, her hands shaking. She slumped to the floor and put her head on her knees. Twenty-four hours ago, everything was going well, even looking better than it had in years. Martin was moving back to Sydney with Ben, her case load had increased, and she'd gained Briony's confidence.

Within a day, Kate had betrayed her by having her followed and Briony had killed herself. Now, Anya knew her private life had been ripped open for public entertainment, and the media vultures were again feeding on the carrion of her sister's disappearance. Her work had been impugned, and, thanks to one newspaper article, Martin would be loath to set foot in Sydney again. She may lose Ben for good. She felt as though a hot knife had torn through her entire being, shredding every good part of her life. For God's sake, why?

Ben's distress and screams played over and over in her mind. She would have given anything to have him back again and hold him, protect him from everything and everyone.

Maybe Briony had been right to leave her child.

That way the little girl would never know the pain of seeing someone she loved destroy her life. Ben was an emotional football and she couldn't begin to imagine the trauma today had caused him.

She could hear herself crying and tried to stop. Like an outsider watching, all she could do was wait until no more tears came. She was still sitting there when darkness fell. With puffy eyes and a splitting headache, she stood up. Legs numb and stiff, she stumbled to the front office and closed the curtains facing the street. After switching on the light, she picked up a keepsake card Elaine kept alongside a family photo: 'Shit happens,' an angel said. The devil replied, 'No it doesn't. It's always created by an arsehole.'

The one thing she always wanted, a real family, was what she'd never have. Changing jobs and working solo was supposed to help get Ben back.

Now her work had pushed him away again, maybe forever. How did she screw up so badly?

Maybe the newspapers were right. She was like a murder magnet. People she touched seemed to suffer. Miriam, Martin, Ben. Now Briony was dead, too, and Anya was partly responsible. That was unchangeable, no matter what anyone said, or did.

After the exposé, she realised, it would be impossible to get work. No-one wanted a scandalous expert witness, recognised by juries thanks to scathing newspaper articles. Someone who supposedly got her sister killed and covered up a murder committed by her husband didn't retain much credibility in a courtroom.

A loud knock on the door startled her. She hesitated and stood in the hallway, not wanting to see anyone.

She kept quiet, hoping whoever was there would leave.

The knocking persisted.

'Who is it?' she said, with a husky voice.

'Dan Brody. Can I come in? It's cold out here.'

'I'm not decent. Can we talk tomorrow?'

'The only light on is the one in the office. If you're in there being indecent, I wouldn't mind seeing!'

Anya wiped her nose with the back of her hand and opened the door.

Brody stood dangling a bottle of red wine, as though the sight of him would entice anyone.

'Now isn't a good time.'

'I can see that. That's why I came. Your answering machine is full.'

Anya folded her arms and opened the door further.

Brody walked straight to the kitchen, opened the top cupboards until he located two wine glasses and began to ferret in the top drawer.

'Bottle opener's in the third one down,' she said, resigned to having a guest. She had no idea why Brody was even there.

He opened the bottle, poured the wine and handed Anya a glass.

They walked into the lounge room and sat on the couch. Anya curled her feet underneath her and pulled her woolly cardigan tight. The wine slipped down her throat and immediately gave her a warm sense of relief.

Brody sat forward, running a finger around the rim of his glass.

'I saw the paper. Thought it must have come out of the blue for you. I had no idea . . . I mean, Brenda never said a word.'

'She didn't know,' Anya said. 'No-one in Newcastle did.'

'Christ, it's a hell of a lot to carry around. I see people all the time keeping secrets, but usually to save their own skins.'

Anya took another sip and waited for the blood rush to her face and hands.

'Why are you here?'

He watched Anya for a moment then sat back. The quiet counsellor wasn't what she'd expected from him. 'Wanted to check you hadn't fled the country on me. I still need you on the Deab case.'

'How is he?' she asked, not really caring.

'No more assaults, but he's clammed up about his daughter's death. He seems to think that shouting out a confession in front of witnesses doesn't mean much. Because he's already on remand, the police have held off charging him.'

Brody pulled a piece of paper from the back pocket of his jeans and handed it to Anya.

She put her glass on the floor and uncrumpled the article.

'Don't worry, you're not mentioned in this one,' he quipped.

The article, dated twelve months prior, discussed multiculturalism and whether Australians should tolerate differing cultural beliefs. It described the death of a Syrian-born girl, chained to her bed and beaten.

'Second page, midway down the third column,' Brody added.

Mohammed Deab, from Greystanes, a friend of the Syrian girl's father, said that if a father found out that his daughter had slept with a man before marriage, he was obliged to kill her: 'I would proudly go to prison if my family were free from shame because of what I did.'

'I'm sorry, Dan. I don't know how I can help anymore. I am thinking of closing up and moving back to Newcastle.'

'Crap. You're just having a hormonal day, or whatever you call it now.'

Anya had no energy to argue, or rise to the bait.

'Come on, where's the bossy, know-it-all smart alec who gives me the shits all the time?'

'Shrouded in scandal, it seems.'

'Anyone worth knowing is controversial. Shit, you're right up there with royalty and our esteemed political leaders. Deab could be facing a murder charge, and from what my sources in the police department tell me, they could link him to a number of suspicious deaths, the ones you've been investigating.'

Anya suddenly recalled the conversation with Kate. 'Not anymore. The DNA taken from two of the dead women doesn't match Mohammed's. The chances of his being implicated in the other deaths are minimal, especially if he doesn't have herpes.'

'Well that's something.' He sat back. 'Do you think Fatima was killed by someone else?'

Grateful for the distraction, she answered honestly, 'I think someone other than Deab did it. As a father, he might have gone there after she'd died and left his cigarette butt, but I think her death is definitely related to the other women.'

'So if we can get him to keep his trap shut and stop confessing . . .' Brody swigged his drink and headed for a refill.

'What about the fibres?' he asked from the kitchen.

'I'm still trying to identify what they are. Don't suppose you know anything about music and speakers?'

'No, if it doesn't have brass or bagpipes, I'm not interested.'

Anya wouldn't be surprised if he played 'The Last Post' during a romantic evening at home.

'Dan, if I'm involved in a coronial inquest into a hospital death that happened this week, the press would eat it up.'

'So, that's what you do, isn't it?'

'Actually, I'm likely to be under investigation.' Anya picked up her glass and gently swirled the contents. 'Someone I had been interviewing in hospital committed suicide. Before she died, I bore the brunt of her anger in front of a nurse. That's bound to come out in the inquest. I'm convinced she survived an attack by the same man who was involved in the fibre deaths.'

'So, your interview technique needs a little work. I already knew that.'

'Dan, I'm serious. My actions contributed to her death.'

'Look, you're not responsible for anyone else's actions. She made the decision herself and if you upset her, she must have been pretty unstable in the first place. If it wasn't you, it would have been someone else.'

He finished the second glass and stood, slapping his hip pockets until he located the car keys.

'Anyway, keep on at those other cases. What you find out might just save Deab's skin. And don't think anyone will care about that rubbish in today's paper. My cat's already crapped on it in the kitty litter box.'

Anya stood up and walked him to the door. 'Thanks for the wine. Hey, you don't happen to represent litigation cases against hospitals or doctors, do you?'

'Doctors and insurance companies? No way. Can't afford to damage my reputation by dealing with those sorts of low-lifes. Give me the crims any day.' He winked and left.

Anya switched on the computer for company. For the amount of work Dan had supplied, he deserved closure with this job. Elaine needed severence pay if the business closed. She'd tell her on Monday morning, to give her time to look for other work.

Anya began to search the Internet for speakers and companies who made them. Someone had to know where those bloody fibres came from.

48

Kate Farrer sat on her lounge room floor wading through print-outs of phone numbers. If something didn't turn up soon, she'd be in deep shit with her commanding officer. With the end of the financial year less than three months away, spending had to be cut to make budget. That meant cutting casual staff and every expense that wasn't vital to a case. Nothing got on Kate's nerves more than money-obsessed COs. Solving homicides didn't get cheaper this time of the year just because money dried up. It just meant that fewer resources were allocated so the numbers would all look good come the end of June. That's all the pricks cared about.

The number of homicides this month was double that for March. With fewer staff, that meant more unpaid overtime, or more unsolved crimes. Despite giving her half-a-dozen cases to 'consult' on and a full case load, the CO was riding her for results. By God, she'd give him one on the case with the dead women. They had the DNA already. What good was expensive technology when you needed a perpetrator to compare it with? Her last hope was finding a link between the women, before they had disappeared.

She'd spent the whole weekend sifting through phone records, trying to find two numbers the same from the Merrylands surgery, from the shifts Fatima Deab worked, the Blakehurst and Finch houses, and the convent in Rouse Hill.

She looked again at the convent's incoming calls in the six months prior to the fall off the cliff. She arched her back and rubbed her neck, numbers swimming in her mind. Every time she closed her eyes, digits flashed across her eyelids.

Shoving the last mouthful of reheated butter chicken into her mouth, she dripped grease onto a page.

'Shit! Shit! Shit!'

With a tissue from her pocket, she cleaned the page and double-checked that the numbers were all visible.

She turned back to the second-last page of Fatima's printout. The third number down seemed similar to the one the grease had almost hidden.

After wiping her fingers on her trousers, she grabbed both pieces of paper and compared them: 9,9, 8,8 . . . All the numbers matched. She took the papers, went into the kitchen and checked again, under stronger light. No doubt about it, someone at the surgery had called the same number as someone from the convent. She checked the time with her own notes from the interviews. The call from the surgery was made at 1 pm, on a

Wednesday, when the doctor was out doing house calls. Fatima had been alone.

The one from the convent was made at 7.30 am on a Monday. Clare didn't catch the train until 8 am so would have had time to make the call. Not many businesses were open that early, which heightened the chances the link was more than a coincidence.

Buoyed by having a number to chase, Kate dragged out the pages from the other two cases, and two and a half hours later, found the number again. This time, on the list from Alison Blakehurt's mobile phone.

She grabbed her own mobile and dialled the number for the duty operations inspector in charge of Police Radio.

'Detective Sergeant Kate Farrer. I need a subscriber check on a number . . . Yes, it is urgent.'

She waited for the inspector to come to the phone. After hours, he wouldn't give it to her unless it involved a life-threatening emergency. She decided to lie to her senior officer and face the consequences later.

'I believe a woman has phoned the number, gone there and is in grave danger.'

She gave her mobile phone number and hung up. In about an hour, she'd know who the women had in common.

Feeling recharged, Kate stripped, and indulged in a long, hot shower, using the water to massage her aching neck. She threw on her favourite tracksuit and combed her hair. Out of reflex, she went to phone Anya but put the receiver down.

By tailing Anya, she thought she'd done the right thing, but Anya didn't see it that way. Doctors and their ethics gave her the shits. Talking to the Lovitt woman was necessary for the investigation. Why couldn't Anya understand that?

As her mobile played the theme from *The Magnificent Seven*, she slipped on the unopened weekend papers lying on the floor, tearing the front pages.

From a sitting position, she grabbed the phone, feeling the impact of the hard floor on her tail-bone. The inspector had identified the subscriber. The phone was listed under the name of a Crisis Centre in town.

Now it made sense. The women had problems in their lives, and had obviously sought counselling. First thing in the morning, she'd find out who answered the phones when the calls were made. If the DNA from any of the counsellors matched, they'd have the bastard who screwed the women and probably killed them.

But how did Debbie Finch and Briony Lovitt fit into the picture? Kate felt uncomfortable not being able to link them to the centre. She rummaged for the white pages and flicked through the 'C' section. Central Crisis Centre had two numbers listed. She scribbled down the alternate number and searched through the phone records again. Debbie Finch had called the other number twice.

By midnight, Kate had the answer she'd wanted. Briony Lovitt had called the centre a week before she disappeared.

Unable to sleep, she decided to e-mail Anya and tell her about the calls. She'd investigate the Crisis Centre in the morning, and find out what she could. She finished off the e-mail saying that Briony's death won't have been in vain and sent it. At 2 am, she crawled under her blanket and fell asleep, fully dressed, having forgotten to turn off the light.

Kate woke up and heard a car revving its engine outside her bedroom. The vehicle sounded badly in need of a tune. She turned off the light and peered through the window. She could make out a blue Corolla, exactly like Anya's. Maybe Anya had read the e-mail and had come over to talk, but was having second thoughts.

'This is stupid,' Kate said aloud. 'We need to sort this out.' She pulled on sandshoes and, huddled against the morning chill, went outside and approached the driver's side.

It wasn't until she reached the window that she realised Anya wasn't driving.

49

Anya didn't notice Elaine arrive.

'No, I don't attend S and M clubs! If you phone here again, I'll call the police.' She slammed down the receiver.

'Not a good morning?'

'It's five past eight and feels like midnight.' Anya slumped into Elaine's chair and rubbed her temples. 'So far we've had calls from radio, print and TV outlets, talk shows, colleagues and, of course, there are the cranks wanting to meet the "fatal attraction" mentioned in the weekend paper.'

'Once it's out of their system, they'll leave you alone. This is just your fifteen minutes in the spotlight.'

As if regretting her comment, Elaine quickly left Anya to answer the door.

'No, she doesn't give out autographs. Good day.' Less than a minute later the bell rang again. 'Oh . . . Good morning . . . Thanks, if you would we'd appreciate it. But I've told you before about the testing lab.'

Anya lifted her head from beneath her hands.

'Sperm Man's standing guard for a while. Doesn't want you getting distracted from his wife's underwear.'

Anya groaned and retreated upstairs with her laptop. 'I don't want to talk to anyone. I'll finish a couple of reports and that's it.'

On her bed, she struggled to concentrate, repeatedly typing the same line about injuries sustained in a domestic violence incident. Sabina Pryor could always find another expert. Within minutes, the incessant ringing made her disconnect the phone from the wall.

After stretching her legs and taking two aspirin, she sat cross-legged on the bed and drafted a letter offering Sabina alternative forensic physicians and their contact details. By midday, that's all she'd managed.

Elaine ventured upstairs with coffee and a sandwich, but Anya's stomach felt like acid had eroded the lining.

'I'm not hungry. Thanks anyway.' Elaine appeared tired. It can't have been easy dealing with the fallout from the weekend. 'How are you coping?'

'Well, you, or should I say, we, have had two marriage proposals, and an obscene caller to round off the morning. Three people want to see what a murder magnet looks like.' She put the tray down on the dressing table. 'Nothing I can't handle. The answering machine's on now so we can have a break. What about you and Martin?'

Anya stood and looked out her small window. 'He took Ben away on Saturday morning. He was so angry, Elaine, he scared me. Ben couldn't stop screaming for me. God, it broke my heart.' She swallowed hard.

Elaine nodded silently. 'You can understand his shock. He'll calm down. He always does.'

'I'm worried what this will do to Ben.'

'That little boy is incredible. I'm sure he'll cope. Still, why don't you phone him if it'll put your mind at ease.'

Anya plugged the line back in as Elaine left.

Nita answered the phone and whispered that Martin didn't want to speak to anyone. Ben had cried until he'd fallen asleep in the car and hadn't said much yesterday morning. He was lying on the carpet with the blue dinosaur, watching a cartoon. In spite of avoiding Nita until now, Anya found herself grateful for the information about her son. This woman sounded as though she genuinely cared about Ben, and Martin, and appreciated Anya's concern. Nita suggested calling back when Martin went for his afternoon surf. That way, they could avoid another argument and Anya could talk to Ben for as long as she wanted.

By four o'clock, the phones had stopped ringing and Elaine called out that she was about to lock the front door. Anya left her upstairs confinement and wandered downstairs, just as her drum teacher arrived.

'Hi. Ready to play something new this week?' Mick Hayes appeared with a pile of sheet music.

Anya had forgotten all about the lesson. The weekend drama put everything else out of her consciousness.

'It's not really a good time. I'm sorry, Mick. I'll pay for your time today, of course.'

'You okay? You look . . .'

'I know, like shit. You can say it. Didn't you see Saturday's paper?'

'No. Played in a gig on Friday night and after that was a write-off.'

Judging by the dark rings under his eyes and the three-day growth on his chin, Friday probably lasted the whole weekend, she thought. Mick played in a band that had sold a number of CDs at venues around town. As he spoke, it occurred to her that he might know someone who knew about sound engineers and speakers.

'Actually maybe you can help me with something. I need to know a bit about sound speakers. So far I know they contain magnets, cardboard and not much else. How can you tell whether a speaker is good or bad quality?'

'That's easy. If it's made by one of the biggest sellers, chances are it's good. Stick to well-known brands and you should be right. You can get some good bargains second hand, if you know what you're looking for.'

'I'll remember that.' Anya smiled for the first time that day. 'By the way, what is it that makes a good speaker? I mean, how would you know if you were making one?'

'Never thought much about it.' He flicked a long fringe out of his eyes. 'But I know a guy who had some stuff tested at a special chamber at the place that does research into acoustics and hearing. Where was it? Lindfield, I think.'

Anya had the spark of an idea. 'Do you know what sort of chamber that is?'

'Kind of like a recording studio, I reckon. With padding to absorb sound.'

Anya had assumed all along that the fibres were contained in the speakers. But it made sense that if the sound engineer had been trying to build the perfect speaker, he would have tested them, perhaps in his own recording studio. Her mental image of a room like the one Mick had described had foam-padded walls to minimise unnecessary sound appearing on recordings. Unintentionally, Mick Hayes had mentioned another possible source of the unidentified fibres. What if they were never in the speakers, but in the testing room instead?

'Thanks, Mick. Let me get my purse and pay you for today.'

He flicked the fringe that Anya would love to have cut or pinned out of his eyes. 'Sure you don't want a lesson?'

'You just taught me more than you realise.'

Kate Farrer dreamt she was a child again, scared and alone. Curled up, her hand groped around for bedclothes to pull up and snuggle under, to protect her from the world. Cold air brushed over her body and each hair stood to attention. Shivering, she opened her eyes to pitch black. Blinking again, she searched for the red glow of the alarm clock by her bed. It wasn't there. Moving her arm, she felt nothing but a chilling hardness underneath.

'What the . . .? Where am I?' she tried to say, mouth too dry to form the words.

Sitting upright, she ran a hand over a metal grid. Between the steel were holes, big enough to fit her fingers through.

Kate's heartbeat drilled in both ears, the only audible sound. Running icy hands over her body, she tentatively moved her legs and feet. Nothing was broken or hurt. Then she realised. Her hands touched nothing but skin. Naked flesh.

'Christ!'

She clutched her belly and dry retched. The skin above her crotch had been shaved.

Kate screamed with despair and panic until her voice croaked. Too frightened to accept what else he might have done, she tried to focus on exactly where she was.

Think, Kate, think. It took all her energy to concentrate. She remembered looking at the phone records and falling asleep. What happened then? *Fuck, why can't I remember*? Drugs. He must have used drugs. Otherwise, she wouldn't be here.

394

'Help me! Someone help!' she screeched.

No matter how loud her cries, no-one answered. The blackness enveloped her and she shivered, uncontrollably.

What the fuck did he do to me? She ran a hand over her eyes and rubbed. Still nothing. No light, no walls, nothing.

Head throbbing, her eyes welled with hot tears that dripped onto her naked chest.

What the fuck did he do? Am I blind? God, no. Don't let me be blind.

With surging nausea, she rubbed her eyes again, willing them to see. Something. Anything! Bile projected out of her mouth and the hot liquid dripped between her legs, the stench unbearable.

Rising hysteria flooded every vein. She shook and screamed in between attempts to catch her breath. Trying to find a way out, she moved on to all fours and crawled in between howls. Using her hands to feel the grid in front, she edged forward, then again. With an outstretched hand feeling for the metal, she became disorientated when the floor disappeared. Her knees still felt the pressure of the grids, which just seemed to end a metre or so in front. Keeping her legs still and balance centred, she ran a hand along what felt like an edge, which led to a taut, thick chain sticking straight upwards.

Hauling herself fully upright using the chain, she realised it went further and must have been attached to the roof. If she could just climb it.

Legs shaking, she took a deep breath and stood on her toes to cling for her life. Instead of gripping the chain, her fingers slipped through wet, oily links. Carefully, she sniffed her hands. Grease. Shit. He'd greased the fucking chain.

Lowering to a crawl position, she slowly mapped out the floor with her hand. The grate was big enough to lie on but not as wide as a bed. Chain ropes attached to the four corners of the platform, each covered in grease at the same level.

Jesus! He'd made it impossible to climb out.

At the other end of the grid, Kate's fingers brushed a small plastic container with a piece of cloth inside, next to a plastic cup with cool, odourless, liquid in it.

With her newfound 'tools', she moved to the centre and squatted. Distributing weight evenly between her legs, she steadied herself and rose to standing again. The first time she toppled and almost fell from the platform. It felt as though the whole floor had slipped. She closed her eyes, hoping it would help, and tried again. This time, she stood to her full height and reached into the air. No ceiling, no walls, nothing to grab on to or touch.

The floor had to be suspended. But how high up? What was this place? Maybe she could lower herself to the ground.

She dropped the full cup over the edge and listened for the sound of its landing. Her ears ached from listening so hard, but the cup didn't make a sound.

God. This was some kind of ledge, up too high to jump from. And she was probably blind. The well of panic overcame her again and trembling, she curled into a foetal position, begging to be let go.

50

Anya entered the atrium of the National Research Centre for Hearing and Acoustics, a large concrete complex obscured from the road by trees and shrubs. After hearing a brief explanation of her need for information, the security officer at the front desk called the head of acoustics and asked Anya to take a seat in a foyer lounge.

The vast areas of carpet and high ceilings reminded her of a hospital design, with natural light the feature. Despite a plethora of colourful artworks, the place had a sterile feel to it. She wondered how many offices and unknown faces beavered at their jobs here, secreted away from the rest of the world.

A bearded gentleman in a tartan tie, tweed jacket and tan trousers strolled down the central stairs and the security man gestured in Anya's direction.

'I'm Godfrey Taggert,' he said. 'How may I help you?'

'I appreciate your seeing me at such short notice. I'm investigating pathology findings in a number of deaths. One of the deceased spent his life building speakers, and, as the materials he used were benign,

I'm now looking into other possible sources, potential environmental allergens, if you like.'

'This research centre has an outstanding record in occupational health and safety,' he said, folding his hands in front of his belt.

Anya hadn't meant to imply otherwise. Obviously, people were sensitive about anyone investigating potential OH and S issues.

'I should explain. I'm not looking into the Centre as such, but the process by which speakers are tested.'

'Ah, I can help you with that. If you'll come this way, I can explain how the centre works.'

Anya walked up the stairs, down a corridor and up another set of stairs. One side of the building had brick walls, and the other, doors, which presumably led to offices.

They stopped at the entrance to what seemed like a maze, with large open doors to one side. 'We study sound, the mechanisms of hearing, and the way the brain interprets sound. This, of course, has many practical applications for musical instruments, singers, speakers, not to mention the hard of hearing.'

The room to the right had a concrete floor, with panels of wood hanging in rows from the ceiling and other rows placed at angles. At first the placement seemed random, but Dr Taggert explained, 'This is our reverberation room. Here, sound bounces off as many surfaces as possible. The effect is quite amazing, especially if you try singing.'

'Is it an echo room?'

'See for yourself. Try singing.'

Anya saw he was quite serious and nervously sang the first line of 'Mary Had a Little Lamb.' She couldn't keep the tune, with the echo of one note distracting her from the next.

In the next room, headphones and microphones lay on tables.

'This is for delayed speech. Put the headphones on and try counting to ten.'

Anya didn't want to waste time, but felt she'd get more information if she at least showed enthusiasm for his party tricks. Putting on the headphones, she counted into the mike.

'One, two, two, two, two.'

Dr Taggert put his hand on her shoulder and tapped on the headphones.

'What did you experience?'

'I heard what I'd said, just after I said it.'

'This records what you say and plays it back to you with an eighth of a second delay. While you're trying to count, your brain is processing what it hears, and interferes with what you want to say. That's why you repeat the same number, like a stutter, or broken record, if you like.'

Embarrassment didn't matter, knowing there was a scientific explanation.

'We rely on auditory feedback, so we listen to make sure we are saying, or singing, what we intended. Distort the feedback, and we struggle to communicate. That leads us to the next facility.'

Anya checked her watch. So far the tour had been interesting, but hadn't included anything helpful to the fibre cases.

Kate tried to think. What had the women been through? Somehow they had all managed to reach the outside world. That's when she'd have the best chance of escape, if she survived in here alone.

Suddenly, a bright white light flashed. She pulled away, shielding her eyes from the pain. It lasted only a second and disappeared, leaving flecks of light flashing across her eyes. As terrifying as it was, it proved she could still see.

Seconds later, the loudest noise she'd ever heard filled the room. Like the sound of a thousand fans or engines switched on. She screamed for it to stop, but couldn't hear her own voice above the din. In the dark, her body vibrated with the movement of the floor beneath her.

She covered her ears and pressed as tightly as she could. The noise wouldn't stop. It just wouldn't stop.

Please make it stop.

Dr Taggert escorted Anya to the roomless side of the building and made his grand gesture. 'Here, we have the opposite of the reverberation room. It absorbs sounds and eliminates echo, or any delay in feedback. Our anechoic chamber.'

Pulling open two large doors, he switched on a light and led the way.

Inside smelt musty, almost mouldy. She walked onto a platform made from what looked like chicken wire.

'You're two storeys up now, and there are two more above your head.'

Looking up, Anya felt claustrophobic, despite the enormity of the room. Large fingerlike projections of foam lined the ceiling, floor and walls, all pointing at her.

As Dr Taggert closed the doors, Anya felt her ears ache. Swallowing hard to equalise the pressure made no difference.

'Why are my ears aching?' Her voice sounded muffled, like it did when her ears were blocked with a head cold.

'Your tympanic membranes, eardrums, are stretching to the maximum, trying to pick up the slightest noise. Because all sound in here is absorbed, this is the closest you can get to real silence.'

He was right. Instead of a relief, the silence was painful. Without any echo, their voices sounded barely recognisable.

She could now imagine deafness, a world completely devoid of sound, and the isolation it could bring.

'Is this where you test speakers?'

'Yes, in the middle is the best place. Unfortunately, the chamber is imperfect, because of the floor you have to stand on, but it's designed to minimise reflection, nonetheless.'

When he stopped speaking, the quiet became almost unbearable.

'What do you call this again?'

'An anechoic, meaning "no echo", chamber.'

Anya moved closer to the door. 'Do they serve any purpose other than testing speakers?'

'The department of psychology at State University has one that's supposedly very old. They're interested in the psychological effects of changes in perception of sound.'

He opened the door and Anya walked quickly towards it, relieved to be back with the natural light. 'May I ask what the chamber is lined with?'

'Some kind of fibreglass padding, not unlike the material used in recording studios and for insulation. This one is state of the art, only six months old. We're quite proud of it. The latest in materials and design.'

Anya caught her heel in the wire and stumbled as she walked to the door.

'Are you all right? I should have told you to watch your step.'

She steadied herself against the wall. 'Fine, just a bit clumsy. It's quite disorienting in here.' As her tour guide offered to take her elbow, Anya dug a fingernail into the foam lining.

'It's impressive,' Anya said as she walked out. 'One last question, Dr Taggert. Do you know where other anechoic chambers are located in New South Wales?'

'They were all the rage in the '50s, when electric

guitars were big on the scene, but the ones I knew of were knocked down or fell apart by the '60s. They took up so much space, and land became too valuable.'

'Could you tell me the locations, exactly where they were?'

'I can't promise, but if you come back to the office, I'll see what I can find for you.'

Anya followed, slipping her fingers into her bag. With another nail, she scraped the foam sample into an empty film container and clicked on the lid.

51

Anya was exhausted by the day. She switched on the answering machine. A message from Detective Constable Brian Hogan asked whether she'd spoken to Kate today. Not likely, Anya thought, her anger still raw.

Tonight the house felt cold and for the first time, really lonely. Eating alone had no appeal. In some ways, she was too tired for an early night. The gym had possibilities, but there was the chance of running into Kate. Instead, she chose to visit the Western Sydney District Hospital library. She wanted to know what psychologists did with anechoic chambers.

An hour later, she sat at a corral, surrounded by tomes on the history of modern psychology. One index mentioned the use of anechoic chambers for behavioural modification. The name B.F. Skinner kept coming up, along with descriptions of experiments on rats and birds.

At the bottom of the pile, a textbook contained pictures of a chamber with a drawbridge that retracted to leave only a small central platform suspended from the ceiling by four chains. The accompanying caption described it as 'a perfect tool for testing effects of noise deprivation on subjects'.

Something further down the paragraph sent a chill through her.

Subjects became particularly disoriented with the addition of light deprivation. They became more likely to comply with examiner's requests when rewarded with short periods of light, or sound. This occurred after periods of as little as two to three days in the chamber.

No wonder Briony agreed to give up her family. In the hands of a psychopath, the chambers were nothing but tools of torture and manipulation. If she couldn't hear any noise inside the National Research Centre's chamber, no-one would ever hear a woman screaming from inside one.

Dr Taggert had supplied the names of companies who used anechoic chambers, and apart from the university, there were only two other possible sites. One at Dural had already been redeveloped. The other, at Annangrove, owned by a guitar maker, was no longer listed in the phonebook. The business could have changed its name, been sold, or closed in the last few years. In the morning she'd drive out to the location and check the property. What if the sound engineer built or had access to his own chamber? Passing through the metal security bar at the library exit, Anya stepped outside and phoned Felix Rosenbaum.

After shouting into the phone, she managed to explain what she'd discovered.

'They test speakers in a chamber lined with foam.'

'Ah,' Dr Rosenbaum said. 'I recall that Phil Abbott had a cousin who had a property not far from him. In those days, of course, one wouldn't just visit for lunch, one would spend the weekend on a property in the north-west of the city. It was all bush, back then.'

She waited patiently for a break in the conversation.

'He was a sound engineer, too,' the doctor continued.

'Could it have been at Annangrove?' she said, holding her breath.

Dr Rosenbaum couldn't be sure, but he thought it sounded possible.

Anya arrived home to find Vaughan Hunter on her doorstep.

He smiled warmly when he saw her. 'I've been phoning and got worried. You didn't answer, and after that appalling piece in the weekend paper, well, I became concerned.'

'I'm fine thanks,' she said, more curtly than she had intended.

'Good. I'm glad.' This time, he was the one who looked awkward. 'Suppose I ought to get going.'

407

Anya waited until he walked past before realising how much she didn't want to be alone.

'Coffee?'

He stopped, grinned and nodded.

Once inside, Anya found herself talking. Being so emotionally wrung-out made her want to talk to an independent listener, one without his own agenda to push. They stood in the kitchen as she made the coffee.

'Ben's the victim in all this. My ex-husband can't seem to settle and that's very difficult for our son, always moving around the state.'

'Can't be easy being called a murderer in the media,' Vaughan said.

'Him or me?' Anya snapped, before realising he was referring to Martin. 'No, it isn't.'

'Are you coping okay with the publicity?'

'Just. I don't understand people who seek it out. It's destructive and fuelled by parasites wanting to create controversy, even when there isn't any. They don't care whose lives get destroyed in the process.'

Vaughan listened intently. Whether he was in professional or friend mode didn't matter to Anya. Talking released the pressure valve inside.

At 11 pm, and two coffees later, she realised that bread and cheese were the only foods in the house yet to pass their expiry date. Toasted sandwiches, it had to be. Her guest didn't seem to mind.

As they ate at the kitchen table, Anya asked if he'd heard of experiments in anechoic chambers.

'I've read about them,' Vaughan said after a

moment. 'Those experiments would never get through the ethics committees today and were pretty much a waste of time. Most of the information and understanding about behavioural modification didn't come from behavioural scientists, anyway. It was gleaned through prisoners of war, especially their experiences in Korea. Interestingly, the captors used the same techniques as men who commit domestic violence.'

Anya had appreciated reading the articles he had given her. She watched him as he spoke now, admiring his extensive knowledge and easy manner. His face not only conveyed information, but empathy. It was easy to imagine anyone feeling comfortable enough to be counselled by him. 'I'm worried that the victims in the cases I'm looking into were kept in one before their deaths.'

'Why don't you go to the police with your information?' he asked, finishing his sandwich.

'That's the tricky part. They don't want to know unless I can prove a crime took place.'

'Oh. So you go up to this property and say, "Excuse me, do you torture women in your chamber, that is, if it's still there?"'

She had to smile. It did sound pretty far-fetched. 'Because it's still a potential hazard to its owners, I can mention the lung diseases associated with the chambers and suggest they seek medical review. If that goes okay, why not ask for a sample of material from inside? Simple.'

'Somehow with you, nothing seems that simple,'

he teased. 'I'm at my Glenhaven rooms in the morning, which is just nearby. How about you pick me up from there? We might look more official as a pair, and I wouldn't mind seeing the chamber if it's still there.' He wrote the address on a business card.

Anya didn't need convincing. The events of the last few days had knocked her confidence to a new lowpoint. 'Fine. I'll see you at about eight.'

Vaughan stood to leave and wished Anya good night. She had to admit, the idea of spending more time with this man had appeal. Right now, she'd settle for friendship and moral support, which he seemed willing to offer.

At the doorstep, light drizzle prevented a drawn-out goodbye. Feeling revived by the coffee, Anya decided to look more closely at the fibres she'd taken from the chamber. At the back of her office sat a microscope her father had given her as a teenager. It was primitive, but still had good magnification. She tipped a tiny amount from the vial onto a clean glass slide and tried to scatter the fibres with a pencil tip. After focusing, she stared down the eyepiece. Moving the slide, she must have examined every fibre in order to be sure. These fibres were longer and thicker than the others, but were definitely hourglass shaped. There was a distinct similarity.

Anya felt her heart rate quicken. She knew the women hadn't been in that particular chamber, but Dr Taggert had said it was built less than a year ago. It didn't exclude the possibility of older chambers using different materials, which the similarities in the shape of the fibres seemed to support. These larger fibres were far less likely to be inhaled into small airways, and therefore, safer.

Before switching out the light, she remembered to check her e-mail, in case Dr Rosenbaum had any more recollections. Peter Latham had confirmed what she had already known: Briony Lovitt's PM found that she had the same fibre in her lungs. Kate's message mentioning the Crisis Centre made her feel more than a little guilty about not passing on the chamber information. Dialling Kate's number, she hung up when she heard the engaged signal. This was not unusual, given that Kate always seemed to be on call. Her mobile didn't answer and failed to divert to voicemail.

After trying a couple more times, Anya phoned directory assistance and asked them to check if Kate's phone was faulty. The operator assured her the phone was simply off the hook – the subscriber was not engaged in a conversation.

Kate bordered on being nocturnal and didn't go to bed before midnight, usually staying up to watch British soccer. If she'd bumped the phone off the hook, work could be trying to contact her and she'd never know. Despite her sense of betrayal, Anya decided to drive the five minutes to Kate's house.

She pulled up behind her friend's car and the front sensor light failed to come on. Tapping was all it took to open the door.

Anya felt a lurch inside her chest. Kate would never leave her door unlocked. Had the place been broken into?

'Kate, are you okay?' she called loudly, trying to scare off any intruder. 'The police are on their way.' Listening carefully, she didn't hear a sound.

Slowly opening the door with her elbow, she cautiously stepped inside. Instead of mess sprawled everywhere, the place had been tidied. Books and papers stacked around the walls. What sort of intruder tidies up? she thought, and relaxed.

'Kate, are you here?'

Looking around the small house, it became clear no-one was home.

She pulled her mobile from her jacket and dialled Brian Hogan.

'What?' a groggy voice challenged.

'Anya Crichton. Listen, I'm at Kate's place. There's no sign of her and her door was open. I'm a little concerned.'

'Not everything's a mystery,' he grunted. She'd either woken him from a deep sleep, or committed coitus telephone interruptus. 'Got a call 'cause she needed time off for personal reasons. Family illness or something.'

Anya didn't know she had any family apart from her father, who lived in Western Australia.

'Did she say who was sick?'

'What is it with you? Don't you people sleep?' he snapped. 'I took the message myself. Good night.' The idiot hung up before Anya could speak.

She hurriedly redialled.

'This had better be good,' he growled.

'Hear me out. Kate's car is out the front, her front door was open and she's not here. Something's wrong.' She had to get through to him. 'What exactly did she say?'

'She didn't say anything, her brother called –'

'Listen to me, Brian. Kate doesn't have a brother. She's an only child!'

52

When the sound abruptly stopped, the silence made Kate's ears ache. She tried to fill the void by singing but couldn't remember the words to any songs, not even nursery rhymes or ad jingles. After the first line, her mind went blank. If she couldn't remember a bloody nursery rhyme, what chance was there of escaping?

What's worse, the shaking wouldn't stop. She had never known terror like this. Not having control. Not knowing what was going to happen. One minute she was freezing; a while ago, it had felt so hot, she almost passed out.

Whatever he had planned, she wished to God he'd show his face and give her a chance to fight.

The noise started up again and suddenly the platform moved, as if it had been bumped. Kate dropped to her knees then lay flat, clinging to the metal grid with all her strength. The whole thing was about to drop. The floor quivered as she held her breath. After a while, it vibrated to a stop. She slowly inhaled and could have sworn she smelt porridge. The light flicked on, off, then on again, long enough for her to see the plate of food beside her. She edged towards it and the noise stopped.

The bastard wanted to play.

'I'm not going to play your stupid mind games!' she shouted.

With a sweep of her leg, she made contact with the plate and kicked it off the platform.

The intolerable noise started again.

53

After two hours with crime scene at Kate's house, Anya had gone home with Brian Hogan's promise to phone the moment he knew anything. By six o'clock she could no longer bear to sit around and headed for the shower. Kate didn't just disappear. Something had happened. It could have been related to any of the homicide cases she had worked on since Kate irritated just about everyone she'd ever met. Hell, even the sandwich shop owner found her offensive. Surely she wouldn't have done something stupid to herself after Briony's death. Determined to remain positive, Anya decided to follow up on the chambers at Annangrove.

Once in traffic, she switched on the radio for any news. An item on a leadership challenge in the opposition party had her thinking about the last time she had spoken to Kate. Why did it have to be a fight?

Every instinct told her that Kate was in trouble and there was nothing she could do. Just like when Miriam vanished.

Traffic flowed reasonably well for peak hour until

Old Northern Road. With light rain, the roads were quickly coated in a film of grease. At yet another traffic light intersection, the car in front accelerated on the green but screeched to a halt with a sudden change to amber. Anya shoved her foot down on the brake pedal. The van behind her did the same, a second too late.

Anya braced herself. The impact snapped her head forward and back, like a rubber band. Before she could take off her seatbelt, the van driver had jumped out of his car and begun yelling obscenities, his tirade of abuse washing over her. She took a mental note of his corporate logo shirt, unclipped her belt, stepped out and walked to the back of her Corolla. The extent of the damage shocked her – tailgate punched inside out, window in the hatch door shattered, rear guards pushed upwards and jammed against the right rear wheel. With a five-hundred-dollar insurance excess, this was something else she didn't need right now.

Seemingly oblivious to the damage he'd caused, the other driver continued to accuse her of incompetence. Cars behind tooted horns, caught in the ensuing traffic jam.

'Listen, *you* smashed into *me*,' she said, trying to sound calm while wanting to scream. 'You are at fault. Before you go anywhere I want your name, driver's licence number and insurance details.' A couple of passers-by offered to help move her car off the road and, looking at the number of cars held up at the lights, she accepted the offer.

Within minutes three tow trucks arrived and their drivers had begun arguing about 'whose tow it was'. Anya phoned the police and her insurance company and refused to participate. One of the drivers became verbally abusive and tried to hook her car up to his truck. She blocked him with her body. A few minutes later, the police arrived and had the traffic under control. The abusive van driver decided to cooperate and exchanged details as drizzle became heavy droplets, then a consistent shower. After a word with the police, the aggressive tow truck driver removed his hook and left, still swearing at Anya as he drove away.

Soaking wet and hating herself for being so helpless, Anya phoned Vaughan and asked if he'd pick her up. She wanted to leave before seeing the Corolla towed.

He arrived quickly, did a U-turn and temporarily blocked the traffic as Anya climbed into the passenger seat of his sedan.

'You okay?' he asked, handing her a towel as he drove off.

Anya nodded. Her neck ached and her head felt like it was being squashed by a vice.

'We're not far, you might as well get dry at my place. It's around the next bend.' He turned the heating up. 'You must be freezing.'

Anya sat, almost anaesthetised, as the car slowed

and indicated a left turn outside a cottage on the main road. A sign out the front read 'Family Counselling Centre'. Instead of pulling into the car park, Vaughan turned down a drive adjacent to the cottage.

'I live up here, you might find it more comfortable to get warm in the house.'

Anya noticed how many trees lined the muddy drive. 'This is beautiful.'

'I think so. I'm close to the rooms and private enough that patients don't know I live here. No need to tell you how important that is.'

At the end of the winding dirt road, they stopped at a house with separate stables and an old-fashioned barn a short walk away.

Mounted on the front verandah were two cameras, one at each end. Vaughan darted towards the house to deactivate the alarm as Anya opened the car door. Wind tore across the front seat, bringing freezing droplets of rain. Shielding her face with the towel, she ran, splashing through a puddle. Muddy water drenched her calf.

'The previous owners had the security installed,' Vaughan volunteered, holding the door open for her. 'You'd be amazed how many people think you're worth robbing if you live on an acreage out this way.'

Self-conscious, Anya took off her muddy shoes outside and pulled off her saturated jacket. A gust of wind forced its way in as she closed the door.

'I'll make a pot of tea,' Vaughan said, disappearing towards the back of the house. 'Bathroom's third on the left.'

Pantyhose wet and dirty, she padded along the polished floor. A series of paintings lined the corridor. One depicted two large women serving a table of Romans soldiers who were gorging themselves. Another showed naked women in a harem guarded by eunuchs. Not quite what she'd expected from Vaughan, but she had long ago decided that taste in art didn't reflect much.

In the bathroom, she removed her pantyhose and towel-dried her hair, which had formed ringlets in the rain. In the mirror she saw the raccoon again, only this time it looked like she had two bruises under her eyes. Bags on top of bags. The last week hadn't just taken an emotional toll. Her face had aged years, it seemed. She checked her mobile for messages. Nothing from Martin or Brian Hogan.

She opened the bathroom door as the kettle whistled. Vaughan had a cooktop kettle, something she hadn't seen for years. She wondered what else he was old-fashioned about. Diagonally across the corridor, Anya could see inside a room lined with wooden bookshelves, stacked with books.

Vaughan reappeared and handed her fresh towels and a fleecy-lined jacket, which she quickly put on. He'd taken off his jumper and replaced it with a pale blue shirt he was buttoning from the

bottom. The collar had twisted. Anya automatically leant forward to turn it down, and gasped
when Vaughan grabbed her wrist hard and pushed
her back.

Stunned, she stared at him, a sudden leap of
fear making it hard to breathe. 'You're hurting me.'

He let go and she saw a series of grossly
distended veins on the left side of his chest.

Rubbing her wrist, she offered, 'I'm sorry, I didn't
mean –'

'Don't touch me again,' he said, breathing
heavily.

She stepped back and for a moment they stood
in awkward silence.

'I don't like anyone seeing them,' he said, and
turned towards the kitchen.

Anya thought about the bulging veins. They
were a classic sign of a mass inside the chest
compressing blood flow in the superior vena cava.
The tourniquet effect caused veins on the chest
wall to engorge and become raised. She hoped she
was wrong. 'Is it something you were born with,
or . . .?'

He stood with his back to her. 'I've got a medi-
astinal tumour blocking the SVC. It's a lymphoma
and I've had chemo and radiotherapy.' He remained
still. 'But it's grown again.'

Anya reached forward and touched his back.
This time he didn't pull away. Lymphoma. God.
No wonder he'd been so short of breath at the
Easter Show. The tumour must have been large to

affect his lungs that much. She wished she hadn't tried to grab his collar and exposed him like that.

'Like you, I value privacy.' He moved away from her touch. 'Let's forget about it and have some tea. I'll bring it into the study.'

He disappeared down the hall. Rubbing her wrist, Anya wondered why he had been so upset about her seeing the veins. He had nothing to be ashamed or embarrassed about. She would have to act as though nothing had been said.

Placing the towels on a chair in the hallway, she entered the study, and stood there impressed by the order and organisation on the shelves lining the walls of the light-filled room. Psychiatric texts filled the shelves, grouped in topic and alphabetical order, according to the author. Unlike her former husband, this man was obsessively tidy. He liked to be in control of his things.

A dark blue thesis stood out: 'Literature review of techniques employed by perpetrators of domestic abuse, by Vaughan M. Hunter'. Lifting it down from the shelf, she carefully opened the front cover and flicked through the contents. The study contained so much of, and about, this man. Anya wanted to explore more.

'How do you have it?' he called from down the corridor.

'Black's fine, thanks.'

'I'm making raisin toast, would you like some?'

'Sounds good,' she shouted.

Returning the thesis to its position Anya surveyed

the shelf. He was behaving as though nothing had happened. Thank God. *Walden* by Thoreau, and *Walden Two* by B.F. Skinner caught her attention. The back blurb on the latter said it was the fictional story of a utopian society. George Orwell's *Animal Farm* and *1984* sat further along, amidst a number of classic high school texts like *Lord of the Flies*. Anya remembered reading that, hating the inhumanity of the boys on the island. The school curriculum had numerous books on repressive and inhumane regimes. True crime books such as *Helter Skelter* sat next to texts on ancient Rome and Greece. Vaughan seemed to have eclectic taste.

On a walnut desk sat a black Bakelite telephone, a micro-cassette recorder and wire in-tray. It struck her as odd that there were no photos in the room. No qualifications framed, or personal touches. She realised she knew nothing about his background, family or friends. He'd always done the listening.

Vaughan appeared in the doorway with two china cups, milk and sugar on a tray. The smell of the buttered toast made her stomach gurgle.

The in-tray contained galley proofs of scientific papers pending publication. She picked them up. 'THE EFFECTS OF SENSORY DEPRIVATION ON PERCEPTION', 'COGNITIVE DISSONANCE – MAKE OR BREAK TIME', one yet to be titled, and 'WHEN BELIEF SYSTEMS ARE SHATTERED AND THE WORLD DOESN'T COME TO AN END'.

'I see you found my most recent works.'

'Hope you don't mind,' she said. 'This room is amazing. When it comes to being tidy, are you sure you're not obsessive?'

'People use that word to medicalise what I prefer to think of as conscientious organisation.'

'Or, you may just lack insight into your obsessive behaviour,' she joked.

'Touché.' He placed the tray on the sideboard beneath the window.

Anya flicked through the papers. 'What exactly is cognitive dissonance?'

He became serious again. 'When people who, for example, believe the teachings of a cult and are convinced the world will end, say, at midnight on a particular day. When that day comes and goes, one of two things happens. Firstly, they might modify their beliefs, which they realise were rubbish. This inevitably leads to depression and what lay people describe as a 'breakdown'. Alternatively, they can justify what happened and reinforce their beliefs. The smart cult leader tells followers the world was saved by their devotion. They are with him for life after that.'

'How bizarre. I think that's what happened with one of the women in the cases I mentioned to you. She committed suicide in hospital.'

Vaughan poured the tea through a strainer. Anya stepped forward to take the cup and trod on something under the desk.

'I'm sorry,' she said, bending down to pick it up and unrolling the glossy paper. The poster looked familiar.

'Don't worry, it's an old one, about to be replaced by another version. We're trying to convince people to seek help when they're being abused. That's part of my work with volunteer programs.'

Anya sipped the piping-hot drink, cupping it in both hands for warmth. She gestured with her eyes towards a pile of papers shoved between two books on the bottom shelf. 'Good to see you're human.'

'I didn't expect you this early.' He put his cup back on the tray, removed the out of place papers and rolled them into a cylinder. They looked like lists of numbers.

Anya recalled the e-mail from Kate mentioning the Crisis Centre that each of the dead women had called. Vaughan might be able to help work out who the women spoke to. 'Do you know much about phone counselling centres?'

He squeezed the papers in his hand. 'They come under the mental health unit's control.'

'How anonymous are callers?'

'What do you mean?' he said, sounding defensive. 'Staff aren't at liberty to divulge callers' names to a third party, unless someone's safety is compromised.'

She blew on the steaming tea. 'Is there a facility for finding out where someone is phoning from in an extreme emergency? What if, for example, a counsellor was talking to a caller who was about to kill her children?'

'Our centres have caller identification and our counsellors are obliged to document phone numbers of callers. That way if someone threatens to kill him or herself, or anyone else, we can immediately notify the police and mental health crisis teams. It's also helpful for identifying the demographic and doing case reviews. It's pseudo de-identified data, you could say.'

So much for anonymous phone calls. Counsellors had information on and access to vulnerable women, revealing their innermost secrets in times of crises. At least the police should be at the Central Crisis Centre by now, trying to find whoever spoke with the dead women.

'How are counsellors screened?'

Vaughan frowned. 'I can only speak for how we do it in the Central Health Service. Candidates go through rigorous testing procedures and routinely debrief using a selection of cases. I do most of the debriefing myself.'

He put down the rolls of paper and offered his guest toast from a floral china plate.

Wondering how Vaughan would feel if one of his staff turned out to be a murderer, Anya selected a slice and decided not to mention it right now. The smell of cinnamon gave the room a homely feel. On the desk, the rolled-up papers unravelled to reveal the lists of numbers. Judging by the length, they were phone numbers. The top page had a greasy stain on it.

She began to feel uneasy. Didn't Central Health Service cover the Central Crisis Centre, which Kate had identified as linking the women? The same centre that was advertised on Vaughan's poster. Anya suddenly remembered where she'd seen the poster before – on the wall at the Merrylands doctor's surgery. Fatima Deab had sat staring at it as she worked. Obviously, she'd called the Crisis Centre and someone there had identified her phone number. It would have been easy to pay an investigator, or phone company worker, to find out the address where the call had originated.

'Everything okay?' Vaughan asked. 'You look like you've seen a ghost again.'

'Just this headache from the accident,' she said, putting down the toast on an empty plate.

Whoever took the women had a good knowledge of manipulative techniques, patterns of abuse and, almost certainly, anechoic chambers. She glanced at the research on the desk and back to the list of numbers. Her head throbbed. Like segments of a jigsaw, a picture began to emerge. Vaughan understood all about behavioural modification and had access to each of the dead women's phone numbers and problems. She remembered the conversation they'd had about being taken out of your comfort zone. Was that some kind of veiled clue for her benefit?

Her neck ached and her temples throbbed. He'd

said he knew her father, too, and what the family had suffered. The pieces fit. And all the art in the hallway depicted women in servitude.

The pain in her neck felt like hot rods driving up to the base of her skull. She had trusted him. He'd even helped with the investigation into Fatima's death.

Anya felt her face and skin on her neck flush as she moved closer to the door. She had to get out of there, without letting him know why.

'I'm not feeling very well,' she told him. 'It could be whiplash but I have a shocking headache.' She put down the cup. 'It's probably a good idea to get it checked out, for insurance reasons.'

'There's no reason to leave.' Vaughan moved towards her. 'I want to help you.'

Her chest tightened. 'They'll probably need to X-ray it, so I might just go to Casualty.'

His face seemed to harden. 'You're not going anywhere,' he said.

She walked towards the door, clutching her head, but he was too quick. He slammed it, shoving her back against the bookshelf. Her head hit a vertical support and a bolt of pain shot through her neck. He squeezed her arms so tightly her hands tingled, then began to lose feeling.

'Sit down before you hurt yourself.' He loosened his grip and she flexed her knee, hard. He side-stepped and avoided the contact with his groin.

'Play nicely,' he whispered in her ear. 'You still

don't know where your friend is.' He yanked her by the arm and pushed her into a chair in front of the desk.

It *was* him. Her body felt numb.

'Why are you doing this?' she stammered. She could feel his hands behind her, hovering over her shoulders.

'There are two types of people in this world – those with fixed beliefs and those who live life flipping from one thing to another, unable to commit to anything. Let's call them spineless, amorphous beings, if you like. I am a purist, a behavioural scientist faced with the challenge of instilling backbones into moral invertebrates.'

She listened for noise in the house and tried to remember what she'd seen as they drove in. 'You think you're just social engineering?'

'That sounds so theoretical. What I do has so many practical implications for the subjects as well as others.'

'You keep people in an anechoic chamber, deprive them of sensory stimuli, distort their perception and then blame them for complying with your sick requests. That's not exactly rocket science. People would do anything to survive.'

His fist slammed against the side of her head, jarring her teeth and jaw. She fell sideways into the arm of the chair, striking her ribs hard against the wood.

'I give people choices. They choose how to react.'

Anya held her breath, determined not to show

weakness. That's what he preyed on. Her face ached and a piercing sound filled her right ear, but she wouldn't let him know it. She had to keep him talking. Slowly, she sat upright.

'Some choice when you push them from a cliff.'

'Ah, that's the beauty of behavioural science. The strong survive, and the weak, well, they take the easy way out. Some would say it is merely natural selection, an extension of the Darwinian theory of evolution.' He scoffed. 'You're talking as though I committed murder.'

'You may not have used your hands to push them, but you sure as hell played with their emotions. Morally, there's no difference.'

If he moved to strike her again, she would run for it. With his tumour, she could outrun him. This time, instead of lashing out, however, he turned, locked the study door and put the key in his trouser pocket.

Shit. He was still strong enough to hold her down. She *had* to talk her way out.

'I believe the law sees things differently. Murder requires either reckless indifference to life, or the intent to kill or inflict grievous bodily harm. I treated these women as patients and put them in therapy, which afforded them choices they previously wouldn't have considered.'

This man was a grotesque psychopath. Anya realised the best chance of escape was by flattering his ego. That's something that working with the police had taught her about eliciting information

430

from suspects. He may just boast about where he had Kate.

'What was it you examined, cognitive dissonance?' she asked, scanning the room for a makeshift weapon.

'We have been listening,' he said snidely from behind her. 'I should be lauded for saving society from these insipid beings, draining the people around them. Look at the ones you've stumbled upon.' He walked around the desk. 'The abuse Fatima suffered would never have stopped, you know, after the arranged marriage. She lived in a fantasy world to escape the beatings. You could say I did her a favour. And the beautiful irony is that I didn't even inject the drugs. Oh, and when her father confessed to you, I have to say, Anya, that was a magnificent piece of work you did; it exceeded my every expectation. After all the vile acts he's committed, he'll be imprisoned for the one crime he didn't commit. That one restored my faith in social justice all around. A good result, you might say.' He stared at the rain tapping on the window. 'And as for you requesting my involvement in the case, to profile him.' He laughed to himself. 'Priceless!'

This man was deluded. She had fallen for his empathy routine, even confided in him. She shuddered with revulsion. He wasn't going to abuse anyone again, if she could help it. Anya wanted Hunter to incriminate himself. He was happy to brag but careful not to admit to any criminal act, so far.

431

She grabbed the arms on the chair. 'If you or Mohammed didn't kill her, who did?'

'Ah, I think you already know.'

Damn right, you bastard. 'You effectively murdered her by giving her herpes. Drug-resistant strains that couldn't be treated.' She stood and Vaughan quickly moved to push her down by the shoulders, hands lingering around her neck.

'Herpes for Fatima was a disaster, but a fascinating outcome. You see, she had no chance of falling pregnant. It seems she had stopped menstruating when her weight plummeted at the same time the beatings increased. Genital herpes, as I recall, is a non-fatal disease. By suggesting that that is what killed her, you're appearing irrational.'

He stroked her neck, threatening to crush it with each movement.

'Phylogenetic analysis confirmed that Alison Blakehurst, Fatima and Briony had the same rare strain, from the same source. Drug-resistance doesn't normally occur in healthy people.' Anya braced herself to gouge his eyes if he tightened his grip. 'That was another miscalculation that you thought no-one would notice. Your lymphoma and treatment suppressed your immune system, which is how *you* managed to be infected with a resistant strain.'

Instead of strangling her, Vaughan let go. He couldn't have known about the analysis. Anya kept talking. 'We can prove you had sexual relations with each woman, and the fibres in their lungs will match the ones in your chamber of horrors.'

He seemed taken aback. 'Clever, I'll admit. That still doesn't prove foul play surrounding their deaths.'

'What made you choose those women in particular?'

'I know what you're doing but I thought it would be obvious, even to you. Present company included,' he chuckled, 'they were all weak, indecisive, with masochistic and self-destructive tendencies. In fact, the difficulty lay in selecting such a small sample.'

She swallowed hard. 'Why the chamber? What happened to them in there?'

'You disappoint me. After I spoon-fed you the information. Sensory deprivation, sleep deprivation, white noise, time destabilisation. The techniques are well documented. In a matter of days, or – in the case of Clare – weeks, the women are so desperate for human contact, they'll do anything. Our species dies without touch. Did you know that?' He stroked her neck again. 'Physical contact speeds healing and is a powerful positive or negative reinforcer. Each one of the subjects in the chamber initiated sexual contact and became addicted to it, you could say. They transferred their emotions to me and made me a saviour for keeping them alive. After that, it took the occasional suggestion about them being better off with me, and they were convinced they'd fallen in love. It's not a crime to have consensual intercourse, or be the object of a woman's desires.'

433

Anya noticed a keyed lock on the window. She'd have to try to break it to get out. The towels could stop her from cutting herself. Shit. She'd left them outside in the hall. Her only chance to survive was to stay calm, and keep him talking.

'Why Clare?'

'Unhappy, doubting God, unable to cope with abuse victims. She was at high risk of post-natal depression, too.' He let go and walked back to his chair behind the desk. 'And what about the poor child? What sort of life would it have had?' He sat down, fingers interlocked on top of his head.

Anya pictured a woman who mutilated her own ears on a cliff. 'What happened to Clare that night she died?'

'Seemed she didn't like hearing the truth when confronted with what she'd done with me.'

'Your truth.' She remembered what Brody had said. Truth was what you could prove in court. The micro-cassette recorder on the table. If only she could switch it on and record everything he said.

Vaughan seemed to be reminiscing. 'Clare was immature. She equated sex with forever-after love and couldn't face reality. She felt she'd been "deflowered". That's a phrase you don't hear very often. When I explained that she had merely been an object for study purposes, she became histrionic.'

Leaning forward, Anya ran both hands along the desk, the recorder, mere centimetres away. 'Why would you pay Clare's bills when you had her locked away?'

'Call me a philanthropist.'

Anya tried again. 'What about Debbie Finch? How did you manage to get her to kill her father first?'

Hunter swung his chair towards the window and laughed. Anya pressed the record button and stood up. 'That had to have been the toughest,' she challenged.

'You don't get it, do you?' he swivelled around again. 'By shaving the pubic region, they were stripped back to the very basics, an almost androgenous state. No pretence, just true nakedness. Now for Debbie, that had an interesting effect, in a remarkably short period of time. Hairless genitalia brought back memories of her father – the repulsion, the hatred. Then she came to want physical contact with me, the touch, vaginal and oral sex. She was almost insatiable and far more experienced than the others.' He gave a wry grin. 'By the time she went home, she couldn't wait to kill him, even took pride in it.'

He seemed to be reliving the moment. 'Then, I suggested having oral sex. She found it too confronting when I covered myself in jam. Seems she might have liked what her father did to her and couldn't face that.'

Anya couldn't believe the twisted logic. 'You became her father?'

'No, I remained the object of her desire. She

435

couldn't reconcile her behaviour with the disgust she'd claimed to harbour for the same act. Cognitive dissonance, remember? Couldn't cope and shot herself.'

'That's when you made your mistake.'

'Mistake?' The side of Hunter's mouth twitched. 'I don't make mistakes.'

Anya took control. 'You left the toilet seat up.'

Vaughan erupted into laughter. 'Now, that *is* a crime!' he finally said. 'This is becoming tiresome. The others are pretty much the same story. I think you get the picture. Dysfunctional people in dysfunctional environments are beyond help. Given the choice, they fuck up every time. That, I have proven, beyond question.'

'Briony managed to get away from you. That must have buggered up your results.'

'She tried to kill herself and couldn't even manage that properly. Pathetic creature. I'm surprised she had the gumption to overdose at all.'

'Were the flowers a threat or just a sick joke?' Anya wanted to know.

He shrugged. 'You tell me. You're the one dissecting my work.'

She had to keep him talking and get him away from the window. 'Results are fallacious when the methodology is flawed. Instead of being objective and giving the women choice, you decided what they'd do in advance and orchestrated things to turn out your way. That broke the most basic tenet of research. Not only did you draw a conclusion

436

and set out to confirm it, your sample was biased and you had no control group. Your results mean nothing.'

He gave a derogatory slow-clap. 'Wrong again. The people interested in my research care nothing for methodology. Just results. Did you know a number of governments are keen to see my papers, including our own? My work has universal implications. This data is invaluable for the interrogation of terrorists, and training in anti-interrogation techniques. Tell that to your recording. Testing, one, two. Are you getting all this?'

The bastard had anticipated her every move – in the investigations and now. It was as though he'd scripted the whole episode, like he had for all the others. His confidence frightened her. Anya knew she had to resist panicking. She no longer felt in control of what would happen next. 'Do you expect me to go into the chamber?'

'No,' he laughed. 'You're a different case – very different.' He clasped both hands behind his head and smiled. 'The others were carefully selected and removed from their environments for the experiment. Except for Kate. She had to be introduced into the study when she found out about the Crisis Centre. Good thing I had tabs on her and your phone calls.' He looked so relaxed, Anya considered pushing him over in the chair to get to the window. He seemed to sense what she was thinking and sat forward.

'I don't have to put you in the chamber. The

experiment was whether or not your own environment could be altered sufficiently for you to change your fixed belief systems.'

He smirked and opened the top drawer of his desk. 'People really do like anonymous callers. In case you hadn't worked it out by now, there is no investigation into your sister's case. I merely phoned your father and he believed everything I said. You'd be amazed how trusting people are, without ever checking a caller's credentials. Your elderly neighbour is a real chatterbox, and not a big fan of yours, either. She was more than happy to tell me about your husband's tantrum and the screaming at your place on Saturday.'

Anya realised he'd phoned the reporter, too. How else would the newspaper have known? He knew how much Ben meant to her and had used that to ruin Martin's job. Just by setting up the article. Manipulating her world hadn't required much effort. She'd even helped him along the way, by confiding in him. God, she'd even let him spend time with Ben.

Anya moved closer to the telephone. Its weight might shatter the window if she threw it hard enough. 'What do you want from me?'

'Simple.' He pulled a cloth parcel from the drawer and placed it on the desk. 'I am curious about your fixed beliefs. In particular, your conviction that killing is wrong. Somehow, I think you're more than capable of killing in cold blood. I intend to test that hypothesis.'

438

Anya had no idea what he had planned, but his callous indifference when he spoke of murder frightened her more than anything he'd said or done so far. She had to keep control, stay calm. He wanted her to panic. If she did, he'd win whatever sick game this was.

'How?' she demanded.

54

Vaughan peeled away the yellow cloth and Anya stepped back. She froze at the sight of the handgun. This was her chance. *Just grab it.*

Anticipating her thoughts, he rose and sat on the desk, beside the 'toy', swinging one leg. The bastard loved every second of this.

'Now, you claim to be against the death penalty, anti-gun and all for life. You're probably thinking you could grab the gun and threaten me with it, but I don't think you'll do it. For one thing, killing me would mean you never see your friend again. By the way, that chamber out at Annangrove? It's a plant nursery now. No more chambers there. I salvaged the materials and rebuilt it.'

Anya's heart lurched, but she tried to make herself breathe deeply and evenly. Stalling for time, she tried to remember how to disengage the safety latch of a gun. She'd seen it done by Ballistics often enough. 'How do I know for sure you've got her?'

Vaughan's eyes turned the darkest black as he leant forward and pulled a hand-held recorder from his pocket. He clicked it on. A woman's screams filled the room. He fast-forwarded the tape and a different voice yelled for help.

'Clare, Fatima, may they rest in peace. I think you get the picture. Now for one you should recognise.'

He kept his gaze on Anya. The tape squealed and stopped. Kate's voice screamed abuse and then became incoherent.

'That's just her begging to go home. Someone really should put that shrew out of her misery.'

Anya punched the recorder out of his hand and grabbed the gun, stumbling against the chair behind her. Her hands trembled as she held it tightly. Hunter made no attempt to stop her. The gun had to be empty.

'Go ahead, it's loaded. If you kill me, you may just have enough time to save your friend.' He checked his watch. 'Did I mention the chamber is airtight? She only has a finite amount of oxygen, especially since I switched on the vacuum device.'

This didn't make sense. Why would he give her the gun, ask her to kill him, no less, unless he wanted to die? What game was he playing?

Anya tightened her grip. 'I won't kill you.'

'I think you might. Why don't I make it easy for you? You just have to follow the cameras.' He paused. 'What's the problem? You'd be killing a dead man. My tumour's recurred and is inoperable.

'It's all on the tape on the desk, Anya. You've got me on record begging you to shoot me, telling

441

you that Kate is dying while you waste time deciding what to do. The safety latch is off, in case you didn't know.'

'You don't deserve a quick death. I won't kill you, but there are other ways.'

Lowering the gun, she held it tightly and squeezed the trigger.

The recoil threw her off balance and the gun dropped. The sound of a wounded animal came out from behind the desk as Hunter fell to the floor.

She fumbled for the gun, grabbed it firmly and took a step forward. The bullet had torn into his thigh.

He whimpered and managed to pull himself into a semi-upright position. 'So naive. You really are a country girl.' He picked up the recorder from the floor, swapped the tape for one from his pocket and clicked the play button.

'I want Mummy. MUMMY!! I'm scared. I want my mummy!'

Ben's voice filled the room. Anya almost dropped the gun again, holding it with two hands, shaking. *He's got Ben.* Suddenly, she felt light-headed and struggled to hold the weapon. Ben kept screaming for her.

Vaughan sneered. 'You can stay here and try to find out where your precious son is, but that would mean killing your friend. Tick, tock, remember?'

Rage filled every vein. If he'd hurt Ben, she would kill him. That's what the sick bastard wanted anyway. He sat there waiting for an answer, the smug prick. He was up to something else. She scrambled to think. This had to be a trick. Jesus. 'Why are you so damn sure I won't kill you?'

'I'm gambling on the fact that you will,' he panted, bleeding from the thigh.

He really did want to die. Shit. 'You did all this because you've got lymphoma and want me to commit euthanasia. Is that it?' In a moment of clarity, Anya knew what she had to do. She took control. 'That was your biggest mistake.'

She stood up to fire again. 'Where is my son?'

'If you shoot me, you'll never find your son. You could get the keys and save Kate now, or she might already be dead. But if you do, can you be sure I'll be here, or even alive, when you return? Then you'd never know what happened to Ben. It's the past all over again. Only this time you could have found out. Whatever you do, I prove that you're a cold-blooded murderer.'

'You're going to pay. But I'm not going to kill you. I won't let you win. We have all the evidence we need to see you go down. Now, give me the keys, you bastard. And for the last time, where the fuck is Ben?'

His forehead beaded with perspiration. 'You *are* going to kill me,' Vaughan said slowly. 'He begged for you to come and help him. Screamed your name until he realised you weren't ever going to show up.' He turned to face Anya, staring smugly at her with soulless black eyes. 'Pity that as I wrapped my fingers around his neck, his veins and those innocent eyes bulged the harder I squeezed. Do you know he took his last breath hearing me say that you never really loved him?'

Ben. Dead. Murdered. Images of her lifeless son flashed through Anya's mind. She struggled to breathe, as if her heart and lungs had ruptured. Without Ben, there was no life. She stepped back and pulled hard on the trigger.

55

Life began to haemorrhage from Vaughan Hunter. His breathing became rapid and colour disappeared from his sweaty face.

A cold detachment took over Anya as she grabbed two sets of keys from his pocket and unlocked the study door. With the gun in her hand, she phoned emergency 000 from the hall phone and requested an urgent ambulance and police attendance. The bastard wouldn't get away with everything he'd done. Without knowing the number of the house, she described the surgery before leaving the phone off the hook and running for the front door. Rain bucketed down. *Think. Think.* He said he owned several acres. Follow the cameras. A surveillance camera on the house's corner caught her eye. From the end of the verandah, she saw another over the barn.

Sprinting in the rain past the stables, she slipped in the muddy drive, barely remaining upright. The barn door had a chain and padlock. She fumbled with the keys, desperately trying to find the right one.

A siren wailed in the distance and grew louder.

As she located a small set of keys and tried one in the lock she prayed the chamber still had an oxygen supply. Damn. That left only four more keys. Fingers numb with cold, she tried again. The third one worked.

Inside the barn was a metal staircase leading to another locked door. That led to a control room with an electronic panel and computer screen. A figure on the monitor lay motionless. *Kate*.

Looking for an entrance to the chamber, she located a door without a frame, flush with the wall. There was no handle. With both hands, Anya pushed hard. Unable to release it, she kicked, punched and yelled, hoping Kate could hear.

Going back to the panel, she scanned the switches. Flicking one on, she saw the figure on the screen flinch and curl up tighter. Pressing a button attached to a microphone, she was almost deafened by the sound of electrical interference. She flicked both switches off. Shit. But at least Kate was alive.

Out of the corner of her eye Anya noticed a small red globe glowing high up on the black wooden wall. It looked like a fuse box with a button attached to the outside. What if that opened the door or controlled the air duct?

She searched the room for something to reach it with. Anything. Pulling the chair over, she climbed up. She was still a couple of inches too short, even at maximum stretch. Ripping the keyboard from its computer attachment, she climbed up again, raised it over her head with both hands and slammed it hard. The keyboard shattered as the button clicked.

Instead of the door moving, air began spewing into the control room. *Jesus! What was that?* What had she done? Shuddering with the cold air over her wet body, Anya flicked all the untried switches on the panel until a hydraulic hiss released the door. Opening on a steel entranceway, she took a step forward in the dark and fell forward, just managing to grab a chain attached to the wall with both hands. She dangled for a moment before finding the floor again.

'Kate. You're okay,' she panted. 'The police are coming.'

Light from the open door filtered through and her eyes readjusted. Inside the chamber was a draw-bridge set-up just like the one she'd seen in the textbook. A metal platform at the door travelled by pulley system to meet the central platform. She jumped onto it, and pulled herself across to Kate. Seeing the naked form, Anya removed her over-sized jacket and covered her friend.

Kate didn't respond.

'It's all over now, you're safe,' she said, cradling the detective. All she could think about was Ben.

Thankfully, the mobile platform took the weight of them both and Anya was able to pull Kate to safety. A police constable appeared as she dragged her drowsy friend through the chamber door.

He immediately called for assistance and an ambulance drove up to the barn. In the control room, an officer covered Kate in a blanket and administered oxygen, explaining that the paramedics were at the house working on the male. With Kate safe, Anya ran back up to the house as fast as her legs would move. If Hunter were alive, he'd have to tell her where Ben was. She had to know.

By the time she arrived at the front door, Hunter had been transferred to the ambulance and a police officer stopped her from seeing him.

'You don't understand! I have to know what he did with my son.' Anya wanted only to hold her child and protect his little body.

'He's conscious, but he won't be talking to anyone but the doctors for now.' The policeman restrained her and she slumped in his arms, crying. The ambulance drove off, siren blaring as it turned onto the main road.

Brian Hogan came out from the house carrying Anya's bag and bent down to her.

'Someone's been ringing you non-stop. It's about your son. He's had some sort of accident.'

Dazed, Anya took the mobile phone and heard Martin's voice.

'Where are you? I've been trying to get you all night. I don't know what to say, it happened so quickly, I couldn't stop it.'

The phone crackled and she instantly recog-nised the voice in the background. 'It's okay, Mummy, it's just a broken arm.'

He's alive! Anya cried with relief.

'It's got a cast on it and the doctor was really nice.'

'Thank God,' she almost laughed.

Hogan signalled her to come inside.

'Darling, Mummy has to go, but I'll call you later. Promise.'

'What the hell happened?' Hogan handed her a clean handkerchief.

She tried to understand what had occurred as she dried her eyes. 'The tape recorder. I taped everything.'

Anya stood outside the study and watched Brian Hogan, with gloved hand, pick up a bloodied recorder from the floor, bring it over and press play.

Ben's voice cried out, 'I'm scared, I want to go back. I want Mummy.' The sound of laughter echoed in the background and someone yelled something about keeping the line moving. *The day at the Easter Show*. The ride. Something had happened up the stairs and Hunter had taped it.

Anya tried to explain what had happened, but Hogan acted as though he were deaf. 'I suggest you wait for legal advice before you say anything,' he muttered so no-one else could hear.

'There's another recorder. On the desk. A larger one.'

'Detective,' a uniformed constable appeared from the room next to the study, 'I think you'd better see this.'

Anya followed but stayed in the doorway. Inside

a room further along the corridor, some electrical equipment and a television were switched on. The scene in the study played on the screen, culminating in her shooting Hunter in the shoulder and fleeing.

The area around the door was out of camera range. Without a wide-angle lens, no-one would have seen him slam her against the wall or lock the door.

'Where's the sound?' Hogan demanded.

There wasn't any.

Anya watched in disbelief as Hunter sat in the chair, looking relaxed, even as she held the gun at him.

The visual images bore no resemblance to the scene she'd just lived through.

'I taped the whole thing,' she said, clutching the handkerchief. 'There was a recorder on the desk.'

Hogan wrote something down in his notebook, rubbed his forehead and hung his head. 'Christ. I hate this job.'

'Brian, it's all on the tape!' she pleaded.

'Anya Crichton, you are under arrest in relation to the attempted murder of Vaughan Hunter.'

56

Inside Castle Hill police station, Hogan and another detective escorted Anya down to the cells and presented her to the duty sergeant, who barely even noticed her as he read out the charge.

'Do you understand the charges?'

Anya mumbled, 'Yes.'

Hogan had been meticulous in reading Anya her rights and kept asking whether or not she understood. She'd said yes, but it all seemed surreal. She had no real comprehension of what had happened at all. From the desk, the custody sergeant opened the perspex cage, or dock, as he called it, and ushered her inside.

'I'd like to speak to my barrister,' Anya said, barely recognising the sound of her voice.

Hogan said, 'Brody's on his way.'

Anya sat on a plastic chair as the custody officer locked the thick plastic door. The place smelt of body odour, and she buried her nose in the sleeve of the black tracksuit, supplied when her clothes had been taken for forensic examination.

She tried to replay the last few hours in her mind, but it all felt like a blur. She watched a man, who looked like a vagrant, hurl abuse at the duty sergeant.

Anya wrapped her arms around herself. Despite perspiring, she felt colder than she'd ever felt before. At least Ben was alive and well, with his father. The broken arm would heal, in time. When Brody arrived, he'd sort out the horrible mess. The police would quickly realise they'd made a mistake. They should have heard the tape by now with Hunter incriminating himself in Kate's abduction.

Within half an hour according to the clock behind the sergeant's desk, Dan Brody's voice boomed in the hallway.

'I wish to interview my client.'

Anya wondered who else he'd come to see. It took a moment to register that she was now the client.

The sergeant accompanied them to an interview room and left. Anya preferred to stand, while Brody, solemn faced, sat at a table.

'The charges are serious and at the moment it looks pretty bad. I need to hear what happened. Exactly.' He placed his briefcase on the table and pulled out a yellow pad and clicked the end of his ballpoint pen. 'They have a recording. A video of Vaughan sitting in the chair. It clearly shows you firing on him. You appear to say something, then shoot him in the leg. On the floor, he fiddles with something in his hand, then a minute later, you stand back and shoot him in the shoulder. That evidence is indisputable.'

452

'I had to do it.' She knelt down next to Brody. 'He said Kate was running out of air and that I'd have to kill him to save her. That was the only way I could get to Kate in time.' Anya realised that was only partly true and didn't know how to explain it to Brody. Something told her to wait before telling him about Ben. Kate was not in her thoughts when she fired that second shot. Her actions could have cost Kate's life, rather than saved it.

For the first time, Brody seemed unsure of himself. 'Why would he want you to kill him?'

'He had cancer and he knew it.'

'That doesn't matter. He could have been dying in ten minutes but if you cut short his life, it's still murder. What happened next?'

Anya struggled to think through the specific order of events. 'I went to his house. No, I didn't mean to go there. I mean –'

'Take your time. It's me you're talking to, remember? I need you to tell me what happened in your own words. As though you're telling a story in a pub.'

Brody sounded authoritative and Anya felt relief flow through her. Brody had a brilliant legal mind. She'd be free in no time. Vaughan Hunter would be the one behind bars.

'Vaughan's the one who abducted the women who committed suicide. The fibres in their lungs must have come from that chamber he kept them in. By depriving them of light and sound, he controlled their behaviour.'

453

Brody took copious notes.

She continued, explaining about the games he'd played and how he had set her up to kill him.

Brody paused. 'He told me he'd only be off work for chemotherapy for a few weeks. He'd taken on new cases. Are you saying he wanted to die?'

God. He even had Brody believing his pathological lies.

She had to make him understand. 'Yes! This man experimented with people's lives. Fatima Deab, Clare Matthews, he named them all.'

She tried to read Brody's face but couldn't. His eyes fixed on the paper.

'Did he admit to killing any of the women?'

Anya shook her head. 'He did say, though, that Mohammed Deab didn't kill Fatima.'

Brody coloured in a row of boxes he'd sketched on top of the page, almost tearing the page with the pen's pressure. 'What did your son have to do with all this?'

'He told me he'd taken Ben and that if I saved Kate, I'd never find out where Ben was, or what had happened to him.' As she spoke, she realised how far-fetched the story sounded. Thank God she had it all on tape.

Brody continued to take notes.

'I refused to kill him – I had to make him tell me where Ben was. He said I was killing Kate anyway, because he'd made sure a vacuum pump sucked air out of the chamber. She only had minutes left.' Anya paused and took a deep breath.

'Then he told me he'd murdered Ben.' She put her face in her hands, and sobbed. 'The bastard lied about that too. He bluffed . . .'

'Hold it together, Anya. You've got to. What did you do next?'

'I shot him again, grabbed the keys to the door, rang the ambulance and police and ran as fast as I could to find Kate. By the time I got her out, the ambulance and police had arrived.'

'So you shot him, believing he'd killed your son?'

'Yes.'

'But the tape he played you wasn't of your son?'

'It was Ben's voice, but he'd taped them at the Easter Show, climbing up stairs of a ride together.'

'You gave him permission to be with your son that time?' He sounded so judgmental.

'Yes.' Anya began to see how guilty she sounded. 'But I didn't know he'd taped Ben. Dan, Vaughan Hunter set me up to kill him. It's what he wanted.'

'Unfortunately, that's a difficult thing to prove.'

'Haven't you heard of suicide by police?' she pleaded. 'Where someone threatens the police, goading them to shoot. That's what he did to me. He used Kate and Ben to get me angry enough to shoot him.'

A knock at the door interrupted them. Brody excused himself and disappeared outside. A few minutes later he re-emerged.

'Anya,' he said, sitting again, 'I have some bad news. The recorder in the study didn't have anything in it.'

God. The bastard must have had enough strength to take the tape out when she phoned the ambulance.

'What about the one in his pocket, with the women screaming on it?'

Brody shook his head. 'Nothing else to corroborate your story. I have to say that without sound, the video is extremely incriminating. Vaughan doesn't even put up a fight. Realistically, we can't plead self-defence.'

'This can't be happening.' She'd left the room with Hunter bleeding from two gunshot wounds. He must have reached up and grabbed the recorder from the table and kept the tape of Kate and the others. They could be anywhere between the house and the hospital. Hunter obviously hadn't intended them to be found. Why couldn't Brody understand? 'I had to shoot him, or Kate would have died.' She had to believe that, herself.

'Luckily, a switch in the control room of the chamber supports your contention that he knew Kate would suffocate. The switch triggered a vacuum system that extracted air from the chamber. They're fingerprinting it now.'

The switch high up on the wall, she thought. It dawned on her that Hunter hadn't turned on the vacuum device at all. She had when she smashed it with the keyboard. That meant that he had been bluffing about suffocating Kate, too. How could she have been so gullible?

'My fingerprints aren't on it,' she said, flatly.

'To be honest, you are lucky there is nothing to confirm that Vaughan threatened your son. If it can be proved you shot him, especially in anger, you're up for attempted murder. We'd better hope he survives.'

Anya listened in disbelief. Hunter had set her up to prove that dysfunctional people fucked up their lives at every opportunity. How could she have fucked up enough to be charged with attempted murder?

Her chest felt like lead, her heart beating so fast that her blood pressure plummeted. She lowered herself to the floor. Hunter had never intended to abduct her. She'd imprisoned herself and become his greatest manipulative triumph.

She thought of Ben. What would happen to him with his mother in prison? Martin would guarantee that she'd never see him again.

'I'll organise a bail hearing for this afternoon. The fact that you called the ambulance and the police as soon as he was shot goes towards your statement that you wanted him to live.'

Yelling came from one of the nearby rooms. She trembled at the thought of going to prison.

Brody touched her shoulder.

'I'm going to argue that you had to inflict harm to save Kate Farrer's life, which you did. Brilliantly, I might say. The shoulder injury was masterful.'

She sighed, relieved that her friend had survived. 'Can we get a sound technician to examine the video and see if there was audio that the equipment didn't play?'

'To be honest, we'd be better off without it. If they can prove you shot out of anger, the chances of mounting a credible defence disappear.'

Brody secured bail and drove Anya home. Overwhelming numbness had replaced distress at the hearing. For the moment, she was free, but she had no idea for how long.

Hunter was out of critical condition, listed as serious, under police guard in hospital. The bastard had to live, to pay for what he'd done. He'd be charged with kidnapping, deprivation of liberty at the very least. Brody felt sure he wouldn't get bail, but doubted whether someone with gunshot wounds and a large chest tumour would ever be fit to stand trial. In case the lymphoma went into remission, kidnapping a policewoman had sealed his fate. For now, in her kitchen, Anya felt safe.

Elaine greeted her with a motherly hug and squeezed her tightly, too tightly. Anya had no idea what to say. Thankfully, Elaine didn't ask.

Brody had decided to talk to the Director of Public Prosecutions and argue that the charges should be dropped, given that Anya's actions had saved a police officer's life.

'Try to get some rest,' he said, and pecked her on the cheek before leaving.

As Elaine poured a cup of coffee, someone came

in through the front door. She headed off to stop whoever it was from coming any further.

'I'm sorry, but Dr Crichton is unavailable right now,' she said in her sternest voice.

'But I have to see her. I have to know what the police found out. So far you have refused to tell me.'

Anya walked to the hallway and faced Anoub Deab.

'It's okay, Elaine. I should talk to him.'

The three stood in the dimly lit space. 'I want to know who left my sister with drugs in the toilet. What did he do to Fatima?'

'He abducted her, kept her in a dark, silent chamber. She had no choice.'

'You know who he is and have spoken to him?' Anoub appeared anxious, hands plucking at the pockets of his jacket. 'What else did he say?'

'He knew your father didn't kill Fatima.'

The young man clenched his fists. 'My father *is* innocent. They have no right to keep him in jail.'

Anya remembered what Hunter had said. If Mohammed Deab had murdered Fatima, his ego wouldn't have let him give credit to anyone else.

'What makes you so sure your father didn't inject Fatima with heroin?'

'My father knows nothing about how to filter and inject drugs.'

Anya shot Elaine a concerned glance. The secretary slowly retreated to the office. Out of the corner of her eye, Anya saw her pick up the phone, ready to dial.

Only the crime scene officer knew about the tampon filter. It didn't appear in the PM report the family had seen.

Anya took a step closer. 'But you do.'

'I don't know what you are talking about.'

After what she'd been through today, Anya was not going to be bullied by the Deabs.

'Fatima didn't use tampons. She had no need to, being too thin to menstruate. You went to the toilet block. I guess you took the drugs with you, or maybe they were already there for Fatima to use. You must have got a tampon from your girl-friend. Am I right?'

He stepped forward, one hand raised, just as his father had done in prison.

Elaine dialled the police as Anya stood firm, refusing to be intimidated. He lowered his hand.

'You do not understand,' he shouted. 'She brought dishonour upon our family. That man tele-phoned our house and told me where she was. He knew she had that disease.'

Anya didn't flinch. Just like his father, he was weak without thugs around him. 'The man who took Fatima forced her to have sex. She did nothing dishonourable.' Anya jabbed a finger into his chest. 'Your sister was innocent and you killed her.'

'You do not understand any of our culture. She was no longer innocent. She had to die.' Deab edged backwards towards the front door. 'She could never marry our cousin. Everybody would know she was not a virgin.'

The rage from the past week rose again. Anya could barely stop herself from hitting him. 'I understand perfectly well. You went there and forced her to inject poison.'

Anoub fidgeted, clenching and unclenching his fists. 'I wanted to protect my family and show my father I know what is right and honourable.'

Anya wanted to know. 'Was he with you when you did it?'

Anoub wiped his eyes with his forearm. 'No. He came later to see where Fatima had died. Instead of being proud,' he faltered, 'my father said I had shamed him. He wanted me to leave home after the police started following us, at the funeral.'

'You were guilty and your father was planning on taking the blame if he had to. So you used me to find out whether the police had any evidence to prove Fatima had been murdered. You honestly thought you'd get away with it?'

Anoub didn't answer. He turned and ran out the front door, and Anya made no attempt to stop him.

57

Two days later, Dan Brody appeared on the doorstep, hands behind his back.

Anya opened the door, fearing the worst. Why else would he have come in person?

'Great news,' he declared. 'You're in the clear. The charges have been withdrawn.' He pulled a bottle of Bollinger from behind his back and invited himself in.

'How?' Anya tried to digest what he'd said. 'When?'

Grinning, Brody explained, 'Crime scene identified only one set of fingerprints on the switch that operated the air vacuum system in the anechoic chamber – Vaughan Hunter's. The police believe he switched the unit on with the intention of killing Kate Farrer. Given that you shot to disable Hunter and phoned for an ambulance, the DPP accepted that the need to save Kate's life justified the shooting.' He paused, waiting for some sort of reaction, then bent closer. 'Congratulations. It's over. You're a free woman!'

'Thank you. I can't believe it.' Anya threw her arms around Brody and hugged his chest. 'Thank you so much.'

He reciprocated without hesitation and she felt the cold bottle in the small of her back.

'Too early for bubbly?'

Anya didn't care about the time. This man was one hell of a lawyer. 'Not today,' she said, pulling two glasses from the drying rack in the kitchen, still there from his last visit. 'What did Hunter tell the police?'

Brody popped the cork, hitting the ceiling. Alcohol flowed down the side of the bottle and Anya caught some in one of the glasses.

'He's refused to speak about the incident, apart from saying he felt sorry for you because he couldn't save you from yourself, or something like that.'

The smug bastard still thought he had won.

Anya felt relieved, but knew her release was purely due to luck and, mostly, her own naivety. If she hadn't switched on the vacuum system by mistake, her story would've had no credibility and she would have been standing trial for attempted murder. Vaughan's third mistake, overestimating her, had given Anya her freedom. Then it occurred to her that she would remain free only if the tape recording of her shooting him could not be found. She felt ill again. What if he ever gave the tape to the police? It proved she'd shot him, wrongly believing he'd killed Ben. With that tape out there somewhere, she'd never be totally free. Maybe that was his plan all along, to have her live in a constant state of dread, never knowing whether a phone call or a knock on the door would mean an end to her freedom.

He'd planned everything else. Even when he died of his lymphoma, the bastard would haunt her from the grave. He would have planned for that too. He had the tapes – somewhere.

Suddenly, Brody's elation at the charges being dropped provided little comfort.

'To you.' Brody clinked his client's glass and took a swig. 'How about we celebrate tonight? I'll take you out to dinner.'

'That sounds great,' Anya said, just as the phone rang. She picked it up.

'We need to talk,' Martin said abruptly. 'Ben really needs to see you.'

'I want to see him, too.' She took a sip and felt her face flush. 'Look, the charges have been dropped. There won't be a trial. The DPP believes I shot in self-defence.'

After a painful silence, he said, 'Good for you. Listen, how about tonight? Can you meet us at Darling Harbour, outside the IMAX theatre at six?'

Anya looked over at Brody, who was mopping up the spill with a dish cloth. 'Um, yeah. Sure. We could all have dinner tonight. I'd like that.'

'I'm glad things worked out for you.' His voice softened. 'Really. For all our sakes.'

Anya hung up. Martin calling was a good start. She had to make the most of it.

Brody came over with the bottle. 'Top up?'

464

She covered her glass with one hand. 'Dan, about tonight.'

'Let me guess. Had a better offer?'

'Martin is going to let me see Ben.'

Brody nodded. 'We can do it another time. Anyway, must go. Clients await.' Placing the bottle on the coffee table, he smiled. 'Congratulations again,' he added, before letting himself out.

Anya held the glass to her chest and switched on the television, in time for the morning news.

Kate Farrer's release from hospital made the bulletin, along with her receiving a commendation from the Police Commissioner. In the group of colleagues welcoming her back, Detectives Ernie Faulkner and Ray Filano shook hands and patted the newly decorated detective on the back. Bloody hypocrites, Anya thought as she watched the charade on TV, grateful not to have her own name mentioned. No doubt Kate would tell her about it at lunch tomorrow. She headed for the shower.

With water streaming down her back, she sat down and clutched her legs to her chest. Charges dropped. She was free. A surge of emotions filled her as hot water teemed over her body. She vowed never to disclose her secret. The police and Brody thought she'd shot only to wound Vaughan Hunter. She knew she hadn't. She'd wanted to kill him, and God knows, she'd tried. The bullet in his shoulder was aimed straight at his heart. He was right. She could kill in cold blood, if she were any more competent with a gun.

And all it took were lies – bluff – to make her do it. Hunter had altered her perception, beliefs and behaviour without ever putting her in the anechoic chamber. It frightened her, too, how attracted to him she'd been and how much she'd wanted him to hold and touch her the day at the Easter Show. Tightening her grip on her legs, she tried to block out the image of him with Ben and thanked Martin for taking their son away from Sydney, out of Hunter's grip.

With fingertips wrinkling as water cascaded over her flexed head, she thought about his other victims and tried to imagine their isolation and desperation in the chamber. They were completely dependent on their captor for life. He probably tormented them with that vacuum switch, sucking out enough air to make them feel they would suffocate, then turning it off just in time. He was a sadist, a sexual predator who maintained a respectable persona in the community. It was still difficult to believe he'd ruined so many lives.

The abducted women weren't the only ones destroyed by Vaughan Hunter's experiments. The Galea boy had done nothing wrong, but would probably suffer permanent brain damage. Alison Blakehurst's husband and kids, Briony Lovitt's daughter and lover, had all been shattered by the decisions of just one man. Clare Matthews' baby and Debbie Finch's father had also been killed by his manipulation. Even Mohammed and Anoub Deab had become his victims. She wondered how many others there had been, that she didn't know about.

With the herpes cultures and DNA from the foetus and sperm, the police would be able to confirm he'd had sex with the women. With Kate's testimony, the chamber and the fibres in all the women's lungs, he'd be facing a stiff prison sentence if he were well enough to stand trial. Proving he killed the women might not be necessary. Maybe a jury would see no moral difference between talking someone to their death and physically pushing them. It was pretty clear his intentions were malicious.

She couldn't forgive herself for being so gullible. Hearing Ben screaming was a nightmare come true. It was like hearing Miriam calling out in so many of Anya's dreams.

Hunter had set out to manipulate her completely, by slowly taking away the things that were most important to her. The article in the paper affected Martin's job offer, and would have ramifications for her work, too, if she ever got work again. The only genuine calls since that article appeared were from the sexual assault services. That's what she'd have to focus on from now on.

Fucking Hunter. She'd proven his hypothesis and almost lost Ben forever in the process. And that's something she was going to have to live with for the rest of her life. She cried, from the gut, and a tidal wave of emotion released itself until long after the hot water had run out.

Once out of the shower, she quickly dressed and headed downstairs, eager to see Ben and be positive for him. She was, after all, free. It was up to her to make the most of life with her son, as privately as possible. Hoping that her make-up hid swollen red eyes, she grabbed her keys and stepped into a pair of black heels inside the door.

Outside, flashes of light blinded her. A throng of reporters shouted loudly, accusing the DPP of bias by dropping the charges. A television camera appeared and a woman's voice demanded answers to the questions that would be asked in Parliament. Someone else asked how the controversy had affected her son. A man shoved a microphone in her face and wanted to know whether she'd had a sexual relationship with Vaughan Hunter before shooting him.

More bulbs flashed.

Anya could almost hear Vaughan Hunter laughing.